Natural Born Charmer

Also by Susan Elizabeth Phillips

Match Me If You Can
Ain't She Sweet
Breathing Room
This Heart of Mine
Just Imagine
First Lady
Lady Be Good
Dream a Little Dream
Nobody's Baby but Mine
Kiss an Angel
Heaven, Texas
It Had to Be You

Natural Born Charmer

Susan Elizabeth Phillips

WM
WILLIAM MORROW
An Imprint of HarperCollins*Publishers*

This book is a work of fiction. The characters, incidents, and dialogue are drawn from the author's imagination and are not to be construed as real. Any resemblance to actual events or persons, living or dead, is entirely coincidental.

HarperCollins books may be purchased for educational, business, or sales promotional use. For information please write: Special Markets Department, HarperCollins Publishers, 10 East 53rd Street, New York, NY 10022.

FIRST EDITION

Designed by Susan Yang

Library of Congress Cataloging-in-Publication Data

Phillips, Susan Elizabeth.
    Natural born charmer / Susan Elizabeth Phillips.—1st ed.
        p.   cm.
ISBN: 978-0-06-073457-2
ISBN-10: 0-06-073457-4
    1. Football players—Fiction.   I. Title.

PS3566.H522N38   2007
813'.54—dc22

                                                                    2006049173

07   08   09   10   11   WBC/RRD   10   9   8   7   6   5   4   3   2   1

To Liam,

a natural born charmer

if there ever was one

Chapter One

It wasn't every day a guy saw a *headless* beaver marching down the side of a road, not even in Dean Robillard's larger-than-life world. "Son of a . . ." Dean slammed on the brakes of his brand-new Aston Martin Vanquish and pulled over in front of her.

The beaver marched right past, her big flat tail bouncing in the gravel, and her small, sharp nose stuck up in the air. Way up. The beaver looked highly pissed.

She was definitely a girl beaver because her beaver head was missing, revealing sweaty, dark hair pulled into a short, scraggly ponytail. He'd been praying for a little distraction from his own depressing company, so he threw open the door and stepped out onto the shoulder of the Colorado road. His newest pair of Dolce & Gabbana boots emerged first, followed by the rest of him, all six feet three inches of steely muscle, razor-sharp reflexes, and unsurpassed gorgeousness . . . or at least that's what his press agent liked to say. Still, it was pretty much true, although Dean didn't have nearly as much personal vanity as he let people believe. But emphasizing the superficial was a good way to keep people from getting any closer than he wanted them to be.

"Uh, ma'am . . . You need some help?"

Her paws didn't break rhythm. "You got a gun?"

"Not with me."

"Then I've got no use for you."

On she marched.

He grinned and set off after her. With his extra-long legs and her shorter, furry ones, it took just a few steps to catch up. "Nice day," he said. "A little warmer than I'm used to for May, but I'm not complaining."

She hit him with a pair of grape lollipop eyes, one of the few curvy things about her. Most of the rest of her came to sharp angles and delicate points, from a set of fragile bladed cheekbones, to a petite, arrow-tipped nose, to a chin keen enough to cut glass. But after that, things got dicey. A razor-edged bow marked the center of a wide and startlingly plump top lip. Her bottom lip was even fuller, giving him the disconcerting feeling that she'd somehow escaped from an X-rated nursery rhyme.

"An actor," she said with the trace of a sneer. "Just my luck."

"What makes you think I'm an actor?"

"You're prettier than my girlfriends."

"It's a curse."

"You're not even embarrassed?"

"Some things you have to accept about yourself."

"Brother . . ." She gave a grunt of disgust.

"Name's Heath," he said, as she picked up the pace. "Heath Champion."

"Sounds phony."

It was, but not in the way she meant.

"What do you need a gun for?" Dean asked.

"Murder an old lover."

"Is he the one who picked out your wardrobe?"

Her big ol' paddle tail smacked him in the leg as she spun on him. "Beat it, okay?"

"And miss all the fun?"

She gazed back at his sports car, a lethal, midnight black Aston Martin Vanquish S with a V-12 engine. The machine had set him back a couple of hundred thousand, but even that hadn't made much of a dent in his net worth. Being the starting quarterback for the Chicago Stars was pretty much like owning a bank.

She nearly poked out her eye as she pushed a sweaty spike of hair away from her cheek with her paw, which didn't seem to be detachable. "I could use a ride."

"Are you going to gnaw my upholstery?"

"Do *not* mess with me."

"Apologies." For the first time all day, he was glad he'd decided to get off the interstate. He tilted his head toward the car. "Hop in."

Even though this was her idea, she hesitated. Finally, she shuffled after him. He should have helped her in—he did open the door for her—but he just stood back to watch the fun.

Mainly it was the tail. The sucker was basically spring-loaded, and as she attempted to wedge herself into the leather passenger seat, it kept smacking her in the head. She got so frustrated she tried to rip it off, and when that didn't work, she stomped on it.

He scratched his chin. "Aren't you being a little tough on the ol' beaver?"

"That's it!" She started to take off again down the road.

He grinned and called out after her. "I apologize. Comments like that are exactly why women have lost respect for men. I'm ashamed of myself. Here, let me help you."

He watched her struggle between pride and necessity and wasn't surprised to see necessity win. When she returned to his side, she let him help fold over her tail. As she clutched it to her chest, he guided her inside. She had to sit on one cheek and peer around the tail to see through the windshield. He climbed behind the wheel. The beaver suit emitted a musky odor that reminded him of a high school locker room. He cracked the window a couple of inches as he pulled back out onto the road. "So where are we off to?"

"About a mile straight ahead. Take a right at the Eternal Life Bible Church."

She was sweating like a linebacker underneath all that malodorous fur, and he turned the AC to full blast. "Are there a lot of career opportunities in beaver work?"

Her derisive look told him she knew exactly how much entertainment he was having at her expense. "I was doing some promotion for Ben's Big Beaver Lumberyard, okay?"

"When you say promotion . . ."

"Ben's business has been down lately . . . or so I was told. I just got to town nine days ago." She nodded straight ahead. "This road leads to Rawlins Creek and Ben's lumberyard. That four-lane highway back there leads to Home Depot."

"I'm starting to get the picture."

"Right. Every weekend, Ben tries to hire somebody to stand out by the highway with a sign to draw some of the shoppers his way. I was his latest patsy."

"Being the new kid in town."

"It's tough to find anybody desperate enough to do this job two weekends in a row."

"Where's the sign? Never mind. You left it with your head."

"I could hardly walk back into town wearing a beaver head."

She pointed this out as if he were slow-witted. He suspected she wouldn't have been walking back into town wearing a beaver suit, either, if she had anything on underneath it. "I didn't see a car parked back there," he said. "How did you get out here in the first place?"

"The owner's wife dropped me off after my Camaro picked this morning to permanently give up the ghost. She was supposed to come back an hour ago to pick me up, but she didn't show. I was trying to figure out what to do when I saw a certain scumsucker whip by in a Ford Focus I helped pay for."

"The boyfriend?"

"Ex-boyfriend."

"The one you're getting ready to murder."

"Keep pretending that I'm kidding." She peered around her tail. "There's the church. Hang a right."

"If I drive you to the crime site, does that make me an accessory?"

"Do you want to be?"

"Sure. Why not?" He turned onto a bumpy, semiresidential street where some scrappy ranch-style homes sat on weedy lots. Although the town of Rawlins Creek was only about twenty miles east of Denver, it didn't seem to be in much danger of becoming a popular bedroom community.

"It's that green house with the sign in the yard," she said.

He pulled up in front of a stucco ranch where a metal deer stood guard over a row of sunflower whirligigs and a sign reading ROOMS TO LET. Except some comedian had drawn a big letter *I* between the TO and LET. A dirty silver Focus sat with the motor idling in the drive. Next to it, a leggy brunette rested her hips against the passenger door and smoked a cigarette. As she saw Dean's car, she straightened.

"That must be Sally," the Beaver hissed. "Monty's latest loser. Me being her predecessor."

Sally was young, thin, with a big rack and lots of makeup, which put the sweaty-haired Beaver at a distinct disadvantage, although showing up in a sporty Aston Martin with him at the wheel might have evened out the playing field. Through the windshield, Dean saw a long-haired, artistic-looking dude in small, wire-rimmed glasses emerge from the house. This could only be Monty. He wore cargos, along with a woven shirt that looked like it had been handmade by a band of South American revolutionaries. He was older than the

Beaver—maybe midthirties—and definitely older than Sally, who couldn't have been more than nineteen.

Monty came to a dead stop when he saw the Vanquish. Sally ground out her cigarette with the toe of a bright pink sandal and stared. Dean took his time climbing out and making his way around the hood to open the passenger door so the Beaver could start her killing spree. Unfortunately, as she tried to swing her paws to the ground, her tail got in the way. She attempted to angle it, only to have it unfold and knock her in the chin. That pissed her off so much that she took a swing at it, which threw her off balance, and she landed flat on her face at his feet, that big brown paddle waving in the breeze over her butt.

Monty stared down at her. "Blue?"

"That's Blue?" Sally said. "Is she a clown or something?"

"Not the last time I saw her." Monty switched his attention from the Beaver, who was trying to climb up on all fours, to Dean. "Who are you?"

The guy had one of those fake upper-crust accents that made Dean want to spit tobacco and say "y'all." "A man of mystery," he drawled. "Loved by some. Feared by many."

Monty looked mystified, but as the Beaver finally made it to her feet, his expression changed to hostility. "Where is it, Blue? What did you do with it?"

"You lying, hypocritical, poetry-spouting jerk!" She shuffled down the gravel drive, sweat glistening on her sharp little face, murder in her eyes.

"I didn't lie." He spoke in a condescending manner that got even Dean's hackles up, so he could only imagine how the Beaver was taking it. "I've never lied to you," he went on. "I explained everything in my letter."

"Which I didn't get until I'd blown off three clients and driven thirteen hundred miles across the country. And what did I find when I got here? Did I find the man who'd spent the last two months begging me to leave Seattle and come out here? Did I find the man who cried like a baby on the phone, talked about killing himself, and said I was the best friend he'd ever had and the only woman he'd ever trusted? No, I did not. What I found was a *letter* telling me that the man who swore I was the only thing keeping him alive didn't need me any longer because he'd fallen in love with a nineteen-year-old. A letter also telling me I shouldn't let this kick up my *abandonment* issues. You didn't even have the guts to talk to me in person!"

Sally stepped forward, her expression earnest. "It's because you're a ballbuster, Blue."

"You don't even know me!"

"Monty's told me everything. And I'm not saying this to be a bitch, but you could benefit from therapy. It'll help you stop feeling so threatened by other people's success. Especially Monty's."

The Beav's cheeks grew bright red flags. "Monty makes his living traveling to poetry slams and writing term papers for college kids who are too lazy to write their own."

Sally's fleeting expression of guilt made Dean suspect this was exactly how she'd met him. But she didn't let herself be thrown off course for long. "You're right, Monty. She is toxic."

The Beaver clenched her jaw and started advancing on Monty again. "You told her I was toxic?"

"Not toxic in general," Monty said, haughty as all hell. "Only to my creative process." He poked his glasses higher on the bridge of his nose. "Now tell me where the Dylan CD is. I know you found it."

"If I'm so toxic, why haven't you been able to write a single poem since you left Seattle? Why did you say I was your fricking *inspiration*?"

"That was before he met me," Sally interjected. "Before we fell in love. Now I'm his inspiration."

"It was two weeks ago!"

Sally tugged on her bra strap. "The heart knows when it meets its soul mate."

"A crap mate is more like it," the Beaver retorted.

"That's cruel, Blue, and very hurtful," Sally said. "You know Monty's vulnerability is what makes him a great poet. And that's exactly why you're attacking him. Because you're jealous of his creativity."

Sally was even getting on Dean's nerves, so he wasn't surprised when the Beav rounded on her. "If you say one more word, I'm decking you. Got it? This is between Monty and me."

Sally opened her mouth, but something in the Beav's expression must have given her pause because she shut it again. Too bad. He'd have enjoyed seeing the Beav take her. Although Sal looked like she worked out.

"I know you're upset," Monty said, "but someday you'll be happy for me."

This guy had graduated right at the top of stupid class. Dean watched the Beav rise up on her paw tips. *"Happy?"*

"I'm not fighting with you," Monty said hastily. "You always want to turn everything into a fight."

Sally nodded. "You do, Blue."

"You are so *right*!" With no more warning than that, the Beav hurled herself through the air, and Monty went down with a thud.

"What are you doing? Stop it! Get off me!"

He was screeching like a girl, and Sally hurried forward to help. "Get off him!"

Dean leaned against the Vanquish to enjoy the show.

"My glasses!" Monty howled. "Watch my glasses!"

He tried to curl himself into a ball as the Beav landed a chop to the side of his head. "I paid for those glasses!"

"Stop it! Get off him!" Sally grabbed the Beav's tail and yanked on it for all she was worth.

Monty was torn between protecting the family jewels and his precious glasses. "You've gone completely crazy!"

"Your influence!" The Beav tried to bitch slap him, but it didn't go well. Too much paw.

Sally had some pretty good biceps, and she started making headway pulling on the tail, but the Beav had game, and she wasn't planning to give up till she drew blood. Dean hadn't seen a pileup this entertaining since the final thirty seconds of last season's Giants game.

"You broke my glasses!" Monty whined, pressing his hands to his face.

"First your glasses. Now your head!" The Beav took another swing.

Dean winced, but Monty finally remembered that he had a Y chromosome and, with Sally's help, managed to push the Beav off and scramble to his feet. "I'm going to have you arrested!" he shrieked like a pussy. "I'm pressing charges."

Dean couldn't take any more, and he ambled forward. Over the years, he'd seen enough film of himself to know the impression he made when he ambled—the way his long physique displayed itself to full advantage. He also suspected the afternoon sun might be setting off some fairly inspirational pyrotechnics in his dark blond hair. Up until he was twenty-eight, he'd sported a honkin' pair of diamond ear studs, but that had been youthful overkill, and now he wore only a watch.

Even with broken glasses, Monty saw him coming and blanched. "You're a witness," poetry boy whimpered. "You saw what she did."

"All I saw . . . ," Dean drawled, ". . . was one more reason we're not inviting you to our wedding." He made his way to the Beav's side, wrapped his arm around her shoulders, and gazed fondly into her startled lollipop eyes. "I apologize, sweetheart. I should have believed you when you said William Shakespeare here didn't deserve closure to your relationship. But I had to go and encourage you to come talk to the poor son of a bitch. Next time, remind me to trust your judgment. But you have to admit that you should have changed out of your costume first like I told you. Our sex life isn't anybody else's business."

The Beav didn't look like the kind of woman who could easily be caught by surprise, but it seemed like he'd done it, and for a man who made his living with words, Monty's verbal well had run dry. Poor Sally could barely manage a croak. "You're marrying Blue?"

"I couldn't be more surprised myself." Dean gave a modest shrug. "Who figured she'd have me?"

And, really, what more could they say after that?

When Monty finally got his breath back, he started whining again about Blue doing something with "it," which Dean finally figured out was an apparently valuable bootleg CD of the original press of Bob Dylan's *Blood on the Tracks* that Monty had accidentally left behind at the rooming house.

"There are only a thousand in existence!" he cried.

"Nine hundred and ninety-nine," the Beav retorted. "Your copy went out with the trash the minute I finished reading your letter."

Monty was pretty much a broken man after that, but Dean couldn't resist twisting the knife. As Poetry Man and Sally began climbing in their car, he turned back to the Beav and spoke just loudly enough for his words to drift in their direction. "Come on, sweet pea. Let's head for the city so we can get a start on buying that two-carat diamond you've got your heart set on."

He swore he heard Monty whimper.

♥

The Beav's triumph was short-lived. The Focus had barely made it out of the driveway before the front door of the ranch house flew open and a heavyset woman with dyed black hair, painted eyebrows, and a doughy face lumbered onto the porch. "What's going on out here?"

The Beav stared at the dust cloud on the road, her shoulders slumping ever so slightly. "Domestic altercation."

The woman crossed her arms over her ample bosom. "I knew the minute I seen you that you was trouble. I never should have let you stay here." She started lambasting the Beav, which gave Dean enough information to piece a few facts together. It seemed that Monty had been living in the rooming house up until ten days ago, when he'd taken off with Sally. The Beav had arrived a day later, found his kiss-off letter, and decided to stay put until she figured out what to do next.

Sweat beads broke out on the landlady's forehead. "I don't want you in my house."

The Beav couldn't seem to regain her fighting spirit. "I'll be out of here first thing tomorrow."

"You'd better have the eighty-two dollars you owe me."

"Of course I have—" The Beav's head shot up. With a muttered oath, she pushed past her landlady and rushed inside.

The woman turned her attention to Dean and then to his car. Generally, the entire population of North America lined up to kiss his butt, but she didn't seem to watch a lot of football. "You a drug dealer? If you got drugs in that car, I'm calling the sheriff."

"Some Extra Strength Tylenol." Plus a few bottles of prescription pain relievers he decided not to mention.

"You're a real wise guy." The landlady shot him a dark look and turned back into the house. Dean regarded her disappearance with regret. Apparently the fun was over.

He didn't look forward to getting back on the road, despite the fact that he'd taken this trip so he could sort out a few things. Mainly the end of an unbroken string of good luck. He'd suffered his share of bumps and bruises playing football, but nothing major. Eight years in the NFL and he'd never broken an ankle, torn an ACL, or shredded an Achilles tendon. Not so much as a broken finger.

But that had ended three months ago with a fourth-quarter sack in the AFC Divisional playoffs against the Steelers. He'd dislocated his shoulder and suffered a SLAP lesion. The surgery was successful. His shoulder would serve him for another few seasons, but it would never be as good as new, and that was the problem. He'd gotten used to thinking of himself as invincible. Injuries happened to other players, not to him, not until now.

His charmed life had come to an end in other ways. He'd started spending too much time in the clubs. Before long, guys he barely knew were moving into his guest rooms, and naked women were passed out in his bathtub. He'd finally decided to take off on a solo road trip, but fifty miles outside the Vegas city limits, he'd concluded that Sin City wasn't the best place to straighten out his head, which was how he happened to be heading east across the state of Colorado.

Unfortunately, he didn't do solitude well. Instead of getting some perspective, he'd only ended up more depressed. The Beav's adventures had been a great distraction that had, sadly, come to an end.

As he began to get back into his car, the shrill sounds of a female argument broke out. The next thing he knew, the screen door flew open, and a suitcase came sailing out. It landed in the yard, where it split open, spewing its contents: jeans and tops, a purple bra, and some orange panties. Next came a navy duffel. And then the Beav.

"Deadbeat!" the landlady shouted just before she slammed the door.

The Beaver had to grab an iron post to keep from falling off the porch. Once she got her balance back, she didn't seem to know what to do, so she sank down on the top step and dropped her head in her paws.

She'd said her car wasn't running, which gave him a good excuse to postpone enduring more of his own lousy companionship. "Need a lift?" he called out.

As she raised her head, she looked surprised to see he was still around. The fact that a woman had forgotten his existence was unusual right there, which further caught his interest. She hesitated, then came awkwardly to her feet. "All right."

He helped her gather up her things, mainly handling the delicate objects that required manual dexterity. Like panties. As something of a connoisseur, he judged hers to be more Wal-Mart than Agent Provocateur, but she still had a nice assortment of bikinis in bright colors and bold prints. No thongs, though. And, most disconcerting, no lace. Since the Beav's delicate, pointed face—minus the sweat and the accompanying fur—belonged in a Mother Goose book, there should have been lace.

"Judging by your former landlady's attitude," he said as he loaded her suitcase and duffel into the Vanguard's trunk, "I'm guessing you're missing eighty-two dollars' rent money."

"More than that. I had two hundred dollars tucked away in that room."

"You've got a string of bad luck going for yourself."

"I'm used to it. Not that it's all just bad luck. Some of it is plain old stupidity." She gazed at the house. "I knew Monty would come back here as soon as I found that Dylan CD under the bed. But instead of hiding my money in the car, I tucked it inside the new issue of *People*. Monty hates *People*. He says only cretins read it, so I was sure the money'd be safe."

Dean wasn't a regular *People* reader, but he had a certain loyalty. During his photo shoot, the staff couldn't have been nicer.

"I'm assuming you want to go to Ben's Big Beaver Lumberyard," he said after he'd helped her inside. "Unless you're trying to set a fashion trend."

"Will you let it go?" The Beav had taken a powerful dislike to him, which was more than a little disconcerting, since she was female and he was . . . well . . . Dean Robillard. She spotted the map he'd tossed down. "Tennessee?"

"I have a vacation place not too far from Nashville." Last week he'd liked the sound of those words. Now he wasn't so sure. He might live in Chicago, but he was a California boy through and through, so why had he bought a Tennessee farm?

"You're a country western singer?"

He thought it over. "Nope. You were nearly right the first time. I'm a movie star."

"I never heard of you."

"Did you see the new Reese Witherspoon film?"

"Yeah."

"I was in the one right before that."

"Sure you were." She gave a long sigh and rested her head against the back of the seat. "You have an incredible car. Expensive clothes. My life gets suckier and suckier. I've fallen in with a drug dealer."

"I'm not a drug dealer!" he retorted hotly.

"You're not a movie star."

"Don't rub it in. The truth is, I'm a semifamous male model with ambitions of being a movie star."

"You're gay." She made it a statement, not a question, which would have upset a lot of jocks, but he had a big gay fan base, and he didn't believe in disrespecting the people who supported him.

"Yeah, but I'm totally in the closet."

Being gay might have some advantages, he decided. Not the reality of it—he couldn't even think about that—but hanging out with interesting women without worrying about leading them on. Over the past fifteen years, he'd expended too much energy convincing some very nice females they weren't going to be the mother of his children, but gay men never had that problem. They could relax and just be pals. He glanced over at her. "Word gets out about my sexual preference, it'll ruin my career, so I'd appreciate you keeping the information to yourself."

She lifted one damp eyebrow. "Like it's some big secret. I knew you were gay five seconds after I met you."

She had to be putting him on.

She started working away at her bottom lip with her teeth. "Do you mind if I tag along with you for a while today?"

"You're leaving your car behind?"

"It's not worth repairing. Ben can have it towed. With the missing beaver head and all, it's a good bet I won't get paid, so he owes me."

Dean thought about it. Sally had called it right. The Beav was a ballbuster, his least favorite kind of female. But she was also entertaining. "We'll try it for a couple of hours," he said, "but I'm not promising more than that."

They pulled up in front of a corrugated metal building painted an unfortunate shade of turquoise. It was Sunday afternoon, and the gravel parking lot at Ben's Big Beaver Lumberyard held only two vehicles, a rusted-out blue Camaro and a late-model pickup. A CLOSED sign swung from a pair of suction cups on the door, which was still wedged open to catch the breeze. Ever the gentleman, he got out to help her. "Watch your tail there."

She gave him a withering glare, managed a slightly more graceful exit, and shuffled to the lumberyard door. As she opened it, he glimpsed a barrel-chested man stacking a display. She disappeared inside.

He'd just finished surveying the unimpressive scenery—a collection of Dumpsters and some power lines—when she stomped back out, a bundle of clothes in her arms. "Ben's wife cut her hand, and he had to take her to the emergency room. That's why she didn't pick me up. Unfortunately, I can't get out of this thing by myself." She shot a disgruntled look toward the guy in the store. "And I refuse to let a professional sex deviant unzip me."

Dean smiled. Who knew there were so many advantages to an alternative lifestyle? "I'll be glad to help."

He followed her around the side of the building where a peeling metal door held the faded silhouette of a beaver wearing a hair bow. The bathroom was a one-seater, not exactly clean, but marginally acceptable, with white, cinder block walls, and a fly-specked mirror bolted above the sink. As she looked around for a clean place to set her bundle of clothes, he lowered the toilet seat lid and—out of respect for his gay brethren—covered it with a couple of paper towels.

She put her clothes down and turned her back to him. "There's a zipper."

In unventilated quarters the beaver suit stank more than a gym locker, but as a veteran of more two-a-day practices than he could count, he'd smelled worse. A lot worse. Some of her damp, baby-fine dark hair had escaped from that sad excuse for a ponytail, and he pushed it away from the nape of her neck, which was milk white except for the faintest trace of a pale blue vein. He poked around in the mangy fur until he found the zipper. He was damn good at undressing women, but he'd barely lowered the tab an inch before it caught in the fur. He worked it free, but after another few inches, it caught again.

It went on that way, stop and start, the parting fur revealing an ever expanding wedge of milky skin, and the longer it took to unzip her, the less gay he felt. He tried to distract himself with conversation. "So what gave me away? How did you know I wasn't straight?"

"Are you sure you won't be offended?" she asked with phony solicitude.

"The truth shall set me free."

"Well, you're totally buff, but those are designer muscles. You didn't get a chest like that roofing houses."

"Lots of men go to the gym." He resisted the urge to blow on her damp skin.

"Yes, but what straight guy doesn't have a chin scar someplace, or a nose bump? Your profile is more chiseled than Mount Rushmore."

It was true. Dean's face had remained remarkably unscathed. His shoulder, however, was another story.

"Then there's your hair. Thick, shiny, blond. How many products did you use on it this morning? Never mind. It'll just make me feel inferior."

The only thing he'd used on his hair that morning was shampoo. Good shampoo, it was true, but, still, shampoo. "It's all in the cut," he said, his cut having been administered by Oprah's hairstylist.

"Those jeans didn't come from the Gap."

Correct.

"And you're wearing gay boots."

"These are not gay boots! I paid twelve hundred dollars for them."

"Exactly," she said triumphantly. "What straight man would pay twelve hundred dollars for boots?"

Not even her asinine assessment of his footwear could cool him off because he'd reached her waist, and, as he'd imagined, she wasn't wearing a bra. The frail bumps of her spine disappeared into the furry V of her costume like a delicate pearl necklace being swallowed by Bigfoot. It took all his considerable willpower not to slip his hands inside, slide them around, and explore exactly what the Beav had going on for herself.

"What's taking you so long?" she asked.

"The zipper keeps getting stuck, that's what." He sounded grouchy, but his jeans hadn't been designed to accommodate what they now needed to accommodate. "If you think you can do this faster, you're welcome to try."

"It's hot in here."

"Tell me about it." With one last tug, he reached the end of the zipper, which was a good six inches below her waist. He took in the curve of her hip along with a narrow band of bright red elastic.

She pulled away, and as she turned to him, she crossed her paws over her chest to hold the suit in place. "I can take it from here."

"Oh, please. Like you have anything I'd be interested in seeing."

The corner of her mouth ticked, but whether from amusement or annoyance, he couldn't tell. "Out."

Oh, well . . . He'd tried.

Before he left, she passed over her keys and asked him, none too politely, to get her stuff from her car. Inside the dented trunk he found a couple of plastic milk crates stuffed with art supplies, some paint-splattered toolboxes, and a big canvas tote. He'd just loaded them in his car when the guy who'd been working inside came out to inspect his Vanquish. He had oily hair and a beer gut. Something told Dean this was the alleged sex deviant who'd earned the wrath of the Beav.

"Man, that is a sweet machine. I saw one of them in that James

Bond movie." And then, as he got a good look at Dean, "Holy shit! You're Dean Robillard. What're you doin' around here?"

"Just passing through."

The guy started sputtering. "Gawdamn. Ben should have made Sheryl drive her own big ass to the hospital. Wait'll I tell him The Boo was here."

Dean's college teammates had stuck him with the moniker because of the amount of time he'd spent at Malibu Beach, which was nicknamed "The Boo" by the locals.

"I saw that sack you took in the Steelers game. How's your shoulder doing?"

"Coming along," Dean replied. It'd be coming along a lot better if he stopped driving around the country feeling sorry for himself and started doing his physical therapy.

The guy introduced himself as Glenn, then launched into a review of the Stars' entire season. Dean nodded automatically, all the while wishing the Beav would hurry up. But a good ten minutes passed before she emerged. He took in her wardrobe.

This was just wrong.

Bo Peep had been kidnapped by a Hells Angels gang. Instead of a ruffly gown, pink bonnet, and shepherd's crook, she'd decked herself out in a faded black muscle shirt, baggy jeans, and the big old work boots he'd seen in the bathroom but mercifully forgotten. Defurred and delicate, she was maybe five four, and as thin as he'd imagined, right down to her chest, which was definitely female, but hardly memorable. Apparently, she'd spent most of her bathroom time washing up, because as she came closer, he smelled soap instead of musty fur. Her wet, dark hair lay flat against her head like spilled ink. She wasn't wearing makeup, not that she needed much with that creamy skin. Still, a little lipstick and a dab of mascara wouldn't have hurt her.

She practically threw her beaver suit at Glenn. "The head and the sign are out at the intersection. I stuck them behind the power box."

"What do you want me to do about it?" Glenn retorted.

"I'm sure you'll think of something."

Dean whipped open the car door before she decided to throw another punch. As she climbed in, Glenn thrust his free hand at Dean. "It's been great talking to you. Wait'll I tell Ben that Dean Robillard was here."

"Give him my best."

"You told me your name was Heath," the Beav said as he pulled out of the parking lot.

"Heath Champion is my stage name. My real name is Dean."

"How did Glenn know your real name?"

"We met last year at a gay bar in Reno." He slipped on a pair of Prada aviators with green lenses and gunmetal frames.

"Glenn's gay?"

"Don't pretend you didn't know."

The Beav's husky laugh had a disconcertingly wicked edge, as if she was enjoying her own private joke. But then, as she turned away to look out the window, her laughter faded and trepidation darkened those grape candy eyes. It made him wonder if the Beav didn't have a few secrets of her own hiding behind that feisty exterior.

Chapter Two

Blue concentrated on counting her breaths, hoping that would calm her, but her panic kept trying to resurface. She gave Pretty Boy a surreptitious glance. Did he honestly expect her to believe he was gay? True, there were the gay boots and those stunning good looks. But, even so, he blasted enough heterosexual megawattage to light up the entire female population. Which he'd undoubtedly been doing since he shot out of the birth canal, glimpsed his reflection in the obstetrician's eyeglasses, and gave the world a high five.

Here she'd thought Monty's betrayal was the final disaster in the rapidly unfolding catastrophe that had become her life, but now she was at the mercy of Dean Robillard. She'd never have gotten in the pro football player's car if she hadn't recognized him. His nearly naked, and incredibly buff, body used to be plastered on billboards everywhere advertising End Zone, a line of men's underwear with the memorable slogan "Get your butt in the Zone." More recently, she'd seen his photo in *People*'s "50 Most Beautiful" edition. He'd been walking barefoot on a beach and wearing a tux with the cuffs rolled up. Although she didn't remember which team he played for, she did know he was the kind of man she avoided at all costs, not that men like him made a habit of popping up in her life. But now he was all that stood between her, a homeless shelter, and a sign that read WILL PAINT FOR FOOD.

Three days ago, she'd discovered that both her savings account, with its eight-thousand-dollar nest egg, and her checking account had been emptied out. Now Monty had stolen her two hundred dollars of security money. All she had left in the world was in her wallet—eighteen dollars. She didn't even have a credit card—a huge miscalculation on her part. She'd spent her adult life making sure she would never be helpless, yet here she was. "What were you doing heading for Rawlins Creek?" She tried to sound as if she were making conversation instead of accumulating information that might help her feel her way with him.

"Following a sign to the Taco Bell," he said, "but I'm afraid meeting your lover made me lose my appetite."

"Ex-lover. Way ex."

"Here's what I don't get. The minute I saw the guy, I knew he was a loser. Didn't any of your Seattle friends bother to point that out?"

"I move around a lot."

"Hell, you could have gone up to a stranger at a gas pump."

"Hindsight."

He gazed over at her. "You're going to start crying any minute now, aren't you?"

It took her a moment to figure out what he meant. "I'm being brave," she said with only a hint of sarcasm.

"You don't have to pretend with me. Go ahead and let it out. Fastest way to heal a broken heart."

Monty hadn't broken her heart. He'd made her furious. Still, he wasn't the one who'd emptied out her bank accounts, and she knew she'd overreacted when she'd attacked him. She and Monty had barely been lovers for two weeks before she'd known she'd rather have him as a friend and she'd permanently kicked him out of her bed.

They had common interests, and despite his self-centeredness, she'd generally enjoyed his company. They'd hung out together, gone to movies and galleries, supported each other's work. She'd known he could be overly dramatic, but his frantic phone calls from Denver had alarmed her.

"I wasn't ever in love with him," she said. "I don't do love. But we watched out for each other, and he sounded more upset every time he called. I started worrying that he'd really kill himself. Friends are important to me. I couldn't turn my back on him."

"Friends are important to me, too, but if one of mine was in trouble, I'd hop on a plane instead of packing up and moving."

She jerked a rubber band from her pocket and snared her hair back into its disheveled ponytail. "I was planning to leave Seattle anyway. Just not for Rawlins Creek."

They passed a sign advertising sheep for sale. She mentally sorted through her closest friends, trying to find someone she could hit up for a loan, but they all had two things in common. Warm hearts and abject poverty. Brinia's newborn had scary medical problems, Mr. Grey could barely scrape by on his Social Security, Mai hadn't recovered from the fire that had wiped out her studio, and Tonya was backpacking in Nepal. Which left her dependent on a stranger. It was her childhood all over again, and she hated the too-familiar fear she felt building inside her.

"So, Beav, tell me about yourself."

"I'm Blue."

"Sweetheart, if I had your dubious taste in men, I wouldn't be too happy, either."

"My name is Blue. Blue Bailey."

"Sounds phony."

"My mother was a little depressed the day she filled out my birth certificate. I was supposed to be Harmony, but a riot had broken out in South Africa, and Angola was a mess . . ." She shrugged. "Not a good day to be a Harmony."

"Your mother must have quite a social conscience."

Blue gave a rueful laugh. "You might say." Her mother's social conscience had led to Blue's currently empty bank account.

He tilted his head toward the rear of the car. She noticed a tiny hole in his earlobe. "Those art supplies I put in the trunk . . . ," he said. "A hobby or an occupation?"

"Occupation. I do portraits of children and pets. Also some murals."

"Isn't it a little tough to build up a clientele moving around like you do?"

"Not really. I locate an upscale neighborhood and stuff the mailboxes with flyers that show samples of my work. It generally does the trick, although not in a town like Rawlins Creek where there isn't an upscale neighborhood."

"Which explains the beaver suit. How old are you, anyway?"

"Thirty. And, no, I'm not lying. I can't help the way I look."

"Safe Net."

Blue jumped as a disembodied female voice invaded the interior of the car.

"Checking in to see if we can be of assistance," the voice purred.

Dean passed a slow-moving tractor. "Elaine?"

"It's Claire. Elaine's off today."

The voice was coming from the car's speakers.

"Hey, Claire. I haven't talked to you in a while."

"I had to go visit my mom. So how's the road treating you?"

"No complaints."

"On your way to Chicago, why don't you stop off in St. Louis? I have a couple of steaks in my freezer with your name on them."

Dean adjusted the sun visor. "You're too good to me, sweetheart."

"Nothing's too good for my favorite Safe Net customer."

When he finally disconnected, Blue rolled her eyes. "You've got them lined up and taking numbers, don't you? What a waste."

He refused to play her game. "Don't you ever get the urge to settle down in one place? Or does the witness protection program keep you on the move?"

"Too much world to see for me to settle down. Maybe I'll start thinking about it when I'm forty. Your lady friend mentioned Chicago. I thought you were going to Tennessee."

"I am. But Chicago's home."

Now she remembered. He played for the Chicago Stars. She gazed longingly at the sports car's impressive instrument panel and gearshift paddles. "I'll be happy to take over the driving."

"It'd be too confusing for you to drive a car that doesn't give off smoke." He turned up the satellite radio, a combination of oldies rock and newer tunes.

For the next twenty miles, she listened to music and tried to appreciate the scenery, but she was too worried. She needed a distraction, and she considered ruffling his feathers by asking him what he found most attractive in a man, but it was to her advantage to maintain the fiction that he was gay, and she didn't want to push him too far. Still, she couldn't resist inquiring if he wouldn't rather find a station that played Streisand.

"I don't mean to be rude," he replied with starchy dignity, "but those of us in the gay community get a little tired of the old stereotypes."

She did her best to sound contrite. "I apologize."

"Apology accepted."

U2 came on the radio, then Nirvana. Blue forced herself to do a little head banging to keep him from suspecting how desperate she felt. He accompanied Nickelback with a mellow and fairly impressive baritone, then joined Coldplay in "Speed of Sound." But when Jack Patriot launched into "Why Not Smile?" Dean switched the station.

"Put that back," she said. " 'Why Not Smile?' got me through my senior year of high school. I love Jack Patriot."

"I don't."

"That's like not liking . . . God."

"Each to his own." The easy charm had vanished. He looked aloof and formidable, no longer the happy-go-lucky pro football star pretending to be a gay model with dreams of movie stardom. She suspected she'd gotten her first glimpse of the real man behind the glittering facade, and she didn't like it. She preferred thinking of him as dumb and vain, but only the last one was true.

"I'm getting hungry." He turned a mental switch that let him revert to the person he wanted her to see. "I hope you don't mind going through a drive-in window. Otherwise, I have to find somebody to watch my car."

"You have to find people to watch your car?"

"The ignition key's computer coded, so nobody can steal it, but it attracts a fair amount of attention, which makes it a big vandalism target."

"Don't you think life's complicated enough without having to hire a babysitter for your car?"

"Living an elegant lifestyle's hard work." He hit a button on the dash and got directions to a picnic spot from someone named Missy.

"What did she call you?" Blue asked after the conversation ended.

"Boo. Short for Malibu. I grew up in Southern California and spent a lot of time at the beach. Some friends picked up on it."

"Boo" was one of those football nicknames. That explained why *People* magazine had photographed him walking on the beach. She poked her thumb toward the car's speaker. "All those smitten women . . . Don't you ever feel guilty about leading them on?"

"I try to make up for it by being a good friend."

He wasn't giving away a thing. She turned her head and pretended to study the view. He hadn't said anything yet about kicking her out of the car, but he would. Unless she made it worth his while to keep her around.

♥

He paid for the fast food with a pair of twenty-dollar bills and told the kid at the window to keep the change. She could barely restrain herself from leaping across the car and snatching the money back. Having worked in the food service industry more than a few times herself, she believed in tipping well, but not that well.

They found the roadside picnic area a couple of miles down the highway, a few tables set under some cottonwood trees. The air had grown cooler, and she dug into her duffel for a sweatshirt while Dean took care of the food. She hadn't eaten since last night, and the smell of the french fries made her mouth water.

"Chow's on," he said as she approached.

She'd ordered the cheapest items she could find, and she set two dollars and thirty-five cents' worth of change in front of him. "This should cover my share."

He gazed with open distaste at the pile of coins. "My treat."

"I always pay my own way," she said stubbornly.

"Not this time." He slid the pile back at her. "You can do a sketch for me instead."

"My sketches are worth a lot more than two dollars and thirty-five cents."

"Don't forget the gas."

Maybe she could make this work after all. As the cars flew by on the highway, she savored every greasy fry and bite of hamburger. He set aside his half-eaten burger and retrieved a BlackBerry. He frowned at the small screen as he checked his e-mail.

"Old boyfriend bothering you?" she asked.

For a moment he looked blank, then he shook his head. "My new housekeeper at the Tennessee place. She sends regular e-mails with detailed updates, but no matter what time I call, all I get is voice mail. It's been two months, and I still haven't talked to her in person. Something's not right."

Blue couldn't imagine owning a house, let alone having a housekeeper.

"My real estate agent swears Mrs. O'Hara's great, but I'm getting tired of doing everything electronically. Just once, I wish the woman would pick up the damn phone." He began scrolling through his messages.

Blue needed to find out more about him. "If you're from Chicago, how did you end up buying a house in Tennessee?"

"I was down there with some friends last summer. I'd been looking for a place on the West Coast, but I saw the farm and bought it instead." He set the BlackBerry on the table. "The place sits in the middle of the most beautiful valley you've ever seen. It has a pond. Lots of privacy. Room for horses, which is something I've always wanted. The house needed a lot of work, so my real estate agent found a contractor and hired this Mrs. O'Hara to oversee everything."

"If I had a house, I'd want to fix it up myself."

"I send her digital pictures, paint samples. She's got great taste and came up with her own ideas. It works out."

"Still . . . That's not the same as being there."

"Exactly why I've decided to surprise her with a visit." He opened another e-mail, frowned, and whipped out his cell. A few moments later, he had his quarry on the line. "Heathcliff, I got your e-mail, and I'm not crazy about this cologne endorsement. After End Zone, I was hoping to get away from that kind of thing." He rose from the bench and walked a few steps away from the table. "I was thinking maybe a sports drink or—" He broke off. Seconds later, his mouth curled in a slow smile. "That much? Damn. My pretty face is as good as an open cash register."

Whatever the other person said in response made Dean laugh, a big, thoroughly masculine sound. He propped his boot on a tree stump. "Got to go. My hairdresser hates it when I'm late, and we're doin' highlights. Give the rug rats my best. And tell your wife she's invited to a sleepover at my place as soon as I get back to town. Just

Annabelle and me." With a crafty laugh, he flipped his phone shut and shoved it back in his pocket. "My agent."

"I wish I had an agent," Blue said. "Just so I could drop the word into a conversation. But I guess I'm not an agent sort of person."

"I'm sure you have other good qualities."

"Tons," she said glumly.

Dean headed for the interstate as soon as they got back on the road. Blue realized she was chewing on her thumbnail and quickly folded her hands in her lap. He drove fast, but he kept a steady hand on the wheel, exactly the way she liked to drive. "So where do you want me to drop you off?" he asked.

The question she'd been dreading. She pretended to think it over. "Unfortunately, there aren't any really big cities between Denver and Kansas City. I guess Kansas City would be fine."

He shot her a who-do-you-think-you're-kidding look. "I was thinking more along the lines of the next decent-size truck stop."

She swallowed hard. "Except you're obviously a people person, and you'll be bored without company. I'll keep you entertained."

His eyes flicked to her breasts. "Exactly how do you intend to do that?"

"Car games," she said quickly. "I know dozens." He snorted, and she hurried on. "I'm also an excellent conversationalist, and I can run interference with your fans. I'll keep all those yucky women from throwing themselves at you."

His blue-gray eyes flickered, but whether from irritation or amusement, she didn't know. "I'll think about it," he said.

♥

Somewhat to Dean's surprise, the Beav was still in his car that night as he exited the interstate somewhere in west Kansas and drove toward a sign for the Merry Time Inn. She stirred as he pulled into the parking lot. While she'd slept, he'd had more than ample time to study the rise and fall of her breasts underneath her muscle shirt.

Most of the women he spent time with had pumped themselves up to four times their normal size, but not the Beav. He knew some guys liked overinflated breasts—hell, he used to like them—but Annabelle Granger Champion had long ago spoiled his fun.

"Every time a man like you ogles a woman with artificial E cups, you encourage some innocent girl with perfectly nice breasts to go under the knife. Women should concentrate on expanding their horizons, not their busts."

She'd made him feel personally responsible for the evils of breast enlargement, but Annabelle was like that. She had a lot of strong opinions, and she didn't pull her punches. Annabelle was his one true female friend, but between her marriage to Heath Champion, his bloodsucker of an agent, and the birth of her second child, she didn't have much time to hang out anymore.

He'd been thinking about Annabelle a lot today, maybe because the Beav had strong opinions, too, and she also didn't seem interested in impressing him. It was odd being with a woman who wasn't coming on to him. Of course, he *had* told her he was gay, but she'd figured out that was bullshit at least a hundred miles ago. Still, she'd kept trying to play him. But Little Bo Peep was way out of her league.

Her mouth froze in midyawn as she spotted the well-lit three-story hotel. As many times as she'd aggravated him today, he still wasn't quite ready to hand her a couple hundred bucks and throw her out. For one thing, he wanted her to ask him for the money. For another, she'd been good company today. And then there was the hard-on that had been plaguing him for the past two hundred miles.

He turned in to the parking lot. "These places will take most any credit card." He should have felt like a bully, but she was so full of tough talk and swagger that he didn't.

Her lips compressed. "Unfortunately, I don't have a credit card."

No big surprise there.

"I abused the privilege a few years ago," she went on, "and haven't trusted myself since." She studied the Merry Time Inn sign. "What are you going to do about your car?"

"Tip the security guy to watch it."

"How much?"

"Why do you care?"

"I'm an artist. I'm interested in human behavior."

He pulled into a parking space. "Fifty dollars now, I guess. Another fifty in the morning."

"Excellent." She held out her hand. "You've got yourself a deal."

"You're not watching my car tonight."

The muscles in her throat worked as she swallowed. "Sure I am. Don't worry. I'm a light sleeper. I'll wake up the minute anybody gets too close."

"You're not sleeping in it, either."

"Don't tell me you're one of those sexist jerks who thinks a woman can't do a job as well as a man."

"What I think is that you can't afford a room." He got out of the car. "I'll sport you."

She shot her sharp little nose up in the air and followed him. "I don't need anybody 'sporting' me."

"Really?"

"What I need is for you to let me guard your car."

"Not going to happen."

He could see her trying to find a way around him, and he wasn't completely surprised when she began reeling off the price list for her portraits. "Even taking out the cost of a hotel room and a few meals," she said when she finished, "you'll have to agree that you're getting the best end of the deal. I'll start sketching you tomorrow over breakfast."

The last thing he needed was another portrait of himself. What he really needed was . . . "You can start tonight." He opened the trunk.

"Tonight? It's . . . awfully late."

"Barely nine o'clock." This team could only have one quarterback, and he was it.

She muttered to herself and started rooting around in the trunk. He pulled out his suitcase and her navy duffel. She reached past him to snatch up one of the toolboxes that contained her art supplies and, still muttering, followed him to the entrance. He negotiated with the inn's sole bellman to watch his car and headed for the reception desk. The Beav stayed at his side. Judging by the live music coming from the bar and the locals spilling out into the lobby, the Merry Time was the small town's Saturday night hot spot. He noted the heads turning in his direction. Sometimes he could go for a couple of days without being recognized, but not tonight. A few people in the crowd openly stared. Those damn End Zone commercials. He set down the suitcases at the front desk.

The clerk, a studious-looking Middle Eastern guy in his twenties, greeted him politely, but without recognition. The Beav jabbed him in the ribs and cocked her head toward the bar. "Your fans," she said, as if he hadn't already noticed the two guys who'd detached them-selves from the crowd and were heading his way. Both were middle-aged and overweight. One wore a Hawaiian shirt that bunched over his belly. The other had a handlebar mustache and cowboy boots.

"Time for me to start work," the Beav said loftily. "I'll take care of this."

"No, you won't. I'll—"

"Hey, there," Hawaiian shirt said. "Hope you don't mind the in-terruption, but me and my buddy Bowman have a bet you're Dean Robillard." He stuck out his hand.

Before Dean could respond, the Beav blocked the man's arm with her small body, and the next thing he knew, she was addressing him in a foreign accent that sounded like a cross between Serbo-Croatian and Yiddish. "*Acht*, this Dean Roam-a-lot, he is very famous man in America, yes? My poor husband"—she curled her fingers around

Dean's arm—"his Eeenglish is veddy, veddy bad, and he does not understand this. But my Eeenglish is veddy, veddy good, yes? And everywhere we go, these pipples—pipples like you—they come up to him and say they think he is this man, this Dean Roam-a-lot. But I say, no, my husband is not famous in America, but veddy famous in our country. He is a veddy famous—how you say?—por-nog-ra-pher."

He just about choked on his spit.

She furrowed her brow. "Yes? Did I say this with rightness? He makes the dirty moo-vees."

Dean was changing identities so fast even he was losing track. Still, the Beav deserved his support for all her hard work—however misguided—so he pulled in his grin and tried to look like he didn't speak English.

She'd thrown the ol' boys for a loss, and they didn't know how to handle it. "We're, uh . . . Well . . . Sorry, there. We thought . . ."

"Is all right," she said firmly. "Happens all the time."

Stumbling over their feet, they made their getaway.

The Beav regarded him smugly. "I'm awfully young to be so gifted. Now aren't you glad I decided to tag along today?"

He gave her high marks for creativity, but since he was in the process of passing over his Visa card to the clerk, her efforts to keep his identity secret were pretty much wasted. "I'll take your best suite," he said. "And a small room by the elevator for my insane companion. If that's a problem, put her next to any old ice machine."

The Merry Time Inn had done a great job training its people, and the desk clerk barely blinked. "Unfortunately, we're very full tonight, sir, and our suite is already occupied."

"No suite?" the Beav drawled. "Will the horror never end?"

The clerk studied his computer screen unhappily. "I'm afraid we only have two rooms left. One, I believe you'll find quite satisfactory, but the other is slated for renovation."

"Aw, hell, the little woman won't mind staying there. I'm sure you got all the bloodstains out of the carpet. Plus, porn stars can sleep just about anywhere. And I do mean anywhere."

He was having one heck of a good time, but the clerk was too well trained to smile. "We will, of course, give you a reduced rate."

Blue leaned on the counter. "Charge him double. Otherwise, he'll be offended."

Once he'd countered that piece of nonsense, they headed for the elevator. As the doors closed, the Beav gazed up at him, her grape lollipop eyes round with innocence. "Those guys who came up to you knew your real name. I had no idea there were so many gay men in the world."

He punched the elevator button. "The honest truth is, I play a little professional football under my real name. Only part-time, though, until my movie career takes off."

The Beav faked looking impressed. "Wow. I didn't realize you could play football part-time."

"No offense, but you don't seem to know much about sports."

"Still . . . A gay man playing football. Hard to imagine."

"Oh, there're a whole bunch of us. Probably a good one-third of the NFL." He waited to see if she'd finally call him on his bullshit, but she wasn't in a hurry to end the game.

"And people think jocks aren't sensitive," she said.

"Just goes to show."

"I noticed your ears are pierced."

"I was young."

"And you wanted to flash your cash, right?"

"Two carats in each ear."

"Tell me you don't still wear them."

"Only if I'm having a fat day." The elevator doors slid open. They headed down the hallway to their rooms. The Beav had a long stride for someone so petite. He wasn't used to pugnacious women, but then she was barely female, despite those curvy little breasts and his stubborn hard-on.

The rooms were adjoining. He opened the first door. Clean, but a little smoky, definitely inferior.

She brushed past him. "Ordinarily, I'd suggest we toss a coin, but since you're paying the bill, that doesn't seem fair."

"Well, if you insist."

She took her duffel and once again tried to hold him off. "I do my best work in natural light. We'll wait till tomorrow."

"If I didn't know better, I'd think you were afraid to be alone with me."

"Okay, you've got me. What if I inadvertently step between you and a mirror? You might turn violent."

He grinned. "See you in half an hour."

When he got to his room, he flipped on the last half of the Bulls game, pulled off his boots, and unpacked his things. He already had more drawings, paintings, and photos of himself than he knew what to do with, but that wasn't the point. He grabbed a beer from the minibar, along with a can of peanuts. Annabelle had once suggested he send some of the glamour shots people had done of him over the years to his mother, but he'd told her to mind her own damned business. He didn't let anybody poke around in that twisted relationship.

He stretched out on the bed in his jeans and the white-on-white button-down Marc Jacobs shirt the designer's PR people had sent him a couple of weeks ago. The Bulls called a time-out. Another night, another hotel room. He owned two condos in Chicago, one not far from the lake and another in the western 'burbs close to Stars headquarters in case he didn't feel like fighting the traffic back into the city. But since he'd grown up in boarding school dorm rooms, no place really felt like home. *Thanks, Mom.*

The Tennessee farm had history and roots that grew deep, everything he lacked. Still, he wasn't usually so impulsive, and he was having second thoughts about buying a place without an ocean nearby. A house with a hundred acres of land around it signaled a permanence he'd never experienced and might not be ready for. Still, it was only a vacation home. If he didn't like it, he could always sell it.

He heard water running next door. A promotion came on for an upcoming story about the drowning death of country western singer Marli Moffatt. They flashed twelve-year-old news footage of Marli and Jack Patriot coming out of a Reno wedding chapel. He hit the mute button.

He was looking forward to getting the Beav naked tonight. The fact that he'd never had anybody like her made the prospect all the more interesting. He tipped a handful of peanuts into his mouth and reminded himself he'd stopped doing one-night stands years ago. The idea that he might be turning into his mother—a woman who'd been so busy snorting coke and giving head that she'd forgotten she had a son—had gotten too depressing, so he limited himself to short-term girlfriends, relationships lasting anywhere from a few weeks to a couple of months. Yet here he was about to violate a decade-long policy against casual hookups and not feeling one bit bad about it. The Beav was hardly a giggling football groupie. Even though they'd only been together for a day—and despite all the ways she raised his hackles—they had a real relationship, one forged by interesting conversation, shared meals, and similar taste in music. Most important, the Beav had proved herself a match for his BS.

The final quarter of the Bulls game had just begun when a knock sounded on the adjoining door. He needed to start the night out right by letting her know who was in the driver's seat. "I'm naked," he called out.

"That's great. I haven't done an adult nude in ages. I need the practice."

She wasn't biting. He smiled to himself and palmed the remote. "Don't take this personally, but the idea of being naked in front of a woman is just plain repulsive."

"I'm a professional. Just like a doctor. You can drape your privates if you're uncomfortable."

He grinned. His *privates*?

"Better yet, we'll wait until tomorrow when you've had a chance to adjust to the idea."

Game over. He took a swig of beer. "That's okay. I'll pull on some clothes." He unfastened the top buttons of his shirt and watched the Bulls' new guard miss a foul shot before he switched off the TV and crossed the room to open the door.

Chapter Three

The Beav's contempt for fashion clearly carried over into nightwear. She wore a maroon man's T-shirt and a pair of faded black track pants that hung in accordion pleats around her small ankles. Nothing remotely sexy about either of those garments, except for the mystery of what they covered up. He stepped back to let her in. She smelled like soap instead of a perfume factory.

He headed for the minibar. "Let me get you a drink."

She yelped. "Ohmygod, you don't actually use that thing?"

He couldn't help it. He looked down at his crotch.

She, however, had her eye on the minibar. She dropped her sketch pad, shot in front of him, and snatched up the price list. "Look at this. Two-fifty for a tiny water bottle. Three dollars for a Snickers bar. A Snickers bar!"

"You're paying for more than the candy," he pointed out. "You're paying for the convenience of having the candy exactly when you want it."

But she'd spotted his peanut can on the bed, and he couldn't talk her down. "Seven dollars. *Seven* dollars! How could you?"

"Do you need a paper bag to breathe into?"

"You should just hand over your wallet."

"Normally I wouldn't mention this," he said, "but I'm rich." And, barring the total collapse of the U.S. economy, he always would be. As a kid, the money had come from substantial child support payments. As an adult, it came from something one hell of a lot better. His own hard work.

"I don't care how rich you are. Seven dollars for a can of peanuts is extortion."

The Beav, he realized, had some serious money issues, but that didn't mean he had to buy into them. "Wine or beer, take your choice. Or I'll choose for you because, one way or another, a bottle's going to get opened here."

She still had her nose buried in the price list. "Could you just give me the six bucks, and I'll pretend to drink the beer?"

He took her by the shoulders and set her aside so he could get to the minibar. "Don't look if this is too painful for you."

She snatched up her sketch pad and retreated to the chair across the room. "There are people starving in the world."

"Don't be a sore loser."

She reluctantly accepted the beer. Fortunately, the room only had one chair, which gave him the perfect excuse to stretch out on the bed. "Pose me any way you want."

He hoped she'd suggest the naked thing again, but she didn't.

"However you're comfortable." She set the beer on the carpet, crossed her ankle over her knee tough-guy style, and balanced the sketch pad on her ratty black track pants. Despite her aggressive posture, she looked nervous. So far, so good.

He propped himself on one elbow and finished unbuttoning his shirt. He'd posed for enough cheesy End Zone photos to know what the ladies liked, but he still didn't entirely understand how they could prefer something lame like this to a game shot of him throwing a perfect spiral. That was women for you.

A spike of inky dark hair had worked free from the Beav's perpetually disorganized ponytail, and it fell across one of her sharp cheekbones as she turned her attention to her sketch pad. He let his shirt fall open far enough to reveal the muscles he'd developed over more than a decade of hard work, but not far enough to reveal his fresh shoulder scars. "I'm not . . . ," he said, ". . . actually gay."

"Oh, honey, you don't need to pretend with me."

"The truth is . . ." Slipping his thumb into the waistband of his jeans, he tugged them lower. "Sometimes, when I go out in public, the demands of fame get to be too much for me, so I resort to extreme measures to hide my identity. Although, in fairness to myself, I never lose my dignity. I wouldn't, for example, go so far as to climb into an animal costume. Do you have enough light over there?"

Her pencil moved across the sketch pad. "I'll bet if you found the right man you'd get past your denial. True love is powerful."

She still wanted to play games. Amused, he temporarily switched tactics. "Is that what you thought you had with ol' Monty?"

"True love, no. I have a missing chromosome. But a real friendship, yes. Would you mind turning to your other side?"

So he'd be facing the wall? No way. "Sore hip." He bent his knee. "All those things Monty was saying about trust and abandonment issues . . . crap?"

"Look, Dr. Phil, I'm trying to concentrate here."

"Not crap, then." She wasn't looking at him. "Me, I've fallen in love half a dozen times. All before I was sixteen, but still . . ."

"Surely there's been somebody since then."

"Well, there you've got me." The fact that he'd never fallen in love drove Annabelle crazy. She pointed out that even her husband, Heath, a head case if there ever was one, had been in love once before he met her.

The Beav's hand swept across the paper. "Why settle down when the world is your playground, right?"

"I'm getting a cramp," he said. "Mind if I stretch?" He didn't wait for an answer but let his legs fall over the edge of the bed. He took his time standing up, then stretched a little, which sucked in his abs and sent his jeans low enough to reveal the top of his gray stretch End Zone boxer briefs.

The Beav kept her eyes glued to her sketch pad.

Maybe he'd made a tactical error bringing up Monty, but he couldn't get over somebody with the Beav's strength of character being attracted to such a dick. He set his hands on his hips, deliberately pushing his shirt out of the way so he could display his pecs. He was starting to feel like a stripper, but she'd finally looked up. His jeans slipped another inch lower, and her sketch pad slid to the floor. She leaned over to pick it up and banged her chin on the chair arm. Clearly, she needed a little time to adjust to the idea of letting him explore her beaver parts.

"I'm going to take a quick shower," he said. "Wash off the road dust."

She pulled her sketch pad back into her lap with one hand and waved him away with the other.

♥

The bathroom door shut. Blue moaned and dropped her feet to the carpet. She should have pretended she had a migraine . . . or leprosy—anything to get out of coming to his room tonight. Why couldn't a nice retired couple have stopped to help her today? Or one of those sweet, artistic guys she was so comfortable with?

The water went on in the shower. She imagined it trickling over that billboard body. He used it like a weapon, and, since no one else was around, he had her in his sights. But men like him were meant to be lusted over from a safe distance.

She took a deep swallow from her beer bottle. She reminded herself that Blue Bailey didn't run. Not ever. She looked delicate, like the faintest gust of wind would blow her over, but she was strong where it counted most. Internally. That's how she'd survived her itinerant childhood.

What does the happiness of one little girl, no matter how beloved, mean against the lives of thousands of little girls threatened by bombs, soldiers, and land mines? It had been a miserable day, and old memories unfolded inside of her.

"Blue, Tom and I want to talk to you."

Blue still remembered the sagging plaid couch in Olivia and Tom's cramped San Francisco apartment and the way Olivia had patted the cushion next to her. Blue had been small for eight, but not small enough to still sit in Olivia's lap, so she'd nestled next to her instead. Tom sat on her other side and rubbed Blue's knee. Blue loved them more than anybody in the world, including the mother she hadn't seen in nearly a year. Blue had lived with Olivia and Tom since she was seven, and she was going to live with them forever. They'd promised.

Olivia wore her light brown hair in a braid down her back. She smelled like curry powder and patchouli, and she always gave Blue clay to play with when she threw her pots. Tom had a big soft Afro and wrote articles for the underground newspaper. He took Blue to Golden Gate Park and let her ride on his shoulders when they went out on the street. If she had a nightmare, she'd climb in their bed and fall asleep with her cheek against Tom's warm shoulder and her fingers twined in Olivia's long hair.

"Do you remember, Punkin'," Olivia said, "how we told you about the baby growing in my uterus?"

Blue remembered. They'd shown her pictures in books.

"The baby's going to be born soon," Olivia went on. "That means lots of things will be different now."

Blue didn't want them to be different. She wanted them to stay exactly the same. "Is the baby going to sleep in my room?" Blue finally had her very own room, and she didn't want to share it.

Tom and Olivia exchanged glances before Olivia said, "No, Punkin'. Something better. You remember Norris, the lady who visited us last month, the weaver who started Artists for Peace? She told you all about her house in Albuquerque and her little boy, Kyle? We showed you where New Mexico was on the map. Do you remember how much you liked Norris?"

Blue nodded in blissful ignorance.

"Well, guess what?" Olivia said. "Your mom and Tom and I arranged for you to go live with Norris now."

Blue didn't understand. She gazed into their wide, fake smiles. Tom rubbed his chest through his flannel shirt and blinked his eyes like he might cry. "Olivia and I are going to miss you very much, but you'll have a yard to play in."

That's when she got it. She started to gag. "No! I don't want a yard. I want to stay here! You promised. You said I could live here forever!"

Olivia rushed her to the bathroom and steadied her head while she threw up. Tom slumped on the edge of the old, chipped bathtub. "We wanted you to stay, but . . . that was before we knew about the baby. Things have gotten complicated with money and everything. At Norris's house, there'll be another kid to play with. Won't that be fun?"

"I'll have a kid to play with here!" Blue had sobbed. "I'll have the baby. Don't make me go. Please! I'll be good. I'll be so good I won't bother you ever."

They'd all started to cry then, but in the end, Olivia and Tom had driven her to Albuquerque in their rusty blue van and sneaked away without saying good-bye.

Norris was fat and showed Blue how to weave. Nine-year-old Kyle taught her card games and played *Star Wars* with her. One month slipped into another. Gradually, Blue stopped thinking so much about Tom and Olivia and started to love Norris and Kyle. Kyle was her secret brother, Norris her secret mother, and she was going to stay with them forever.

Then Virginia Bailey, her real mother, came back from Central America and took her away. They went to Texas, where they stayed with a group of activist nuns and spent every spare minute together. She and her mother read books, did art projects, practiced Spanish, and had long talks about everything. A whole day would pass without Blue thinking about Norris and Kyle. Blue fell back in love with her gentle mother and was inconsolable when Virginia left.

Norris had gotten married again, so Blue couldn't go back to Albuquerque. The nuns kept her until the school year ended, and Blue transferred her love to Sister Carolyn. Sister Carolyn drove Blue to Oregon, where Virginia had arranged for her to stay with an organic farmer named Blossom. Blue clung so desperately to Sister Carolyn when she tried to drive off that Blossom had to pull her away.

The cycle started all over again, except this time Blue held a little of herself back from Blossom, and when she had to leave, she discovered it wasn't as painful as before. From then on, she was more careful. With each subsequent move, she distanced herself more from the people she stayed with until, finally, the leaving barely hurt at all.

Blue gazed toward the hotel room bed. Dean Robillard was horny, and he expected her to accommodate him, but he didn't know how deep her aversion ran to casual hookups. In college, she'd watched her girlfriends, high on *Sex and the City*, sleep with whomever they wanted whenever they'd pleased. But instead of feeling empowered, most of them had ended up depressed. Blue had suffered from enough short-term relationships during her childhood, and she wasn't adding to the list. If she didn't count Monty, which she didn't, she'd only had two lovers, both artistic, self-absorbed men happy to leave her in charge. It worked better that way.

The bathroom doorknob turned. She had to be careful how she dealt with Dean for fear he'd leave tomorrow morning. Unfortunately, tact wasn't her forte.

He came out of the bathroom, a towel looped low around his hips. He looked like a Roman god taking a breather in the middle of an orgy while he waited for the next temple virgin to be sent his way. But as the light hit him, her fingers constricted around her sketchbook. This was no flawless, marble-carved Roman divinity. He had a warrior's body—highly functional, powerfully built, and ready for battle.

He saw her taking in the trio of thin scars on his shoulder. "Pissed-off husband."

She didn't believe that for a minute. "The perils of sin."

"Speaking of sin . . ." His lazy smile oozed seduction. "I've been thinking . . . Late night . . . two lonely strangers . . . a comfortable bed . . . I can't come up with a better way to entertain ourselves than to make use of it."

He'd abandoned subtlety to make a dash for the goal line. His gorgeous face and athletic fame gave him a sense of entitlement when it came to women. She understood that. But not this woman. He moved closer. She smelled soap and sex. She considered bringing up the gay thing again, but, at this point, why bother? She could plead a headache and flee the room . . . or she could do what she always did and face up to the challenge. She uncurled from the chair. "Here's the way it's going to be, Boo. You don't mind if I call you 'Boo,' do you?"

"As a matter of fact—"

"You're gorgeous, sexy, and ripped. You've got more charm than any man should have. You have great taste in music, and you're rich—huge bonus points there. You're also very smart. Don't think I haven't noticed. But the thing is, you don't turn me on."

His eyebrows slammed together. "I . . . don't turn you on?"

She tried to look apologetic. "It's not you. It's me."

He blinked, more than a little stunned. She couldn't blame him. He'd undoubtedly used that "It's not you. It's me" line a thousand times himself, and it must be disconcerting to have it thrown back in his face.

"You're kidding me, right?"

"The unvarnished truth is that I'm more comfortable with losers like Monty, not that I intend to make that mistake again. If I went to bed with you—and I've thought long and hard about this—"

"We only met eight hours ago."

"I have no boobs, and I'm not pretty. I'd know you were just using me because I'm all that's available, which would make me feel like crap, which would be the start of another one of my downhill spirals, and frankly, I've spent enough time in mental institutions."

His smile had an edge of calculation. "Anything else?"

She gathered up her sketch pad, along with the beer. "Bottom line, you're a man who lives to be adored, and I don't do adoration."

"Who says you're not pretty?"

"Oh, it doesn't bother me. I have so much character that adding beauty to the mix would be greedy. Honestly, until tonight, it hasn't been an issue. Well, except for Jason Stanhope, but that was seventh grade."

"I see." He continued to look amused.

As casually as possible, she made her way to the connecting door and opened it. "You should feel like you've dodged a bullet."

"What I mainly feel is horny."

"Which is why hotel rooms offer porn." She quickly closed the door and drew her first clean breath. The trick to staying half a step in front of Dean Robillard was to keep him off balance, but whether she could manage that as far as Kansas City was as problematic as what she'd do once she got there.

♥

The Beav must have stayed up late because she had the drawing ready the next morning. She waited till they'd stopped for a break at a central Kansas truck stop before she set it in front of him. Dean stared down at the finished product. No wonder she was broke.

The Beav suppressed a yawn. "If I'd had more time, I could have done it in pastels."

Considering how much damage she'd performed with her pencil, it was probably just as well. She'd drawn his face, all right, but with the features seriously out of whack: eyes too close together, his hairline set back a good two inches, and a couple of extra pounds, giving him jowls. Most damaging, she'd reduced the size of his nose just enough to make it look squashed on his face. He was seldom at a loss for words, but the image she'd drawn left him speechless.

She took a bite of her chocolate glazed doughnut. "Fascinating, isn't it, how easily it could all have gone wrong for you?"

That's when he realized she'd done this deliberately. But she looked more thoughtful than smug. "I hardly ever get to experiment," she said. "You were the perfect subject."

"Glad to be of service," he said dryly.

"Naturally, I did another one." She pulled a second drawing from the folder she'd carried into the truck stop and flicked it dismissively onto the table, where it landed next to his uneaten muffin. It showed him lounging on the bed, knee cocked, shirt falling open over his chest, exactly how he'd arranged himself for her. "Predictably gorgeous," she said, "but boring, don't you think?"

Not just boring, but a little sleazy, too—his pose too calculated, his expression too cocky. She'd seen right through him, and he didn't like it. He still found it hard to believe she'd walked out on him last night. Was it possible he'd lost his touch? Or maybe he'd never had one. Since women tended to drop into his lap, he didn't have a whole lot of experience being the sexual aggressor. He needed to fix that.

Once again, he studied the first drawing, and as he took in his altered face, he began thinking about all the ways his life would have been different if he'd been born with the face the Beav had given him. No lucrative endorsement for End Zone, that was for sure. Even when he was a kid, his looks had given him a lot of free passes. He'd understood that theoretically, but her drawing made it concrete.

The Beav's face clouded. "You hate it, don't you? I should have known you wouldn't get it, but I thought . . . Never mind." She reached for the paper.

He snatched it back before she could touch it. "It took me un-aware, that's all. I probably won't hang it over my fireplace, but I don't hate it. It's . . . thought provoking. As a matter of fact, I like it. I like it a lot."

She studied him to figure out if he was sincere. The longer he was with her, the more his curiosity grew. "You haven't told me much about yourself," he said. "Where did you grow up?"

She broke off a section of her doughnut. "Here and there."

"Come on, Beav. You'll never run into me after this. Spill your secrets."

"My name is Blue. And if you want secrets, you have to go first."

"I'll give it to you in a nutshell. Too much money. Too much fame. Too good-looking. Life's a bitch."

He'd intended to make her smile. Instead, she studied him so intently he grew uncomfortable. "Your turn," he said quickly.

She took her time polishing off her doughnut. He suspected she was trying to decide how much she wanted to tell him. "My mother is Virginia Bailey," she said. "You've probably never heard of her, but she's famous in peace circles."

"Pee circles?"

"*Peace* circles. She's an activist."

"You don't want to know what I was imagining."

"She's led demonstrations all over the world, been arrested more times than I can count, and served two stints in a federal maximum security prison for trespassing on nuclear missile sites."

"Wow."

"That's not the half of it. She nearly died during the eighties when she went on a hunger strike to protest U.S. policy in Nicaragua. Later, she ignored U.N. sanctions to take medicine into Iraq." The Beav rubbed a dab of frosting between her fingers, her expression distant. "When the American soldiers entered Baghdad in 2003, she was already there with an international peace group. In one hand, she held up a protest sign. With the other, she passed out water bottles to the soldiers. For as long as I can remember, she's deliberately kept her income below thirty-one hundred dollars to avoid paying income tax."

"Cutting off your nose to spite your face, isn't it?"

"She can't bear the idea of her money being spent on bombs. I don't agree with her about a lot of things, but I do think the federal government should let taxpayers check off boxes stipulating where they want their tax money to go. Wouldn't you like to make sure all those millions you give Uncle Sam went to schools and hospitals instead of nuclear warheads?"

As a matter of fact, he would. Playgrounds for big kids, preschool programs for little ones, and mandatory LASIK surgery for NFL refs. He set down his coffee mug. "She sounds like a real character."

"Like a kook, you mean."

He was too polite to nod.

"She's not, though. Mom's the real thing, for better or for worse. She's been nominated twice for the Nobel Peace Prize."

"Okay, now I'm impressed." He leaned back in his chair. "What about your father?"

She dipped part of her paper napkin into her water glass and wiped the doughnut icing from her fingers. "He died a month before I was born. A well he was digging in El Salvador caved in. They weren't married."

One more thing he and the Beav had in common.

So far, she'd given him a lot of facts without revealing much that was personal. He stretched his legs. "Who took care of you while your mother was out saving the world?"

"An assortment of well-intentioned people."

"That can't be good."

"It wasn't terrible. They were mostly hippies—artists, a college professor, some social workers. Nobody beat me or abused me. When I was thirteen, I lived with a Houston drug dealer, but in Mom's defense, she had no idea Luisa was still in the business, and except for the occasional drive-by shooting, I liked being with her."

He hoped Blue was kidding.

"I lived in Minnesota for six months with a Lutheran minister, but Mom's a devout Catholic, so I spent a lot of time with various activist nuns."

She'd had a childhood even less stable than his own. Hard to believe.

"Fortunately, Mom's friends tend to be benevolent. I also learned a lot of skills most people don't have."

"Like."

"Well . . . I read Latin, a little Greek. I can put up drywall, plant one hell of an organic garden, use power tools, and I'm a kickass cook. I'll bet you can't match that."

He spoke damn good Spanish and liked using power tools himself, but he didn't want to spoil her fun. "I threw four touchdown passes against Ohio State in the Rose Bowl."

"And set those Rose Princesses' hearts a-fluttering."

The Beav loved taking shots at him, but she did it with such open relish that she never came across as bitchy. Odd. He drained his coffee. "With so much moving around, school must have been a challenge."

"When you're constantly the new kid, you develop fairly sophisticated people skills."

"I'll bet." He was beginning to see where her confrontational attitude came from. "Any college?"

"A small liberal arts school. I had a full scholarship, but I quit at the beginning of my junior year. Still, it's the longest I spent in one place."

"Why'd you leave?"

"Wanderlust. I was born to roam, babe."

He doubted that. The Beav wasn't a natural hard-ass. Raised differently, she would have been married by now, probably teaching kindergarten with a couple kids of her own.

He tossed a twenty on the table, and when he didn't wait for change, she reacted with predictable outrage. "Two cups of coffee, a doughnut, and one uneaten muffin!"

"Get over it."

She snatched up his muffin. As they headed across the parking lot, he studied the drawings she'd done of him and realized he'd gotten the best end of their deal. For the price of a couple of meals and a night's lodging, he'd received some food for thought, and how often did that happen?

♥

As the day advanced, Dean noticed the Beav growing more fidgety. When he stopped for gas, she took off for the restroom and left her grungy black canvas purse behind. He capped off the tank, thought about it for half a second, then went on an exploratory mission. Ignoring her cell phone and a couple of sketch pads, he pulled out her wallet. It contained an Arizona driver's license—she really was thirty—library cards from Seattle and San Francisco, an ATM card, eighteen dollars in cash, and a photograph of a delicate-looking middle-aged woman standing with some street kids in front of a burned-out building. Although the woman's hair was pale, she had the Beav's same small, sharp features. This had to be Virginia Bailey. He dug deeper in her purse and unearthed both a checkbook and a savings account passbook issued by a Dallas bank. Fourteen hundred dollars in the first and a lot more in the second. He frowned. The Beav had a nice nest egg, so why was she acting as though she was broke?

She returned to the car. He put everything back in her purse, closed it, and handed it over. "I was looking for breath mints."

"In my wallet?"

"Why would you have breath mints in your wallet?"

"You were snooping in *my* purse!" Her expression indicated that snooping in general didn't bother her, only when it was directed against her. A pointed reminder to keep his own wallet close to his body. "Prada makes purses," he said as he pulled away from the gas station and headed back to the interstate. "Gucci makes purses. That thing looks like it came with a set of socket wrenches and a girly calendar."

She bristled with indignation. "I can't believe you snooped."

"I can't believe you hit me up for a hotel room last night. You're not exactly destitute."

He was greeted with silence. She turned to stare out the window. Her small stature, those narrow shoulders, the delicate elbows emerging from beneath the sleeves of her ridiculously oversize black T-shirt—all those signs of fragility should have aroused his protective instincts. They didn't.

"Someone emptied out my bank accounts three days ago," she said flatly. "I'm temporarily broke."

"Let me guess. Monty the snake."

She tugged absentmindedly on her ear. "Yeah, that's right. Monty the snake."

She was lying. She hadn't said a word about bank accounts when she'd launched her assault against Monty yesterday. But her dismal expression testified that someone had robbed her. The Beav needed more than a ride. She needed money.

He prided himself on being the most generous guy in the world. He treated the women he dated like queens and sent lavish presents when the relationships ended. He'd never two-timed, and he was a damned unselfish lover. But the way Blue kept resisting him tempered his natural inclination to open his wallet. He took in her disheveled hair and sorry excuse for an outfit. She wasn't even close to being a knockout, and under ordinary circumstances, he'd never have noticed her. But last night, she'd held up a big red stop sign, and the game was on.

"So what are you going to do?" he asked.

"Well . . ." She nibbled at her bottom lip. "I don't actually know anyone in Kansas City, but I have an old college roommate who lives in Nashville. Since you're going right through there . . ."

"You want a ride to Nashville?" He made it sound like the moon.

"If you wouldn't mind."

He didn't mind at all. "I don't know. Nashville's a long way off, and I'd have to pay for all your meals plus another hotel room. Unless . . ."

"I'm not sleeping with you!"

He gave her a lazy smile. "Is sex all you think about? I don't want to hurt your feelings, but, frankly, it makes you seem a little desperate."

It was sucker's bait, and she refused to bite. Instead, she slammed on a pair of cheap aviator sunglasses that made her look like Bo Peep about to take command of an F-18. "Just drive and look gorgeous," she said. "No need to tax your brain by talking."

She had more nerve than any woman he'd ever met.

"The thing is, Blue, I'm not only a pretty face, I'm also a businessman, which means I expect a return on my investment." He should feel as smarmy as he sounded, but he was enjoying himself too much.

"You're getting an original Blue Bailey portrait," she said. "You're also getting a security guard for your car and a bodyguard to hold off your fans. Honestly, I should charge you. I think I will. Two hundred dollars between here and Nashville."

Before he could tell her what he thought of that idea, Safe Net interrupted.

"Hi, Boo, it's Steph."

Blue leaned toward the speaker. "Boo, you devil. What did you do with my panties?"

A long silence followed. He glowered at her. "I can't talk now, Steph. I'm listening to an audiobook, and somebody's about to get stabbed to death."

The Beav pulled the aviators down on her nose as he disconnected and peered at him over the top. "Sorry. I was bored."

He cocked an eyebrow at her. She was at his mercy, but she refused to give an inch. Intriguing.

He turned up the radio and helped out the Gin Blossoms with a damn good drum fill on the steering wheel. Blue, however, stayed lost in her own world. She didn't even comment when he flipped the station after Jack Patriot came on again with "Why Not Smile?"

♥

Blue barely heard the radio playing in the background. She was so far out of her element with Dean Robillard that he might have been from a different universe. The trick was not letting him realize she knew it. She wondered if he'd bought into her lie about Monty and the bank accounts. He didn't give much away, so it was hard to tell, but she couldn't bear having him know her own mother was the villain.

Virginia was Blue's only relative, so it had been natural for her to be the cosigner on all Blue's accounts. Her mother was the last person to steal from anyone. Virginia happily bought her clothes at Salvation Army thrift stores and slept on friends' couches when she was in the States. Only a humanitarian crisis of epic proportions could have made her take Blue's money.

Blue had discovered the theft on Friday, three days ago, when she'd tried to use her ATM card. Virginia had left a message on her cell.

"I only have a few minutes, sweetheart. I got into your bank accounts today. I'll write as soon as I can to explain everything." Her mother rarely lost control, but Virginia's soft, sweet voice had broken. *"Forgive me, my love. I'm in Colombia. A group of girls I've been working with was kidnapped yesterday by one of those armed bands of marauders. They'll be . . . raped, forced to become killers themselves. I—I can't let that happen. I can buy their freedom with your money. I know you'll see this as an unforgivable breach of trust, my darling, but you're strong and others aren't. Please forgive me and—and remember how much I love you."*

Blue stared blindly at the flat Kansas landscape. She hadn't felt so helpless since she was a kid. The nest egg that had given her the only security she'd ever known had become ransom money. How did she start over with only eighteen dollars? That wouldn't even pay for new advertising flyers. She'd feel marginally better if she could call Virginia and scream at her, but her mother didn't own a phone. If she needed one, she simply borrowed.

"You're strong and others aren't." Blue had grown up hearing those words. *"You don't have to live in fear. You can make your own way. You don't need to worry about soldiers breaking into your house and dragging you off to prison."*

Blue also didn't have to worry about soldiers doing much worse.

She tried never to think about what her mother had once endured in a Central American prison. Her sweet, kind mother had been a victim of the unspeakable, yet she'd refused to hold on to hatred. Every night she prayed for the souls of the men who had raped her.

Blue gazed across the passenger seat toward Dean Robillard, a man who took being irresistible for granted. She needed him right now, and maybe the fact that she hadn't fallen at his feet gave her a weapon, although admittedly a fragile one. All she had to do was keep him interested, and herself fully clothed, until they got to Nashville.

♥

At an early evening rest stop just west of St. Louis, Dean watched Blue standing by a picnic table with her cell. She'd told him she was calling her old roommate in Nashville to make arrangements for a place to meet tomorrow, but she'd just kicked a charcoal grill and slammed her phone back into her purse. His spirits rose. The game wasn't over after all.

A few hours earlier he'd made the mistake of taking a call from Ronde Frazier, an old teammate who'd retired to St. Louis. Ronde had insisted they get together that night, along with a couple other players in the area. Since Ronde had protected Dean's ass for five seasons, he couldn't beg off, even though it screwed up his plans for a night with Blue. But it didn't look as though things were working out the way she wanted. He took in her disgruntled expression and watched her limp back toward him. "Problem?" he said.

"No. No problem." She reached for the door handle then dropped her arm. "Well, maybe, a small one. Nothing I can't handle."

"Like you've been doing such a good job of handling things so far?"

"You could be just a little supportive." She jerked open the door and glared at him over the roof of the car. "Her phone's been disconnected. Apparently, she moved without letting me know."

Life had just handed him a frosty mug of cold beer. Surprising how satisfying it was to have a woman like Blue Bailey at his mercy. "I'm sorry to hear that," he said with all kinds of sincerity. "What are you going to do now?"

"I'll come up with something."

As he pulled back out on the interstate, he decided it was too bad Mrs. O'Hara didn't believe in answering her phone or he could have told her that he was on his way to the farm . . . and bringing along his first overnight guest.

"I've been considering your current difficulties, Blue." He shot past a red convertible. "Here's what I'm going to suggest . . ."

Chapter Four

April Robillard closed out her e-mail. What would Dean say if he knew the real identity of his housekeeper? She couldn't bear thinking about it.

"You want the stove hooked up. Right, Susan?"

No, dude, let's pop a geranium in it and make a planter. "Yes, hook it up as soon as you can."

She stepped over the shredded remnants of the dancing copper kettle wallpaper the painters had stripped from the kitchen walls. Cody, who was younger than her son, wasn't the only workman who invented excuses to talk to her. She might be fifty-two years old, but the boys didn't know that, and they kept swarming. It was as if they could still smell sex on her. Poor babies. She no longer gave away her goodies so easily.

She grabbed her iPod so she could drown out the noise with some vintage rock, but before she stuck in the earpieces, Sam, the head carpenter, poked his head through the kitchen door. "Susan, check out the upstairs bathrooms. I want to make sure you're okay with the exhaust fans."

She'd checked out the exhaust fans earlier that morning with him, but she followed him into the hallway, maneuvering around a compressor and a pile of drop cloths to get there. The house had been built in the early nineteen hundreds and rehabbed during the seventies, when the plumbing and electrical had been updated and air-conditioning installed. Unfortunately, that modernization had also included avocado green bath and kitchen decor, cheap paneling, and gold vinyl floors grown dingy and cracked from use. For the past two months, she'd dedicated herself to erasing those mistakes and restoring the place to what it should be, a traditional farmhouse, luxuriously updated.

The early afternoon sunshine streaming through the new sidelights caught floating dust particles, but the worst of the construction mess was over. Her sandals with their jeweled T-straps clicked on the hallway's hardwood floor. The bangles on her wrists jingled. Even amid all the dirt and disorder, she dressed to please herself.

A dining room that had once been a parlor opened off to her right, and a newly enlarged living area, part of a later addition, off to her left. The frame and stone house had been built in the Federal style, but the various additions had turned it into a hodgepodge, and she'd knocked out walls to make the space more livable.

"If you take long showers, you want a good exhaust fan to keep the steam from building up," Sam said.

Dean liked his showers long and hot. She remembered that much from his teenage years, but for all she knew, he could have become one of those men who took short showers and dressed in five minutes. Painful to know so little about your only child, although she should be used to it by now.

Several hours later April managed to slip away from all the noise. As she stepped out the side door, she drew in the scent of the late May afternoon. The distant whiff of manure from a neighboring farm drifted her way, along with the fragrance of the honeysuckle growing in a happy ramble around the farmhouse's stone foundation. It fought for space with overgrown day lilies, floppy peony bushes, and a leggy tangle of hearty shrub rose planted by farm wives too busy growing the pole beans and corn that would carry their families through the winter to fuss with demanding ornamentals.

She stopped for a moment to survey the weed-choked garden laid out decades earlier in the no-nonsense square common to rural households. Just beyond it a newly poured concrete slab extended from the back of the house, where the carpenters would soon begin erecting the screen porch. In the far corner, she'd etched her initials *A.R.* in tiny letters, so she could leave something permanent behind. One of the painters working upstairs gazed down at her from the window. She pushed a blade of long blond hair away from her face and hurried past the old iron pump before someone tried to stop her with more unnecessary questions.

The former Callaway farm sat in a gentle valley surrounded by rolling hills. It had once been a prosperous horse farm, but now the only animals roaming its seventy-five acres were deer, squirrel, raccoon, and coyote. The property—pasture, paddock, and woods— also held a barn, a dilapidated tenant cottage, and a secluded, spring-fed pond. An old grape arbor, overgrown like everything else, sat at the end of a broken flagstone path. The weathered wooden bench nearby suggested Wilma Callaway, the farm's last occupant, might have come out here when her work was done. Wilma had died last year at ninety-one. Dean had bought the farm from a distant relative.

April kept tabs on her son through an elaborate network of connections. That's how she'd learned that he intended to hire someone to supervise rehabbing the house. Right away, she'd known what she had to do. After all these years, she would finally make a home for her son. Leaving her work behind in L.A. had been complicated, but getting the job here had been surprisingly easy. She'd manufactured some references, bought a skirt and sweater at Talbots, found a clip-on headband to pull her long, choppy hair back from her face, and invented a story that explained her presence in East Tennessee. Dean's real estate agent had hired her ten minutes into the interview.

April had a love-hate relationship with the conservative woman she'd created to keep her identity anonymous. She imagined Susan O'Hara as a widow who was now on her own. Poor, but valiant, Susan had no marketable skills beyond the ones she'd gained raising a family, which included handling household accounts, teaching Sunday school, and helping her beloved, deceased husband rehab houses.

Susan's conservative taste in clothes, however, had to go. On April's first day in Garrison, she'd declared the widow a new woman and reverted to her own wardrobe. April loved mixing vintage with cutting-edge fashion, matching designer pieces with thrift shop finds. Last week she'd gone into town wearing a Gaultier bustier with Banana Republic chinos. Today, she'd dressed down in a reconstructed dark brown Janis Joplin T-shirt, ginger-colored cropped pants, and her bijou jeweled sandals.

She took the path that led into the woods. White violets were beginning to bloom, along with Queen Anne's lace. Before long, she could see the sun-dappled surface of the pond through a ring of mountain laurel and flame azalea. She found her favorite place on the bank and kicked off her sandals. On the other side of the pond, just out of sight, was the ramshackle tenant's cottage where she'd taken up residence.

She pulled her knees to her chest. Sooner or later, Dean was going to uncover her deception, and that would be the end of it. He wouldn't scream at her. Screaming wasn't his way. But his unspoken contempt was more cutting than angry shouts or vicious words. If only she could finish his house before he saw through her charade. Maybe once he moved in he'd feel at least a little of what she wanted to leave behind—her love and regret.

Unfortunately, Dean wasn't a big believer in redemption. She'd cleaned up her act over ten years ago, but his scars ran too deep to forgive. Scars she'd put there. April Robillard, the queen of the groupies . . . The girl who knew all about having fun, but nothing about being a mother.

"Stop talking about yourself like that," her friend Charli said whenever they discussed the bad old days. *"You were never, ever a groupie, April. You were their freakin' muse."*

That's what they all told themselves. Maybe, for some of them, it had been true. So many fabulous women: Anita Pallenberg, Marianne Faithfull, Angie Bowie, Bebe Buell, Lori Maddox . . . and April Robillard. Anita and Marianne had been the girlfriends of Keith and Mick; Angie was married for a while to David Bowie; BeBe was involved with Steven Tyler; Lori with Jimmy Page. And for over a year, April had been Jack Patriot's lover. All the women were smart and beautiful, more than capable of forging their own way in the world. But they'd loved the men too much. The men and the music they made. The women offered counsel and companionship. They stroked egos, smoothed brows, overlooked infidelities, and entertained with sex. Rock on.

"You weren't a groupie, April. Look at how many you turned down."

April had been discriminating in her way, refusing the men she didn't fancy, no matter how high on the charts their albums hit. But she'd dogged those she wanted, willing to shrug off the drugs, the rages, the other women.

"You were their muse . . ."

Except a muse had power. A muse didn't lose years of her life to alcohol, pot, Quaaludes, mescaline, and, finally, cocaine. Most of all, a muse wasn't so afraid of corrupting her little boy that she'd virtually abandoned him.

It was too late to fix what she'd done to her Dean, but at least she could do this. She could make him a home and then once again disappear from his life.

April rested her head on her knees and let the music wash over her.

Do you remember when we were young,
And every dream we had felt like the first one?
Baby, why not smile?

♥

The farm belonged to the valley. Dean and Blue arrived at sunset when low clouds of orange, lemon, and purple draped the surrounding hills like ruffles on a cancan dancer's skirt. A curving, bumpy drive led from the highway to the house. As Blue caught sight of it, her current disasters slipped from her mind.

The house—big, rambling, and weather-beaten—spoke to her of America's roots: of planting and harvest, Thanksgiving turkeys and Fourth of July lemonade, of hardworking farm wives snapping beans into chipped white enamel pans, and hardworking men stomping the mud from their boots at the back door. The oldest and largest part of the house was built of stone with a deep front porch and long, double-hung windows. An abbreviated wooden ell, a newer addition, bumped back on the right. The low-pitched roof held a ramble of eaves, chimneys, and gables. This had been no hardscrabble farm but a once prosperous enterprise.

Blue took in the mature trees and overgrown yard, the barn, fields, and pastures. She couldn't imagine a more unlikely spot for a big-city celebrity like Dean. She watched him head toward the barn with the easy, loping grace of a man at home in his body, and then she returned her attention to the house.

She wished she could have come here under different circumstances so she could enjoy this place, but the farm's isolation made her situation more difficult. Maybe she could get hired by one of the crews working on the house. Or she'd find something in the nearby town, although it was barely a dot on the map. Still, she only needed a few hundred dollars. Once she had that, she'd set out for Nashville, rent a cheap room, print up new flyers, and start all over again. The trick was getting Dean to let her stay here rent free while she put her life back together.

She had no illusions about why he'd brought her to the farm. By not tearing off her clothes for him that first night, she'd turned herself into a challenge—a challenge he'd forget about the instant one of the local southern beauties caught his eye. That meant she'd needed to find another way to make herself useful to him.

Just then, the front door opened and one of the most amazing creatures Blue had ever seen stepped out. Amazon tall and slender, she had a bold, square face and long, uneven blades of poker-straight, streaky blond hair. Blue remembered photos she'd seen of the great fashion models of the past, women of the sixties and seventies like Verushka, Jean Shrimpton, and Fleur Savagar. This woman had that same presence. Smoky blue eyes peered out from a dramatic square-jawed face, almost masculine in its strength. As the woman reached the front step, Blue saw a faint set of lines bracketing that wide, sensuous mouth and realized she wasn't as young as she'd first thought, maybe in her early forties.

Narrow jeans perched on bladed hip bones. The strategically placed rips at the thighs and knees hadn't been put there by wear, but by a designer's calculated eye. Metallic threads edged the suede shoulder straps of her crocheted, cantaloupe-colored camisole. Copper leather blossoms bloomed on the toes of her slides. Her look was both boho funky and chic. Was she a model? An actress? Probably one of Dean's girlfriends. With such dramatic beauty, a few years' age difference hardly signified. Although Blue didn't care about fashion, she was suddenly conscious of her own shapeless jeans, baggy T-shirt, and unkempt hair, which drastically needed a decent cut.

The woman took in the Vanquish, and her wide, crimson-slashed mouth curved in a smile. "Lost?"

Blue bought a little time. "Well . . . I know where I am geographically, but, frankly, my life's kind of a mess right now."

The woman laughed, a low, husky sound. There was something familiar about her. "I know all about that." She came down the steps, and Blue's sense of familiarity grew. "I'm Susan O'Hara."

This sexy, exotic creature was Dean's mysterious housekeeper? No way. "I'm Blue."

"Damn. I hope it's temporary."

Right then, Blue knew. *Holy shit.* That square jaw, those blue-gray eyes, that quick brain . . . Holy, holy shit.

"Blue Bailey," she managed. "It was a . . . uh . . . bad day in Angola."

The woman regarded her with interest.

Blue made a vague, meaningless gesture with her hand. "Plus South Africa."

Boot heels struck the gravel.

As the woman turned, the fading light picked out long strands of blond and fawn in her hair. Her red lips parted, and the delicate fans of strain at the corners of her eyes constricted. The boot heels came to an abrupt stop, and Dean stood silhouetted against the barn, his legs braced, arms tensed at his side. The woman might have been his sister. But she wasn't. Not his girlfriend, either. The woman with the stricken ocean blue eyes was the mother he'd dismissed so brusquely just that morning when Blue had asked about his family.

He stopped for only a moment, and then his boots ate up the ground. Ignoring the brick path with its uneven edges like broken teeth, he stalked across the overgrown lawn. "Mrs. Fucking O'Hara."

Blue flinched. She couldn't imagine blasting her mother with the f-word, no matter how angry she got. But then, her mother was impervious to verbal attacks.

This woman wasn't. The bangles slipped on her wrist and a trio of delicate silver rings caught the light as she touched her throat. Long seconds ticked by. She turned away and went inside without a word.

The dazzling charm Dean employed so skillfully was gone. He

looked stony and remote. She understood his need to withdraw, but now wasn't the time for it. "If I were a lesbian," she said to break the tension, "I would totally go for her."

The shuttered look vanished and outrage took its place. "Thanks for nothing."

"I'm just being honest. And I thought *my* mother drew a lot of attention."

"How do you know she's my mother? Did she tell you?"

"No, but the resemblance is hard to miss, although she must have been twelve when she had you."

"A skin-deep resemblance, that's for damn sure." He mounted the steps and headed for the front door.

"Dean . . ."

But he was already gone.

Blue didn't share her mother's intolerance for violence—witness her recent contretemps with Monty—but the idea of that exotic creature with the wounded eyes being its victim bothered her, and she followed him into the house.

Evidence of the renovation was everywhere. A staircase with an unfinished banister rose on the right, along with a wide, plastic-draped opening that must lead to the house's primary living area. On her left, beyond a pair of sawhorses, lay the dining room. The smell of fresh paint and new wood permeated everything, but Dean was too intent on finding his mother to check out the changes.

"Believe me," Blue said, "I understand what it's like to have serious maternal issues, but you're not in the best state of mind to deal with this. Maybe we should talk it through first?"

"Let's not." Shoving aside the plastic, he peered into the living room only to hear footsteps overhead. He headed for the stairs.

She had more than enough trouble of her own, but instead of letting him go, she stayed at his heels. "I'm just saying that I think you need to give yourself a little time to cool off before you confront her."

"Beat it."

He'd already reached the top with Blue only a few steps behind. The smell of paint was stronger up here. She peered around his broad back into the big, irregularly shaped hallway. All the doors were missing, but, unlike the downstairs, this area had been painted, new electrical sockets waited for sconces, and the old wide-plank floors gleamed. Just past Dean's shoulder, Blue glimpsed a bathroom that had been carefully restored with white honeycomb tile, freshly painted tongue-and-groove wainscoting, an antique medicine cabinet, and pewter fixtures.

His mother emerged from a bend in the hallway, a slouchy metallic tote stuffed with papers in her hand. "I'm not sorry." She met his eyes defiantly. "I've worked harder than any real housekeeper."

"I want you out of here," he said in a cold steel voice that made Blue flinch.

"As soon as I get everything organized."

"Now." He moved deeper into the hallway. "This is bullshit, even for you."

"I've done a good job."

"Pack up."

"I can't go now. Tomorrow, the men are coming with the kitchen countertops. I have electricians showing up and painters. Nothing will be done right if I'm not here."

"I'll risk it," he snapped.

"Dean, don't be stupid. I'm staying at the tenant's cottage. You won't even know I'm around."

"You couldn't be invisible if you tried. Now get your crap together and get out of here." He brushed past Blue and headed downstairs.

The woman stared at his retreating back. Her head came up, her shoulders straightened, but then her weight seemed too much for her. The tote dropped from her fingers. She bent down to pick it up, then sat on the floor instead, her spine pressed to the wall. She didn't do anything as dramatic as bursting into tears, but she looked so sad that Blue's heart went out to her.

The woman bent her knees and wrapped her arms around them, the silver rings showing off her slender fingers. "I wanted . . . to make a home for him. Just once."

Blue's own mother would never have thought of anything like that. Virginia Bailey understood nuclear disarmament treaties and international trade agreements, but she knew nothing of homemaking. "Don't you think he's a little old?" Blue said softly.

"Yes. Too old." The long blunt ends of her hair fell over the crocheted whirls of her camisole. "I'm not a horrible person. Not now."

"You don't seem horrible."

"You probably think I shouldn't have done this, but, as you can see, I didn't have anything to lose."

"Still, hiding your identity probably wasn't the best way to manage a reconciliation. If that's what you're looking for."

The woman drew her knees closer to her chest. "It's too late for that. I just wanted to fix up this place for him, then get away before he figured out I was his Mrs. O'Hara." With a self-conscious laugh, she lifted her head. "I'm April Robillard. I haven't even introduced myself. This must be embarrassing to you."

"Not as much as it should be. I have an unhealthy curiosity about other people's business." She noticed a little color returning to April's pale cheeks, so she kept talking. "I don't actually buy the tabloids, but if I walk into a Laundromat and see one lying around, I'll dive over a row of washers to get to it."

April gave a shaky laugh. "There's a certain fascination in reading about other peoples' screwups, isn't there?"

Blue smiled. "Would you like me to get you something? A cup of tea? A drink?"

"Would you . . . just sit with me for a minute? I miss being around women. The men who work here are great, but they're men."

Blue had a feeling April didn't easily ask for help. She understood all about that. The smell of fresh lumber drifted up the stairs as she sat on the floor across from April and searched for a neutral topic. "I like what you've done."

"I tried to make the renovations fit the bones of the house. He's so restless. I wanted him to be able to relax here." She gave a choked laugh. "I guess tonight wasn't the best way to get a start on that."

"He seems pretty high maintenance."

"He gets it from me."

Blue ran her hand over the worn, polished floorboards. In the sunlight, they'd gleam like honey. "You've accomplished a lot."

"I've loved doing it. You should have seen what it looked like when I got here."

"Tell me about it," Blue said.

April described what she'd found when she arrived and the changes she'd made. As she spoke, her love for the house shone through. "We're further along up here than downstairs. All the beds have been set up, but there's not much else. I was planning to attend some estate sales soon to supplement the furniture he's already ordered."

"Where are the doors?"

"Being stripped and refinished. I couldn't stand the idea of putting in new ones."

Downstairs, the front door opened. April's expression clouded, and she quickly rose to her feet. Blue needed to leave them alone, so she stood, too.

"I have to call the contractor," April said as Dean came up the stairs.

"Don't bother. I'll figure it out."

April's jaw set. "Spoken like someone who's never renovated a house."

"I think I can handle it," he said tightly. "If I have any questions, I'll be sure to send you an e-mail."

"I need at least a week to get everything organized before I can leave."

"Forget it. I want you out of here tomorrow." He propped his foot on the top step, blocking Blue's exit point. He stared coldly at his mother. "I made a reservation for you at the Hermitage in Nashville. If you'd like to stay there a few extra days, put it on my tab."

"I can't leave that fast. There's too much going on."

"You'll have tonight to get organized." He deliberately turned his back on her so he could inspect the bathroom.

The first hint of entreaty came into April's voice. "I can't walk away from this job, Dean. Not when I have so much invested in it."

"Hey, you're good at walking away. Remember how it was? The Stones arrived in the States. You were gone. Van Halen played Madison Square Garden. Hello, Big Apple. Be out of here by tomorrow night."

Blue watched April lift her chin. She was a tall woman. Even so, she had to look up at him. "I don't like to drive at night."

"You used to tell me that night was the best time to be on the road."

"Yeah, but I was stoned then."

Her response was so in-your-face that Blue couldn't help feeling at least a little admiration.

"The good old days." A corner of Dean's mouth curled unpleasantly, and he headed back down the steps.

April followed him, addressing the back of his neck, her show of rebellion fading. "A week, Dean. Is that too much to ask?"

"We don't ask things from each other, remember? Hell, of course you remember. You're the one who taught me that."

"Just . . . let me finish here."

Blue watched from the top of the stairs as April reached for his arm, only to draw back before she touched him. The fact that she couldn't touch her own son struck Blue as sad beyond words.

"The tenant's cottage is out of sight of the house." April stepped in front of him, forcing him to acknowledge her. "I'll be with the workmen during the day. I'll stay out of your way. Please." Her chin came up again. "This . . . means a lot to me."

Dean was unmoved by her pleas. "If you need money, I'll write you a check."

April's nostrils flared. "You know I don't need money."

"Then I guess we don't have anything more to say to each other."

April finally realized she'd been beaten and pushed her trembling hands in the pockets of her jeans. "Sure. Enjoy the place."

Blue couldn't bear watching April's heartbreaking attempt to hold on to her dignity. Even as she told herself this wasn't her affair, the unplanned, ill-advised words came spilling out.

"Dean, your mother is dying."

Chapter Five

April's lips parted in shock. Dean stiffened. "What are you talking about?"

Blue had sort of meant it figuratively—that April was dying inside—but Dean didn't seem to be in a figurative turn of mind. She never should have spoken. But, honestly, how could things get any worse?

She came slowly down the stairs. "Your mother— The, uh, doctors—" She tried to put it together. "There's this hole in her heart. Your mother's dying, but she doesn't want you to know."

April's blue-gray eyes widened.

Blue reached the bottom and curled her fingers around the banister. Okay, so maybe she'd gone a tiny bit overboard, but when it came to maternal relationships, she was too screwed up to be held accountable.

Dean's complexion had grown ashen. He gazed at his mother. "Is this true?"

April's lips moved, but no sound came out. Blue's grip on the rail tightened. Finally, April's throat muscles began to work, and she swallowed. "It . . . might not be fatal."

"But the doctors aren't making any promises," Blue said quickly.

Dean shot Blue a hard look. "How do you know about this?"

How indeed? "I don't think your mother meant to tell me, but she had sort of a . . . mini-breakdown up here."

April took offense. "I *didn't* have a breakdown. Mini or not. I just . . . dropped my defenses for a second."

Blue regarded her sadly. "So brave."

April shot her a lethal glare. "I don't want to talk about this, and I'd appreciate it if *you* didn't talk about it, either."

"I apologize for breaking your confidence, but it seemed cruel not to tell him."

"It's not his problem," April shot back.

If Blue had harbored any hope that Dean would instantly take his mother in his arms and tell her the time had come to work out their differences, he quickly disillusioned her by stalking out the front door. As his footsteps faded, Blue fixed a chipper expression on her face. "I think that went well, don't you? All things considered."

April did everything but lunge for her throat. "You're a lunatic!"

Blue took a quick step backward. "Yet you're still here."

April threw up her hands, bangles jingling, rings flashing. "You've made everything worse."

"Frankly, it didn't look like things could get much worse. But then, I'm not the one with a hotel reservation in Nashville tomorrow night, so I might be missing something."

The Vanquish's engine roared to life, and the tires spun in the gravel. Some of the fire left April. "He's going out to celebrate. Free drinks for everybody in the bar."

"And I thought I had a twisted relationship with my mother."

April's eyes narrowed. "Who are you, anyway?"

Blue hated questions like this. Virginia would have answered that she was a child of God, but Blue doubted the Almighty was all that anxious to claim Virginia's daughter right now. And explaining about Monty and the beaver costume wouldn't exactly be putting her best foot forward. Fortunately, April had come up with her own explanation.

"Never mind. My son's effect on women is legendary."

"I'm a painter."

Her eyes swept from Blue's untidy ponytail to her scuffed black motorcycle boots. "You're not his usual type of girlfriend."

"Once again, my three-digit IQ separates me from the pack."

April sank down on the next to last step. "What the hell am I going to do now?"

"Maybe you could try to reconcile with your son while you wait for the results from your latest round of tests. Considering the amazing strides doctors have made treating heart disease, I'm fairly confident you'll get good news."

"It was a rhetorical question," April said dryly.

"Only a suggestion."

♥

April set off for the tenant's cottage shortly after, and Blue wandered through the quiet, dusty rooms. Even the home's renovated kitchen couldn't cheer her up. No matter how pure her motivation, she had no business indulging her fairy godmother fantasy when it came to other people's family messes.

By nightfall, Dean still hadn't returned. As darkness settled around the house, Blue made the unpleasant discovery that only the kitchen and bathrooms had any working light fixtures. She sincerely hoped Dean returned soon because the house, so cozy a few hours earlier, had grown eerie. The plastic hanging over the doorways crackled like dry bones. The old floors creaked. Since there were no doors, she didn't have the option of locking herself in a bedroom, and with no car, she couldn't even drive into town and hang out at a convenience store. She was stuck. There was nothing to do but go to sleep.

She wished she'd made up a bed while she could still see. She fumbled around in the dark, feeling her way along the dining room chair rail to get to the trouble light the carpenters had left coiled in the corner. Ominous shadows leaped up the dining room walls as she flicked it on. She unplugged it and crept upstairs, holding on to the banister while the long yellow power cord dragged behind her like a tail.

Five bedrooms opened off the hallway's nooks and crannies, but only one had a private bath with a working light fixture. By the time she reached it, she was so jumpy from the grotesque shadows shooting across the walls that she couldn't go any farther. True, only a few faint threads of illumination spilled from the bathroom, but it was better than nothing. She propped the trouble light in a corner and unpacked the linens stacked on the mattress. The new, queen-size sleigh bed had a curving cherry headboard but no footboard. The bed, along with a matching triple dresser, were the only pieces of furniture. Six bare windows watched her like staring eyes with a big stone fireplace forming a gaping mouth.

She pushed the stepladder the painter had left in the hallway in front of the door to let Dean know this room was already occupied for the night. The ladder would hardly keep him out if he decided he wanted to come in, but why should he? After the earthshaking news he'd received about his mother, he'd hardly be in the mood for seduction.

She carried the trouble light into the small bathroom and washed her face. Since Dean had driven off with her stuff, she had to brush her teeth with her finger. She pulled her bra through the armhole of her T-shirt and kicked off her boots but left everything else on in case she needed to flee the house screaming. She wasn't a jumpy person when it came to dealing with urban boogeymen, but she was out of her element here, and she took the trouble light with her as she slipped into bed. Only after she'd settled in did she turn it off and stick it under the covers where she could get to it quickly.

A branch rubbed the side of the house. Something rustled in the chimney. She imagined bats lining up for a 5K through the house. *Where was Dean? And why couldn't this place have some doors?*

She wished she'd gone to the cottage with April, but she hadn't been invited. Maybe Blue had been a little heavy-handed, but at least she'd bought Dean's mother some time, which was more than April had been able to do for herself. The helplessness of the naturally beautiful.

Blue tried to concentrate on being ill-used, but she wasn't good at lying to herself. She'd interfered with something she should have left alone. On the bright side, dealing with other people's troubles had distracted her from worrying about her own.

A floorboard creaked. The chimney moaned. She curled her fingers around the handle of the trouble light and stared at the gaping doorway.

Minutes ticked away.

Gradually, her fingers relaxed, and she fell into a restless sleep.

♥

An ominously creaking floorboard jolted her awake. Her eyes shot open to see a menacing shape looming over her. Her hand convulsed around the trouble light. She yanked it from under the covers and swung.

"Shit!" A familiar masculine bellow pierced the night quiet.

Her fingers found the switch. Miraculously the bulb in the plastic cage hadn't broken, and harsh light flooded the room. A very angry multimillionaire quarterback hovered above her. He was bare-chested, furious, and rubbing his arm just above the elbow. "What the *hell* do you think you're doing?"

She shot up in the pillows, trouble light clutched high. "Me? You creep in here—"

"It's *my* house. I swear to God, if you screwed up my passing arm . . ."

"I had the door blocked! How could you sneak up on me like that?"

"Sneak? You had this place lit up like a frickin' Christmas tree."

She wasn't stupid enough to mention the jumping shadows and staring windows. "Only two measly bathroom lights."

"Plus the kitchen." He whipped the trouble light from her hands. "Give me that and stop being a chickenshit."

"Easy for you to say. You weren't attacked when you were sound asleep."

"I didn't attack you." He flicked off the light, plunging the room into darkness. The insensitive jerk had even turned off the bathroom light.

She heard the whoosh of sliding denim as he pulled off his jeans. She went up on her knees. "You're not sleeping here."

"It's my room, and this is the only bed with sheets."

"A bed I'm already occupying."

"And now you have company." He crawled in.

She took a deep breath and reminded herself he had too big an ego to attack her. If she scrambled around in the dark for another place to sleep, she'd look like a wuss. *Show no weakness.* "You stay on your side," she warned him, "or you won't like the consequences."

"Going to hit me with your tuffet, Miss Muffet?"

She had no idea what he was talking about.

The smell of toothpaste, skin, and the leather upholstery of a very expensive car drifted toward her. He should have smelled like liquor. A grief-stricken man coming home at two o'clock in the morning should be drunk. His bare leg brushed her thigh. She stiffened.

"Why do you have your jeans on?" he said.

"Because my luggage was in your car."

"Yeah, right. You kept them on because you were afraid the boogeyman would get you. What a chickenshit."

"Sticks and stones."

"That's mature."

"Like you're not all about seventh grade," she retorted.

"At least I don't have to sleep with the lights on."

"You might have second thoughts about that when the bats start flying out of the chimney."

"Bats?" He grew still.

"A colony."

"You're a bat expert?"

"I heard them rustling around. Making bat noises."

"I don't believe you." He was a crossways bed sleeper, and his knee poked her calf. Unaccountably, she'd begun to relax.

"I might as well sleep with a damn mummy," he grumbled.

"They're staying on."

"Don't think I couldn't get them off you if I put my mind to it. Thirty seconds max, and they'd be gone. Unfortunately for you, I'm off my game tonight."

He shouldn't be thinking about sex when his mother was dying. Her opinion of him plummeted. "Shut up and go to sleep."

"Your loss."

The wind picked up outside. A friendly branch tapped at the window. As his breathing grew deep and regular, slivers of moonlight crept across the old wooden floors, and the chimney gave a contented sigh. He stayed on his side of the bed. She stayed on hers.

For a while . . .

♥

In a house with almost no doors, a door banged. Blue's eyes inched open, disturbing the most delicious, erotic dream. Threads of gray light had crept into the room, and she let her eyes slip shut again, trying to reclaim the feeling of long fingers curling around her breast . . . a hand nuzzling inside her jeans. . . .

Another door banged. Something hard pressed against her hip. Her eyes sprang open. A gravely voice near her ear muttered an obscenity, a hand that didn't belong to her cupped her breast, and another pressed inside her jeans. A rush of alarm brought her fully awake. This was no dream.

"The carpenters are here," a woman said from not all that far away. "If you don't want company, you'd better get up."

Blue shoved at Dean's arm, but he took his time extricating himself from her clothes. "What time is it?"

"Seven," April replied.

Blue yanked her shirt down and buried her face in the pillow. This hadn't been part of her plan to stay ahead of him.

"It's the middle of the night," he protested.

"Not for a construction crew," April replied. "Good morning, Blue. Coffee and doughnuts downstairs." Blue rolled over and gave a weak wave. April waved back and disappeared.

"This sucks," he muttered. And then he yawned. Blue didn't like that. The least he could do was express a little sexual frustration.

She realized she hadn't entirely shaken off the aftereffects of her dream. "Pervert." She threw herself out of bed. She absolutely couldn't let herself be turned on by this man, not even in her sleep.

"You're a liar," he said from behind her.

She looked back. "What are you talking about?"

The covers fell to his waist as he sat up, and sunlight from the bare windows skipped across his biceps, gilding the hair on his chest. He rubbed his bad shoulder. "You told me you had, quote, 'no boobs.' Turns out, you were dead wrong about that."

She wasn't awake enough for a good comeback, so she glared at him and stalked into the bathroom, where she turned both faucets on full force for privacy. When she emerged, she found him standing in front of an expensive suitcase he'd set on the bed. He was wearing only a pair of navy knit boxers. She stumbled, silently cursed herself, then pretended she'd done it on purpose. "For the love of God, warn me next time. I think I'm having a heart attack."

He glanced over his shoulder, blasting her with all his stubbled, rumpled glory. "From what?"

"You look like an ad for gay porn."

"You look like a national disaster."

"Exactly why I have dibs on that shower." She headed for her grungy duffel, which he'd deposited in the corner. She unzipped it and rummaged for clean clothes. "I don't suppose you'd stand guard in the hall while I clean up?"

"Why don't I just go in there and keep you company?" It sounded more like a threat than a come-on.

"Amazing," she said. "A superstar like you still willing to help out the little people."

"Yeah, well, that's the way I'm made."

"Forget it." She grabbed her clothes, a towel, and some toiletries and headed for the bathroom. Once she was absolutely sure he wouldn't try to join her, she shampooed her hair and shaved her legs. Dean didn't know his mother wasn't really dying, but he seemed more belligerent than sorrowful. She didn't care what April had done to him. That was cold.

She dressed in a pair of clean but faded black bike shorts, a roomy camouflage T-shirt, and flip-flops. After a quick blast with his hair dryer, she pulled her hair up with a red ponytail elastic. The shorter ends refused to cooperate and straggled down her neck. For April's sake she'd have added lip gloss and mascara if they hadn't both gone missing three days ago.

As she came downstairs, she saw an electrician perched on a ladder in the dining room wiring an antique chandelier. The plastic had been taken off the living room doorway, and Dean stood inside, talking to the carpenter repairing the crown molding. Dean must have showered in the other bathroom because his hair was damp and beginning to curl. He wore jeans and a T-shirt that matched his eyes.

The living room extended the depth of the house and had a stone fireplace larger than the one in the master bedroom. A new set of French doors opened onto what looked like a freshly poured concrete slab that jutted out from the back of the house. She headed for the kitchen.

Last night she'd been too unnerved to appreciate everything April had done here, but now she paused in the doorway to take it in. The vintage appliances, along with nostalgic white bead-board cabinets bearing cherry red ceramic knobs, made her feel as though she'd stepped back into the forties. She imagined a woman in a freshly ironed cotton dress, hair rolled neatly at the nape of her neck, peeling potatoes over the farmhouse sink while the Andrews Sisters harmonized in "Don't Sit Under the Apple Tree" on the radio.

The fat white refrigerator with its rounded edges was probably a reproduction, but not the vintage white enamel gas stove, which had double ovens and a shallow, built-in metal shelf above the burners to hold salt and pepper shakers, canisters, maybe a Mason jar stuffed with wildflowers. The countertops hadn't yet been installed, so she could see that the bead-board cabinets weren't original but beautiful reproductions. The black-and-white checkerboard floor was also new. A paint sample taped to the wall announced the kitchen's final color scheme: sunny yellow walls, white cupboards, bright red accents.

Don't sit under the apple tree . . .

Light flooded the room from two sources: a wide window over the sink and longer windows that had been added to the squared-off breakfast nook and still bore the manufacturer's stickers. A clutter of doughnut boxes, abandoned Styrofoam cups, and papers sat on top of a chrome kitchen table with a cherry red Formica top.

April stood with one hand resting gracefully on the back of a bentwood chair, the other curled around a phone. She wore yesterday's ripped jeans with a garnet baby doll top, silver earrings, and sage green snake charmer flats. "You were supposed be here at seven, Sanjay." She nodded at Blue and gestured toward the coffeepot. "Then you'll have to get another truck. These countertops need to be installed by the end of the day so the painters can get in here."

Dean wandered in. His expression revealed nothing as he made his way to the doughnut box, but when he reached the table, the sunbeam dancing off his hair caught April's, and Blue was struck with

the crazy notion that God had created a special spotlight just to follow these two golden creatures around.

"We're not holding up the installation," April said. "You'd better
be here in an hour." She switched to another call, transferring the
phone from her right ear to her left. "Oh, hi." She lowered her voice
and turned away from them. "I'll call you back in ten minutes. Where
are you?"

Dean drifted toward the breakfast nook windows and gazed out
at the backyard. Blue found herself hoping he was trying to come to
terms with April's imminent demise.

April made another call. "Dave, it's Susan O'Hara. Sanjay's going
to be late."

The electrician who'd been wiring the dining room chandelier
ambled in. "Susan, come look at this."

She made a wait-a-minute gesture as she finished up her conversation, then flipped her phone shut. "What's up?"

"I ran into more old wiring in the dining room." The electrician's
eyes were all over her. "It's going to have to be replaced."

"Let me see." She followed him out.

Blue dumped a teaspoon of sugar in her coffee and went over to
examine the stove. "You'd be so screwed right now if she weren't
here."

"Yeah, you're probably right." Dean passed over the powdered
doughnuts and took the only glazed doughnut left in the box, exactly
the one she'd had her eye on.

A power drill screeched. "This kitchen is incredible," she said.

"It's okay, I guess."

"Okay?" She ran her thumb across the words O'Keefe & Merritt
on the front panel of the stove and threw out a lure. "I could spend
the whole day in here baking. Homemade bread, a fruit cobbler . . ."

"You really can cook?"

"Of course I can cook." The white enamel stove was a passport to
another era. Maybe it could also be her passport to temporary security.

But he'd lost interest in food. "Don't you own anything pink?"

She looked down at her bike shorts and camouflage T-shirt. "What's wrong with this?"

"Nothing, if you're planning to invade Cuba."

She shrugged. "I'm not into clothes."

"Now there's a surprise."

She pretended to think it over. "If you really want to see me in pink, I guess I could borrow something from you."

His smile wasn't all that friendly, but if she didn't keep challenging him, he'd start confusing her with one of his sexual handmaidens.

April returned to the kitchen and closed her phone. She addressed Dean with cool formality. "The driver's on his way with the wagon. Why don't you check around outside and decide where you want it?"

"I'm sure you have a suggestion."

"It's your house."

He regarded her stonily. "Give me a hint."

"The wagon doesn't have a toilet or running water, so don't put it too far away." She called into the hallway over her shoulder. "Cody, is the plumber's truck out there yet? I have to talk to him."

"Just pulled up," Cody called back.

"What kind of wagon?" Blue asked as April disappeared.

"Something *Mrs. O'Hara* talked me into in one of her many e-mails." He grabbed his coffee and the doughnut to go outside. Blue picked up a powdered doughnut and followed him through a refurbished laundry room to the side door.

When they reached the yard, she extended the powdered doughnut. "I'll trade you."

He took a big bite out of his glazed one, handed it over, and grabbed hers. "Okay."

She gazed down at it. "Once again, I'm forced to live on other people's leftovers."

"Now you're making me feel bad about myself." He sank his teeth into the fresh doughnut.

They walked around the back. Blue studied the overgrown garden with her artist's eye, imagining it alive with banks of color, maybe an herb garden by the iron pump, old-fashioned hollyhocks against the side of the house, a rope clothesline with laundry snapping in the warm breeze. *Gonna take a sentimental journey . . .*

Dean inspected a shady area just beyond the garden. Blue joined him. "A covered wagon?" she asked. "A paddy wagon?"

"I guess you'll see."

"You don't know yourself, do you?"

"Sort of."

"Show me the barn," she said. "Unless there are mice."

"Mice? Hell, no. That's the only barn in the known universe without them."

"You've been very sarcastic all morning."

"Gosh, I'm sorry."

Maybe he was covering up his grief. For the sake of his soul, she found herself hoping.

A flatbed truck pulled in, carrying what looked like a small covered wagon heavily wrapped in black plastic. She stayed where she was while Dean walked over to talk to the driver. Before long, the man was slapping him on his injured shoulder and calling him "Boo." Finally they got down to business. With Dean directing, the driver backed the flatbed toward the trees and began unloading the wagon. Once they'd jimmied it into position, he began stripping away the black plastic.

The body of the wagon was red, but it had bright purple wheels with gilt patterns on the spokes like a circus calliope. Painted spindles decorated the sides, and every surface displayed flowing vines and fanciful flowers in bright blue, indigo, buttery yellow, and sunny orange. At the front of the wagon, a gilt unicorn danced on a royal blue door. The bowed top of the wagon formed a small overhang supported by lemon yellow gingerbread brackets. The wagon's flat, spindled sides slanted outward from bottom to top and held a small window with miniature royal blue shutters.

Blue sucked in her breath. Her heart hammered. This was a gypsy wagon. A home for wanderers.

"Dibs," she said softly.

Chapter Six

As the driver pulled away, Dean tucked his thumbs in his back pockets and circled the wagon as if it were a new car. She didn't wait for him but pulled down a hinged step and climbed up to open the door.

The dark red interior was as magical as the exterior. Every surface, from the beams curving across the bowed ceiling, to the wooden ribs on the walls, to the panels between the ribs, had been painted with the same dancing unicorns, wandering vines, and fanciful flowers as the exterior. Across the rear of the wagon, a silky curtain trimmed in loopy fringe had been swagged at one side, revealing a bed that reminded Blue of a ship's berth. Another bed formed a top bunk along the left side, with a painted double-door cupboard beneath. Small pieces of furniture had been upended for transport and wrapped in brown paper.

The wagon had two miniature windows, one in the center of the side wall above the table, and another over the rear bed. Both had white lace doll's-house curtains drawn back with loops of purple braid. Near the baseboard on one side, a painted brown rabbit munched a tasty tuft of clover. It was so cozy, so absolutely perfect, that Blue wanted to cry. If she hadn't forgotten how, she might have.

Dean came in behind her and gazed around. "Unbelievable."

"This must have cost you a fortune."

"She got a deal."

No question who *she* was.

Only the center of the wagon rose high enough for him to stand upright. He started unwrapping the protective paper from a wooden table. "There's a guy in Nashville who specializes in restoring these caravans. That's what they call them. Some record mogul backed out of the deal after he'd ordered it."

Caravan. She liked the word. It hinted of the exotic. "How did April talk you into buying it?"

"She told me it would be a good place to stick drunken guests. Also, some of my friends have kids, and I thought it would be fun for them."

"Plus, you decided it would be a cool thing to own. The only gypsy caravan in the neighborhood and all that."

He didn't deny it.

She ran her hand over the walls. "A lot of this has been stenciled, but there's some handwork. It's a good job."

He began poking around, opening the cupboard, pulling out the built-in drawers, and investigated a wrought-iron wall sconce shaped like a seahorse. "These are wired for electricity, so I'll need to get some power out here. I'd better talk to the electrician."

Blue wasn't ready to leave, but he held the door open for her, so she followed him out into the yard. The electrician squatted in front of a junction box, the radio at his side playing an old Five for Fighting song. April stood a few feet away, holding a notebook and studying the concrete slab jutting from the rear of the house. Dean still hadn't mentioned anything today about her leaving. The Five for Fighting song came to an end and segued into the opening chords of "Farewell,

So Long," one of Jack Patriot's ballads. Dean's gait faltered, the change
of rhythm so slight Blue doubted she would have noticed if April's
head hadn't come up at the same time. She snapped the notebook
closed. "Turn it down, Pete."

The electrician glanced over at her but didn't immediately move.

"Never mind." April tucked her notebook under her arm and
headed inside. At the same time, Dean set off for the front yard, his
mission to talk to the electrician abandoned.

Blue poked around the overgrown garden. Instead of figuring out
how she'd get into town so she could look for a job, she thought over
what she'd just witnessed. "Farewell, So Long" came to an end, and
the Moffatt Sisters' "Gilded Lives" began to play. Even some of the
adult contemporary stations had been playing a few of the Moffatts'
country hits since Marli's death, generally pairing the songs with Jack
Patriot's "Farewell, So Long," which Blue found a little crass, since
they'd been divorced for years. She turned it all over in her mind as
she headed inside.

Three men speaking a language she didn't understand were in the
kitchen installing charcoal soapstone countertops. April sat in the
dining nook, frowning at a notebook page. "You're an artist," she said
as Blue came in. "Help me with this. I'm great with clothes, but not
as good drawing architectural details, especially when I'm not sure
what I want."

Blue had been hoping to snag another doughnut, but the box held
only a dusting of confectioners' sugar and a couple of jelly stains.

"It's the screen porch," April said.

Blue sat next to her and took in the drawing on the notebook
page. As the men chattered in the background, April explained what
she envisioned. "I don't want this porch looking like it belongs on a
broken-down fishing cabin. I see big sunburst windows set above the
screening to let in plenty of light and moldings to break up all the
height, but I'm not sure what kind."

Blue thought it over and began sketching some simple trims.

"I like that one," April said. "Can you draw the end wall for me? With the windows?"

Blue sketched each wall as April described it. They made some adjustments and came up with a more balanced arrangement. "You're good at this," April said when the workers headed outside for a cigarette break. "Would you mind doing some interior sketches for me? But maybe I'm assuming too much. I'm not exactly sure how long you're staying or what your relationship is with Dean."

"Blue and I are engaged," Dean said from the doorway.

Neither of them had heard him approach. He set his empty coffee mug by the stove and walked over to pick up Blue's sketch. "She'll be staying as long as I'm here."

"Engaged?" April said.

He didn't look up from the sketch. "That's right."

Blue could barely resist rolling her eyes. This was an obvious gotcha on his part. He wanted to remind his mother how little she meant to him, to show her he hadn't considered her important enough to let her know he was getting married. What a totally crappy thing to do to someone on her deathbed.

"Congrats." April set down her pencil. "How long have you known each other?"

"Long enough," he said.

Blue couldn't keep pretending that what April had witnessed a few short hours ago hadn't happened. "Last night was an aberration. Just so you know, I was fully clothed when I went to bed."

April's eyebrow formed a skeptical arch.

Blue tried to look demure. "I took a virginity vow when I was thirteen."

"A what?" April asked.

Dean sighed. "She didn't take a virginity vow."

As a matter of fact, Blue had done exactly that, although even at thirteen she'd had her doubts about keeping it. But she'd long ago made her peace with God, if not Sister Luke, who'd coerced her into the whole thing. "Dean doesn't agree, but I think a wedding night should mean something. That's why I'm moving into the caravan tonight."

He snorted. April gazed at Blue for a long time, then at him. "She's . . . lovely."

"That's all right." He set down the sketch. "You can say what you really think. Believe me, I've said a lot worse."

"Hey!"

"The first time I saw her was at a street carnival." He walked over to inspect the countertops. "She had her face stuck through one of those wooden cutouts, so naturally she caught my attention. You've got to admit that face is something. By the time I saw the rest of her, it was too late."

"I'm sitting right here," Blue reminded them.

"There's nothing exactly wrong with her." April's statement didn't carry much conviction.

"She has a lot of other wonderful qualities." He inspected the hinges on a cupboard door. "I try to turn a blind eye."

Blue had a fairly good idea where the conversation was headed, so she ran her finger over the sugar in the bottom of the doughnut box.

"Everybody isn't into fashion, Dean. It's not some big sin." Spoken by a woman who could have hopped up from the table at exactly that moment and waltzed down a runway.

"Once we're married, she's promised she'll let me buy her clothes," he said.

Blue's gaze wandered to the refrigerator. "Are there maybe some eggs in there? A little cheese for an omelet?"

April's silver earrings tangled in a ribbon of blunt-cut hair. "You'll have to live with this, Blue. When he was three years old, he'd throw a fit if his Underoos weren't a perfect match. In third grade everything had to be Ocean Pacific, and he spent most of junior high in

Ralph Lauren. I swear he learned to read by sounding out clothing labels."

April's trip down memory lane was a mistake. Dean's top lip thinned. "I'm surprised you remember so many details from the blackout years." He wandered back to Blue, and the possessive way he curled his fingers around her shoulder made her wonder if his engagement ruse might also be designed to send out the silent message that he had someone indisputably in his corner. He didn't realize he'd fallen in with Benedict Arnold.

"In case Dean hasn't gotten around to sharing," April said, "I was a junkie."

Blue had no idea how to respond to that.

"And a groupie," April added bluntly. "Dean spent his childhood either with nannies or in boarding school so I could follow my dream of getting high and nailing as many rock stars as possible."

Blue *really* had no idea how to respond to that. Dean dropped his hand from her shoulder and turned away.

"Uh . . . how long have you been clean?" Blue said.

"A little over ten years. Respectably employed most of them. Working for myself the last seven."

"What do you do?"

"I'm a fashion stylist in L.A."

"A stylist? Wow. What exactly does that involve?"

"For God's sake, Blue . . ." Dean snatched up his empty coffee mug and carried it to the sink.

"I work with actresses, Hollywood wives—women with more money than taste," April said.

"It sounds glamorous."

"It's mainly a diplomat's job."

Blue could understand that. "Convincing a fifty-year-old soap star to give up her minis?"

"Watch it, Blue," Dean said. "You're getting personal. April's fifty-two, but you can bet she has a closet full of minis in every color."

Blue took in his mother's endlessly long legs. "I'll bet every one of them looks fantastic."

He moved away from the sink. "Let's go into town. I have some things I need to get."

"Pick up groceries while you're there," April said. "I have food at the cottage, but there's nothing much here."

"Yeah, we'll do that." With Blue in tow, he headed for the door.

♥

Blue broke the thick silence as Dean shot out onto the highway. "I'm not lying to her. If she asks the color of our bridesmaids' dresses, I'm telling her the truth."

"No bridesmaids, so no problem," he said caustically. "We're eloping to Vegas."

"Anybody who knows me knows I'd never elope to Vegas."

"She doesn't know you."

"Presumably you do, and getting married there is like admitting to the world that you're too disorganized to come up with a better plan. I have more pride."

He turned up the radio to drown her out. Blue hated misjudging people, especially men, and she couldn't get past his callousness toward his mother's fatal illness. She turned the volume back down to punish him. "I've always wanted to go to Hawaii, but, until now, I couldn't afford it. I think we'll get married there. On the beach of some ritzy resort at sunset. I'm so glad I found a rich husband."

"We're not getting married!"

"Exactly," she shot back. "Which is why I don't want to lie to your mother."

"Are you on my payroll or not?"

She sat up straighter. "Am I? Let's talk about that."

"Not now." He looked so irritable that she temporarily fell silent.

They passed an abandoned cotton mill nearly swallowed up by undergrowth, then a well-maintained mobile home park, followed by a golf course that advertised karaoke Friday nights. Here and there an old plow or a wagon wheel held up a mailbox. She decided to make a stealth attack on her fake fiancé's private life. "Since we're engaged, don't you think it's time you told me about your father?"

His knuckles tightened ever so slightly on the steering wheel. "No."

"I'm fairly good at connecting the dots."

"Un-connect them."

"It's hard. Once I get an idea in my head . . ."

He shot her a killer glare. "I don't talk about my father. Not to you. Not to anybody."

She argued with herself for only a moment before she went for it. "If you really want to keep his identity a secret, you should probably stop going all stony-faced every time Jack Patriot comes on the radio."

He uncurled his fingers and draped them over the top of the wheel, the gesture a little too casual. "You're overdramatizing. My father was a drummer in Patriot's band for a while. That's all there is to it."

"Anthony Willis is the only drummer the band has ever had. And since he's black . . ."

"Check your rock history, babe. Willis sat out most of the Universal Omens tour with a broken arm."

Dean might be telling the truth, but somehow Blue didn't think so. April had been open about her rock and roll past, and Blue had seen the way they'd both frozen up when "Farewell, So Long" came on the radio. The possibility that Dean might be Jack Patriot's son made her head spin. She'd had a crush on the rock star since she was ten. No matter where she'd lived, she'd kept his tapes stacked by her bed and magazine pictures of him pasted inside her school notebooks. His lyrics made her feel less alone.

A city limits sign announced that they'd reached Garrison. A second sign just below it declared that the town was for sale and that anyone interested in buying it should contact Nita Garrison. She twisted in her seat as they whipped past. "Did you see that? How can anybody sell a town?"

"They sold one on eBay a while back," he said.

"That's right. And remember when Kim Basinger bought that little town in Georgia? I keep forgetting this is the South. All kinds of weird crap happens here that couldn't happen anywhere else."

"A sentiment best kept to yourself," he said.

They drove past a Greek Revival funeral home and a church. Most of the tan sandstone buildings in the three-block downtown area looked as though they'd been constructed early in the twentieth century. The wide main street had diagonal parking on both sides. Blue spotted a restaurant, a drugstore, a resale shop, and a bakery. A stuffed deer with an OPEN sign hanging from an antler stood guard near the door of an antique store named Aunt Myrtle's Attic. Just across the street, old trees shaded a park with a four-sided clock and black iron lampposts topped with white globes. Dean pulled into a parking space in front of the pharmacy.

Blue didn't have much faith in his comment about her being on his payroll, and she wondered if she could find a job in such a small town. "Do you notice anything strange?" she said as he flicked off the ignition.

"Other than you?"

"No fast food." She took in the shabby but quaint main street. "I didn't see any chain restaurants out on the highway, either. This place isn't big, but it's big enough for a NAPA Auto Parts store or a Block-buster. Where are they? If you took away the cars and ignored peoples' clothes, it would be hard to figure out what year it is."

"Interesting you should mention clothes." He studied her black bike shorts and camouflage T-shirt. "I guess you didn't get the dress code memo that came with your new job."

"That piece of crap? I tossed it out."

A woman's face popped up in the window of Barb's Tresses and Day Spa next to the pharmacy. At the insurance agency on the other side, a balding man peered out from behind a church rummage sale poster. She imagined similar heads popping up across the street. In a town this small, the news of their famous new neighbor's arrival would spread quickly.

She followed Dean into the pharmacy, keeping a respectful three paces behind, which further annoyed him, even though he'd brought it on himself with his attitude. He disappeared to the back of the store while she talked to the cashier and discovered there were no job openings. Two women rushed in, one black and one white. The man from the insurance agency entered, followed by an older woman with wet hair. Next came a skinny guy with a plastic name tag that identified him as Steve.

"There he is," insurance man said to the others.

They all craned their necks to stare at Dean. A woman in a bright pink business suit came charging in, her taupe pumps clicking on the tile floor. She looked as though she was around Blue's age, too young for her hair to be so stiffly sprayed, although Blue had no room to criticize anyone's hairstyle. She'd have gotten hers cut if she hadn't left Seattle so abruptly. She edged toward the mascara display just as the woman called out to Dean, uttering his name on a long, adoring breath. "Dean . . . I just heard that you'd shown up at the farm. I was on my way out to welcome you."

Blue peered around the mascara in time to watch Dean's blank expression shift to recognition. "Monica. Nice to see you." He held nail clippers, an Ace Bandage, and a package of what looked like gel shoe inserts. No condoms.

"Goodness, the town is buzzin'," Monica said. "Everybody's been waiting for you to show up. Isn't Susan O'Hara amazing? Don't you love what she's done to the house?"

"Amazing, all right."

Monica drank him in like a frosty glass of sweet tea. "I hope you're staying for a while."

"I'm not sure. Depends on a couple of things."

"You can't leave till you've had a chance to meet all of Garrison's movers and shakers. I'll be happy to throw a little cocktail party and introduce you to everybody." She curled her fingers around his arm. "You are just going to love it here."

He was used to having his personal space invaded, and he didn't pull away but tilted his head toward the cosmetics instead. "I have someone I want you to meet. Blue, come over here so I can introduce you to my real estate agent."

Blue checked her impulse to duck farther behind the mascara. Maybe this woman could help her find a job. She slapped on her friendliest smile and made her way over. Dean pulled away from his real estate agent's overly possessive hand to wrap his arm around her. "Blue, this is Monica Doyle. Monica, my fiancée, Blue Bailey."

Now he was just being lazy.

"We're getting married in Hawaii," he said. "On the beach at sunset. Blue wanted to go to Vegas, but I'm too well organized for that."

He was perfectly capable of fending off women without resorting to an imaginary fiancée, but apparently he didn't want the tedium of dealing with all those panties being thrown at him. She had to admit she was surprised.

Monica's face had fallen, but she did her best to hide her disappointment behind some rapid eye blinks and a quick survey of Blue's appearance. The real estate agent took in the camouflage T-shirt Blue had appropriated from her apartment building's laundry room after it had been thumbtacked to the bulletin board for a month. "You are the cutest thang, now aren't you?"

"Dean thinks so," Blue said modestly. "I'm still not sure how he managed to overcome my aversion to aging frat boys."

His warning squeeze pulled her into his armpit, which smelled deliciously of one of those expensive male deodorants that came packaged in phallic-shaped glass bottles stamped with designer logos. She stayed there a few beats too long before she poked her head back out. "I noticed the For Sale sign when we came into town. What's that all about?"

Monica pursed her penciled and glossed lips. "Nita Garrison being her normal hateful self, that's all. Some people aren't worth talking about. We do our best not to pay her any mind."

"Is it true?" Blue asked. "The town's really up for sale?"

"I suppose it depends on how you define town."

Blue started to ask how they defined this one, but Monica was already calling over the people lurking in the aisles so she could introduce them.

Ten minutes later, they finally escaped. "I'm breaking this engagement," Blue grumbled as she followed Dean to the car. "You're too much trouble."

"Now, sweetheart, surely our love is strong enough to survive a few bumps in the road of life." He stopped at a newspaper vending machine.

"Introducing me as your fiancée made you look ridiculous, not me," she said. "Those people aren't blind. We look bizarre together."

"You have some serious self-esteem issues." He dug in his pocket for change.

"Me? Try again. Nobody's going to believe a brainiac like Blue Bailey would fall for a mental lightweight like you." He ignored her and pulled out a paper. She stepped in front of him. "Before we head for the grocery, I need to make inquiries about a job. Why don't you have some lunch while I look around?"

He tucked the paper under his arm. "I already told you. You're working for me."

"Doing what?" She squinted up at him. "And how much are you paying?"

"Don't you worry about it."

He'd been irritable with her all morning, and she didn't like it. It wasn't her fault his mother was dying. All right, so it *was* her fault, but he didn't know that, and he shouldn't punish her for April's medical tragedy.

When they reached the grocery store, the introductions started all over again as one person after another welcomed him to the town. He was cordial to everybody, from the pimple-faced produce clerk to a crippled old man in a VFW cap. The older kids were in school, but he rubbed bald baby heads, shook a slobbery fist, and engaged in an encouraging conversation with an adorable three-year-old named Reggie who didn't want to use a potty. Dean was the weirdest combination of ego and decency she'd ever met in one person, although his decency seemed to stop with her.

While he handled PR, she slipped away to do the grocery shopping. The store didn't carry a wide selection, but she found the basics. He met up with her at the checkout line, where she had to stand silently by as he whipped out his Visa card. This couldn't go on. She had to make some money.

♥

Dean unloaded the groceries and left Blue the job of deciding where to put them while he went back outside to move his car into the barn. Even Annabelle didn't know the identity of his real father, but Blue had dug it up after spending only four days with him. She was the most intuitive person he'd ever met, not to mention the most devious, and he had to play a smarter game.

After he'd cleared out a space in the barn for his car, he poked around in the shed for a shovel and hoe and started attacking the weeds growing near the house's foundation. As he breathed in the smell of honeysuckle, he remembered exactly why he'd bought this place instead of the Southern California beach house he'd always imagined. Because being here felt right. He loved the old buildings, the way the hills sheltered the farm. He loved knowing this land had been part of something more lasting than a football game. But most of all, he loved the privacy. No crowded Southern California beach could give him that, and when he needed his ocean fix, he could always fly to the coast.

He barely knew what privacy felt like. First, growing up in boarding schools, then embarking on a college athletic career that had brought him instant recognition. After that, he'd turned pro. Finally, with those damned End Zone ads, even people who weren't football fans recognized him. He stiffened as he heard the jingle of bracelets. Bitterness curdled his stomach. She was trying to ruin this like she'd tried to ruin everything else.

"I was planning to hire a landscape crew," his mother said.

He jabbed the shovel into a clump of weeds. "I'll deal with it when I'm ready." He didn't care how long she'd been sober. Every time he looked at her, he remembered tear-streaked makeup, slurred speech, and the weight of her arms dragging on his neck during her drunken, drugged-up pleas for his forgiveness.

"You've always been happiest outside." She came closer. "I don't know much about plants, but I think you're trying to take out a peony bush."

Considering the life she'd led, his mother should have looked like Keith Richards, but she didn't. Her body was toned, her jawline a little too smooth to be entirely natural. Even her long hair offended him. She was fifty-two, for chrissake. Time to cut it off. As a teenager, he'd been forced into more than a few fights when one of his classmates gave a too detailed description of her ass or whatever other body part she'd chosen to show off on one of the rare days she condescended to visit him at school. With the toe of her shoe, she unearthed a flattened tin can. "I'm not dying."

"Yeah, I figured that out last night." And Blue was going to pay for her lie.

"Not even sick. There goes your big celebration."

"Maybe next year."

She didn't flinch. "Blue has a big heart. She's an interesting person. Different than I would have expected."

She'd gone on a fishing expedition, but she wasn't going to catch anything. "That's why I asked her to marry me."

"She has those big innocent eyes, but there's something sexy about her, too."

An X-rated nursery rhyme . . .

"She's not beautiful," April went on, "but she's . . . something better. I don't know. Whatever it is, she doesn't seem to have a clue about it."

"She's a train wreck." Too late, he remembered he was supposed to be smitten. "Just because I'm in love doesn't mean I'm blind. It's the fact that she's her own person I'm attracted to."

"Yes, I can see that."

He grabbed the hoe and began hacking at some weeds around a rosebush. He knew it was a rosebush because it had a couple of flowers.

"You heard about Marli Moffatt," she said.

The hoe struck a rock. "Hard to avoid. It's all over the news."

"I guess her daughter will go to Marli's sister. God knows Jack won't do anything but write a check."

He tossed down the hoe and picked up the shovel again.

She toyed with one of her bracelets. "I hope you've figured out by now that kicking me out isn't a good idea, not if you want to live here in any kind of comfort this summer. I'll be out of your life permanently in three or four weeks."

"That's what you said in November when you showed up at the Chargers game."

"It won't happen again."

He stabbed the shovel into the dirt, then worked it free. She'd been on top of everything today. It was hard to reconcile her efficiency with the drugged-out woman who'd regularly misplaced her kid. "Why should I believe you this time?"

"Because I'm sick of living with guilt. You're never going to forgive me, and I'm not asking again. Once the house is done, I'm gone."

"Why are you doing this? Why the fucking charade?"

She shrugged, looking bored—the last woman in the bar after the fun had ended. "I thought it would be a kick, that's all."

"Hey, Susan!" Mr. Horny Electrician poked his head around the corner. "Can you come here for a minute?"

Dean dug up another rock as she walked away. Now that he saw how many tasks she was juggling, he knew he'd be hurting himself more than her if he made her leave. He could always head back to Chicago, but the idea of letting her drive him away stuck in his craw. He didn't run from anybody, especially not from his mother. But he also couldn't stand the idea of being alone with her, even on a hundred acres of property, and that was why keeping Blue around had become a necessity, not just an impulse. She'd be his buffer.

He envisioned Blue's head and guillotined a thistle with one clean blow. Her lie about April stepped over more boundaries than he could count. Although he'd met a lot of manipulative women, he'd never met one with more gall, but before he confronted her, he intended to let her swing in the breeze.

By the time the carpenters left for the day, he'd cleared the worst of the weeds from the foundation without doing too much damage to what he finally figured out were the peony bushes. His shoulder ached like a son of a bitch, but he'd been cooped up too long, and he didn't care. It felt good using his body again.

As he emerged from the toolshed, the smell of something savory drifted his way from the open kitchen window. Blue had decided to cook, but he had no intention of sitting through a cozy dinner that included his mother, and he didn't doubt for a moment that Blue would invite her.

On his way into the house, his thoughts abruptly returned to Marli Moffatt's death and the eleven-year-old daughter she'd left behind. His half sister. The idea was unreal. He knew what it felt like to be an orphan, and one thing was for damn sure. That poor kid had better be able to look after herself because Jack Patriot wouldn't do it for her.

Chapter Seven

Riley Patriot lived in Nashville, Tennessee, in a white brick house with six white columns, white marble floors, and a gleaming white Mercedes-Benz in the garage. In the living room, a white grand piano sat near a pair of matching white sofas on an all-white carpet. Riley hadn't been allowed in the living room since she'd squirted a box of grape Juicy Juice there when she was six.

Even though Riley was eleven now, her mother had never forgiven or forgotten—not just the grape Juicy Juice, but a lot of things—and now it was too late. Ten days ago, a whole bunch of people had seen her mom, Marli Moffatt, fall through a broken railing into the Cumberland River from the top deck of the paddle wheeler *Old Glory*. She'd banged her head on something when she hit the water, it was night, and they didn't find her until it was too late. Ava, Riley's ten millionth au pair, woke Riley up to break the news.

Now, a week and a half later, Riley was on the run to find her brother.

Although she'd only walked a block from her home, her T-shirt was already sticking to her skin, so she unzipped her puffy pink jacket. Her lavender corduroys were a size twelve chubbo, but they were still too tight. Her cousin Trinity was a size eight slim, but just Riley's bones without any skin were bigger than a size eight slim. She switched her heavy backpack to her other arm. Her load would have been a lot lighter if she'd left the scrapbook behind, but she couldn't do it.

The houses on Riley's street sat well back from the road, some behind gates, so there weren't any sidewalks, but there were street-lights, and Riley dodged them as best she could. Not that anybody was going to come looking for her. Her legs started to itch, and she tried to scratch through the corduroy, but that only made the itching worse. By the time she saw Sal's beat-up red car at the end of the next block, they were on fire.

He'd parked under a streetlight, like a moron, and he was smok-ing a cigarette in quick, jerky puffs. When he spotted her, he started looking around, like he thought the police might show up at any minute. "Gimme the money," he said when she got to the car.

Riley didn't like standing under the light where anybody driving by could see them, but arguing would take longer than giving him the money. Riley hated Sal. He worked on his dad's landscape crew when he wasn't in school, which was how Riley knew him, but that wasn't why she hated him. She hated him because he rubbed himself when he didn't think anybody was looking, and he spit, and he said nasty stuff. But he was sixteen, and ever since he got his license four months ago, Riley had been paying him to take her places. He was a crappy driver, but until Riley turned sixteen herself, she didn't have a lot of choices.

She pulled the money out of the front pocket of her green back-pack. "A hundred dollars now. I'll give you the rest after we get to the farm." She'd watched a lot of old movies, so she knew all about how you were supposed to divide up the money.

He looked like he wanted to grab her backpack, but it wouldn't have done him any good, because she'd hidden the rest of the money

in her sock. He counted the bills, which she thought was rude because she was standing right in front of him, and it was like calling
her a big cheater. Finally, he stuffed the money in his jeans pocket.
"If my old man finds out about this, he's going to beat the shit out
of me."

"He's not going to find out from me. You're the only blabber-
mouth."

"What did you do about Ava?"

"Peter's staying over. She won't notice." Riley's au pair had come
from Hamburg, Germany, two months ago. Peter was Ava's boyfriend, and all they did was make out. When Riley's mom was alive,
Ava hadn't been allowed to have Peter in the house, but with her
mom dead, he'd been sleeping over about every night. It would be
breakfast before Ava figured out Riley was gone, and maybe not even
then, because they didn't have school tomorrow for end-of-the-year
teachers' conferences. Riley had stuck a Post-it note on her door saying she had an upset stomach and not to wake her up.

Sal still didn't get in the car. "I want two-fifty. I forgot about
gas."

She tugged on the car door, but he had it locked. She scratched
her legs. "I'll give you twenty dollars extra."

"You're rich. You don't have to be so cheap."

"Twenty-five, and that's all. I mean it, Sal. I don't want to go that
bad."

A big lie. If she didn't get to her brother's farm, she'd lock herself
in the garage and turn on her mom's Benz—she knew how—and sit
in the car until she suffocated to death. Nobody could make her come
out, not Ava, or her Aunt Gayle, or even her dad—like he'd even care
if she died.

Sal must have believed her because he finally unlocked the car
doors. She dropped her backpack on the floor of the front seat, then
got in and fastened her seat belt. The inside of the car smelled like
cigarettes and stale hamburgers. She pulled the directions she'd got

from MapQuest out of the zipper pocket of her backpack. He peeled away from the curb without even looking to see if a car was coming.

"Watch out!"

"Relax. It's midnight. There's nobody around." He had stringy brown hair, and some hairs growing on his chin that he thought made him look cool.

"You're supposed to go to Interstate Forty," she said.

"Like I don't know that." He tossed his cigarette out the open window. "They're playing the Moffatt Sisters' CD on the radio all the time now. I bet you're going to make about a million bucks."

All Sal ever wanted to talk about was money or sex stuff, and Riley definitely didn't want him to talk about sex stuff, so she pretended to study the MapQuest papers, even though she'd already memorized everything.

"You're so lucky," Sal went on. "You don't have to work or anything, and you get all this money."

"I can't spend it. It goes in my trust fund."

"You can spend the money your dad gives you." He was only driving with one hand, but if she said anything about it, he'd just get mad. "I saw your dad when he was here for the funeral. He even talked to me. He's a lot nicer than your mom. Seriously. Someday I'm going to have cool clothes like him and ride around in a limo."

Riley didn't like it when people talked about her dad, which they always wanted to do, like they thought she'd introduce them or something when she hardly ever saw him. Now that her mom was dead, he planned to transfer Riley to Chatsworth Girls, which was a boarding school where everybody would hate her because she was fat and nobody would want to be her friend except to get near her dad. She went to Kimble now, but it wasn't a boarding school, and even being in the same classes with her cousin Trinity was better than a sleepover school. She'd begged her dad to let her stay at Kimble and live with Ava in an apartment or something, but he'd said that wouldn't work out.

Which was why she had to find her brother.

He was really her half-brother, and he was a secret. Only a few people knew Riley and he were related, and even Riley wouldn't have known that her dad had this other kid a long, long time ago if she hadn't overheard her mom's old boyfriend talking to her mom about it. Her mom was one of the Moffatt Sisters, along with Aunt Gayle, Trinity's mom. They'd been performing together since they were fifteen, but they hadn't had a hit on the country charts in six years, and their new CD *Everlasting Rainbows* hadn't been doing too good, which was why they'd gone on the paddle wheeler that night, to do a promotion for a bunch of radio people visiting Nashville for a conference. Now, with all the publicity about her mom drowning, the CD was at the top of the charts. Riley thought her mom would be happy about this, but she wasn't sure.

Her mom had been thirty-eight when she died, two years older than Aunt Gayle. They were both skinny with blond hair and big boobs, and a couple of weeks before the accident, Riley's mom had gone to Aunt Gayle's face doctor and gotten these shots in her lips that made them big and puffy. Riley thought she'd looked like a fish, but her mom had told Riley to keep her stupid opinions to herself. If Riley had known her mom was going to fall off the riverboat and drown, she would never have said anything.

The corner of the scrapbook jabbed her ankle through her backpack. She wished she could take it out and look at the pictures. That always made her feel better. She grabbed the dashboard. "Watch where you're going, will you? That's a red light."

"So what? No cars are coming."

"If you get in an accident, you're going to lose your license."

"I'm not getting in no accident." He turned up the radio but then turned it down again. "I'll bet your dad screwed about ten thousand girls."

"Will you just shut up!" Riley wished she could close her eyes and pretend she was somewhere else, but if she didn't watch Sal's driving, he'd probably wreck.

For about the millionth time, she wondered if her brother knew about her. Last year, when she'd found out about him, it had been the most exciting thing that had ever happened to her. She'd started her secret scrapbook right away, pasting in articles off the Internet, plus pictures of him she found in magazines and newspapers. He always looked happy in his pictures, like he never thought nasty things about people, and like he could appreciate everybody, even if they weren't beautiful or skinny or eleven years old.

Last winter, she'd sent him a letter at Chicago Stars headquarters. She never heard back, but she knew people like her dad and her brother got so much mail they didn't read it themselves. When the Stars had come to Nashville to play the Titans, she'd made up this plan to meet him. She was going to sneak away and find a taxi to drive her to the stadium. Once she got there, she'd figure out which door the players came out of and wait for him. She imagined calling his name and how he'd look over at her, and she'd say, "Hi, I'm Riley. I'm your sister." And his whole face would be happy, and once he got to know her, he'd tell her to come live with him or even just stay with him on school vacations so she wouldn't have to stay with Aunt Gayle and Trinity like now.

But instead of going to the Titans football game, she'd gotten strep throat and had to spend a whole week in bed. Since then, she'd called Stars headquarters a bunch of times, but no matter what she told the operator, they'd never give her his phone number.

They reached the outside of Nashville, and Sal turned up the radio so loud Riley's seat vibrated. She liked loud music, too, but not tonight when she was so nervous. She'd found out about her brother's farm the day after the funeral when she'd heard her dad talking to somebody about it on the phone. When she'd looked up the town he'd mentioned and seen it was in East Tennessee, she was so excited she got dizzy. But her dad didn't say exactly where the farm was, only that it was near Garrison, and since she couldn't ask him, she used her detective skills.

She knew people bought houses and farms from real estate sales-men because that's what her mother's old boyfriend had been, so she'd looked up all the real estate companies around Garrison on the Inter-net. Then she'd started calling them and saying she was fourteen and doing this report about people who had to sell their farms.

Most of the real estate people were really nice and told her all kinds of history about some of the farms, but since they were all still for sale, she knew they weren't her brother's. Two days ago, though, she reached a lady who was this secretary, and she told Riley about the Callaway farm and how a famous athlete had just bought it, but she wasn't at liberty to say who. The lady told her where the farm was, but when Riley asked if the famous athlete was there now, she started getting suspicious and said she had to go. Riley took that to mean he was. At least she hoped so. Because if he wasn't, she didn't know what she'd do.

Sal wasn't driving too bad for once, maybe because the interstate was pretty straight. He jabbed his thumb toward her backpack and yelled over the music. "You got anything to eat?"

She didn't want to share her snacks, but she didn't want him to stop, either. He'd only make her pay, plus the trip would be longer, so she dug in her backpack and handed him some Cheese Nips. "What did you tell your dad?"

He ripped the package open with his teeth. "He thinks I'm spend-ing the night at Joey's house."

Riley had only met Joey once, but she thought he was nicer than Sal. She told Sal the exit number where he had to get off, even though it would be a long time before they got there. But she was afraid if she fell asleep he'd drive right past it because the more she looked at the white lines on the road, the harder it was to keep her eyes open. . . .

The next thing she knew, she was jolted awake as the car skidded and started to spin. Her shoulder banged against the door, and her seat belt grabbed her chest. On the radio 50 Cent was yelling, and this billboard was coming right at them. She screamed over the music, and all she could think of was that now she'd never see her brother or own a puppy farm when she grew up.

Right before they hit the billboard, Sal jerked the steering wheel, and the car lurched to a stop. She saw his face in the dashboard light. His lips were open and his eyes big and scared. She didn't want to die, no matter what she'd thought about her mom's Benz and the garage.

Outside, quiet settled around the car. Inside, 50 Cent was rapping, but Riley was making these crying sounds, and Sal was sort of gulping to breathe. The interstate ramp was behind them, and the road was dark except for one big light shining down on a billboard for Captain G's Market. BAIT. BEER. POP. SUBS. As much as she wanted to find her brother, she wished she was home in bed. The clock on the dashboard said 2:05.

"Stop acting like a baby!" Sal burst out. "Just read the stupid directions."

He turned the car around right in the middle of the dark country road, so she knew they'd spun all the way in the opposite direction. Her armpits were sweaty, and her hair was damp against her scalp. Her hands shook as she smoothed out the MapQuest directions. He turned the radio off without her asking, and she read what they had to do, ending with going 5.9 miles on Smoky Hollow Road, then turn right on Callaway Road for 1.3 miles, which was where the farm was supposed to be.

Sal made her give him another pack of Cheese Nips. She ate one herself and then, because she was still so scared, she ate some Rice Krispies Treats. She had to pee really bad, but she couldn't tell Sal that, so she held her legs together and hoped they got there soon. Sal wasn't driving fast like he had before. After almost wrecking, he had both hands on the steering wheel, and he kept the radio off. They missed Smoky Hollow Road because it was too dark to see the sign and had to turn back.

"Why are you jumping around so much?" Sal still sounded really mad, like it was her fault he hadn't slowed down when he got off the interstate.

She couldn't say she had to pee. "Because I'm glad we're almost there."

She was looking as hard as she could for the sign for Callaway Road when Sal's cell rang. They both jumped. "Shit." He banged his elbow on the door trying to get the phone out of his jacket pocket. He looked really scared, and when he answered, his voice kind of squeaked. "Hello?"

All the way on the other side of the car, Riley could hear his dad yelling, asking Sal where the hell he was and telling him if he didn't get home right now, he'd call the police. Sal was afraid of his dad, and he looked like he was going to cry. When his dad finally hung up, Sal stopped the car right in the middle of the road and started scream-ing at Riley. "Give me the rest of the money! Right now!"

He looked like he was going sort of crazy. Riley shrank back against the door. "As soon as we get there."

He grabbed her jacket and shook her. A little bubble of slobber popped at the corner of his mouth. "Give it to me or you'll be sorry."

She jerked away, but he'd scared her so much that she kicked off her shoe. "I got the money here."

"Hurry up. Give it to me!"

"Take me to the farm first."

"If you don't give it to me now, I'm going to hit you."

She knew he meant it, and she grabbed at her sock and pulled out the bills. "I'll give this to you when we get there."

"Give it to me now!" He twisted her wrist.

She smelled the Cheese Nips on his breath, plus something sour. "Let go!"

He pried open her fingers and grabbed the money. Then he yanked her seat belt free, reached across her, and threw open her car door. "Get out!"

She was so scared she started to cry. "Take me to the farm first. Don't do this. Please."

"Get out right now!" He shoved her hard. She tried to grab the door, but she missed and fell out on the road. "Don't you tell anybody," he shouted. "If you tell anybody, you'll be sorry." He threw her backpack out, pulled the door shut, and took off.

She lay in the middle of the road until the sound of the engine disappeared. All she could hear was herself crying. It was so dark, the darkest night in her whole life. There weren't any streetlights like in Nashville, and she couldn't even see the moon, just this gray place in the clouds where the moon must be behind. She heard scuffing noises and remembered this movie she'd seen where a guy jumped out of the woods and kidnapped this girl and took her back to his house and cut her all up. That scared her so much that she snatched her backpack and ran across the road to where the field was.

Her elbow throbbed where she'd hit it when she fell, her leg hurt, and she had to pee so bad she'd wet her pants a little. Biting her lip, she fumbled with the zipper on her cords. Because they were so tight, she had a hard time pulling them down. She kept her eye on the woods across the road as she peed. By the time she'd finished and found a tissue, she could see a little better in the dark, and no man had come out of the trees, but her teeth were chattering.

She remembered the MapQuest directions. Callaway Road couldn't be that much farther, and when she found it, all she had to do was walk 1.3 miles to get to the farm; 1.3 miles wasn't far. Except she didn't remember which direction they'd been going.

She swiped at her nose with the sleeve of her jacket. Somehow when Sal had pushed her out of the car, she'd rolled a little and gotten mixed up. She looked for a sign through the dark, but because the road was going uphill, all she could see was darkness. Maybe a car would come? But what if a kidnapper was driving it? Or a serial killer?

She thought they'd maybe been going uphill when Sal's dad

called. Even though she wasn't sure, she picked up her backpack and started walking because she couldn't stay here. The nighttime was a lot louder than she'd ever imagined. A spooky owl hooted, wind cracked in the trees, and things made slithery noises that she hoped wasn't snakes because she was very afraid of snakes. No matter how hard she tried to hold them back, these little whimpery sounds kept coming out of her mouth.

She started thinking about her mom. Riley'd thrown up in her wastebasket when Ava had told her the news. At first, all she could think about was herself and what would happen to her. But then she'd thought about how her mom used to sing silly songs to her. That was when Riley had been a cute little kid, before she got fat and her mom stopped liking her. During the funeral, Riley kept imagining how scared her mom must have been when she felt her lungs filling up with water, and she'd started crying so hard that Ava'd had to take her out of the church. Afterward, her dad said she wasn't allowed to go to the graveyard for the burial, and him and Aunt Gayle had a big fight about it, but her dad wasn't afraid of Aunt Gayle like everybody else, so Ava took Riley home, and let her eat all the Pop-Tarts she wanted, and put her to bed.

The wind whipped Riley's hair, which was bushy brown, not shiny blond like her mom's and Aunt Gayle's and Trinity's. *"It's a pretty color, Riley. Like a movie star's."*

That's what Riley imagined her big brother would say about her hair. He would be like her best friend.

The farther she got up the hill, the harder it was to breathe, and the more the wind kept trying to push her back. She wondered if her mom was up there in heaven looking down at her now and maybe trying to figure out how to help her. But if her mom was in heaven, she'd be talking to her friends on the telephone and smoking.

Riley's legs were burning from where they were rubbing together, and her chest hurt, and if she was going in the right direction, she would have seen the sign by now. Her backpack got so heavy she had to drag it. If she died here, she wondered if a wolf would eat her face before anybody found her, and then maybe nobody would know it was her, Riley Patriot.

She still hadn't reached the top of the hill when she saw a bent metal sign. CALLAWAY ROAD. It went uphill, too. The blacktop was crumbling at the sides, and she stumbled. Her cords ripped, and she started to cry, but she made herself get up. This wasn't straight like the other road but had curves that scared her because she didn't know what was on the other side.

She almost didn't care if she died now, but she didn't want a wolf to eat her face, so she kept going. Finally, she got to the top of the hill. She tried to look down and maybe see the farm, but it was too dark. Her toes jammed against the front of her sneakers as she started downhill. Finally, the woods opened up a little, and she saw this wire fence. The wind blew cold against her cheeks, but she was sweaty under her puffy pink jacket. It seemed like she'd already walked a hundred miles. What if she'd walked past the farm and didn't even know it?

At the bottom of the hill, she saw a shape. A wolf! Her heart hammered. She waited. It felt like it should be morning, but it wasn't. The shape didn't move. She took a cautious step forward and then another, getting closer and closer until she saw that it was an old mailbox. Something might be written on the side, but it was too dark to read, and it probably wouldn't be her brother's name anyway, since people like her brother and her dad tried not to let everybody know where they lived. Still, it had to be his farm, so she turned in.

This road was the worst of all, gravel without any blacktop and big trees making it even darker. She fell again, and the heels of her hands stung from the gravel. Finally, she came around a curve where the trees stopped and spotted a house, but there weren't any lights on. Not even one. Her house in Nashville had motion lights, so if a burglar came close at night it would light up. She wished this house had motion lights, but she didn't think they had those in the country.

She hoisted up her backpack and walked closer. She saw more buildings. The shape of a barn. She should have thought about what she'd do if nobody was awake. Her mom hated getting woken up too early. Maybe her brother would, too. Worst of all, what if her brother wasn't really here? What if he was still in Chicago? That was the one thing she'd been trying hardest not to think about.

She needed a place to rest until it got to be morning. She was scared to go to the barn, so she gazed toward the house. Slowly, she made her way up the path.

Chapter Eight

The faintest threads of morning light crept through the lace curtains in the tiny window above Blue's head. It was too early to get up, but she'd foolishly drunk a big glass of water before she went to bed, and the gypsy caravan, for all its cozy charms, had no bathroom. Blue had never slept in a more wondrous place. It had been like falling asleep in the middle of a fairy tale that came complete with a wild, blond-haired gypsy prince who'd danced with her around the campfire.

She couldn't believe she'd dreamed about him. True, Dean was exactly the kind of man to inspire outrageous female fantasies, but not from a realist like her. Ever since yesterday morning, she'd been too aware of him in all the wrong ways, and she needed to snap out of it.

The wagon's bare wooden floor was cool under her feet. She'd slept in an orange T-shirt that said BODY BY BEER and a pair of deep purple tie-dyed yoga pants that had never seen a yoga class but were super comfy. After she'd slipped into her flip-flops, she stepped outside into the cucumber chill. Only the birds' dawn songs broke the quiet—no clatter of garbage cans, shriek of sirens, or piercing warnings from trucks backing up. She headed for the house and let herself in the side door. In the morning light, the white kitchen cabinets and their bright red knobs gleamed against the new soapstone counters.

Don't sit under the apple tree . . .

Dean had taped black plastic over all the bathroom doors before he went out last night, and she made her way to the downstairs powder room partially tucked under the stairs. Like everything else in the house, this room had been designed for him, with a high sink and a partially raised ceiling to accommodate his height. Blue wondered if he'd noticed how much his mother had personalized everything. Or maybe she'd simply done as he'd asked.

While the coffee brewed, she located some bowls from the boxes of new kitchenware waiting to be unpacked after the kitchen was painted. The clean plates sitting on the new countertop reminded her of the dinner she'd shared with April last night. Dean had begged off, saying he had things to do. Blue bet those things included a blonde, brunette, and redhead. She pulled open the refrigerator door to get milk and saw that he'd made a big dent in the shrimp Creole leftovers. Judging from how little of the dish remained, all that sex had worked up his appetite.

She splashed water in the sink to wash some dishes for breakfast. The white bowls had red mattress-ticking stripes around the edge, and the mugs were printed with a cluster of bright red cherries. She poured her coffee, added a splash of milk, and wandered toward the front of the house. When she reached the dining room, she paused in the doorway. Last night, April had told her she was considering having some landscape murals painted in here and asked if Blue did that kind of thing. Blue said no, which wasn't exactly true. She did a fair amount of mural work—pets on rec room walls, business logos in offices, the occasional Bible verse on a kitchen wall—but she refused to paint landscapes. Her college professors had given her too much grief about the ones she'd done for her classes, and she hated anything that made her feel incompetent.

She let herself out the front door. Sipping her coffee, she ambled toward the steps and enjoyed the mist swirling in the hollows. As she turned to watch a platoon of birds perch on the barn's roof, she jerked and splashed coffee on her wrist. A child lay huddled in the corner of the porch fast asleep.

The girl looked like she might be thirteen or so, although she hadn't lost her baby fat, so she could have been younger. She wore a dirty pink jacket with a Juicy logo and muddy lavender cords that had a V-shaped tear at the knee. Blue put her wrist to her mouth to lick up the coffee. The child's wild, curly brown hair tumbled over a round, grimy cheek. She'd fallen asleep awkwardly, her back wedged against the dark green backpack she'd shoved into the porch corner. She had olive-toned skin, bold, dark eyebrows, and a straight nose she hadn't quite grown into. Her polished blue fingernails were bitten to the quick. But despite her grime, her clothes looked expensive, as did her sneakers. This kid had BIG CITY written all over her, which meant another wanderer had shown up at Dean's farm.

Blue set down her mug and made her way to the child's side. Crouching down, she gently touched her arm. "Hey, you," she whispered.

The girl jumped, and her eyes shot open. They were the toasty brown of caramelized sugar.

"It's okay," Blue said, trying to calm the fear she saw there. "Good morning."

The child struggled to sit up, and a morning croak deepened her soft southern accent. "I—I didn't hurt anything."

"Not a whole lot out here to hurt."

She tried to shove the hair out of her eyes. "I wasn't . . . supposed to fall asleep."

"You didn't pick a very comfortable bed." She looked too skittish for Blue to cross-examine just yet. "Would you like some breakfast?"

The child's front teeth sank into her bottom lip. They were straight, but still a little big for her face. "Yes, ma'am. If that's okay?"

"I was hoping someone would show up to keep me company. My name is Blue."

The child struggled to her feet and picked up her backpack. "I'm Riley. Are you the help?"

Obviously, she came from a privileged background. "Help or hindrance," Blue replied. "It depends on my mood."

Riley was too young to appreciate an adult smart-ass. "Is . . . like anybody here?"

"I am." Blue opened the front door and gestured for Riley to enter.

Riley peered around as she came inside. Her voice quivered with disappointment. "It's not done. There isn't any furniture."

"A little. The kitchen's almost finished."

"So . . . nobody's living here now?"

Blue decided to dodge the question until she figured out what the kid was up to. "I'm so hungry. How about you? Do you feel like eggs or cereal?"

"Cereal, please." Dragging her heels, Riley followed her down the hallway to the kitchen.

"The bathroom's right there. It doesn't have a door yet, but the painters won't be here for a while, so if you'd like to wash up, nobody'll bother you."

The girl gazed around, looking toward the dining room and then the stairs before she and her backpack headed into the bathroom.

Blue had left all the nonperishable groceries in sacks until the painters finished. She went into the pantry and dug out some cereal boxes. By the time Riley returned, dragging her backpack and jacket behind her, Blue had everything set out on the table, including a small cow-pitcher filled with milk. "Choose your poison."

Riley filled her bowl with Honey Nut Cheerios and three teaspoons of sugar. She'd washed her hands and face, and some of her curls stuck to her forehead. Her lavender cords fit too tightly, as did her white T-shirt, which had FOXY written across it in purple glitter script. Blue couldn't imagine a less appropriate word to describe this serious child.

She fried an egg for herself, made a piece of toast, and carried her plate to the table. She waited until the child had satisfied the worst of her hunger before she started digging. "I'm thirty. How old are you?"

"Eleven."

"That's a little young to be on your own."

Riley set down her spoon. "I'm looking for . . . somebody. Kind of a relative. Not—not like a brother or anything," she said in a rush. "Just . . . like maybe a cousin. I—I thought he might be here."

Right then, the back door opened, bracelets jingled, and April came in. "We have company," Blue said. "Look who I found asleep on the porch this morning. My friend Riley."

April cocked her head, and a big silver hoop peeked through her hair. "On the porch?"

Blue abandoned her toast. "She's trying to find one of her relatives."

"The carpenters should be here soon." April smiled at Riley. "Or is your relative one of the painters?"

"My—my relative doesn't work here," Riley mumbled. "He's . . . He's supposed to live here."

Blue's knee banged the table leg. April's smile faded. "Live here?" The girl nodded.

"Riley?" April's fingers convulsed around the edge of the counter. "Tell me your last name."

Riley dipped her head over the cereal bowl. "I don't want to tell you."

April's complexion lost its color. "You're Jack's kid, aren't you? Jack and Marli's daughter."

Blue nearly choked. It had been one thing to suspect Dean's connection to Jack Patriot, but another thing to have it confirmed. Riley was Jack Patriot's daughter, and despite her clumsy attempt to hide it, the relative she was looking for could only be Dean.

Riley tugged on a coil of her hair, pulling it over her face while she stared into her cereal bowl. "You know about me?"

"I— Yes," April said. "How did you get here? You live in Nashville."

"I sort of got a ride. With this friend of my mother's. She's thirty."

April didn't call her on her obvious lie. "I'm sorry about your mother. Does your father know you're—" April's expression hardened. "Of course he doesn't. He hasn't got a clue, does he?"

"Not most of the time. But he's very nice."

"Nice . . ." April rubbed her forehead. "Who's supposed to be taking care of you?"

"I have an au pair."

April reached for the notebook she'd left on the counter last night. "Give me her number so I can call her."

"I don't think she'll be out of bed yet."

April locked eyes with her. "I'm sure she won't mind if I wake her up."

Riley looked away. "Could you tell me . . . Is anybody . . . Is like maybe my . . . cousin living here? Because it's very important for me to find him?"

"Why?" April said tightly. "Why do you need to find him?"

"Because . . ." Riley swallowed. "Because I need to tell him about me."

April drew a shaky breath. She gazed down at the notebook. "This isn't going to work the way you want."

Riley stared at her. "You know where he is, don't you?"

"No. No, I don't," April said quickly. She looked at Blue, who was still trying to absorb what she was hearing. Dean bore no resemblance to Jack Patriot, but Riley did. They had the same olive skin tone, mahogany brown hair, and straight bladed nose. Those darkly rimmed caramelized sugar eyes had stared back at her from countless album covers.

"While Riley and I talk," April said to Blue, "would you take care of that matter upstairs?"

Blue got the message. She was supposed to keep Dean away. As a child, she'd felt the pain of withheld secrets, and she didn't believe in shielding kids from the truth, but this wasn't her call to make. She pushed back from the table, but before she could get up, a firm set of footsteps approached from the hall.

April grabbed Riley's hand. "Let's go outside and talk."

It was too late.

"I smell coffee." Dean walked in, freshly showered, unshaven, a *GQ* ad for hip country casual in blue bermudas, a pale yellow mesh T-shirt with a Nike swoosh, and high-tech lime green sneakers as streamlined as race cars. He spotted Riley and smiled. "Morning."

Riley sat paralyzed, drinking him in with her eyes. April pressed a hand to her waist, as if her stomach ached. Riley's lips parted ever so slightly. Finally, she found her tongue. "I'm Riley." Her voice came out in a papery croak.

"Hi, Riley. I'm Dean."

"I know," she said. "I—I have a scrapbook."

"You do? What kind of scrapbook?"

"A—about you."

"No kidding?" He headed for the coffeepot. "So you're a football fan."

"I'm sort of . . ." She licked her dry lips. "I'm sort of like . . . maybe your cousin or something."

Dean's head came up. "I don't have a—"

"Riley is Marli Moffatt's daughter," April said stonily.

Riley kept her focus glued entirely on him. "Jack Patriot is . . . like my dad, too."

Dean stared at her.

Riley's face flushed with agitation. "I didn't mean to say that!" she cried. "I never told anybody about you. I swear."

Dean stood frozen. April couldn't seem to move. Riley's stricken eyes filled with tears. Blue couldn't stand witnessing so much pain, and she rose from her chair. "Dean just rolled out of bed, Riley. Let's give him a few minutes to wake up."

Dean shifted his gaze to his mother. "What's she doing here?"

April stepped back against the stove. "Trying to find you, I guess."

Blue could see this meeting wasn't playing out as Riley had imagined. Tears spiked the child's lashes. "I'm sorry. I won't ever say anything again."

Dean was the grown-up, and he needed to take charge, but he stood silent and rigid. Blue moved around the table toward Riley. "Somebody hasn't had his coffee yet, and it's made him a grouchy bear. While Dean wakes up, I'll show you where I slept last night. You won't believe it."

When Blue was eleven years old, she'd have challenged anybody who tried to close her out, but Riley was more accustomed to blind obedience. She ducked her head and reluctantly picked up her backpack. The kid was a walking heartache, and Blue's own heart contracted in sympathy. She slipped an arm around Riley's shoulders and steered her toward the side door. "First, you have to tell me what you know about gypsies."

"I don't know anything," Riley muttered.

"Fortunately, I do."

♥

Dean waited for the door to shut. In less than twenty-four hours, two people had confronted him with the secret he'd been able to keep for so many years. He spun on April. "What the hell is going on? Did you know about this?"

"Of course I didn't know," April retorted. "Blue found her asleep on the porch. She must have run away from home. Apparently she only has an au pair watching her."

"Are you telling me that selfish son of a bitch left her alone less than two weeks after her mother died?"

"How would I know? It's been thirty years since I talked to him in person."

"Un-frickin'-believable." He thrust his finger at her. "You find him right now and tell him to get one of his flunkies over here this morning to pick her up." April didn't like being ordered around, and she set her jaw. Too bad. He headed for the door. "I'm going to talk to her."

"Don't!" Her intensity stopped him. "You saw the way she was looking at you. It's easy to see what she wants. Stay away, Dean. It's cruel to raise her hopes. Blue and I'll handle this. Don't do anything to let her get attached to you unless you're going to see it through."

He couldn't hide his bitterness. "The April Robillard school of child rearing. How could I have forgotten?"

His mother could be a real hard-ass when she wanted to, and her chin shot up. "You turned out all right."

He threw her a disgusted look and left by the side door. But halfway across the yard he slowed. She was right. Riley's needy eyes said she wanted everything from him that she knew she wouldn't get from her father. The fact that Jack had abandoned the kid so soon after her mother's funeral spelled out her future in big capital letters—an expensive boarding school and vacations spent with a series of glorified babysitters.

She'd still have it better than him. His vacations had taken place in luxury villas, fleabag hotels, or seedy apartments, depending on where April had been with her men and her addictions. Over time he'd been offered everything from marijuana to booze to hookers and generally had accepted it all. In fairness, April hadn't known about most of it, but she should have. She should have known about a lot of things.

Now Riley had come after him, and unless he grossly misread the yearning on her face, she wanted him to be her family. But he couldn't do that. He'd kept his connection with Jack Patriot secret for too long to have it blown now. Yes, he felt sorry for her, and he hoped like hell things got better, but that was as far as it went. She was Jack's problem, not his.

He ducked inside the gypsy caravan. Blue and Riley sat on the unmade bed in the back. Blue was her customary fashion disaster, her pointy nursery rhyme face at odds with a pair of tie-dyed purple pants that had to be somebody's idea of a joke, and an orange T-shirt big enough to house a circus. The kid gazed up at him, a world of misery inscribed on her round little face. Her clothes were too tight, too fussy, and the script FOXY on her T-shirt looked obscene over the innocent buds of her breasts. She wouldn't believe him if he tried to convince her she was wrong about his connection to Jack.

Seeing so much desperate need in Riley's expression brought back too many bad memories, and he spoke more harshly than he meant to. "How did you find out about me?"

She glanced at Blue, afraid to reveal more than she already had. Blue patted Riley's knee. "It's okay."

The kid poked at the lavender wales on her corduroy pants. "My—my mom's boyfriend told her about you last year. I sort of heard them talking. He used to work for my dad. But he made her swear not to tell anybody, not even Aunt Gayle."

He braced his hand on one of the caravan's ribs. "I'm surprised your mom knew about the farm."

"I don't think she did. I heard my dad talking to somebody on the phone about it."

Riley seemed to overhear a lot of things. Dean wondered how his father had found out about the farm. "Give me your phone number," he said, "so I can call your house and tell them you're all right."

"There's only Ava, and she doesn't like when the phone wakes her up too early. It makes Peter mad." Riley picked at the blue nail polish on her thumb. "Peter's Ava's boyfriend."

"So Ava must be your au pair?" he said. *Nice work, Jack.*

Riley nodded. "She's pretty nice."

"And incredibly competent," Blue drawled.

"I didn't tell anybody about—you know," she said in earnest. "I know it's a big secret. And I don't think Mom did, either."

Secrets. Dean had spent his early childhood years believing Bruce Springsteen was his father. April had even invented an elaborate story about Bruce writing "Candy's Room" about her. But it had all been wishful thinking. When Dean was thirteen and April had been high on God-knew-what, she'd blurted out the truth, and his already chaotic world had turned upside down.

Eventually, he'd found the name of Jack's lawyer in April's stuff, along with a collection of photos of April and Jack together, plus evidence of the support money Jack was paying out. He'd called the lawyer without telling April. The guy had tried to stonewall him, but Dean had been as stubborn then as he was now, and finally, Jack had called him. It was a brief, uncomfortable conversation. When April found out, she went on a weeklong bender.

Dean and Jack had their first face-to-face encounter, a secretive, awkward meeting in a bungalow at the Chateau Marmont, during the L.A. segment of the Mud and Madness tour. Jack had tried to act like Dean's best friend, but Dean hadn't bought it. After that, Jack had insisted on seeing him a couple of times a year, and each secretive visit was more miserable than the last. At sixteen, Dean rebelled.

Jack left him alone until Dean's sophomore year at USC, when his face started popping up in *Sports Illustrated.* Jack had started calling again, but Dean had frozen him out. Still, Jack occasionally ran him to ground, and Dean sometimes heard that Jack Patriot had been spotted at a Stars game.

He got down to business. "I need a phone number, Riley."

"I . . . kind of forget."

"You forgot your own phone number?"

She nodded, a quick jerk of her head.

"You look like a pretty smart kid to me."

"I am . . . but . . ." She gulped. "I know a lot about football. Last year, you completed three hundred forty-six passes, and you only got sacked twelve times, and you threw seventeen interceptions."

Dean usually requested that people not use the *i*-word around him, but he didn't want to agitate her more than necessary. "I'm impressed. It's interesting you can remember all that and not remember your phone number."

She pulled her backpack into her lap. "I've got something for you. I made it." She opened the zipper and removed a blue scrapbook. The pit of his stomach contracted as he gazed down at the cover, which had been painstakingly hand decorated. Using puffy paint and marking pens, she'd drawn the Stars' aqua and gold logo and an elaborate 10, his jersey number. Hearts with wings and banners that said "The Boo" decorated the border. He was glad Blue spoke because he couldn't think of a damn thing to say.

"That's some pretty good artwork."

"Trinity's better," Riley replied. "She's neat."

"Neatness doesn't always count so much in art," Blue said.

"My mom says neatness is important. Or . . . she used to say that."

"I'm so sorry about your mom," Blue said quietly. "This is a really hard time for you, isn't it?"

Riley rubbed one of the puffy hearts on the scrapbook cover. "Trinity's my cousin. She's eleven, too, and she's very beautiful. Aunt Gayle is her mom."

"I'll bet Trinity's going to be worried when she finds out you're missing," he said.

"Oh, no," she replied. "Trinity'll be glad. She hates me. She thinks I'm a weirdo."

"Are you?" Blue asked.

He didn't see the point of rubbing it in, but Blue ignored his dirty look.

"I guess," Riley said.

Blue beamed. "Me, too. Isn't that wild? Weirdos are the only truly interesting people, don't you think? Everybody else is so boring. Trinity, for example. She might be beautiful, but she's boring, right?"

Riley blinked. "She is. All she wants to talk about is boys."

"Yuck." Blue screwed up her face way more than she needed to.

"Or clothes."

"Double yuck."

"Look who's talking," he muttered.

But Riley was totally tuned in to Blue. "Or puking so you don't get fat."

"You've got to be kidding me." Blue wrinkled her small, sharp nose. "How does she know about that?"

"Puking's real important to Aunt Gayle."

"Gotcha." Blue shot Dean a quick look. "So I'm guessing Aunt Gayle is pretty boring, too."

"Totally. She always says 'huggy huggy' when she sees me and makes me kiss her, but it's fake. She thinks I'm a fat weirdo, too." Riley tugged on the hem of her T-shirt, trying to pull it over the little roll of flesh showing above the waistband of her cords.

"I feel sorry for people like that," Blue said earnestly. "People who are always judging. My mother, who's a very, very powerful woman, taught me that you can't do extraordinary things in the world if you're spending your time criticizing others because they don't look or behave the way you think they should."

"Is your mom . . . like . . . alive?"

"Yes. She's in South America helping protect some girls from getting hurt." Blue's expression turned grim.

"That doesn't sound boring," Riley said.

"She's a pretty great woman."

A great woman, Dean thought, who'd abandoned her only kid to be raised by strangers. But at least Virginia Bailey hadn't spent her nights getting high and fucking rock stars.

Blue rose and stepped around him to retrieve her cell from the table. "I need you to do something for me, Riley. I can see you don't want to give Dean your phone number, and privacy's okay up to a point. But you have to call Ava yourself and tell her you're okay." She held out her phone.

Riley gazed at it but didn't take it.

"Do it." Blue might look like an escapee from the Magic Kingdom, but she could be a drill sergeant when she wanted, and Dean wasn't surprised to see Riley take the phone and punch in a number.

Blue sat next to her. Several seconds ticked by. "Hi, Ava, it's me. Riley. I'm okay. I'm with grown-ups, so you don't have to worry about me. Say hi to Peter." She disconnected and gave the phone back to Blue. Her eyes, bottomless pools of need, returned to Dean. "Would you . . . like to see my scrapbook?"

He did not want to hurt this fragile kid by raising false hopes. "Maybe later," he said brusquely. "I've got some work to do." He looked at Blue. "Give me a hug before I go, sweetheart."

She got up, compliant for the first time since he'd met her. Riley's appearance had put a crimp in his plan to deal with her lie about April, but only temporarily. He moved to the middle of the caravan so he didn't bump his head. She wrapped her arms around his waist. He considered copping a feel, but she must have read his mind because she pinched him hard through his T-shirt. *"Ouch."*

She smiled up at him as she pulled away. "Miss me, dreamboat."

He glared at her, rubbed his side, and left the caravan.

As soon as he was out of sight, he reached into his back pocket and pulled out the cell she'd transferred over to him. He flicked through the menus, redialed the last call, and got voice mail for a Chattanooga insurance company.

The kid was no dummy.

While he had Blue's phone, he thumbed through the log until he found the date he wanted. He dialed up her voice mail and entered the password he'd watched her punch in a couple of days earlier. She hadn't gotten around to clearing out her mailbox, and he listened to her mother's message with interest.

♥

Inside the caravan, Blue watched Riley slowly return the scrapbook to her backpack. "I didn't know he was your boyfriend," she said. "I thought you were like the cleaning lady or somebody."

Blue sighed. Even at eleven, this child knew the Blue Baileys of the world weren't in the same league with the Dean Robillards.

"He likes you a lot," Riley said wistfully.

"He's just bored."

April poked her head in. "I have something I forgot at the cottage. Would the two of you like to come with me while I get it? It's a nice walk."

Blue still hadn't made it to the shower, but keeping Riley away from Dean for a while seemed like a good idea, and she suspected that was April's intention. Besides, she wanted to see this cottage. "Sure. We weirdos like new adventures."

April lifted an eyebrow. "Weirdos?"

"Don't worry," Riley said politely. "You're too pretty to be a weirdo."

"Stop right there," Blue said. "We can't be prejudiced against people just because they're pretty. Being a weirdo is a state of mind. April has a lot of imagination. She's kind of a weirdo, too."

"I'm honored," April said dryly. And then she gave Riley a stiff smile. "Do you want to see my secret pond?"

"You have a secret pond?"

"I'll show you."

Riley grabbed her backpack, and they both followed April from the caravan.

Chapter Nine

The small, weathered cottage sat behind a dilapidated picket fence. Pine needles dusted the tin roof, and four spindly candlestick posts held up the rickety porch. The once white paint had grayed, and the shutters had faded to a dull green.

"You live here all by yourself?" Riley said.

"Only for the past couple of months," April replied. "I have a condo in L.A."

As Blue took in the silver Saab with California plates parked in the shade at the side of the house, she decided the fashion stylist business was good.

"Don't you get scared at night?" Riley said. "Like what if a kidnapper or serial killer tries to get you?"

April led them up onto a creaky wooden porch. "There are enough real things in life to worry about. The chances of a serial killer making his way here are pretty slim."

A flap of screening had come loose from the door. April hadn't locked it, and they walked into the living area, which had bare wooden floors and two windows draped with shabby lace curtains. Bright rectangular patches on the blue and pink cabbage rose wallpaper showed where pictures had once hung. The room had little furniture: an overstuffed sofa topped with a quilt, a painted three-drawer chest, and a table holding an old brass table lamp, an empty water bottle, a book, and a stack of fashion magazines.

"Renters lived here until about six months ago," April said. "I moved in as soon as I got the place cleaned up." She headed for the kitchen, just visible at the back. "Feel free to look around while I find my notebook."

There wasn't a lot to see, but Blue and Riley peeked into the two bedrooms. The larger one had a charming bed with a curlicue iron headboard covered in chipped white paint. A pair of old-fashioned pink ribbon-glass boudoir lamps sat on mismatched tables. April had spruced up the bed with an assortment of pillows and a lavender bedspread that matched the nosegays splashed over the faded aqua wallpaper. With a rug and a few more furnishings, the room could have been a magazine layout for flea market chic.

The bathroom with its sea foam green fixtures wasn't as charming, nor the kitchen, which had worn counters and fake red-brick linoleum. Still, a wicker basket of pears and the earthenware vase of flowers sitting on the out-of-date butcher-block table provided a homey touch.

April came into the kitchen behind them. "I can't find my notebook anywhere. I must have left it at the house after all. Riley, there's a blanket in the bedroom closet. Bring it out, will you? We might as well enjoy the pond before we go back. I'll pour us some iced tea."

Riley dutifully fetched the blanket while April poured iced tea into three blue glasses. They carried them outside. Behind the cottage, the pond glistened in the sunshine, and the willows lining the banks trailed their leafy fringe in the water. Dragonflies buzzed through the cattails, and a family of baby ducks swam near a fallen tree that formed a natural pier. April directed them toward two dented red metal lawn chairs with scalloped backs that faced the water. Riley studied the pond warily. "Are there snakes?"

"I've seen a couple sunning themselves on that tree that's fallen into the water." April settled in one chair while Blue took the other. "They seem pretty content. Did you know snakes are soft?"

"You *touched* them?"

"Not those exact snakes."

"I would *never* touch a snake." Riley dropped her backpack and the blanket next to the chairs. "I like dogs. When I grow up, I'm going to have a puppy farm."

April smiled. "That sounds nice."

It sounded nice to Blue, too. She imagined blue skies, puffy white clouds, and a grassy meadow filled with scampering puppies.

Riley began spreading out the blanket. Without looking up, she said, "You're Dean's mom, aren't you?"

The tea glass stilled in April's hand. "How do you know that?"

"I know his mom's name is April. That's what Blue called you."

April took a slow sip before she answered. "Yes, I'm his mother." She didn't try to lie to Riley but simply stated that she and Dean had a difficult relationship and briefly explained the Susan O'Hara charade. Riley understood celebrity privacy issues and seemed satisfied.

All these secrets, Blue thought. She tugged on her BODY BY BEER T-shirt. "I haven't made it to the shower yet. Although you won't see that much difference after I do. I don't care about clothes."

"You care in your own way," April said.

"What do you mean?"

"Clothes are great camouflage."

"With me, it's not so much camouflage as comfort." Not exactly true, but she was only willing to reveal so much.

April's cell rang. She glanced at the screen and excused herself. Riley lay on the blanket and rested her head on her backpack. Blue watched a pair of ducks go bottoms-up looking for food. "I wish I'd brought my sketch pad," she said when April returned. "It's so pretty here."

"Are you formally trained?"

"Yes and no." Blue briefly outlined her academic career and the highlights of her less than satisfactory experience with the college art department. A soft wheezy sound drifted their way. Riley had fallen asleep on the blanket.

"I reached her father's manager," April said. "He promised someone would be here by the end of the day to pick her up."

Blue couldn't believe she was sitting with a person who knew how to reach Jack Patriot's manager. April nudged a dandelion with the toe of her raffia sandal. "Have you and Dean set a date?"

Blue wouldn't perpetuate Dean's lie, but she also didn't intend to clean up after him. "It hasn't gotten nearly to that point."

"As far as I know, you're the only woman he's ever asked to marry him."

"He's only attracted to me because I'm different. Once the newness wears off, he'll find a way out."

"You believe that?"

"I hardly know anything about him," she said truthfully. "I didn't even know for sure who his father was until today."

"He hates talking about his childhood, or at least the parts of it that involve me and Jack. I don't blame him. I lived a totally irresponsible life."

Riley sighed in her sleep. Blue cocked her head. "Was it really so bad?"

"Yeah, it was. I never called myself a groupie because I didn't put out for everybody. But I put out for way too many of them, and there are only so many rockers you can take on before you cross the line."

Blue would have loved asking exactly who those rockers had been. Fortunately, she still had some self-restraint left. But the double standard behind what April had just said bothered her. "How come nobody wags a finger at the rockers who were doing the groupies? Why is it always the women?"

"Because that's the way the world's made. Some women embrace their groupie past. Pamela Des Barres has written books about it. But it was wrong for me. I let them use my body like a garbage can. I *let* them. Nobody forced me. I didn't respect myself, and that's what shamed me." She tilted her face into the sun. "I fed off the lifestyle. The music, the men, the drugs. I let it imprison me. I loved dancing in the clubs all night, then blowing off my modeling assignment the next day to hop on a private plane and fly across the country, conveniently forgetting I'd also promised to visit my son at school." She gazed at Blue. "You should have seen Dean's face when I actually kept one of my promises. He'd drag me from one friend to the next, showing me off to everyone, talking so fast he'd get red in the face. It was like he had to prove to his friends that I really existed. That stopped somewhere around thirteen. A little kid will forgive his mother just about anything, but once he gets older, you've pretty much lost your chance at redemption."

Blue thought of her own mother. "You straightened your life out. You have to feel good about that."

"It was a long journey."

"I think it would be good for Dean to forgive you."

"Don't, Blue. You can't imagine what I put him through."

Blue could imagine it. Maybe not in the way April meant, but she knew what it felt like not being able to count on a parent. "Still . . . At some point he has to see you're not that same person. He should at least give you a chance."

"Stay out of it. I know you mean well, but Dean has every reason to feel the way he does. If he hadn't figured out how to protect himself, he'd never have become the man he is now." She checked her watch, then rose from the chair. "I need to talk to the painters."

Blue glanced down at Riley, who'd curled into a comma on the blanket. "Let's let her sleep. I'll stay."

"You don't mind?"

"I'll sketch for a while, if you have some paper."

"Sure. I'll get it for you."

"And maybe use your bathtub while I'm at it. If you don't mind."

"Take whatever you need from the medicine cabinet. Deodorant, toothpaste." She paused. "Makeup."

Blue smiled.

April smiled back. "I'll put out some clothes you can change into."

Blue couldn't imagine anything designed for April's willowy body fitting her, but she appreciated the offer.

"My car keys are on the counter," April said. "There's a twenty in the drawer next to my bed. When Riley wakes up, would you mind driving her into town for lunch?"

"I'm not taking your money."

"I'll bill it to Dean. Please, Blue. I want to keep her away from him until Jack's people get here."

Blue wasn't sure that keeping the eleven-year-old away was the best thing for either Riley or Dean, but she'd already been called to task for meddling, so she reluctantly nodded. "All right."

♥

April had laid out a delicate pink camisole and a frothy little after-thought of a ruffled skirt. She'd hastily modified both garments with some kind of double-sided tape to make them smaller. Blue knew she'd look adorable in the outfit. Way too adorable. The fluff-ball who wore those clothes might as well be wearing a SCREW ME OVER sign. This was the problem Blue always faced whenever she got around to fixing herself up, the main reason she'd stopped doing it.

Instead of the clothes on the bed, Blue appropriated a navy T-shirt. It did little to improve her purple tie-dyed yoga pants, but even she couldn't stomach appearing in public in her orange BODY BY BEER sleeping T-shirt. Vanity reared its ugly head, and she dipped into April's makeup—a swipe of soft pink tint on her cheeks, a little lip stain, and enough mascara to make it apparent exactly how long her lashes were. Just once, she wanted Dean to see that she was perfectly capable of looking decent. She simply didn't care to.

"You look nice with makeup," Riley said from the passenger seat of April's Saab as she and Blue headed into town. "Not so washed out."

"You've spent too much time around that awful Trinity."

"You're the only person who thinks she's awful. Everybody else loves her."

"No, they don't. Okay, probably her mom. The rest are just pretending."

Riley gave a faint, guilty smile. "I like it when you talk bad about Trinity."

Blue laughed.

Since Garrison lacked a Pizza Hut, they picked Josie's, the restaurant across from the pharmacy. Josie's was short on charm, the food was lousy, and it lacked employment opportunities—Blue asked about a job first thing—but Riley liked it. "I never ate anyplace like this. It's different."

"It definitely has character." Blue had settled on a BLT, which turned out to be more L than B or T.

Riley pulled a translucent sliver of tomato off her burger. "What does that mean?"

"It means it's only like itself."

Riley thought it over. "Sort of like you."

"Thanks. You, too."

Riley stuffed a French fry in her mouth. "I'd rather be pretty."

Riley had left on her FOXY T-shirt, but exchanged the dirty lavender cords for a pair of too-tight denim shorts that squeezed her stomach. They'd settled into a cracked brown vinyl booth that afforded a good view of a bad collection of western landscape art displayed on nauseating pastel blue walls along with some dusty ballerina figurines resting in shadow box frames. A pair of blond, fake wood ceiling fans stirred the smell of fried food.

The door opened and the lunchtime buzz stilled as a formidable-looking older woman limped in, supporting herself with a cane. She was overweight, overpowdered, and overdressed in bright watermelon pink slacks and a matching tunic. Multiple gold chains accented a plunging V-neck, and the stones in her dangling earrings looked as though they might be real diamonds. She'd probably once been beautiful, but she hadn't permitted herself to age gracefully. The sprayed mass of teased platinum hair that curled, waved, and swooped around her face had to be a wig. She'd drawn in her eyebrows with a light brown pencil but abandoned restraint with thick black mascara and frosted blue eye shadow. A small mole, which might once have been seductive, sagged at the corner of her bright pink lips. Tan orthopedic oxfords supporting badly swollen ankles were the only concession she'd made to her age.

None of the lunch crowd seemed happy to see her, but Blue regarded her with interest. The woman surveyed the crowded restaurant, her disdainful gaze flicking over the regulars, then settling on Blue and Riley. Seconds ticked by as she openly studied them. Finally, she bore down, her pink tunic molding to a formidable set of breasts held high by an excellent bra.

"Who," she said, when she reached their table, "are you?"

"I'm Blue Bailey. And this is my friend Riley."

"What are you doing here?" The faintest trace of Brooklyn colored her speech.

"We're enjoying a little lunch. How about you?"

"I have a bad hip, in case you haven't noticed. Were you planning to ask me to sit?"

Her imperious manner amused Blue. "Sure."

Riley's panicky expression suggested she didn't want the woman anywhere near her, so Blue slid over to make a place on her side of the booth. But the woman shooed Riley aside with her fingers. "Move over." She placed a big straw purse on the table and lowered herself slowly into the booth. Riley plastered her body against her backpack, sliding as far away as she could.

The waitress appeared with silverware and a glass of iced tea. "Your regular's coming right up."

The woman ignored her to concentrate on Blue. "When I asked what you were doing here, I was talking about in this town."

"We're visiting," Blue replied.

"Where are you from?"

"Well, I'm basically a citizen of the world. Riley's from Nashville." She tilted her head. "We've introduced ourselves, but you have us at a disadvantage."

"Everyone knows who I am," the woman replied querulously.

"We don't." Although Blue had a strong suspicion.

"I'm Nita Garrison, of course. I own this town."

"That's great. I've been wanting to ask somebody about that."

The waitress popped up with a plate holding a scoop of cottage cheese and a quartered canned pear resting on shredded iceberg lettuce. "Here you go, Miz Garrison." Her syrupy voice belied the dislike in her eyes. "Anything else I can get for you?"

"A twenty-year-old body," the old woman snapped.

"Yes, ma'am." The waitress hurried off.

Mrs. Garrison inspected her fork, then poked at the canned pear as if she were looking for a worm hiding under it.

"Exactly how does anybody own a town?" Blue asked.

"I inherited it from my husband. You're very odd-looking."

"I'll take that as a compliment."

"Do you dance?"

"Whenever I get the chance."

"I used to be an excellent dancer. I taught at the Arthur Murray Studio in Manhattan during the fifties. I met Mr. Murray once. He had a television show, but *you* wouldn't remember." Her haughty manner suggested it was Blue's stupidity at fault rather than her age.

"No, ma'am," Blue replied. "So . . . when you inherited this town from your husband, would that be the whole town?"

"All the parts of it that count." She plunged her fork into the cottage cheese. "You're staying with that stupid football player, aren't you? The one who bought the Callaway farm."

"He's not stupid!" Riley exclaimed. "He's the best quarterback in the United States."

"I wasn't talking to you," Mrs. Garrison snapped. "You're very rude."

Riley wilted, and Nita Garrison's high-handedness no longer amused Blue. "Riley has very nice manners. And she's right. Dean has his faults, but stupidity isn't one of them."

Riley's stunned expression indicated she wasn't used to anyone sticking up for her, which Blue found sad. She noticed the other customers were openly eavesdropping.

Instead of backing down, Nita Garrison puffed up like an angry cat. "You're another one of those people who lets kids behave however they want, aren't you? Lets them say whatever they want. Well, you aren't doing her any favors. Just look at her. She's fat, but you let her sit there wolfing down French fries."

Riley's face turned bright red. Mortified, she dipped her head and stared at the tabletop. Blue had heard more than enough. "Riley is perfect, Mrs. Garrison," she said quietly. "And her manners are a lot better than yours. Now I'd appreciate it if you'd find another table. We'd like to finish our lunch alone."

"I'm not going anywhere. I own this place."

Even though they hadn't finished eating, Blue had no choice but to get up. "All right then. Come on, Riley."

Unfortunately, Riley was trapped in the booth and Mrs. Garrison wasn't moving. She sneered, revealing lipstick-smeared teeth. "You're as disrespectful as she is."

Now Blue was burning. She jabbed her finger toward the floor. "Out, Riley. Right now."

Riley got the message and managed to squeeze from under the

table with her backpack. Nita Garrison's eyes narrowed to irate dashes. "Nobody walks away from me. You'll be sorry."

"Wow, I'm scared. I don't care how old you are, Mrs. Garrison, or how rich. You're just plain mean."

"You'll regret this."

"No, I really won't." She threw down April's twenty, which about killed her, since their lunch had only come to twelve-fifty, wrapped her arm around Riley's shoulders, and led her through the now silent restaurant and out onto the sidewalk.

"Do you think we could go back to the farm now?" Riley whispered when they'd moved far enough past the door.

Blue had hoped to make some more job inquiries, but that would have to wait. She hugged Riley. "Sure we can. Don't let that old woman bother you. She feeds off being mean. You could see it in her eyes."

"I guess."

Blue continued trying to soothe her as they got in the Saab and pulled out onto the main street. Riley made all the right responses, but Blue knew the hurtful words had struck home.

They'd nearly reached the city limit sign when she heard the siren. She glanced into the rearview mirror and saw a police squad car bearing down. She wasn't speeding, and she hadn't run any red lights, so it took her a moment to figure out the cop was after her.

An hour later, she was in jail.

Chapter Ten

April and Dean both came into town to get her. April handed over Blue's driver's license and claimed the Saab. Dean bailed Blue out of jail and yelled at her. "I leave you alone for a couple of hours, and what do you do? You get yourself arrested! I feel like I'm living in an *I Love Lucy* rerun."

"I was framed!" Blue's shoulder banged against the door of the Vanquish as he took a curve too fast. She was so angry she wanted to hit something, starting with him for not being as indignant as she was. "Since when have you heard of anybody being thrown in jail for driving without a license? Especially somebody who has a perfectly valid license."

"Which you didn't have on you at the time."

"But which I could have produced if they'd given me half a chance."

The police hadn't questioned Blue's statement that Riley was a family friend visiting the farm, and while Blue had been seething in her cell, Riley was sipping a Coke and watching Jerry Springer on the waiting room television. Still, it had been one more scary experience for the eleven-year-old, and April had driven her back to the farm as soon as the police turned over the Saab's keys.

"This whole thing was totally bogus." Blue glared across the passenger seat at Dean, whose blue-gray eyes had turned the exact color of an ocean storm.

He wheeled around another curve. "You had no license, and you were driving an out-of-state car registered to someone else. How does that constitute being framed?"

"I swear to God, all those fashion magazines have destroyed your brain. Think about it. Ten minutes after I went head to head with Nita Garrison, the police pulled me over with a lame excuse about random seat belt checks. How do you explain that?"

He switched from anger to condescension. "So what you're saying is that you got into a fight with an old lady, who then forced the police to arrest you?"

"You haven't met her," she countered. "Nita Garrison is mean to the bone, and she has the town in her pocket."

"You're a walking catastrophe. Ever since I picked you up on—"

"Stop making such a big deal out of it. You're a professional football player. You have to have spent some time in jail yourself."

He bristled. "I have *never* been in jail."

"Dude. The NFL won't let you on the field if you haven't been arrested at least twice for assault and battery—double points if you beat up a wife or girlfriend."

"You're not even mildly amusing."

Probably not, but she'd made herself feel better.

"Start at the beginning," he said, "and tell me exactly what happened with the old lady."

Blue described their encounter in detail. When she finished, he was silent for a few moments before he spoke. "Nita Garrison was way out of line, but don't you think you could have been a little more tactful?"

Blue bristled all over again. "No. Riley doesn't have a lot of people standing up for her. Or any, for that matter. It was time to fix that."

She waited for him to tell her she'd been right, but instead, he turned into the freaking town historian. "I talked to the painters about Garrison being up for sale and got the whole story." A few hours earlier, she'd been anxious to hear this, but not when he still hadn't said she was right.

He shot past a Dodge Neon that had unwisely decided to pull out in front of him. "A carpetbagger named Hiram Garrison bought a couple of thousand acres around here after the Civil War to build a mill. His son enlarged it—that abandoned brick building we passed on the highway—and established the town, all without selling an acre. If people wanted to build houses or businesses, they had to lease the land from him, even the churches. Eventually, he passed every-thing to his son Marshall. Your Mrs. Garrison's husband."

"Poor guy."

"He met her a couple of decades ago on a trip to New York. He was fifty at the time, and she was apparently hot."

"Let me tell you those days are gone." His civics lecture had started to make her wary. She had the feeling he was buying time. But for what?

"Marshall apparently shared his ancestors' aversions to selling even a quarter acre. And since they had no children, she inherited it all when he died—the land the town's built on and most of the busi-nesses."

"That's way too much power for one mean-spirited woman." She separated her ponytail to tighten the rubber band. "Did you find out how much she's asking for it?"

"Twenty million."

"That rules me out." She gazed at him sideways. "Does it rule you out?"

"Not if I sell my baseball card collection."

She hadn't really expected him to divulge his net worth. Still, he didn't need to be so sarcastic about it.

A dairy farm flashed past as he took advantage of the straightening road. "East Tennessee is a growing area. Popular with retirees. She had an offer for fifteen million from a group of Memphis businessmen but turned it down. People suspect she doesn't really want to sell." The car nearly fishtailed as he took the turn onto Callaway Road. "Without any national franchises, Garrison is pretty much a time capsule—quaint, but frayed at the edges. The local business leaders want to capitalize on that quaintness, spruce everything up so it's a tourist destination, but Nita refuses to cooperate."

As he raced past the lane that led to the farm, she straightened. "Hey! Where are you going?"

"Someplace private." The road turned into a dirt track. His jaw tensed. "Where we can talk."

Her heartbeat kicked up. "We already talked. I don't want to talk anymore."

"Too late." The bumpy track abruptly ended at a rusted barbed wire fence bordering an overgrown pasture. He flicked off the ignition and caught her in those ocean storm eyes. "Topic number one on our agenda. April's impending death . . ."

She gulped. "Tragic."

He waited. His charm had disappeared, leaving behind the nononsense man who made his living being quicker, smarter, and tougher than everyone else. She should have seen this coming and been better prepared. "Sorry," she said.

"Oh, we both know you can do better than that."

She tried to open the door to get some air and discovered it was locked. The old sense of helplessness sent a rush of adrenaline through her, but just as her fighting instincts kicked in, the lock clicked open. She got out, and so did he. She walked away from him toward the rusty fence. "I know I shouldn't have meddled," she said carefully. "It was none of my business. But she looked so sad, and I'm a total head case when it comes to maternal relationships."

He came up behind her, caught her by the shoulders, and turned her around. His grim features locked into final countdown. "Don't *ever* lie to me. If it happens again, you're out of here. Understand?"

"That's not fair. I like lying to you. It makes my life easier."

"I mean what I say. You crossed the line."

She gave up. "I know. I apologize. Really." She felt a weird urge to poke at the forbidding corners of his mouth until she'd rearranged them into the charming grin she was accustomed to. "I don't blame you for being mad. You have every right." She couldn't resist asking. "When did you figure it out?"

He released her shoulders but stayed where he was, looming over her. "About half an hour after I left the house last night."

"Does April know you know?"

"Yes."

Blue wished April had chosen to share that information with her.

"At least there's one good thing about my mother . . ." He studied her intently. "I don't have to worry about April emptying out my bank accounts."

A crow shrieked in the distance. She took a step back from him. "How do you know about that?"

"Two can play the meddling game. Stay out of my private business, Blue, and maybe I'll stay out of yours."

He must have gotten into her voice mail when she'd given him her phone. She could hardly protest, no matter how much she hated him knowing about Virginia. He finally moved away from her to survey the pasture. A covey of birds shrieked as they flew up from the long grass. "So what are you going to do about Riley?" she said.

He whirled around. "I don't believe you! Didn't we just talk about your meddling?"

"Riley's not your private business. I'm the one who found her, remember?"

"I'm not doing anything," he declared. "April got hold of one of Mad Jack's serfs a couple of hours ago. Someone's coming to pick Riley up."

"Just like so much garbage." She began walking back to the car.

"That's the way he works," he said from behind her. "His responsibility stops with writing checks and hiring people to do his dirty work."

She turned. He hadn't moved away from the fence. "Are you going to . . . talk to her?" she asked.

"And say what? That *I'm* going to take care of her?" He delivered a sharp kick to the rotting post. "I can't do that."

"I think it would help if you'd at least promise to stay in touch with her."

"She wants a lot more from me than that." He came toward her. "Don't give me any more trouble, okay? I've already bailed you out of jail *and* paid your traffic fine."

Just like that, he was on the attack again. She had to squint against the sun to return his gaze. "I'll repay you as soon as I can."

"We're bartering, remember?"

"Remind me how that works?"

Instead, he surveyed her critically. "Have you considered letting a professional work on your hair as opposed to a kindergartner with a set of plastic scissors?"

"Too busy."

"Stop being such a hard-ass." His hand curved around her shoulder, and he hit her with a smoky-eyed look that made her knees go weak. She knew he'd given that same look to a thousand women, but the long day had made her defenses sluggish. Their eyes locked, his as dark as the sea. She understood his danger. He had an innate sense of entitlement and an arsenal of lethal sexuality. But she still didn't move. Not an inch.

His head dipped, their mouths meshed, and the sounds of birds and breeze faded away. Her lips parted on their own. He touched her with his tongue. Silky threads of pleasure unwound inside her. The kiss deepened, and dazzling colors began swirling in her head. She'd turned herself over to him just like all the others. She'd been swept away.

The knowledge chilled her. Having a nighttime fantasy about a gypsy prince was one thing, but acting on it was something else entirely. She pushed away, blinked her eyes, and came up swinging. *"That* was a disaster. Jeeze, I'm sorry. If I'd known the truth, I'd never have kidded you about the gay thing."

The corner of his mouth cocked, and his lazy eyes trickled over her as intimately as a lover's hand. "Keep fighting, Bluebell. You'll only make the victory sweeter."

She wanted to dump a bucket of cold water over her head. Instead, she gave him a dismissive wave and headed for the dirt track that led to the house. "I'm walking back. I need to be alone so I can have a long, hard talk with myself about being so insensitive."

"Good idea. I need to be alone so I can picture you naked."

She flushed and picked up her pace. Fortunately, the farm was less than a mile away. Behind her, the Vanquish roared to life. She heard him back up and turn around. Before long, the car drew up next to her, and the driver's window slid down. "Hey, Bluebell . . . I forgot something."

"Yeah, what's that?"

He slipped on his sunglasses and smiled. "I forgot to thank you for defending Riley against the old lady."

And then he was gone.

♥

Riley barely touched the dinner Blue fixed that evening. "It'll probably be Frankie who comes to get me," she said, pushing aside a fig Blue had added to the chicken and dumplings. "He's my dad's favorite bodyguard."

April reached across the table and pressed her hand over Riley's. "I'm sorry I had to tell them you were here."

Riley ducked her head. One more disappointment in her young life. Earlier, Blue had tried to distract her with an invitation to bake brownies, but that had gone sour when Dean had come in and brusquely refused Riley's eager plea to look at her scrapbook. He thought he was doing the right thing, but Riley was his flesh and blood, and Blue wished he'd spare a small corner of his life for her. She knew what he'd say if she pressed him. He'd say Riley wanted more than a small corner, and he'd be right.

It was just as well he'd driven off. Now she had space to get her equilibrium back and straighten out her priorities. Her life was complicated enough right now without putting herself at more of a disadvantage by becoming another of Dean Robillard's easy conquests.

Riley reached for the plate of brownies Blue had ended up baking alone, then stopped herself. "That woman was right," she said softly. "I am fat."

April set down her fork with a clink. "People need to concentrate on what's right about themselves. If you only think about what's wrong, or about all the mistakes you've made, you get paralyzed. Are you going to fill up your head with garbage—everything you don't like about yourself—or are you going to be proud of who you are?"

April's intensity made Riley's lip tremble. "I'm only eleven," she said in a tiny voice.

April made a business of wadding her napkin. "That's right. I'm sorry. I guess I was thinking about someone else." She gave Blue an overly bright smile. "Riley and I'll clean up while you relax."

They ended up working together. April tried to distract Riley with talk of clothes and movie stars. One of Riley's offhand remarks revealed that Marli had deliberately bought Riley's clothes too small, hoping to shame her into losing weight. Soon after, April excused herself to go to the cottage. She tried to convince Riley to come with her until her father's assistant arrived, but Riley was still hoping Dean would return.

Blue set Riley up at the kitchen table with a set of watercolors. Riley studied the blank paper. "Would you draw some dogs for me so I can paint them?"

"Wouldn't you rather draw them yourself?"

"I don't think I have enough time for that."

Blue squeezed her arm and drew four different dogs. As Riley started to paint, Blue grabbed some clothes upstairs and took them out to the caravan. On her way back inside, she stopped in the dining room and gazed at the four blank walls. She imagined them covered with dreamy landscape murals, the kind of work her art professors had so tactfully criticized her for painting.

"A bit derivative, don't you think, Blue?"

"You need to start stretching yourself. Pushing the boundaries."

"I'm sure an interior decorator would love what you've done," her only female professor had said, more bluntly. *"But sofa paintings don't make good art. This isn't a real statement. It's sentimental claptrap, an insecure girl looking for a romanticized world to hide in."*

Her words made Blue feel as though she'd been stripped naked. She'd given up her dreamy landscapes and begun producing bold mixed-media pieces using motor oil and Plexiglas, latex and broken beer bottles, hot wax and even her own hair. Her professors were delighted, but Blue knew the work was phony, and she left school at the beginning of her junior year.

Now the blank dining room walls wanted to lure her back to those dreamy places where life was simple, where people stayed in place, where only good things happened, and where she would finally feel safe. Disgusted with herself, she went outside to sit on the porch steps and watch the sunset. Maybe painting kids' portraits didn't inspire her, but she was good at it, and she could have built up a respectable business in any of the cities where she'd lived. She never did, though. Sooner or later, she started feeling panicky, and she knew the time had come to move.

The porch post felt warm against her cheek. The sun reminded her of a shimmering copper globe hanging low over the hills. She thought about Dean and their kiss. If the timing were different . . . If she had a job, an apartment, money in the bank . . . If he were more ordinary . . . But none of that was true, and she'd spent too many years living at the mercy of others to put herself any further under his control. As long as she resisted, she had power. If she gave in, she'd have nothing.

The noise of an engine intruded on her thoughts. Shielding her eyes, she saw two cars approaching down the lane. Neither of them was Dean's Vanquish.

Chapter Eleven

Two SUVs with tinted windows pulled up in front of the farmhouse. The back door of the lead vehicle opened, and a man dressed entirely in black stepped out.

His shaggy dark hair was threaded with gray, his weather-beaten face creased from too many long nights riding the glory trail. As he moved away from the car, his gunslinger's arms hung loosely at his sides ready to draw—not a six-shooter—but the blazing Fender Custom Telecaster he'd used to conquer the world. If Blue hadn't already been sitting, her knees would have buckled. As it was, she couldn't squeeze a single particle of air into her lungs.

Jack Patriot.

Car doors began to open behind him, and men in sunglasses spilled out, along with a long-haired woman carrying a designer purse and a water bottle. They stayed by the cars. His boot heels hit the brick walk, and Blue turned into every screaming fan who'd knotted her fingers through a chain-link fence, pressed her body against a police barricade, chased a stretch limo, or stood vigil outside a five-star hotel praying for a glimpse of her rock idol. Except, instead of screaming, she couldn't make a sound.

He stopped less than eight feet away. Small silver skulls adorned his earlobes. Beneath the cuff of his black, open-neck shirt, she saw a leather bracelet with a beaten silver sleeve. He nodded. "I'm looking for Riley."

Ohmygod! Jack Patriot was standing right in front of her. Jack Patriot was talking to her! She scrambled to her feet. She wheezed for air, choked on nothing, and started to cough. He waited patiently, the silver skulls turning to rust in the sunset. Her eyes began to tear. She pressed her fingers to her throat, trying to clear the air passage.

Rock star legends understood overwrought females, and he took in the house while he waited. She balled her hand into a fist and struck her chest. He finally spoke again in the familiar smoke-and-gravel voice that still held remnants of his native North Dakota. "Could you get Riley for me?"

As she struggled to pull herself together, the front door opened, and Riley came out. "Hi," she muttered.

Only his lips moved. "What's this all about?"

Riley gazed toward the silent entourage gathered around the SUV. "I dunno."

He tugged on his earlobe, the silver skull disappearing between his fingers. "Do you have any idea how worried everybody's been?"

Her head came up slightly. "Who?"

"Everybody. Me."

She studied the toes of her sneakers. She wasn't buying it.

"Who else is here?" he asked, scanning the house.

"Nobody. Dean drove away, and April went to her cottage."

"April . . ." He spoke her name as if he were conjuring up a not-too-pleasant memory. "Get your things together. We're leaving."

"I don't want to go."

"I'm sorry about that," he said flatly.

"I left my jacket at the cottage."

"Go get it then."

"I can't. It's dark. I'm too scared."

He hesitated, then rubbed his hand over his jaw. "Where's this cottage?"

Riley told him about the path through the woods. He turned to Blue. "Can I drive there?"

Yes, you sure can. Take the lane back toward the highway, but just before you get there, you'll see a road going off to your left. It's not much more than a track, really, and easy to overlook, so keep your eyes peeled. But none of that came out of her mouth, and he looked back at Riley, who shrugged. "I don't know. I guess."

Blue had to say something. Anything. But she couldn't adjust to having the man she'd had a crush on since she was ten years old standing in front of her. Later, she would ponder the fact that he hadn't kissed or hugged his daughter, but for now, she focused on willing her mouth to open.

It was too late. He'd signaled both Riley and his entourage to stay where they were and headed toward the path his daughter had pointed out. Blue waited until he disappeared, then slumped down on the top step. "I'm an idiot."

Riley sat down next to her. "Don't worry. He's used to it."

♥

As dusk settled in, April finished her last phone call, slipped her cell into the beaded pocket of her jeans, and wandered down to the edge of the pond. She loved it here at night, the soothing lap of water, the throaty croak of a frog striking a bass note against a cricket chorus. The pond smelled different at night, musky and fecund, like something feral.

"Hello, April."

She spun around.

The man who'd shattered her world stood in front of her.

It had been three decades since she'd seen him in person, but even in the dusky light, every feature in that angular, excess-lined face was as familiar as her own: the long, aquiline nose; the deep-set eyes, black at the rims but with golden brown irises; his swarthy skin and knife-blade jaw. Silver threaded the dark hair that used to fly in a midnight storm cloud around his head. It was shorter now—just above his collar—and wirier, but still thick. She wasn't surprised he'd made no effort to cover the threads of gray. He had little personal vanity. Although he'd always been tall for a rocker, now he seemed even taller because he was so thin. The sockets beneath those gaunt cheekbones were deeper than she remembered, the grooves at the corners of his eyes more sharply etched. He looked every one of his fifty-four years.

"Hey, little girl. Is your mother around?"

His voice was whiskey-soaked gravel. For the briefest moment, she felt the old breathlessness claim her. This man had once been her world. She'd flown across the ocean on an hour's notice to be with him. London, Tokyo, West Berlin. It didn't matter where. Night after night as he'd come offstage, she'd stripped the tight, sweat-soaked costume from his body, smoothed his long, damp hair with her fingers, parted her lips, parted her thighs, made him feel like a god.

But in the end, it was only rock and roll.

Their last face-to-face communication had taken place the day she'd told him she was pregnant. From then on, everything had been handled through an intermediary, including the blood test after Dean was born. How bitterly she'd resented Jack for that.

She pulled herself back together. "Just me and the frogs. How have you been?"

"My hearing's shot, and I can't get it up anymore. Otherwise . . ."

She only believed the first part. "Lay off the booze, cigarettes, and teenagers. You'll be amazed how good you'll feel." She didn't need to mention drugs. Jack had cleaned up his act years before she'd been able to.

A leather and silver bracelet slipped down on his wrist as he ambled forward. "No more teenagers, April. Cigarettes, either. I haven't smoked for a couple of years. And hasn't that been a mission from hell? As for the booze . . ." He shrugged.

"I guess you geezer rockers need at least one vice."

"I have a few more than that. How about you?"

"I got a speeding ticket on my way to Bible study a few months ago, but that's about it."

"Bullshit. You've changed, but not that much."

He hadn't always been able to see through her so easily, but he was older now and, presumably, wiser. She shrugged her hair from her face. "I don't have much interest in vice anymore. Too busy making a living."

"You look great, April. Really."

Better than he did. For the last decade she'd worked hard to repair the damage she'd done to herself, detoxifying with endless cups of green tea, hours of yoga, a little nip and tuck.

He tugged on a small skull earring. "Do you remember how we used to laugh at the idea of a rocker over forty?"

"We used to laugh at the idea of anybody ever reaching forty."

He stuffed a hand in his pocket. "AARP wants me to pose for the cover of their fucking magazine."

"Damn their black hearts."

His crooked smile hadn't changed, but she wasn't going to wander down memory lane with him. "Did you see Riley?"

"A couple of minutes ago."

"She's a sweet kid. Blue and I have been quite taken with her."

"Blue?"

"Dean's fiancée."

He pulled his hand from his pocket. "Riley came here to see him, didn't she?"

April nodded. "Dean's tried to stay away, but she's persistent."

"I wasn't the one who told Marli about him. She had a fling with my former business manager last year and weaseled out the information. Until I got your message, I didn't know Riley had found out."

"This is a hard time for her."

"I know. I had some things I needed to take care of. Marli's sister was supposed to be watching out for her." He glanced toward the cottage. "Riley said she left her jacket."

"No. She wasn't wearing her jacket when she came here."

"She was stalling, then." He slipped his hand in his shirt pocket, as if he were looking for cigarettes. "I could use a beer."

"Afraid you're out of luck. I've been a teetotaler these many moons."

"You're not serious."

"I lost the urge to die."

"Not all bad, I guess." He had a way of looking at people as though he really saw them, and he turned that intensity on her. "I hear you've done well for yourself."

"No complaints." She'd built her career one client at a time, with no one to rely on but herself, and she was proud of that. "What about Mad Jack? Now that you've won the rock wars, what do you do for an encore?"

"The rock wars can't ever be won. You know that. There's always another album, another shot at the top of the charts, and, if that doesn't happen, the inevitable reinvention." He made his way to the edge of the pond, picked up a rock, and flung it far out into the pond, where it made a quiet splash. "I'd like to see Dean before I leave."

"So you can reminisce about the good times? Lots of luck. He hates you almost as much as he hates me."

"Then what are you doing here?"

"It's a long story." Something else she wouldn't go into with him.

He turned back to her. "One big happy family, aren't we?"

Before she could reply, a flashlight beam ricocheted toward them, and Blue shot out of the path. "Riley's gone!"

♥

To keep herself from falling mute again, Blue pretended Jack Patriot didn't exist and focused only on April. "I've searched the house, the caravan, that mousy barn." She shuddered. "She can't have gone far."

"How long has she been missing?" April said.

"Maybe half an hour. She said she wanted to finish her painting before she had to go. I went out to burn the trash like you showed me, and when I came back, she'd disappeared. I gave flashlights to the men who came with"—*Mr. Patriot* sounded ridiculous, and *Jack* too familiar— "with Riley's father—and they're looking now."

"How could she do this?" Jack said. "She's always been so quiet. She's never caused any trouble."

"She's scared," April told him. "Take my car and look along the lane."

Jack agreed. After he set off, Blue and April searched the cottage then struck out for the farmhouse, where they found Jack's entourage poking ineffectively around the garden while the lone woman sat on the back step, smoking a cigarette and talking on her cell. "There are a hundred places Riley could hide," April said. "Assuming she's still somewhere on the property."

"Where else could she go?"

April searched the house again while Blue rechecked the caravan and toolshed. They met up on the front porch. "Nada."

"She took her backpack," April said.

Jack pulled up to the house and climbed out of April's Saab. Blue retreated into the shadows so she didn't embarrass herself in front of him again. Dean should be coping with this, not her.

"No sign of Riley," Jack said as he approached the porch.

"I'll bet she's watching the house," April said quietly. "Waiting for you to leave before she comes out."

He shoved a hand through his wiry hair then glanced over at his bodyguards emerging from the barn. "We'll leave. Then I'll circle back on foot."

Only after the cars had pulled away did Blue emerge from the corner. "Wherever she is, I'm sure she's scared."

April rubbed her temples. "Do you think we should call the po-lice . . . the sheriff . . . whoever?"

"I don't know. Riley's hiding; she hasn't been abducted, and if she sees a police car pull up . . ."

"That's what worries me."

Blue gazed into the darkness. "Let's give her some time to think this through."

♥

Dean slowed as his headlights picked out a man walking down the side of the lane toward the farmhouse. He flicked on his high beams. The man turned and shielded his eyes. Dean looked closer. Mad Jack Patriot . . .

He couldn't believe Jack had come after Riley himself, but here he was. Dean hadn't talked to him in a couple of years, and he sure as hell didn't want to talk to him now. He fought his instinct to goose the accelerator and shoot past him. Years ago, he'd fixed his strategy for dealing with his father, and he saw no reason to change. He pulled up and slid down the car window. Keeping his expression carefully neutral, he propped his elbow on the frame. "Jack."

The son of a bitch nodded. "Dean. It's been a long time."

Dean nodded back. No digs or wisecracks. Total indifference.

Jack rested the heel of his hand on the roof of the car. "I came to get Riley, but she ran away after she saw me."

"Really?" It didn't entirely explain why he was out here walking alone, but Dean wouldn't ask.

"I don't suppose you've seen her."

"No."

The silence between them lengthened. If Dean didn't offer to drive him to the house, he'd be showing the son of a bitch exactly how much he hated him. Still, he had to force out the words. "Need a lift?"

Jack stepped back from the car. "I don't want her to see me. I'll walk."

"Suit yourself." He slid the window up and pulled slowly away. No spinning tires or flying gravel. Nothing to show the depth of his anger. When he reached the house, he headed inside. The electrician had finished installing most of the fixtures today, and they finally had some decent light. He heard footsteps overhead. "Blue?"

"Upstairs."

Just the sound of her voice made him feel better. She'd distract him from worrying about Riley, from his tension over Jack. She'd make him smile, make him mad, turn him on. He needed to keep her here.

He found her in the second-largest bedroom, which had a fresh coat of light tan paint, a new bed and dresser, but not much else, no rugs, no curtains, no chairs, although Blue had found a paint-spattered gooseneck desk lamp somewhere and set it on the dresser. She was smoothing a blanket over the sheets she'd just tucked in. Her T-shirt fell loosely away from her body as she leaned forward, and locks of hair had escaped from her ponytail and drifted down her neck like spilled ink.

She looked up, twin worry lines between her eyebrows. "Riley's run away."

"I heard. I ran into Jack on the road."

"How did that go?"

"It went fine. Not a big deal. He doesn't mean anything to me."

"Right." She didn't believe him, but she didn't challenge him, either.

"Don't you think somebody should be out looking for her?" he said.

"We've looked everywhere. She'll be back when she's ready."

"You're sure about that?"

"Reasonably optimistic. Plan B involves calling the sheriff, and that'd scare her too much."

He forced himself to consider what he'd so far been reluctant to face. "What if she walked out to the highway and hitched a ride?"

"Riley isn't stupid. She has a highly developed fear of strangers from all the movies she shouldn't have seen. Also, April and I don't think she's completely given up on you."

He tried to mask his guilt by walking over to the window. It was too dark for an eleven-year-old girl to be out there alone.

"Would you make another sweep of the yard? There's a flashlight in the kitchen. She might come out if she sees you." Blue regarded the room with dissatisfaction. "I wish there was at least a rug in here. I'm sure he's not used to anything this spartan."

"He?" Dean's head snapped up. "Forget it. Jack is not sleeping here." He stalked into the hall.

Blue came after him. "What's the alternative? It's getting late, and his entourage has driven off. There aren't any hotels in Garrison, and he's not going anywhere until Riley's been found."

"Don't bet on it." Dean wanted all this to go away. If only he'd driven off first thing this morning.

Blue's cell rang. She snatched it from her jeans pocket. He waited. "You found her?" she said. "Where was she?" He took a deep breath and leaned against the doorframe.

"But we looked there." She wandered back into the bedroom and sat on the side of the bed. "Yes. All right. Yes, I'll do that." She flipped the phone shut and looked up at him. "The eagle-ette has landed. April found her asleep in the back of her closet. We looked there, so she must have waited till we left to go inside."

The front door opened downstairs, and heavy, measured footsteps sounded in the foyer. Blue's head shot up. She jumped to her feet and spoke in a rush. "April said to tell Riley's father that she'll keep Riley at the cottage for tonight, and he can stay here in the house, and he should wait until morning to talk to her."

"You tell him."

"I don't think . . . The thing is—"

More footsteps from below. "Anyone here?" Jack called out.

"I can't," she hissed.

"Why not?"

"I just . . . can't."

Jack's voice carried up the steps. "April?"

"Crap." Blue's hands flew to her cheeks, and she rushed out, but instead of going downstairs, she dashed into the master bedroom. Only seconds later—too short a time for her to have undressed—the shower went on. That's when he realized the fearless Beav had gone into hiding. And not over him.

♥

Blue stalled as long as she could in the bathroom, brushing her teeth and washing her face, then she sneaked out to grab her yoga pants and BODY BY BEER T-shirt. Finally she managed to creep outside without being detected. Tomorrow morning, if Jack was still here, this idiocy was coming to an end, and she'd behave like a grown woman. At least Jack Patriot's appearance had been a diversion from her real problem. She stepped inside the gypsy caravan and stopped cold. Her real problem had come for a visit.

A surly-looking gypsy prince lay sprawled on the rear bed, the oil-burning lamp on the table casting a golden glow over him. He'd propped his shoulders against the side of the wagon, cocked one knee, and dangled the other calf over the side of the bed. As he lifted the beer bottle to his lips, his T-shirt rode up to reveal a taut wedge of muscle above the low-riding jeans. "You, of all people," he said with a disparaging sneer.

Feigning ignorance would be wasted effort. How could someone who'd known her for only a few days see through her so quickly? She lifted her chin. "I need a little time to adjust, that's all."

"I swear to God, if you ask for his autograph . . ."

"I'd have to speak to him for that to happen. So far, that hasn't been possible."

He snorted and took a swig of beer.

"I'll pull it together by tomorrow." She pushed the chair back under the painted table. "You got out here awfully fast. Did you even talk to him?"

"I told him about Riley, pointed in the direction of the bedroom, and then politely excused myself to find my fiancée."

She eyed him warily. "You're not sleeping in here."

"Neither are you. I'll be damned if I give him the satisfaction of driving me out of my own house."

"And yet, here you are."

"I came to get you. In case you've forgotten, those bedrooms don't have any doors, and there's no way I'm letting him see that my beloved doesn't sleep with me."

"In case *you've* forgotten, I'm not your beloved."

"For now, you are."

"Once again, my virginity vow seems to have slipped your mind."

"Fuck your virginity vow. Are you working for me or not?"

"I'm your cook. And don't pretend you're not eating. I saw what you did to those leftovers last night."

"Yeah, well, I don't need a cook. What I need is somebody to sleep with tonight." He gazed at her over the rim of the beer bottle. "I'll pay you."

She blinked. "You want to pay me to sleep with you?"

"Nobody's ever accused me of being cheap, either."

She pressed her palm to her chest. "Hold on. This is such a proud moment that I want to savor it."

"What's your problem?" he asked, all innocence.

"A man I once respected is offering me money to sleep with him. Let's start with that."

"*Sleep,* Beav. Get your mind out of the gutter."

"Right. Like we *slept* last time?"

"I don't know what you're talking about."

"You were all over me," she said.

"You wish."

"You had your hands down my jeans."

"The overheated imagination of a sex-starved female."

She wouldn't let him manipulate her. "You're sleeping by your-self."

He set the beer bottle on the floor, rested his weight on one hip, and pulled out his wallet. Without a word, he withdrew two bills and wordlessly fanned them between his fingers.

A pair of fifties.

Chapter Twelve

Half a dozen indignant responses raced through Blue's mind before she reached the obvious conclusion. She could be bought. Yes, she'd be putting herself in harm's way, but wasn't that part of this game they were playing? Finally having money in her wallet justified the risk. Besides, this gave her a chance to show him exactly how immune she was to his charms.

She grabbed the bills. "All right, you rat bastard, you win." She stuffed the money in her back pocket. "But I'm only taking it because I'm greedy and desperate. *And* because there's no door on that room so you can't get too frisky."

"Fair enough."

"I mean it, Dean. If you try to cop even one feel . . ."

"Me? What about you?" His eyes slid over her like cool icing on hot spice cake. "How about this? Double or nothing."

"What are you talking about?"

"You touch me first, I keep the hundred. I touch you first, you get two hundred. Nobody touches anybody, the deal stands as is."

She thought it over, but couldn't see any immediate loopholes other than the threat of her inner slut emerging, and she could darned well control that little bitch. "Deal."

"First, though . . ." She wasn't spending any more time in that bedroom with him than she had to, so she swiped his beer and propped herself at the opposite end of the bed. "You're awfully bitter about your parents. I'm beginning to think your childhood was as twisted as mine."

He brushed his toe against the hollow below her ankle bone. "The difference being that I've recovered, and you're still a fruitcake."

She moved her foot. "Yet of all the women on the planet, you've chosen me to marry."

"There's that." He eased onto one hip and slipped his wallet back in his pocket. "Before I forget . . . Apparently you've now decided we're going to Paris instead of Hawaii to tie the knot."

"And why is that?"

"Hey, I'm not the one who can't make up her mind."

"Poor Dean. Fending off all the women you're meeting in the bars at night is pretty much a full-time job, isn't it?" His calf grazed the side of her leg. "Just out of curiosity, why *are* you fending them off?"

"Not interested."

Meaning they're married or old. "So what was it like growing up the way you did?"

Sure enough, she'd broken the mood, and his brow furrowed. "It was just fine. I had a series of babysitters looking out for me until I went off to a very good boarding school. You'll be disappointed to know I wasn't beaten or starved there, and I also learned to play ball."

"Did you ever see him?"

He snatched his beer back, which involved moving his leg away. "I really don't want to talk about this."

She wasn't above a little subtle manipulation. "If it's too painful . . ."

"Hardly. I didn't even realize he was my father until I was thirteen. Before that, I thought the Boss had done the deed."

"You thought Bruce Springsteen was your father?"

"April's drunken fantasy. Too bad it wasn't true." He drained the bottle and set it on the floor with a clink.

"I can't imagine her drunk. She's so controlled now. Did Jack know about you from the beginning?"

"Oh, yeah."

"That's crappy. If April was an addict, shouldn't he have been just a little worried about her pregnancy?"

"She cleaned up her act when she was pregnant. Probably hoping he'd marry her. Fat chance of that." He rose and shoved his feet into his shoes. "Stop stalling. Let's go."

She rose reluctantly. "I mean it, Dean. No contact."

"I'm starting to get offended."

"No, you're not. You just want to give me a hard time."

"Speaking of hard . . ." He set his hand in the small of her back, just where it was most sensitive.

She moved a step away and gazed up at the front bedroom window. "The light's out."

"Mad Jack in bed by midnight. That's gotta be a first."

Her flip-flops squeaked in the damp grass. "You don't look anything like him."

"Thanks for the compliment, but there were blood tests."

"I wasn't insinuating—"

"Could we talk about something else?" He held the side door open for her. "Why you're so afraid of sex, for example?"

"Only with you. I have an allergy to your beauty cream."

His husky laugh drifted out into the warm Tennessee night.

♥

By the time Dean came out of the bathroom, she was settled in bed. She pulled her eyes away from the noticeable bulge in his End Zone forest green knit boxers, but only got as far as his ridged abdomen and an arrow of golden hair pointing the way to Armageddon before he took in the enormous wall of pillows she'd arranged down the middle of the bed. "Don't you think that's a little childish?"

She dragged her gaze away from his Garden of Earthly Delights. "Stay on your side of the bed, and I'll apologize in the morning."

"If you think I'm going to let him see how juvenile you are, you're wrong." He spoke in a low whisper to avoid waking his unwanted houseguest.

"I'll wake up early and tear it down," she said, thinking about the one hundred dollars.

"Like you did yesterday morning?"

Was it only yesterday morning he'd had his hand down her jeans? He flicked off the chipped white ginger jar lamp April had brought over from the cottage. Moonbeams penetrated the room, painting his body in light and shadow. As he approached the bed, she reminded herself he was a player, and this was a game to him. By saying no, she'd waved a green flag.

"You're not that irresistible." He threw back the sheet and climbed in. "You know what I think?" He propped himself on an elbow and glared at her over the pillow wall. "I think it's yourself you're afraid of. You're afraid you won't be able to keep your hands off me."

He wanted to spar. But their sparring felt like foreplay, and she bit off every smart-ass retort that sprang to mind.

He lay back . . . and reared right up again. "I don't have to put up with this!" With a sweep of his arm, pillows flew, and her wall came crashing down.

"Wait!" She tried to sit up only to have his weight press her back into the mattress. She braced herself for an attack, but she should have known better. His mouth nuzzled softly against hers, and for the second time that day, he began teasing her lips.

She decided to let him kiss her for a while—he was so good at it—but only for a few minutes.

His hand slipped under her T-shirt, and his thumb found her

nipple. She tasted toothpaste and sin. Heat began spreading through her body. His erection pressed against her leg.

A game. This was only a game.

He dipped his head and began suckling her nipples through her T-shirt. As long as she kept her clothes on . . . He teased her with the hot, wet cotton, then pressed his hand between her thighs, against the fabric. Her knees slowly fell open. He toyed and dallied, thinking they had all the time in the world. But he played too long. Her head fell back. The moonlight shimmered then splintered into a thousand silver slivers. Through her barely muffled cry, she heard a soft, answering groan and felt him shudder along with her. Only as she came back to herself did she grow aware of something damp against her leg.

With a curse, he rolled off her, flung himself out of bed, and disappeared into the bathroom. She lay there—sated, angry, self-destructive. So much for her willpower.

Eventually he emerged from the bathroom. Naked. His soft growl drifted across the room. "Don't you say one word. I mean it. That is the single most embarrassing thing that's happened to me since I was fifteen."

She waited until he'd resettled before she propped her head on her elbow and gazed down at him "Hey, Speed Racer . . ." She leaned forward and brushed his lips with a quick, casual kiss that told him their encounter meant nothing to her. "You owe me another hundred bucks."

♥

The birds woke her the next morning. She'd slept as far from him as she could to guard against any middle-of-the-night coziness, and her leg dangled over the edge. She slipped out of bed without waking him. His skin looked golden against the stark white sheets, and a patch of pale hair grew on his chest between formidable pecs. She took in the tiny hole in his earlobe and remembered the silver skulls Jack had been wearing. She had no trouble imagining Dean doing the same. Her gaze moved lower and came to rest on the mound pushing against the sheet. All that could be hers . . . if she'd only leave her brain behind.

He didn't stir as she headed for the shower. She turned her face into the spray to clear her head. This was a new day, and as long as she didn't make a big deal out of the relatively innocent events of last night, he couldn't rack up any points on that scoreboard he carried around in his head. It was true that she still had no job, but she did have a temporary bargaining chip until she found work. He wanted to keep her right here at the farm, standing between him and the people who'd invaded his world.

As she dried off, she heard the water go on in the hallway bathroom. When she came out, the bed was empty. She hurriedly pulled a sleeveless black T-shirt from her duffel and a pair of jeans she'd cut off at midthigh. She felt a bump in her pocket and discovered her missing mascara and lip gloss. She made use of both, but only because there was a good chance she'd see Jack Patriot before he left for Nashville.

On her way downstairs, she smelled coffee, and as she walked into the kitchen, she saw Mad Jack himself sitting at the table, sipping from one of the white china mugs decorated with cherries. The same light-headedness that had rendered her mute when she'd met him last night struck again.

He wore yesterday's clothes, along with some rocker stubble. The flecks of gray in his hair only made him sexier. He observed her with the familiar, heavy-lidded eyes she'd memorized from a dozen album covers. "Good morning."

Somehow she managed to squeeze out a wheezy, "M-morning."

"You're Blue."

"B-Bailey. B-Blue Bailey."

"Sounds like that old song."

She knew what he meant, but her face had frozen, so he clarified.

"*Won't you come home, Bill Bailey?* You're probably too young. April tells me you and Dean are getting married." He didn't quite hide his curiosity. She wondered if he'd looked in on them sleeping or if Dean had wasted two hundred dollars. "Have you set a date?" he asked.

"Not yet." She squeaked like Minnie Mouse.

His cool survey continued. "How did you meet?"

"I was, uh, doing some . . . promotional work for a lumber company."

Seconds ticked by. When she realized she was staring, she stumbled toward the grocery bags in the pantry. "I'll bake panmakes. *Make!* I'll *make* pancakes."

"All right."

She'd had adolescent sexual fantasies about this man. While her classmates argued over who had dibs on Kirk Cameron, she'd imagined losing her virginity to Dean's father. *Ew. Ick.*

Still . . .

She sneaked another glance at him as she came out of the pantry with the pancake mix. Despite his olive skin, he was pale, as if he hadn't spent enough time outside lately. Even so, he radiated the same kind of sexual magnetism as his son, but Jack's allure felt a lot safer. As she opened the box, she reminded herself to give Dean as hard a time as possible today.

She concentrated on mixing the ingredients without screwing up the measurements. Usually, she made pancakes from scratch, but this wasn't the morning to attempt it. Jack took pity on her and didn't ask any more questions. As she poured the first batch on the new griddle, Dean sauntered in, all scruffy high style, his jock stubble as rugged as his father's rocker stubble. Maybe it was genetic. The perfect number of wrinkles creased his periwinkle T-shirt, and his khaki cargo shorts fell on his hips at exactly the right point. He didn't look at Jack. Instead, he took her in from head to toe before he settled on her face. "Makeup? What happened? You look almost female."

"Thanks. You look almost straight."

Behind them, Jack chuckled. Ohmygod, she'd made Jack Patriot laugh.

Dean leaned down and kissed her—long, cool, and so premeditated that she barely let herself get worked up about it. This was his opening move in another game, the one he played with the parents he hated. He was marking her as his teammate so that Jack knew it was now two against one.

Only after he drew away did he acknowledge his father's presence with a crisp nod. Jack nodded back and tilted his head toward the windows in the dining niche. "This is a nice place. I never figured you for a farmer."

When Dean didn't bother to respond, Blue broke the tense silence. "First batch of pancakes coming up. Dean, see if you can find syrup in those bags in the pantry. And grab some butter, will you?"

"Be glad to, sweetheart." He pecked her forehead with another strategic kiss. As she reached for the plates, she wondered if her life could get any weirder. Her life savings had been handed over to a band of South American guerrillas, she had a phony engagement to a famous football player, she was homeless and jobless, *and* she was making breakfast for Mad Jack Patriot.

As Dean came out of the pantry, Jack gestured toward Blue. "Where's the engagement ring?"

"She hated the first one I got her," Dean said. "The stones were too small." He had the nerve to tweak her chin. "Nothing but the best for my sweetheart."

She hummed the *Speed Racer* theme song.

By avoiding looking at Jack, she managed to deliver his pancakes without sliding them into his lap. Dean ate his standing up, hips resting against the counter. He talked to her as he ate, but made sure he directed an occasional comment to Jack so he couldn't be suspected of ignoring him. She'd practiced the strategy too often herself not to recognize it. *Don't let anyone see the hurt.* She didn't like how well she understood him.

Since she couldn't imagine eating her pancakes across the table from Jack Patriot, she ate standing up, too. The back door opened, and April came in. She wore khakis, a coral top with a ribbon tie, and her sandals with a rainbow wedge. Riley followed, her damp brown hair parted in the center and pulled back from her forehead with a series of iridescent blue clips that April must have arranged. With Riley's curls tamed a little, her pretty toasted-sugar eyes were more noticeable. She'd exchanged yesterday's FOXY T-shirt for a black one just as tight with a woman's pouty, crimson lips on the front. Dean turned away to make a trip into the pantry. As Riley spotted her father, she stopped where she was.

Jack rose but, once he was on his feet, didn't seem to know what to do next. He settled on the obvious. "There you are."

Riley picked at a remnant of fingernail polish.

"I made pancakes," Blue said brightly.

April avoided looking at either Jack or her son. "We ate cereal at the cottage."

"I hope you thanked April," said the man who'd once kicked a drum set across the stage and told a cop to fuck himself.

Dean came out of the pantry, an unnecessary jar of peanut butter in his hand. This might be the first time he'd been in the same room with both of his parents. He stood stony and silent. Although he didn't need anyone's protection, she went to his side anyway and slipped her arm around his waist.

Jack reached in his pocket. "I'll call Frankie to pick us up."

"I don't want to go," Riley mumbled. And then, as he pulled out his cell, "I—I'm not going."

He looked up from the phone. "What are you talking about? You've already missed a week of school. You have to get back."

Her chin came up. "Summer vacation starts next week, and I finished my work. Ava has it."

He'd obviously forgotten, but he tried to cover. "Aunt Gayle is expecting you. She arranged for you and your cousin to go to that camp in two weeks."

"I don't want to go to camp! It's stupid, and Trinity will get everybody to make fun of me." She dropped her pink jacket and backpack. Red blotches sprang up on her cheeks. "If you try to make me, I'll—I'll just run away again. And I know how to do it."

Riley's show of rebellion took him aback, but Blue wasn't surprised. This was the same kid who'd managed to get from Nashville to her half-brother's farm in the dead of night. Dean's muscles had gone rigid beneath his T-shirt. Blue rubbed the small of his back with her fingertips.

Jack palmed the phone. "Look, Riley, I understand it's been really hard for you, but things will get better."

"How?"

He was out of his element, but he put up a good effort. "Time will make it better. After a while it won't hurt so much. I know you loved your mother, and—"

"I didn't love her!" Riley cried. "She thought I was ugly and stupid, and the only person she liked was Trinity!"

"That's not true," Jack said. "She loved you very much."

"How do you know?"

He faltered. "I—I know, that's all. Now I don't want to hear any more. You've caused enough trouble, and you'll do what I tell you."

"No, I won't." Dry-eyed and furious, she curled her hands into fists. "I'll kill myself if you make me go back! I will! I know how. I can find Mom's pills. And Aunt Gayle's, too. I'll swallow all of them. And—and I'll cut myself like Mackenzie's big sister. And then I'll die!"

Mad Jack was clearly shaken. Dean had gone pale, and April tugged on her silver rings. Riley started to cry and rushed toward her. "Please, April! Please, let me stay with you." April's arms instinctively curled around her.

"April can't take care of you," Jack said brusquely. "She has things to do."

Tears rolled down Riley's cheeks. She was staring at the ribbon tie on April's top, but she was talking to her father. "Then you stay. You stay and take care of me."

"I can't do that."

"Why not? You could stay for like two weeks." In a display of youthful courage, she regarded April with pleading eyes. "That would be okay, wouldn't it, April? If he stayed for two weeks?" She took a tentative step toward her father. "You don't have any gigs or anything until September. I heard you say you need to get away somewhere so you can work on some new songs. You could get away here. Or at the cottage. April's cottage is really, really quiet. You could write your new songs there."

"It's not my cottage, Riley," April said gently. "It's Dean's. So is this house."

Riley's chin trembled. She dragged her gaze from April and focused on Dean's chest. Blue felt his skin burning through his T-shirt.

"I know I'm fat and everything," Riley said in a small voice. "And I know you don't like me, but I'll be quiet, and Dad will be, too." She lifted those heartbreaking eyes so she was looking directly at Dean. "He doesn't pay attention to anybody when he's writing songs. He wouldn't bother you or anything. And I could even help. Like, I could—I could sweep up stuff and wash the dishes maybe." Dean stood frozen as Riley's tears blurred her next words. "Or . . . if you . . . if you needed somebody to throw the football so you could practice and everything—I could maybe try."

Dean squeezed his eyes shut. He barely seemed to be breathing. Jack snapped open his phone. "I don't want to hear any more. You're coming with me."

"No, I'm not!"

Dean jerked away from Blue, and his voice cracked like an ice dam breaking. "Can't you give the kid two lousy weeks out of your big, busy schedule?"

Riley went still. April's head came slowly up. Jack didn't move.

"Her mother just died, for chrissake! She needs you. Or are you going to run away from her, too?" Dean realized what he'd said and stalked toward the door. The window over the sink rattled as he slammed the door behind him.

A tiny muscle ticked at the corner of Jack's jaw. He cleared his throat, shifted his weight. "All right, Riley, you've got one week. One, not two."

Riley's eyes widened. "Really? I can stay? You'll stay here with me?"

"First, we're going back to Nashville to pack up. And you have to promise me that you won't ever try to run away again."

"I promise!"

"We'll come back on Monday. And you'd better keep that promise, because if you try anything like this again, I'll send you to school in Europe, someplace where it won't be so easy to run away. I mean it, Riley."

"I won't! I promise."

Jack shoved his cell back in his pocket. Riley gazed around the kitchen, as if she were seeing it for the first time. April slipped to Blue's side. "See if he's all right," she said softly.

Chapter Thirteen

Blue finally located Dean in the weeds behind the barn. He had his hands on his hips, and he was gazing at the rusted frame of a red pickup truck. Through the gaping hole where the passenger door had once been, she could see springs poking through what was left of the upholstery. A pair of dragonflies flitted over the rotted wood, bald tires, and unidentifiable pieces of farm machinery that littered the truck bed. She followed the path he'd made through the weeds. As she got closer, she spotted the remnants of a bird's nest roosting on the steering wheel column. "I know it's tempting to trade in your Vanquish now that you've seen this," she said, "but I'm against it."

His hands fell from his hips. His eyes were bleak. "It just gets better and better, doesn't it?"

"There's nothing like a little drama to get your adrenaline pumping." She resisted the urge to put her arm around him again. "Jack told Riley he'd stay for a week," she said softly. "But he's taking her to Nashville for the weekend. We'll see if he comes back."

His face contorted. "How did this fucking *happen*? All these years

I've kept him away from me, and now, in a few seconds, I blow the whole thing."

"I thought you were wonderful," she said. "And this is coming from someone who loves to find fault with you."

She couldn't eke out even the trace of a smile. He kicked the rusted fender. "You think I did Riley a favor in there?"

"I do. You stood up for her."

"I've only caused her more trouble. Jack doesn't care about anything but his career, and all I did for Riley was set her up for another letdown."

"She's spent a lot more time with him than you, so she probably knows him fairly well. I doubt her expectations are very high."

He snatched up a piece of rotted wood and hurled it into the truck bed. "The son of a bitch had better stay out of sight. I don't want any link between us."

"I'm sure the last thing he'll do is advertise his presence." She hesitated, trying to figure out how to put this, but Dean was already there.

"Don't say it. Do you think I haven't figured out I'm the real reason she wants to stay here? She gave up on Jack long ago. I should have driven away the minute I saw April come out that front door."

Blue didn't want him revisiting the part she'd played in keeping him here. She picked at a fleck of rust. "Let's look on the positive side."

"Oh, all right. Let's hurry up and do that."

"This is the first time you've had your mother and father together. That's monumental."

"You're not thinking there's going to be some grand reconciliation, are you?"

"No. But maybe you can lay a few ghosts to rest. The brutal truth is, they're your family, for better or worse."

"You're so wrong." He began gathering up some of the junk that had fallen in the woods and tossing it into a pile. "The team is my family. It's been that way ever since I started playing ball. If I pick up the phone and say the word, I know a dozen guys who'll hop on a plane, no questions asked. How many people can say that of their relatives?"

"You won't be playing football forever. What happens then?"

"It won't matter. They'll still be there." He kicked at the axle of the truck. "Besides, I've got a lot of time left."

Not so much, she thought. In football years, Dean was on his way to becoming a senior citizen.

A dog began barking, a high-pitched yipping sound. She glanced over her shoulder in time to see a filthy white fur ball scamper out of the weeds. The critter stopped in its tracks as it saw them. Its tiny ears drew back and its yipping grew more ferocious. Matted hair hung over the dog's small face, and briars clung to its legs. To Blue's trained eye, the stray looked like some kind of Maltese mix, the kind of dog that should be named Bonbon and have a pink bow in its topknot. But this little critter hadn't been pampered in a very long time.

Dean went down on one knee. "Where did you come from, big guy?"

The yipping stopped, and the dog regarded him suspiciously. Dean held out his hand, palm up. "It's a wonder you haven't been eaten up by a coyote."

The dog cocked its head, then came cautiously forward to sniff him.

"Not exactly your typical farm dog," Blue said.

"I'll bet somebody abandoned him. Tossed him out of a car and drove away." He poked around in the grubby fur. "No collar. Is that what happened, killer?" He ran his hand along the dog's side. "His ribs are poking through. How long since you've eaten? I'd like five minutes in an alley with whoever dumped you off."

The critter rolled to his back and splayed his—*her*—legs.

Blue gazed down at the little trollop. "At least make Dean work for it."

"Ignore Bo Peep. She's sex starved, and it's made her bitter." Dean stroked the animal's hollow, filth-covered tummy. "Come on, killer. Let's get you something to eat." With a last pat, he rose to his feet.

Blue set off after the two of them. "Once you feed a dog, it's yours."

"So what? Farms need dogs."

"Shepherds and border collies. That is not a country dog."

"Kindly Farmer Dean believes everyone deserves a chance."

"A word of warning," she called out to his back. "That is a gay man's dog, so if you want to stay in the closet . . ."

"I'm turning you in to the P.C. police."

At least the mangy little yipper had taken Dean's mind off the drama at the house, and Blue kept up the distraction by bickering with him until they reached the front yard.

The trucks that should have been clogging the lane were nowhere in sight. No din of hammers or scream of power drills disturbed the sound of the birds. He frowned. "I wonder what's going on."

April emerged from the house, her cell in hand. The dog greeted her with furious yelps. "Quiet!" Dean said. The animal recognized leadership and fell silent. Dean surveyed the yard. "Where is everybody?"

April came off the porch. "It seems they've fallen mysteriously ill."

"All of them?"

"Apparently."

Blue started putting the pieces together and didn't like what she saw. "It's not because . . . No, I'm sure it isn't."

"We've been boycotted." April threw up one hand. "How did you make that woman so mad?"

"Blue did what she needed to," Dean said sharply.

Riley flew out onto the porch. "I hear a dog!" The mutt went bonkers at the sight of her. She hurried down the steps but slowed as she got closer. Kneeling, she extended her hand just as Dean had. "Hey, doggie."

The filthy fur ball regarded her suspiciously but condescended to be petted. Riley looked up at Dean, her perpetual worry line digging deeper into her forehead. "Is she yours?"

He thought it over for a moment. "Why not? There'll be a caretaker around when I'm not here."

"What's its name?"

"She's a stray. She doesn't have a name."

"Can I like . . . call her . . ." She studied the dog. ". . . maybe Puffy?"

"I, uh, was thinking something on the order of Killer."

Riley studied the dog. "She looks more like a Puffy."

Blue couldn't harden her heart against the stray a moment longer. "Let's go find Puffy something to eat."

"Get the contractor on the phone," Dean said to April. "I want to talk to him."

"I've been trying. He's not picking up."

"Then maybe I'd better pay him a personal visit."

♥

April wanted Puffy defleaed by a vet, and she somehow convinced Jack to take the dog with him when he and Riley left for Nashville. Blue secretly doubted having the dog in the house would ever be a problem. Regardless of what Jack had promised, Blue didn't believe he'd keep his word and bring Riley back. She gave the eleven-year-old an extra hug before she left. "Don't take any crap from anybody, okay?"

"I'll try?" Riley answered with a question mark.

Blue intended to hitchhike into town and look for a job, but April needed help, so she spent the rest of the day trying to earn her keep by cleaning out kitchen cupboards, arranging dishes, and setting up a linen closet. Dean e-mailed April that the contractor had disappeared. A "family emergency," according to a neighbor.

Late in the afternoon, April made her take a break, and Blue went outside to explore. She wandered through the woods and followed the creek that led to the pond, staying out longer than she'd planned. When she returned, she found a note from Dean waiting for her on the kitchen counter.

Sweetheart,

I'll be back Sunday night. Keep the bed warm for me.

Your Loving Fiancé
P.S. Why did you let Jack take my dog?

She threw the note in the trash. One more person she'd grown to care about had taken off without warning. But so what? She didn't care that much.

It was only Friday afternoon. Where had he gone? An ominous foreboding claimed her. She raced upstairs, grabbed her purse, and pulled out her wallet. Sure enough, the hundred dollars he'd given her the night before had disappeared.

Her loving fiancé wanted to make sure she stayed put.

♥

Annabelle Granger Champion gazed at Dean across the living room of the spacious contemporary home in Chicago's Lincoln Park that she shared with her husband and two children. Dean was still sprawled on the floor from an earlier bout of roughhousing with Trevor, her three-year-old son, who was now napping.

"There's something you're not telling me," Annabelle said from her perch on the roomy sofa.

"There's a lot I'm not telling you," he retorted, "and I intend to keep it that way."

"I'm a professional matchmaker. I've heard it all."

"Good. Then you don't need to hear any more." He got up and walked toward the wedge of windows that looked out over the street. He had an evening flight back to Nashville, and he damned well intended to be on it. He wasn't going to be driven away from his own home, and as long as he kept Blue in place as his buffer, he could make it work.

But Blue was more than his buffer. She was his—

He didn't know what she was. Not exactly a friend, although she understood him better than people he'd known for years, and she entertained him as much as any of them, maybe more. Also, he didn't want to fuck his friends, and he definitely wanted to fuck her.

Yeah, he was a real stud, all right. Memories of his mortifying performance on Thursday night made him cringe. He'd been messing around with her, getting them both warmed up, but then he'd heard those throaty moans, felt her convulse, and he'd lost it. Literally. Blue had been throwing him off stride since the moment they'd met. Speed Racer, indeed. Next chance he got, he was going to make her eat those words.

Annabelle was staring at him. "There's something going on with you," she said, "and it involves a woman. I've been sensing it all afternoon. Something more than another one of your meaningless sexual escapades. You've been very distracted."

He arched his eyebrow at her. "All of a sudden you're some big psychic?"

"Matchmakers have to be psychic." She turned to her husband. "Heath, go away. He won't tell me a thing while you're hanging around." Annabelle had met Dean's agent not long after she'd taken over her grandmother's matchmaking business when Heath had accidentally hired her to find him a beautiful, sophisticated society wife. Annabelle wasn't exactly any of those things. But her big eyes, feisty personality, and riot of curly red hair had captivated him, and they had one of the best marriages Dean had ever seen.

Heath, who was nicknamed the Python for his habit of consuming his enemies whole, curled his mouth in a snake's smile. He was a good-looking guy, about Dean's height, with an Ivy League degree and a street scrapper's mentality. "The Boo tells me everything, Annabelle. Except for you, he's my closest friend."

Dean snorted. "The depth of your friendship, Heathcliff, is purely based on how much revenue I generate for Champion Sports Management."

"He's got you there, Heath," Annabelle said cheerfully. And then, to Dean, "Privately, you drive him crazy. You're too unpredictable."

Heath tucked their sleeping infant daughter into the crook of his neck. "Now, now, Annabelle, no pillow talk in front of my grossly insecure clients."

Dean loved these guys. Well, he loved Annabelle, but he also knew his professional life couldn't be in better hands than Heath's.

Annabelle was like a bloodhound when she felt she was on the track of something interesting. "You're never distracted, Dean. I've lost five pounds, and you didn't even notice. What's wrong? Who is she?"

"Nothing's wrong. If you want to nag somebody, nag Bozo over there. Do you know he's planning to take fifteen percent for that cologne deal?"

"I want a new car," she said. "Now stop dodging. You've met somebody."

"Annabelle, I left Chicago less than two weeks ago, and until I got to the farm, I spent most of my time in the car. How could I have met someone?"

"I don't know, but I think you did." Annabelle dropped her bare feet to the floor. "This shouldn't be happening when I'm not around to supervise. You're too swayed by appearances. I'm not saying you're shallow because you're not. It's just that you're always attracted by the superficial, and then you're disappointed when the women don't live up to your expectations. Although I have made several excellent matches from your castoffs."

Dean could see exactly where this discussion was going, and he tried to head it off. "So, Heath, has Phoebe signed Gary Candliss yet? When I talked to Kevin, it sounded like a done deal."

But Annabelle was picking up steam. "*Then* when I set you up with someone who's *perfect* for you, you won't give her a chance. Look what happened with Julie Sherwin."

"Here we go," Heath murmured.

Annabelle ignored him. "Julie was smart, successful, beautiful— one of the sweetest women I've ever met—but you dumped her after two dates!"

"I dumped her because she took everything I said literally. You've got to admit, Annabelle, that's just disconcerting. I made her so nervous she couldn't eat, not that she did much of it anyway. It was an act of mercy."

"You do that to women. I know you try not to, but it still happens. It's your looks. Except for Heath, you're my most challenging client."

"I am not your client, Annabelle," he retorted. "I don't pay you a cent."

"Pro bono," she chirped, looking so pleased with herself that both Dean and Heath laughed.

Dean grabbed his rental car keys from the coffee table. "Look, Annabelle. I came back to the city for the weekend so I could pack some things to ship to the farm and catch up on all the business your husband has been throwing at me. There's nothing earthshaking going on in my life."

Now that was a lie.

As he drove to the airport, he thought about Blue and contemplated how easily he'd given himself over to the dark side. And for what? Emptying out her wallet didn't guarantee she'd stay in place. If she made up her mind to leave the farm, she'd do it, even if it meant sleeping on a park bench. She'd only stayed around this long because so much had happened. He hoped April had been able to drag her to those estate sales in Knoxville over the weekend because he didn't want to think about returning to the farm and finding Blue gone.

♥

Blue sat on the porch step, cradling her second cup of Monday morning coffee and trying to appear relaxed as she watched Dean riding toward her down the lane. She'd spotted his car keys on the kitchen counter when she'd gotten up this morning, but he hadn't come to the caravan, and this was the first time she'd seen him since he'd taken off on Friday.

He was riding a high-tech gunmetal gray road bike that could have carried Lance Armstrong up the Champs-Élysées. He looked magnificent, almost futuristic, as though he belonged in a big budget sci-fi movie. Sunlight bounced off an aerodynamic silver helmet, and powerful leg muscles rippled beneath a pair of skintight electric blue bike shorts. Her own leg muscles felt wobbly just watching, and an unacceptable pang of longing pierced her heart.

He drew up to the end of the old brick walk. It was barely eight o'clock, but judging from the sweat glistening on his neck and the damp cling of the green mesh shirt to that amazing chest, he'd been doing some serious riding. Blue forced herself to get a grip. She nodded toward the bike. "Nice. How long have the training wheels been off?"

"Big talk from somebody who looks like she lives in a toy box." He swung his leg over the frame and walked the bike toward her. "I decided it was time I stopped messing around and started getting back in shape."

She couldn't help gaping. "You were out of shape?"

"Let's just say I've slacked off more than I should have since the season ended." He pulled off his helmet and hung it over the handlebars. "I'm turning that back bedroom into a weight room. I don't believe in showing up for training camp flabby and overweight."

"Not to worry."

He smiled and tunneled his fingers through his sweaty, flattened hair, which instantly rearranged itself into a sexy rumple. "April e-mailed me photos of the paintings and antiques the two of you found in Knoxville this weekend. Thanks for going with her. The pieces will look good with the new furniture I ordered."

Blue had seriously considered setting her pride aside and asking April for a small loan. With all Knoxville's great neighborhoods, she wouldn't have had any trouble finding clients, and she could have re-paid April in no time. But she hadn't asked. Just like a kid playing with matches, she'd come back. She had to see what would happen next.

"So how was your weekend?" She managed to set aside her cup without slopping any coffee over the rim.

"Filled with alcohol and rampant sex. Yours?"

"Pretty much the same."

He smiled again. "I flew to Chicago. I had some business to take care of. And Annabelle was the only woman I spent any time with while I was there, in case you're interested."

She was very interested. She curled her lip. "Like I care."

He pulled a water bottle from the bike and tilted his head toward the barn. "I had the shop deliver two bikes. The second one's a smaller hybrid. Use it whenever you want."

She stood up so she could give him her best hard-ass look. "I'd thank you for that, but my gratitude ran out when I discovered that my hooker money is missing from my wallet. You wouldn't happen to know anything about that, would you?"

"Yeah, sorry." He propped his foot on the bottom step and took a slug from the bottle. "I needed some change."

"Fifty-dollar bills aren't change."

"They are in my world." He snapped the cap back on.

"You are so obnoxious! I should have stayed in Knoxville."

"Why didn't you?"

She sauntered down the steps, or at least she hoped it looked like sauntering. "Because I'm praying Jack will come back. Talk about a once-in-a-lifetime opportunity. I'm almost positive I'll be able to work up the nerve to ask for his autograph."

"I'm afraid you'll be too busy for that." He gave her a long, lazy look. "Keeping me satisfied in bed's going to be a full-time job."

The picture that flashed through her mind was so sizzling that he and his bike were halfway to the barn before she got her voice back. "Hey, Dean."

He glanced over his shoulder. She shaded her eyes from the sun. "If you're serious about getting it on again, be sure to give me some advance notice, so I can grab my appointment calendar and block out three minutes."

He didn't laugh. Not that she'd exactly expected him to. But neither had she expected to see the way he looked at her, as if the national anthem had just ended and they were starting a brand-new game.

♥

A little later, while Blue was cleaning up the kitchen, she heard Dean drive off. April came in dressed in old clothes and lugging a pile of drop cloths. "Apparently Dean didn't manage to run down the contractor on Friday," she said, "because no one has shown up this morning, and I'm not sitting around all day waiting for them to get to this kitchen. I have the paint. Want to help?"

"Sure."

They'd barely gotten set up before April disappeared to take another of her mysterious phone calls. When she came back, she put on Gwen Stefani, and by the time Gwen belted out "Hollaback Girl," it had become apparent that April's dance skills far exceeded her painting experience, so Blue directed the job.

As they finished the prep work, they heard a car, and a few minutes later, Jack Patriot ambled in, wearing worn jeans and a tight-fitting SCORCHED T-shirt from his last tour. Blue hadn't expected him to come back, and she stumbled on nothing. He grabbed her just as she was about to step into the roller pan. April, who'd been doing some X-rated grinds to "Baby Got Back," immediately stopped dancing. Jack set Blue on her feet. "Any idea what it might take for you to get past this?" he said.

"I—Yes—I—Oh, God . . ." She flushed from her roots down. "Sorry. I'm sure a lot of people say they're your number one fan, but I really am." She pressed a hand to her hot cheek. "I . . . well . . . I had sort of an itinerant childhood, but your songs were always there, no matter where I was or who I was living with." Now that she'd gotten started, she couldn't stop herself, even as he drifted toward the cof-feepot. "I own every album. All of them, even *Outta My Way*, which I know the critics trashed, but they're wrong because it's wonderful, and 'Screams' is one of my favorite songs, like seeing right into my heart the way I was then, and, oh shit, I know I'm babbling like a fool, but in the real world Jack Patriot doesn't just pop into your life. I mean how is anybody supposed to prepare for this?"

He stirred in a teaspoon of sugar. "Maybe I could autograph your arm."

"Really?"

He laughed. "No, not really. I don't think Dean would take it too well."

"Oh." She licked her lips. "I guess not."

He tilted his head toward April. "Help us out here."

April tossed her hair. "Sleep with him, Blue. That'll bring you down to earth real fast. He's a huge disappointment."

A slow grin curled the corner of his mouth. "I'll buy the huge part . . ."

April dropped her eyes to his crotch. "There are some things a man can't buy, no matter how rich he is."

He propped one shoulder against the doorjamb and let his eyes play a hot lick down her body. "I still get inspired by sharp-tongued women. Grab a piece of paper for me, April. I feel a song coming on."

Sex blistered the air between them. They might be in their fifties, but teenage lust simmered in that kitchen. Blue half expected the walls to start sweating, and she began to ease out of the room, only to stumble on the drop cloth.

The movement broke the spell, and April turned away. Jack inspected the ceiling where Blue had cut in the paint. "Let me get my stuff unloaded and I'll help out."

"You know how to paint?" Blue said.

"My dad was a carpenter. I did a lot of construction work when I was a kid."

"I'm going to check on Riley." April pushed past him and headed for the side door.

Blue gulped. She was getting ready to paint a kitchen with Jack Patriot. Her life got more bizarre by the minute.

Chapter Fourteen

When Dean got back that afternoon, he discovered Jack and April silently painting opposite walls of his kitchen while Coldplay blared in the background. Bright yellow paint splattered April from head to toe, but Jack had only a few smears on his hands. Until yesterday, Dean had never seen the two of them together. Now they were painting his fucking kitchen.

He stalked off to find Blue. On the way, he pulled out his Black-Berry to check his messages. April had sent the latest ten minutes ago.

We only have a gallon of yellow paint left. Go buy more.

He found Blue in the dining room, working on the ceiling. She looked like a pocket-size Bo Peep with a paint roller in her hand. Her splattered green T-shirt hung nearly to her hips, covering up the trim body she was determined to hide from him. Not for long, however. He jabbed his thumb toward the kitchen. "What's going on in there?"

"Exactly what it looks like." The plastic drop cloth rustled under her feet as she moved a few steps to the side. "Fortunately, Jack knows his way around a paintbrush, but I've had to watch April like a hawk."

"Why didn't you stop them?"

"Until that wedding ring is on my finger, I don't have any real authority here." She set down the roller and studied the longest wall. "April wants me to paint a mural."

She didn't sound happy about it, but he liked the idea of Blue painting a mural a hell of a lot better than he liked having his parents painting his kitchen. It would also keep her in place for a while longer. "I'll have my PR people send you a dozen of my best action shots," he said. "You can pick the most flattering."

She smiled as he'd hoped, but then the furrow between her eyebrows crept deeper. "I don't do landscapes anymore."

"Too bad." He opened his wallet and pulled out two hundred dollars in cash. "Here's the hundred dollars I borrowed plus the other hundred from that ill-advised bet. I believe in clearing up my debts."

As he expected, she didn't leap to take the money but studied it instead.

"A deal's a deal," he said, all innocence. "You earned it." When she still didn't take it, he slipped the bills into the pocket of her saggy T-shirt, lingering only a moment longer than necessary. She might not have a whole lot there, but she had enough for him. Now all he needed was unlimited access.

"A deal with the devil," she said glumly. He concealed his triumph as she retrieved the money, stared at it for a moment, then shoved it into his pocket, unfortunately without lingering at all. "Give this to a charity that keeps women off the streets."

Poor Beav. He could have told her when he placed the bet that her scruples would keep her from holding on to the cash, but he hadn't made All Pro by being stupid. "Well, if you're sure."

She turned back to peruse the walls. "If you think I could unfold some groundbreaking artistic vision in here, you'd be in for a big disappointment. My landscapes are beyond ordinary."

"As long as you don't paint anything too girly, I'd be happy. No ballet dancers or old-time ladies carrying around umbrellas. And nothing with dead rabbits lying on plates."

"No worries there. Ballet dancers and dead rabbits would be way too innovative for me." She turned away. "Life's too short. I'm not doing it."

Now that she'd planted the idea in his head, he wasn't ready to set it aside, but he'd wait a while before he pressed her. "Where's my dog?"

She kneaded her shoulder, working out a kink. "I believe your manly companion Puffy is having a picnic in the backyard with Riley."

He pretended to be leaving but turned around just before he got to the hallway. "I should have remembered to tell you this, especially when I know how anxious you are to get those doors back on. Before I left for Chicago, I paid a visit to the man who's refinishing them. He lives in the next county—out of boycott range—so I was able to convince him to speed things along. They'll be done any day now."

Her eyes flashed. "You bribed him."

"Merely an incentive bonus."

"Life sure is easier when you're rich."

"And a natural born charmer. Don't forget that part."

"How could I?" she retorted. "It's the only thing we have in common."

He smiled. "That bedroom door had better fit nice and tight. Just the way I like it."

♥

By the time Dean got back from his paint run, it was well after five. The house was quiet, and except for the dining nook, the kitchen had a fresh coat of yellow paint. Jack's black SUV was missing, so he and Riley must have taken off for dinner. So far today, Dean had managed to avoid all of them, and he intended to keep it that way. He breathed in the smell of fresh paint and new wood. He'd pictured himself owning a home with palm trees and a view of the Pacific, but he loved this farmhouse with its one hundred acres. As soon as he got rid of his houseguests, it would be perfect. Except for Blue. He'd missed her this weekend, and he wasn't ready for her to go anywhere yet.

As he set the paint in the kitchen, he heard the shower go on. He retrieved the packages he'd left in his car then went upstairs, where he set the sacks on the floor by his suitcases and gazed toward the bathroom door. Blue's paint-spattered clothes lay in a puddle on the floor. Only a real pervert would push back that plastic she'd insisted he hang over the door, and nobody had ever accused him of being a pervert. Instead, he'd leave the plastic alone and wait here like the gentleman he was for her to come out.

Hopefully naked.

The water stopped. He stripped off his shirt and tossed it aside, a cheesy move, but she liked his chest. He gazed at the fluttering plastic and told himself not to get his hopes up. There was a distinct possibility she'd come out in combat boots and camouflage gear.

He was in luck. She wore only a white towel hiked up to her armpits. Not nearly as good as naked, but at least he could see her legs. His gaze followed a trickle of water sliding down the inside of one trim thigh.

"Out!" Looking like a provoked water nymph, she stabbed her finger toward the hallway.

"My room," he said.

"I have dibs."

"How do you figure?"

"Possession. Nine-tenths of the law. Out."

"I need a shower."

She gestured toward the bathroom door. "I promise not to bother you."

He ambled closer. "I'm seriously starting to worry about you." As he drew up next to her, he caught the scent of his favorite shampoo. It smelled better on her. Her wet hair lay against her head, and the flicker in her eyes told him he was making her nervous. Excellent. He gave her a slow once-over. "I mean it, Blue. I'm seriously starting to believe you might be frigid."

"Really?"

He circled her, taking in the soft, damp nape of her neck where her hair parted, the gentle curve of her narrow shoulders. "I don't know . . . Have you thought about seeing a sex therapist? Hell, we could go together."

She grinned. "I haven't had a boy try to get into my panties by telling me I was frigid since I was fifteen. I feel like a kid again. No, wait. That's you."

"You're right." He touched her shoulder with the tip of his index finger and had the satisfaction of seeing her skin pebble. "Why go to a therapist when we can fix that dysfunction here and now?"

"The gap. You keep forgetting about that gap we have going. Remember? You, gorgeous and useless? Me, smart and hardworking?"

"It's called chemistry."

Her derisive snort told him he'd done it again. Instead of keeping his focus on the goal line, he couldn't resist sparring with her. It was a tactical error he'd never have made if he'd had any actual practice seducing women. Hell. Up until now, just saying hello had been good enough. He frowned. "How about you stop being a wiseass and get ready for our date?"

"We have a date?"

He pointed to the sacks. "Pick out any old thing to wear."

"You bought me clothes?"

"You don't think I'd let you shop for yourself."

She rolled her eyes. "You're such a chick."

"You might want to ask the Packers defense about that." It was way past time to remind her who was in charge. He dropped his hands to the waistband of his shorts. "Or maybe you'd like to peek in the shower and see for yourself." He flipped open the tab.

Her eyes went right to the goal post. He played with the top of the zipper. She seemed to have a hard time raising her head, and when she finally did, he hit her with the same condescending smile he used on rookies who couldn't back up their trash talk. Then he stepped into the bathroom.

♥

Blue watched the plastic fall back into place after him. The man was a devil. Her fingers twitched. She wanted to throw off her towel, march in there, and get it on. Dean was her once-in-a-lifetime chance to play with the pros, and if her mother hadn't chosen this particular time to empty out her bank accounts, Blue might have been able to overcome her aversion to meaningless sex and rationalize a one-time trip to the locker room.

She kicked aside the sacks, resisting the temptation to peek inside and see what he'd bought. Instead, she pulled on clean jeans and her freshly laundered black muscle shirt. She semidried her hair in the hallway bathroom, snagged it into a ponytail, thought for a moment, then dabbed on some mascara and lip gloss.

She made her way downstairs to wait for him on the front porch. If they'd been a real couple, she could have sat on the bed and watched him get dressed. And what a glorious sight that would have been. With a sigh of regret, she gazed toward the overgrown pasture. By this time next year, horses would be grazing there, and she wouldn't be around to see them.

He was ready in record time, but as he came out on the porch, she spotted a filmy lavender top dangling from his fingers. He passed the garment from one hand to the other, not saying a word, letting it speak for itself. The late afternoon sun caught a sprinkle of tiny silver beads, like bubbles in a froth of lavender sea. The fabric swayed from his fingers like a hypnotist's watch.

"The thing is," he finally said, "you probably don't have the right bra. I've seen girls in clubs with tops like this, and they wear a bra with lacy straps. Maybe a contrasting color. I'm thinkin' pink would be nice." He shook his head. "Aw, heck, I've embarrassed us both." Not looking the slightest bit embarrassed, he dangled the lavender confection a few inches closer. "I tried to buy you something with spikes and leather, but, I swear, if there's an S&M shop around here, I sure as hell couldn't find it."

She'd entered the Garden of Eden, except this time Adam was holding the treacherous apple. "Go away."

"If you're afraid to claim your womanhood, I understand."

She was tired, hungry, and feeling more than a little sorry for herself or she wouldn't have let him bait her. "Fine!" She grabbed the lavender temptation. "But you gave up a Y chromosome to do this!"

When she got upstairs, she whipped off her muscle shirt and pulled Satan's garment over her head. A ruffle fell softly at the hem, where it brushed the waistband of her jeans. Delicate ribbon ties curled over her shoulders. Her bra straps showed; he'd been right about that. Of course, he'd been right. He was an expert on women's undergarments. Fortunately, her own bra was pale blue, and although the straps weren't lace, they weren't white either, which even she knew would have been an unforgivable fashion faux pas to Mr. Vogue Magazine downstairs.

"There's a skirt in one of those sacks," he called up the stairs, "just in case you're interested in getting rid of those jeans."

Ignoring him, she kicked off her sandals, pulled on her scuffed black biker boots, and headed downstairs.

"That's just juvenile," he said as he took in her footwear.

"Are you ready to go or not?"

"I don't think I've ever met a woman more afraid of being female. When you see that shrink—"

"Don't start. It's my turn to drive." She held out her hand, palm up, and nearly choked as he passed over the keys without arguing.

"I understand," he said. "You need to assert your masculinity."

He'd scored way too many verbal hits today, but she was so entranced with the idea of driving the Vanquish that she let this one pass.

The car performed like a dream. She'd watched him maneuver the paddles on the transmission, and he only winced a couple of times before she got the hang of shifting gears. "Head for town," he said as they reached the highway. "Before we eat, I want to pay an unfriendly call on Nita Garrison."

"Now?"

"You don't seriously believe I'm going to let her get away with this? Not my style, Bluebell."

"I could be missing something, but I don't think I'm exactly the best person to go see Nita Garrison with you."

"Which is why you're waiting in the car while I charm the old bat." Without warning, he reached over and started playing with her earlobe. Her ears were incredibly sensitive, and she nearly drove off the road. Just as she opened her mouth to tell him to keep his hands to himself, he slipped something into the tiny hole. She glanced into the rearview mirror. A purple droplet winked at her.

"It's all in the accessories," he said. "I'll do the other one when we stop."

"You bought earrings for me?"

"Had to. I was afraid you'd show up wearing lug nuts."

Suddenly, she had her own fashion stylist, and it wasn't April. She wondered if he saw the connection. His contradictions added to her fascination. A man with such over-the-top masculinity shouldn't love beautiful things so much. He should only love sweaty things. She hated when people refused to fit into pigeonholes. It made life murky.

"Unfortunately, those aren't real stones," he said. "My shopping options were limited."

Real or not, she loved them.

Nita Garrison's stately home sat on a shady street two blocks from the downtown area. Built of the same tan crab orchard stone as the bank and the Catholic church, it had a low, hipped roof and a formidable, Italianate facade. Stone pediments topped nine large, double-hung windows—four on the ground floor and five above, with the one in the middle wider than the rest. The grounds were almost too well maintained, with severely delineated beds of ruthlessly trimmed shrubbery.

Blue pulled up in front. "Cozy as a penitentiary."

"I stopped by earlier, but she wasn't home." His arm brushed the back of her neck and his opposite thumb grazed her cheek as he slipped the other earring in her lobe. She shivered. It felt more intimate than sex. She forced herself to break the spell. "I'll share if you want to wear them for part of the evening."

Instead of returning her volley, he rubbed the earring and her lobe gently between his fingers. "Very nice."

She was about to expire from lust when he let her go. He opened the door and stepped out, then leaned down to peer back in at her. "This car had better be sitting here when I come out."

She tugged on the purple earring. "I wasn't going to strand you. Just a quick spin around the block to keep from getting bored."

"Or not." He shot her with the old index finger pistol.

She leaned back in the comfortable seat and watched him walk up the path to the front door. A curtain fluttered in a corner window. He pressed the bell and waited. When no one answered, he pressed it again. Still nothing. He rapped on the door with his knuckles. She frowned. Nita Garrison wouldn't take well to that. Had he forgotten Blue's arrest four days ago?

He came back down the front steps, but her relief was short-lived because, instead of giving up, he took off around the side of the house. Just because Nita was elderly and female, he thought he could badger her. She'd probably already summoned her private police force. Garrison wasn't Chicago. Garrison was the stuff of Yankee nightmares, a small southern town with its own set of rules. Dean would end up in jail, and Blue would never get her dinner. She was struck by an equally alarming thought. They'd impound his beautiful car.

She jumped out. If she didn't stop him, the Vanquish would end up in one of those police auctions. He was so used to his famous name unlocking every door that he thought he was invincible. He'd completely underestimated this woman's authority.

She followed a brick path around the side of the house and found him peering in a window. "Don't do that!"

"She's in there," he said. "I can smell the brimstone."

"Clearly, she doesn't want to talk to you."

"Tough. I want to talk to her." He took off around the corner. Gritting her teeth, she headed after him.

A square patch of manicured grass and a row of rigidly clipped shrubs grew in front of the garage, which was made of the same tan stone as the house. Not a flower in sight, just an empty concrete birdbath. Ignoring her protests, he walked up a set of four steps to the back door, which sat under a short overhang supported by the same carved brackets that ornamented the eaves. As he turned the knob and pushed open the door, Blue started hissing like a wet cat. "Nita Garrison's going to call the police on you! Give me your wallet before you're arrested."

He glanced over his shoulder. "What do you want with my wallet?"

"Dinner."

"That's cold, even for you." He poked his head inside. A dog gave a low, creaky bark, then fell silent. "Mrs. Garrison! It's Dean Robillard. You left your back door unlocked." And he walked right in.

Blue stared at the open door, then slumped down on the back step. Not even the Garrison Police Department could arrest her if she didn't go inside, could they? She propped her elbows on her knees, ready to wait him out.

A querulous female voice shattered the evening quiet. "What do you think you're doing? Get out of here!"

"I know this is a small town, Mrs. Garrison," Dean said from inside, "but you should really keep your doors locked."

Instead of retreating, her voice grew louder and shriller. Once again, Blue detected a trace of Brooklyn. "You heard me. Get out!"

"As soon as we talk."

"I'm not talking to you. What are you doing out there, girl?"

Blue whipped around to see Mrs. Garrison looming over her in the doorway. She wore full makeup, a big platinum wig, wide-leg blue jersey slacks, and a matching boatneck tunic she'd accessorized with gold pendants. This evening, her heavy ankles spilled over a pair of worn magenta slippers.

Blue got right to the point. "What I'm *not* doing is breaking and entering."

"She's afraid of you," Dean said from someplace inside. "I'm not."

Mrs. Garrison propped both hands on her cane and regarded Blue as if she were a cockroach. Blue reluctantly came to her feet. "I am not afraid of you," she said, "but I haven't eaten since breakfast, and all I saw in that jail was a vending machine, and— Never mind."

Mrs. Garrison gave a contemptuous snort and shuffled toward Dean. "You've made a big mistake, Mr. Hotshot."

Blue peeked inside. "Not his fault. He's taken one too many hits to the head." Giving in to her curiosity, she crossed the threshold.

Unlike the stark exterior, the inside of the house was cluttered and unkempt. Stacks of newspapers sat by the back door, and the gold-flecked ceramic floor tiles could have used a good scrubbing. Mail lay scattered across the French provincial table, which also held an empty cereal bowl, a coffee mug, and a banana peel. Although the house wasn't scary filthy, it had a musty smell and a sour, untended look. A very old, overfed black Lab with a grizzled muzzle lay sprawled in the corner where some of the seams on the gold-striped wallpaper had begun to curl. The gilded kitchen chairs and small crystal chandelier gave the kitchen a gaudy Las Vegas ambience.

Nita raised her cane. "I'm calling the cops."

Blue couldn't take it any longer. "A word of warning, Mrs. Garrison. Dean seems like a nice guy on the surface, but the brutal truth is, there's not a player in the NFL who isn't half animal. He just hides it better than most of them."

"Do you really think you can scare me?" Nita sneered. "I grew up on the streets, sweetie."

"I'm merely pointing out the reality of the situation. You've upset him, and that's not good."

"This is my town. He can't do a thing to me."

"That's what you think." Blue stepped past Dean, who'd crouched down to pet the ancient black Lab. "Football players are a law unto themselves. I know you're used to having the local police force in your back pocket—and that was a nasty trick you pulled last week—but the minute Dean starts signing autographs and flashing a fistful of game day tickets, those cops won't remember your name."

Blue had to hand it to the old bat. Instead of backing off, she smirked at Dean. "You think that'll work, do you?"

Dean shrugged and rose. "I like cops, so I might stop at the station for a visit. But, frankly, I'm more interested in what my lawyer says about this little boycott of yours."

"Lawyers." She spat out the word, then started in on Blue again, which was beyond unfair, since Blue was trying to mediate. "Are you ready to apologize for the way you spoke to me last week?"

"Are you ready to apologize to Riley?"

"For telling the truth? I don't believe in coddling children. People like you want to solve every little problem for them so they never learn how to take care of themselves."

"That particular child just lost her mother," Dean said with deceptive mildness.

"Since when has life been fair?" Her mean eyes narrowed, further crinkling her blue frosted eye shadow. "It's better they understand how things are when they're young. When I was her age, I spent my nights sleeping on the fire escape to get away from my stepfather." She bumped the table with her hip, and the coffee mug rolled to the floor, followed by a stack of junk mail. Nita made a vague gesture toward the mess. "Nobody in this town is willing to do housework anymore. Now all the black girls go off to college."

Dean rubbed his ear. "That damned Abe Lincoln."

Blue reined in a smile.

Nita looked him up and down. "You're a real wise guy, aren't you?"

"Yes, ma'am."

The practiced way she took him in suggested she'd assessed more than her fair share of good-looking men. At the same time, there was nothing coquettish in her manner. "Do you dance?"

"I don't think we're getting on well enough for that."

Her lips thinned. "I taught at Arthur Murray in Manhattan for many years. Ballroom dancing. I was quite beautiful." She gazed at Blue, her distaste making it clear that Blue wasn't. "You're wasting your time mooning over him. You're too plain."

Dean lifted an eyebrow. "She's not—"

"That's what he likes about me," Blue said. "I don't steal his lime-light."

Dean sighed.

"You're a fool," Nita sneered. "I've known men like him all my life. In the end, they always picked women like me—like I used to be. Big boobs, blond hair, and long legs."

Nita had hit the nail on the head, but Blue wouldn't give up without a fight. "Unless they're into cross-dressing. Then, it's all about the woman with the prettiest lingerie."

"You'll let me know when you're done?" Dean said.

"Who are you, anyway?" The old woman lobbed the question at Blue like a stink bomb.

"I'm a portrait painter. Dogs and children."

"Really?" Her eyes flickered with interest. "Well, then. Maybe I'll hire you to paint Tango." She tilted her head toward the ancient dog. "Yes, I think I will. You can start tomorrow."

"She already has a job, Mrs. Garrison," Dean said. "She works for me."

"You've been telling everybody in town that she's your fiancée."

"She is. And I know she'll be the first to say that I'm a full-time job."

"Rubbish. You're just leading her on so she'll keep sleeping with you. The minute you get bored with her, you'll dump her."

He didn't like that. "Out of respect for your age, Mrs. Garrison, I'm going to let that pass. Now you have twenty-four hours to call off your dogs."

Ignoring him, she turned back to Blue. "I want you here at one o'clock tomorrow to start painting Tango's portrait. Once you show up, I'll tell the men to get back to work."

"Blackmail is supposed to be a little more subtle," Blue said.

"I'm too old to be subtle. I know what I want, and I make sure I get it."

"You don't understand, Mrs. Garrison," Dean said. "What you're going to get is a lot of trouble for yourself." He grabbed Blue's elbow and steered her out the door.

♥

When they got back to the car, Dean didn't say much beyond ordering Blue never to go near Mrs. Garrison again. Since Blue hated orders, she was tempted to argue with him on principle, but she had no intention of letting the old woman inflict more torment on her. Besides, she wanted to enjoy the evening.

They pulled up in front of a one-story blue shingled building with a yellow sign over the front entrance that said BARN GRILL. "I thought this place would be a real barn," she said as they walked toward the door.

"I did, too, the first time I came here. Then I found out it was the current owner's idea of a joke. In the eighties, it was Walt's Bar and Grill, but the native tongue of Tennessee shortened it."

"To Barn Grill. I've got it."

The sound of Tim McGraw singing "Don't Take the Girl" drifted through the door as they stepped into an entry area with dark brown latticework walls and an aquarium that had a Day-Glo orange castle sitting on a bed of fluorescent blue rocks. The roomy restaurant was divided into two sections, with a bar at the front. Beneath a pair of fake Tiffany lampshades, a bartender who looked like Chris Rock filled a pair of beer mugs. He called out a greeting as he spotted Dean. The bar patrons turned on their stools and immediately sprang to life.

"Hey, Boo, where you been all weekend?"

"That is a fabulous shirt."

"We've been talkin' about next season, and—"

"Charlie thinks you should go to the run-and-shoot."

They acted as though they'd known him forever, although Dean had told her he'd only eaten here twice. The instant intimacy people showed toward him made her glad she wasn't famous.

"Ordinarily, I'd love to talk sports with you boys, but tonight I promised my fiancée I wouldn't." Dean draped his arm around her shoulders. "It's our anniversary, and you know how sentimental the ladies get."

"What anniversary is that?" the Chris Rock lookalike asked.

"Six full months since my little darlin' hunted me down and drug me home."

The men laughed. Dean steered her past the bar and into the rear section of the restaurant. "I *drug* you home?" she said. "Since when did you give up your Yankee citizenship?"

"Since I became a southern landowner. Automatically made me bilingual."

A half wall topped with more brown latticework and a row of straw Chianti bottles divided the restaurant from the bar. He shepherded her to a vacant table and held out a chair. "Those ol' boys at the bar? One's a county judge, the big man's the high school principal, and the bald guy's an openly gay hairdresser. I love the South."

"It's a good place to be an oddball, I'll grant you that." She reached across the red vinyl tablecloth for the cracker basket and grabbed a packet of saltines. "I'm surprised they'll serve you. Nita Garrison must have slipped up."

"We're outside the town limits, and this is one property she doesn't own. There also seems to be a general 'what she don't know won't hurt her' attitude."

"Are you really going to sic your lawyer on her?"

"I'm not sure. The good news is, I'll win. The bad news is, it'll take months."

"I'm not painting Tango."

"Damn right you aren't."

She discarded the stale saltine. Even though it was Monday night, three-quarters of the tables were full, and most of the occupants were studying her. It wasn't hard to figure out why. "This seems like a big crowd for a Monday."

"No place else to go. On Monday nights it's either the Barn Grill or Bible study at Second Baptist. Or maybe Tuesday is Second Baptist. The Bible study schedule in this town is more complicated than the Stars' offensive line stunts."

"You like it here, don't you? Not just the farm. Small town life."

"It's different."

The waitress appeared with the menus. Her thin, sour face immediately twisted into a simpy smile for Dean. "My name's Marie, and I'll be your server tonight."

Blue wished somebody would pass a law that made it illegal for a person who worked in a place with Tabasco bottles on the table to introduce herself.

"Real nice to meet you, Marie," Redneck Dean drawled. "What's good tonight?"

Marie ignored Blue to recite the specials just for him. Dean settled on the barbecue chicken with a side salad. Blue chose the fried catfish, along with something called "dirty potatoes," which proved to be a concoction of mashed potatoes, sour cream, and mushrooms smothered in gravy. While she lapped it up, Dean ate his chicken without the skin, added only a small pat of butter to his baked potato, and refused dessert, all the time chatting amiably with the assorted townspeople who interrupted his meal. He introduced her to everyone as his fiancée. When they finally had a moment alone, she addressed him over a big, gooey serving of mud pie. "How are you going to explain our broken engagement after I leave?"

"I'm not. As far as this town's concerned, I'm staying engaged until there's a good reason for me not to be engaged."

"Which will be the minute a breathtakingly gorgeous, incredibly stacked, and marginally intelligent twenty-year-old catches your eye."

He stared at her dessert. "Where are you *putting* all that food?"

"I haven't eaten since breakfast. No funny stuff, Dean. I mean it. You can't break off our engagement by giving me a fatal disease or saying you caught me with another man. Or a woman," she added quickly. "Promise me."

"Just out of purely salacious curiosity, have you ever been with a woman?"

"Stop screwing around. I want your word."

"Okay, I'll say you dumped me."

"Like anybody's going to believe that." She scooped up another bite of mud pie. "So has it ever happened to you?"

"What? Being dumped? Sure."

"When?"

"Sometime. I don't remember exactly."

"Never. I'll bet you've never once been dumped."

"Sure I have. I'm pretty sure." He sipped his beer and thought it over. "I remember. Annabelle dumped me."

"Your agent's wife? I thought you said you never dated her."

"I didn't. She said I was immature, which I'll admit was true at the time, and she refused to date me."

"I don't see how that constitutes being dumped."

"Hey, work with me here."

She grinned, and he smiled back, and something inside her melted, right along with the last bite of mud pie. She quickly excused herself and headed for the ladies' room.

Which was when the trouble started.

Chapter Fifteen

She'd noticed the woman earlier, bony and bitter-faced, with harsh makeup and dyed black hair. She and the grizzly-looking man sharing her table had been drinking steadily all evening. Unlike so many other restaurant patrons, neither of them had approached Dean. Instead the woman had been staring a hole through Blue. Now, as Blue passed her table, she called to her in a drunken slur, "Get over here so I can talk to you, Pee Wee."

Blue ignored her and entered the restroom. She'd just latched the stall when the outer door banged open and that same belligerent voice intruded. "What's the matter, Pee Wee? You think you're too good to talk to me?"

She began to tell the woman that she didn't talk to drunks when a familiar male voice intruded. "Leave her alone." Dean the charmer had been replaced by the field general who demanded instant obedience.

"You touch me, asshole, and I'll scream rape," the woman snarled.

"Oh, no, you won't." Blue stomped out of the stall. "What's your problem?"

The woman stood in the harsh yellow light by the sinks, with Dean's big, broad-shouldered frame filling the open doorway off to her left. Her sneer, the jut of her hip, the coil of her dead, dyed hair, all signaled someone embittered with the world and determined to pin her failures on Blue. "You walked right pas' me, that's my problem."

Blue slammed a hand on her hip. "Lady, you are drunk."

"So what? All night you been sitting there looking like you're better than every woman here, just because you're fuckin' Mr. Hot Shit."

Blue stalked forward only to have Dean snake his arm around her waist and pull her back. "Don't do it. She's not worth it."

Blue hadn't intended to fight her, merely enlighten her. "Let me go, Dean."

"Hiding behind your big bad boyfriend?" the woman jeered as Dean steered Blue toward the door.

"I don't have to hide behind anybody." Blue planted her feet and shoved at his arm. It didn't budge.

The grizzly bear the woman had been sitting with loomed in the doorway. He was barrel-chested, with a lantern jaw and biceps that looked like tattooed beer kegs. The woman was too focused on Blue to notice. "Your big, rich boyfriend wants to make sure you don't get too messed up for him to fuck tonight."

Dean scowled in the mirror. "Lady, you are one foul-mouthed, sorry excuse for a human being."

Someone in the crowd gathering behind Grizzly Bear thoughtfully wedged the door open so nobody missed anything. Grizzly Bear leaned in. "What you doin' in there, Karen Ann?"

"I'll tell you what she's doing," Blue retorted. "She's trying to pick a fight with me because she's screwed up her life, and she wants to pin all her misery on somebody else."

The woman grabbed the edge of the sink to support herself. "I work for a living, bitch. I don't take handouts from nobody. How many times did you have to blow Big Shot so he'd pay for your dinner?"

Dean dropped his arm. "Take her, Blue."

Take her?

Karen Ann lurched forward. She was a head taller and at least thirty pounds heavier than Blue, but she was also staggeringly drunk. "Come on, Pee Wee," she sneered. "Let's see if you fight as good as you suck cock."

"That does it!" Blue didn't know why Karen Ann had declared war on her, and she didn't care. She shot across the tile floor. "I strongly recommend you apologize, lady."

"Fuck you." Curling her fingers into claws, Karen Ann made a grab for Blue's hair. Blue ducked and drove her shoulder into the woman's middle.

With an oomph of pain, the woman lost her balance and hit the floor.

"Goddamn it, Karen Ann! Get your ass up!" Grizzly Bear pushed forward only to have Dean block his way.

"Stay out of it."

"Who's going to make me?"

Dean's mouth curled in a lethal facsimile of a smile. "You don't seriously think you're going through me, do you? Isn't it enough that Pee Wee over there just kicked your girlfriend's ass?"

That wasn't exactly true. "Pee Wee over there" had merely given the drunken woman one push, but it had been exceptionally well placed, hitting Karen Ann right in the solar plexus. Now Karen Ann was curled into a comma and wheezing for air.

"You're asking for it, asshole." Grizzly Bear swung.

Dean blocked the punch without even moving his feet. The crowd hooted, including, Blue noticed, the man Dean had said was a county judge. Grizzly staggered and hit the doorframe. His eyes narrowed, and he charged again. Dean sidestepped, which sent Grizzly into the towel dispenser. Grizzly righted himself and came at Dean again.

This time he got lucky and connected with Dean's bad shoulder, which Dean didn't like at all. Blue jumped out of the way as her fake fiancé stopped playing games and got serious.

A horrible exhilaration crept through her as she watched his surgically efficient counterattack. Few things in life were as black and white as this, and seeing justice being dispensed so swiftly filled her with longing. If only Dean, with his great strength, quick reflexes, and odd chivalry, could right all the evils in the world, then Virginia Bailey wouldn't have to.

As Grizzly lay on the floor, the big, balding man Dean had pointed out earlier as the high school principal pushed through the crowd. "Ronnie Archer, you still don't have the brains of a flea. Pull yourself together and get out of here."

Grizzly tried to roll to his back but didn't get far. Karen Ann, in the meantime, had crawled into a stall to heave.

The hairdresser and the bartender pulled Grizzly to his feet. Judging by their expressions, he wasn't the most popular guy in town. One of the men shoved a paper towel at him to staunch the blood while the other led him out the door. Blue made her way to Dean's side, but other than a scraped elbow and some dirt on his designer jeans, he didn't seem any the worse for wear.

"That was fun." He gave her the once-over. "You okay?"

Her fight had ended before it had begun, but she appreciated his concern. "I'm fine."

The sound of retching finally stopped, and the principal disappeared into the stall. He emerged with a pasty-faced Karen Ann wobbling at his side. "The rest of us do not appreciate having the two of you make us look like a bunch of drunken hillbillies in front of strangers." He led her through the crowd. "Do you intend to spend the rest of your life picking fights with every short woman who reminds you of your sister?"

Blue and Dean traded glances.

After the drunks were disposed of, the county judge, Gary the hairdresser, the principal, and a woman everybody called Syl, who turned out to own the local resale shop, insisted on buying Dean and Blue a drink. They quickly learned that Ronnie was stupid, but not bad. That Karen Ann was just plain mean—as one look at her split ends and bad dye job testified—and that she'd been mean even before her pretty, petite younger sister Lyla ran off with both Karen Ann's husband and, most damning, Karen Ann's red Trans Am.

"She sure did love that car," Judge Pete Haskins said.

Sister Lyla, it turned out, was just about Blue's size and also had dark hair, although hers had a tad more shape to the cut, Gary tactfully pointed out.

"Tell me about it," Dean muttered.

"Karen Ann went after Margo Gilbert a couple of weeks ago," Syl pointed out, "and she doesn't look nearly as much like Lyla as Blue does."

Just before Blue and Dean left, the Chris Rock lookalike bartender, whose real name was Jason, agreed not to serve either Ronnie or Karen Ann more than one drink a night, not even during Wednesday's All You Can Eat Italian Buffet, which was Ronnie's favorite.

♥

The smell of scotch tickled April's nostrils as she took a seat at the bar. She needed a drink and a cigarette in exactly that order.

Just for today.

"Club soda with a twist," she told the hunky young bartender as she sucked in the secondhand smoke. "Thrill me and serve it in a martini glass."

He smiled and let his boy-child's eyes roam. "You got it."

Not so much anymore, she thought. She gazed down at her salmon Marc Jacobs flats. She was getting a bunion. My Life in Shoes, she thought. Five-inch platforms; boots of every size and shape; stilettos, stilettos, more stilettos. And now, flats.

She'd needed to get away from the farm tonight, away from Dean's disdain, but mostly, she needed to get away from Jack. She'd driven to the next county to find solitude at this upscale steak house. Although she hadn't planned on stopping in the half-empty bar before she ate, old habits had drawn her in.

All day, she'd felt like a homemade sweater unraveling inch by inch. She hadn't imagined anything could be more difficult than Dean's appearance, but spending hours painting that kitchen with Jack today had sent too many ugly emotions struggling to break through the surface of her hard-earned serenity. Fortunately, Jack hadn't been any more anxious to talk than she, and they'd kept the music loud enough to make conversation impossible.

Every man in the bar had noticed her arrival. As bad elevator music played, two Japanese businessmen studied her. *Sorry, guys. I don't work in pairs anymore.* A man in his late forties with more money than taste preened for her. *Not your lucky day.*

What if, after all her hard work, all the healing she'd done, Jack Patriot once again managed to cast his spell over her? He'd been her folly, her madness, the beginning of her ruin. What if that happened again? But it couldn't. She controlled men these days. They didn't control her.

"You sure you don't want a double?" hunky bartender said.

"Can't. I'm driving."

He grinned and added a fresh shot of club soda. "You need anything else, you let me know."

"I'll do that."

The bars and clubs were where she'd lost her life, and sometimes she needed to go back so she could remind herself that the drugged-out party girl eager to debase herself with any man who caught her eye no longer existed. Still, it was a dangerous practice. The dim lights, the clink of ice cubes, the enticing smell of liquor. Fortunately, this wasn't much of a bar, and the cheesy instrumental version of "Start Me Up" grated so badly that she wasn't tempted to linger. Whoever recorded shit like that should be thrown in jail.

Her cell vibrated in her pocket. She checked the caller ID and quickly answered. "Mark!"

"God, April, I need you so much. . . ."

♥

April returned to the cottage a little before midnight. In the old days, the party would have just been starting. Now all she wanted to do was sleep. But as she stepped out of the car, she heard music coming from the backyard. A lone guitar and that familiar raspy baritone.

"When you are alone at night,
Do you ever think about me, darling,
Like I think about you?"

The rasp had more gravel now, and he held the words further back in his throat, as if he couldn't bear letting them go. She went inside the cottage and set down her purse. For a moment, she stood where she was, eyes closed, listening, trying to hold herself back. Then, she did as she always had and followed the music.

He sat facing the dark pond. Instead of a lawn chair with its metal arms, he'd dragged out an armless straight-back kitchen chair. A chunky candle sat on a saucer in the grass not far from his feet so he could see to jot down a lyric on the pad of paper lying next to it.

"Baby, if you ever knew
The heartache that you've put me through,
You'd cry,
Cry like I do."

The years slipped away. He curled over the guitar just as she remembered—stroking, persuading, inflaming. Candlelight flickered off a pair of reading glasses lying on top of his notebook pad. The wild, long-haired, rock-and-roll rebel of her youth had turned into an elder statesman. She could have—should have—gone back inside, but the music was too sweet.

> *"Do you ever wish for rain*
> *So you don't feel alone again?*
> *Do you ever wish the sun away?"*

He saw her, but he didn't stop. Instead, he played to her as he used to, and the music rippled over her skin like warm, healing oil. When the last chord finally drifted into the darkness, he let his hand fall to his knee. "What do you think?"

The wild girl she'd once been would have curled at his feet and ordered him to play the bridge again. She would have told him he needed to clean up the chord change at the end of the first verse and that she could hear a Hammond B3 sweeping into the chorus. The grown woman gave a dismissive shrug. "Vintage Patriot."

It was the cruelest thing she could have said. Jack's obsession with exploring new musical trails was as legendary as his scorn for the lazy rock idols who only repeated their old tricks. "You think so?"

"It's a good song, Jack. You know that."

He leaned down to lay his guitar back in the case. The candlelight outlined that bladed nose. "Do you remember how it used to be?" he said. "You heard a song once, and you knew whether it was good or bad. You understood my music better than I did."

She wrapped her arms around herself and gazed out over the pond. "I can't listen to those songs anymore. They remind me of too many things I've left behind."

His voice drifted toward her like cigarette smoke. "Is all the wildness gone, April?"

"Every bit of it. I'm a boring L.A. career woman now."

"You couldn't be boring if you tried," he said.

A deep weariness overcame her. "Why aren't you at the house?"

"I like to write by the water."

"It's not exactly the Côte d'Azur. I hear you have a place there."

"Among others."

She couldn't do this. She unclasped her arms. "Go away, Jack. I don't want you here. I don't want you anywhere near me."

"I'm the one who should be saying that."

"You can take care of yourself." Old bitterness bubbled to the surface. "It's so ironic. All the times I needed to talk to you, you wouldn't take a single call. Now, when you're the last person in the world I want to—"

"I couldn't, April. I couldn't talk to you. You were poisonous to me."

"So poisonous that you wrote your best music when we were together?"

"I wrote my worst, too." He stood. "Remember those days? I was washing pills down with vodka."

"You were drugging before I met you."

"I'm not blaming you. I'm only saying that living in a jealous frenzy made it worse. No matter who I was with—even my own band—I kept wondering whether you'd gotten to them first."

Her fists curled at her sides. "I loved you!"

"You loved them all, April. As long as they rocked."

Not true. He was the only one she'd truly loved, but she wouldn't be drawn into defending those ancient, misplaced feelings. She also wouldn't let him shame her. His sexual body count was as high as her own.

"I was wrestling my own demons," he said. "I couldn't wrestle yours, too. Remember those ugly fights? Not just ours. I was punching out fans, photographers. I was burning up."

And taking her with him.

He wandered past her toward the edge of the pond. Only in the way he moved, with the same lithesome, long-legged grace as his son, could anyone have guessed they were related. They didn't look alike. Dean had taken after her blond Nordic ancestors. Jack was night, dark as sin. She swallowed and said softly, "We had a son together. I needed to talk to you about him."

"I know. But my survival depended on staying away."

"Maybe at first, but what about later on? What about then?"

He met her gaze full on. "As long as I was signing the checks on time, I gave myself a pass."

"I never forgave you for that blood test."

He gave a sharp bite of a laugh. "Give me a break. How many lies had I caught you in? You were wild, out of control."

"And Dean was the one who paid."

"Yeah, he was the one who paid."

She rubbed her arms. She was so tired of having her past shape the present. *Fake it till you make it.* It was time to take her own advice. "Where's Riley?"

"Asleep."

She glanced toward the cottage windows. "Inside?"

"No. At the farmhouse."

"I thought Dean and Blue went out."

"They did." He grabbed the kitchen chair to carry it inside.

"You left Riley alone?"

He headed for the back door. "I told you. She was asleep."

"What if she wakes up?"

He picked up his step. "She won't."

"You have no way of knowing that." She went after him. "Jack, you don't leave a skittish eleven-year-old alone in a big house like that at night."

He'd never liked being put on the defensive, and he set the chair down hard in the grass. "Nothing's going to happen. She's safer there than in the city."

"She doesn't feel that way."

"I guess I'm a better judge of my own child than you are."

"You don't have any idea what to do with her."

"I'll figure it out," he said.

"Do it fast. She might only be eleven, but trust me when I tell you time is running out."

"Now you're the big expert on motherhood?"

A rush of anger sent another crack into the rocky landscape of her serenity. "Yes, Jack, I am. Nobody's a better expert than someone who's made every mistake in the book."

"You're right about that." He grabbed the chair and stalked inside.

The crack split into a chasm. Only one person had the right to condemn her, and that was Dean. She shot after him. "Don't you dare judge me. You, of all people."

He wouldn't retreat. "I don't need you telling me how to take care of my daughter."

"You only think you don't." Riley had touched something inside her, and she couldn't let this go, not when the little girl's future was at stake, and not when Jack so clearly understood he was wrong. "Life doesn't hand out a lot of second chances, but you've got one with her. Except you're going to blow it. I can already see it. Mr. Rock Star is fifty-four years old and still too self-indulgent to let his life be disrupted by a needy little kid."

"Don't try to paint me with the brush of your sins." His words were tough, but the lack of conviction in his voice told her she'd struck a nerve. He shoved the chair under the table and brushed past her. The door slammed. She watched through the window as he grabbed his guitar and bent over the candle flame. Seconds later, the backyard fell into darkness.

♥

Dean enjoyed watching Blue enjoy the Vanquish. She was still behind the wheel as they drove up to the farmhouse. "Explain it to me one more time," she said. "Explain how you knew I wouldn't end up being permanently paralyzed by a psychotic woman who was two feet taller than me and fifty pounds heavier."

"Stop exaggerating," he said. "She had you by maybe four inches and thirty pounds. And I've seen you fight. Besides, she wasn't psychotic. She was so drunk she could hardly walk."

"Still . . ."

"Somebody had to teach her manners. I couldn't do it. And that's what teamwork's all about." He grinned. "You've got to admit you enjoyed it."

"I hate that."

"You can't help it, Blue. You're a natural born badass."

He could see she appreciated the compliment.

He got out to open the barn door so she could park the Vanquish. He was beginning to understand her strange inner workings. Growing up with no one but herself to rely on had made her fiercely independent, which was why she couldn't tolerate being beholden to him. His old girlfriends took dinners at luxury restaurants and expensive presents for granted. But even those cheap earrings galled Blue. He'd seen her steal more than a few glances at herself in the rearview mirror, so he knew she liked them, but he also knew she would have given them back in an instant if she could have figured out how to do it and keep her dignity. He had no idea how to handle a woman who wanted so little from him, especially when he wanted so much from her.

She pulled the Vanquish in and got out. Today he'd carted away several wheelbarrow loads of old feed sacks and other debris from the barn and stables to make room for the car. He couldn't do much about the pigeons roosting in the rafters except keep the car covered, but once he built a garage, that wouldn't be a problem.

He slid the barn door back. Blue came up next to him, the purple glass earrings bobbing at her ears. He wanted to slip her in his pocket, among other things. "You're used to it, aren't you?" she said. "Not just the fighting, but strangers buying you drinks and everybody trying to be your best friend. You don't even seem to resent it."

"Considering the obscene amount of money they pay me for basically doing nothing, I've got no right."

He expected her to agree, but she didn't. Instead, she studied him so steadily that he got the feeling she knew exactly how much mind-numbing pain he endured. Even in the off-season, he watched so much game film that it played in his sleep. "Professional sports is entertainment," he said. "Anybody who loses sight of that is kidding himself."

"But it has to be a drag sometimes."

It was. "You won't hear me complaining."

"One of the things I like about you." She squeezed his arm, one friend to another, which set his teeth on edge.

"It has a lot more positives than negatives," he said a tad too belligerently. "People know who you are. It's hard to be lonely when you're even middling famous."

She pulled her hand away. "Because you're never an outsider. You don't know what that feels like, do you?" Her face fell. "I'm sorry. The way you grew up . . . Of course, you do. That was a crappy thing to say." She rubbed her cheek. "It's because I'm dead on my feet. I'll see you in the morning."

"Wait, I—"

But she was off to the caravan, the beads on her sparkly lavender top twinkling in the dark like tiny stars.

He wanted to shout out that he didn't need anybody's sympathy. But he'd never chased after a woman in his life, and not even Blue Bailey could make him start. He stalked inside.

The house was quiet. He wandered into the living room, then stepped out through the French doors onto the concrete slab that would hold his screen porch when the carpenters came back. A stack of lumber waited for them. He tried to enjoy the stars, but his heart wasn't in it. The farm was supposed to be his refuge, the place where he could kick back and relax, but now Mad Jack and Riley were asleep upstairs, and he only had Blue to protect his blind side. Everything in his life had gone off balance, and he didn't know how to straighten it out.

He wasn't used to feeling unsure of himself, so he went back inside and headed for the stairs.

What he saw at the top brought him to a dead stop.

Chapter Sixteen

Riley sat huddled on the top step, a butcher knife clutched in her small fist, Puffy at her side. The knife couldn't have looked more out of place with her pink, candy-heart pajamas and round child's face. He did not want to deal with this. Why wasn't Blue here? She'd know exactly how to handle Riley. She'd say just the right thing.

He had to force himself to mount the stairs. When he reached the top, he nodded toward the knife. "What were you planning to do with that?"

"I—I heard noises." She drew her knees tighter against her chest. "I thought there might be . . . like . . . maybe a murderer or something."

"It was just me." He leaned down and took the knife from her. Puffy, looking considerably cleaner and better fed than on Friday, gave a wheezy sigh and closed her eyes.

"I heard noises before you came in." She gazed at the damned knife as if she thought he might use it on her. "At ten-thirty-two. Ava packed my alarm clock."

"You've been sitting here for two hours?"

"I think I woke up when Dad left."

"He's not here?"

"I think he went to see April."

It didn't take much imagination to figure out what Mad Jack and dear old Mom were up to. He strode down the hallway to Jack's room and pitched the knife on his bed. Let him figure out how it got there.

When he returned, Riley was right where he'd left her, still huddled over her knees. Even the dog had deserted her. "After Dad left, I heard creaking sounds," she said. "Like somebody was trying to break in, and maybe they had a gun or something."

"This is an old house. They all creak. How did you get the knife?"

"I sneaked it up to my bedroom before I went to sleep. My—my house at home has security alarms, but I didn't think there are any alarms here."

She'd been sitting here armed with a butcher knife for two hours? The idea made him crazy. "Go to sleep," he said more harshly than he intended. "I'm here now."

She nodded, but she didn't move.

"What's wrong?"

She picked at her fingernail. "Nothing."

He'd found her with a butcher knife, and he was mad at Blue, and he hated knowing April was getting it on with Mad Jack, so he took it out on the kid. "Say it, Riley. I can't read your mind."

"I don't have anything to say."

But she didn't move. Why wouldn't she get up and go to bed? He had endless patience with the most bumbling rookie, but now he felt himself losing it. "Yes, you do. Spit it out."

"I don't want anything," she said quickly.

"Fine. Then sit there."

"Okay." Her head dipped lower, her tangled mass of curly hair hung further over her face, and her defenselessness was a rope dragging him back to the darkest corners of his childhood. His lungs compressed. "You know, don't you, that you can't count on Jack for anything but money. He's not going to be there for you. If you want something, you'll have to take care of it because he won't be around to fight your battles. If you don't stand up for yourself, the world will roll right over you."

Misery muffled her quick response. "Okay, I will."

Friday morning in the kitchen she'd managed to stand up for herself just fine. Unlike him, she'd bent her father to her will, but now, seeing her like this made him crazy. "You're just saying what you think I want to hear."

"I'm sorry."

"Don't be sorry. Just tell me what the *hell you want*!"

Her small shoulders trembled, and the words came out in a rush. "I want you to see if a murderer is hiding in my bedroom!"

He sucked in his breath.

A tear dropped on the leg of her pajamas, right next to a candy heart that said KISS ME STUPID.

He was the biggest shithead who'd ever lived, and he couldn't do this any longer. He couldn't steel himself against her just because she was an inconvenience. He sank down on the step next to her. The dog came trotting out from his bedroom and nosed between them.

All his adult life, he'd kept his childhood baggage from dragging him down. Only on the football field did he let that dark cauldron of leftover emotions erupt inside him. But now he'd allowed his anger to spill over onto the person who least deserved it. He'd punished this sensitive, defenseless kid for drawing him back to that place of helplessness. "I'm a jerk," he said softly. "I shouldn't have yelled at you."

"It's okay."

"No, it's not okay. I wasn't mad at you. I was mad at myself. Mad at Jack. You haven't done one thing wrong." He could feel her taking the words in, running them through that complex brain of hers, probably looking for a way she could still blame herself. He couldn't stand it.

"Go ahead and punch me," he said.

Her chin came up, and her teary eyes widened in shock. "I couldn't ever do that."

"Sure you could. It's . . . what sisters do when their brothers act like jerks." It wasn't easy for him to say the words, but he needed to stop acting like a self-centered ass and step up to the plate.

Her lips parted in shock that he might finally be willing to claim her. Hope kindled in her damp eyes. She wanted him to live up to her illusions. "You're not a jerk."

He had to get this right, or he couldn't live with himself. He slipped his arm around her shoulder. Her back stiffened, as if she were afraid to move for fear he'd pull away. She was already beginning to count on him. With a sense of resignation, he drew her closer. "I don't know how to be a big brother, Riley. I'm pretty much a kid at heart."

"So am I," she said earnestly. "I'm a kid at heart, too."

"I didn't mean to yell at you. I was just . . . worried. I know a lot about what you're going through." He couldn't say any more, not now, so he stood and pulled her to her feet. "Let's go check your room for murderers so you can get to sleep."

"I feel better now. I don't really think there are any murderers in there."

"Neither do I, but we'd better check anyway." An idea came to him, a stupid way to begin making up for some of the pain he'd caused her. "I've got to warn you . . . The big brothers I know are pretty rotten to their sisters."

"What do you mean?"

"Well . . . They might open their sister's closet and scream like they really saw a monster in there just to scare her."

A smile started in Riley's eyes and played with the corner of her mouth. "You wouldn't do that."

He felt himself smiling back. "I might. Unless you beat me to it."

And she did. She ran ahead of him into the bedroom, screaming all the way. He had himself a sister, whether he wanted one or not.

Puffy joined the melee, and, in the commotion, Dean missed the sound of running feet. The next thing he knew, something hit him in the back, he lost his balance, and fell. As he rolled over, he saw Jack hovering above him, his face twisted with anger. "You leave her alone!"

Jack grabbed Riley, who was now screaming for real while the dog raced in shrill, yipping circles around them. Jack pulled her to his chest. "It's okay. I won't let him get near you again. I promise." He stroked her tangled hair. "We're getting out of here. Now."

An unwieldy mix of rage, resentment, and disgust churned inside Dean. This chaos was what currently passed for his life. He came to his feet. Riley clutched Jack's shirt, gulping for air and trying to talk, but too hysterical to frame the words. The revulsion in Jack's face gave Dean a queer kind of satisfaction. *That's right. It's all out in the open now. And right back atcha.*

"Get out of here," Jack said.

Dean wanted to punch him, but Riley still had a death grip on Jack's shirt. She finally found her voice. "It wasn't— He's not— It's all my fault! Dean saw the—the knife."

Jack caught her head in his hands. "What knife?"

"I got it . . . from the kitchen." She hiccupped.

"What were you doing with a knife?" Jack raised his voice over the noise of the barking dog.

"I was— It was—"

"She was afraid." Dean wanted the words to fester, but Riley let it all tumble out.

"I woke up and there wasn't anybody in the house, and I was scared . . ."

Dean didn't stay to listen but headed for his bedroom. His shoulder already ached from his fight with Ronnie, and he'd just landed on it again. Two fights in one night. Brilliant. The barking stopped as he popped a couple of Tylenol. He stripped off his clothes, got in the shower, and turned the water on as hot as he could tolerate.

Jack was waiting in the bedroom when he came out. The house was quiet. Riley and Puffy had presumably been tucked in for the night. Jack tilted his head toward the hall. "I want to talk to you. Downstairs." Without waiting for a response, he left.

Dean threw off his towel and tugged a pair of jeans over his damp legs. It was way past time to have this out.

He found Jack in the empty living room, his fingers stuffed in his back pockets. "I heard her screaming," he said, gazing out the window. "It looked bad."

"Hell, I'm just glad you finally got around to remembering you left her alone. Good job, Jack."

"I know when I fuck up." Jack turned, his hands dropping to his sides. "I'm feeling my way with her, and sometimes I get it wrong— like tonight. When that happens, I do my best to fix it."

"Admirable. Very admirable. I'm humbled."

"You never did anything wrong in your life?"

"Hell, yes. I threw seventeen interceptions last season."

"You know what I mean."

Dean hooked his thumb in the waistband of his jeans. "Well, I've got a bad habit of picking up speeding tickets, and I can be a sarcastic son of a bitch, but I haven't left any old girlfriends pregnant, if that's what you're driving at. No bastard kids running around. I'm embarrassed to say it, Jack, but I don't seem to be in your league." Jack flinched, but Dean wanted to annihilate him, and he needed more. "Just to make sure you understand . . . The only reason I'm letting you stay here is because of Riley. You're nothing but a sperm donor to me, pal, so keep out of my way."

Jack wouldn't back off. "No problem. I'm good at that." He moved closer. "I'm only going to say this once. You got a raw deal, and I'm sorrier about that than you could ever imagine. When April told me she was pregnant, I ran as fast and as far as I could. If it had been up to me, you'd never have been born, so factor that in the next time you let her know how much you hate her."

Dean felt sick, but he refused to look away, and Jack sneered. "I was twenty-three, man. Too young for responsibility. All I cared about was music, getting high, and getting laid. My lawyer was the guy who looked out for you when April couldn't. He was the one who made sure there was a nanny on duty just in case your mother snorted too many lines or forgot to come home after she'd spent the night entertaining some glam rocker in gold lamé pants. My lawyer was the one who kept track of your grades. He was the one the school called when you got sick. I was too busy forgetting you existed."

Dean couldn't move. Jack's lips curled. "But you have your retribution, pal. I get to spend the rest of my life seeing the man you've become and knowing—if it had been up to me—you'd never have drawn your first breath. How cool is that?"

Dean couldn't handle any more, and he turned away, but Jack had one last missile to toss at his back. "I promise you one thing. I won't ever ask you to forgive me. I can at least do that."

Dean rushed into the foyer and out the front door. Before he knew it, he'd reached the caravan.

♥

Blue had just fallen asleep when the door of her peaceful habitat blew open. She fumbled for her flashlight and finally managed to flip it on. He was bare-chested, and his eyes glittered like midnight ice. "Not a word," he said, slamming the door so hard the wagon shook. "Not one word."

Under other circumstances, she would have taken issue, but he looked so tortured—so magnificent—that she was temporarily struck speechless. She eased up into the pillows, her comfy haven no longer feeling quite so safe. Something had deeply upset him, and for once, she didn't think it was her. He cracked his head on the caravan's curved roof. A blistering blasphemy split the air followed by a gust of wind that shook the wagon.

She licked her lips. "Uhm, it's probably not good to take the Lord's name in vain until the weather's a little calmer."

"Are you naked?" he demanded.

"Not at this precise moment."

"Then hand it over. Whatever ugly piece of crap you're wearing." The slivers of moonlight coming through the window carved his face into blunt planes and enigmatic shadows. "The game's gone on long enough. Give it to me."

"Just like that?"

"Just like that," he said flatly. "Hand it over, or I'm coming in to get it."

If another man had talked to her like this, she'd have screamed her head off, but he wasn't any man. Something had cracked his shiny facade, and he was hurting. Even though she was jobless, penniless, and homeless, he was the needy one. Not that he'd admit it. Neither of them played the game that way.

"You're on the pill." Last week, he'd initiated a pointed discussion about blood tests and sexual health, and he already knew this.

"Yes, but—" Once again, she had to keep herself from admitting she took it more for her complexion than for her sex life. In the meantime, he walked over to the cupboard, slid open a built-in drawer at the bottom, and pulled out a pack of condoms she hadn't put there. She didn't like his premeditation. At the same time, she appreciated his common sense.

"Give me that." He pulled the flashlight from her fingers, tossed the condoms down, and whipped back the sheet that covered her. The beam of light hit her BODY BY BEER T-shirt. "You'd think by now I'd have lowered my expectations, but I keep hoping."

"File a complaint with the fashion police."

"How about I take the law into my own hands?"

She braced herself—hoped for?—some bodice ripping, but he

disappointed her by dragging the flashlight beam along her bare legs instead. "Very nice, Blue. You should show these off more often."

"They're short."

"And sweet. They do the job just fine." He pushed up the hem of her T-shirt. Just a few inches. Just far enough to expose the only other garment she wore, some unimaginative, nude-colored, hip-hugger panties.

"I'm buying you a thong," he said. "Red."

"Which you'll never see."

"How do you figure?" He moved the beam across the panties from one hip bone to the other, then back to home base.

"If I do this—"

"Oh, you're doing it all right."

"*If* I do it," she said, "it's a one-shot deal. And I'm on top."

"Top, bottom, upside down. I'll bend you more ways than you can imagine."

A bolt of erotic lightning buzzed through her. Her toes curled.

"But first . . ." He touched the working end of the flashlight to the crotch of her panties, rubbed the hard case over the nylon for a few tantalizing seconds, then used it to push up the hem of her T-shirt. The cold plastic came to rest on the skin just beneath her breasts, sending a dim pinwheel across her bare rib cage. He cupped one breast through the soft cotton. "I can't wait to taste."

She nearly moaned. Her libido was way out of touch with her sexual politics.

"Which part of you am I going to unwrap first?" The flashlight beam danced over her. She watched as if she were hypnotized, waiting to see where the beam would land. It played across her covered breasts, her bare midriff, the crotch of her panties. Then it hit her square in the eyes. She squinted, the mattress sagged, and his denim-clad hip brushed her own as he dropped the flashlight onto the bed.

"Let's start here." His words fell across her cheek as his mouth dipped to meet hers, and she lost herself in the craziest kiss she'd ever experienced, soft one second, tough the next. He teased and tormented, demanded and seduced. She reached up to wrap her arms around his neck, but he drew away. "Don't do that again," he said with a rough gasp. "I see right through your tricks."

She had tricks?

"You're determined to distract me, but it's not going to work." He pulled her T-shirt over her head and tossed it aside, leaving her only in her panties. He whipped up the flashlight and shone it on her breasts. Being less than a D-cup wasn't always a bad thing, she decided. Her barely Bs sat up firm and ready for whatever was to come.

Which was his mouth.

His bare chest rubbed against her ribs as he suckled her, and her fingers dug into the mattress. He took his time, using his lips, his tongue. The careful scrape of his teeth stimulated her until she couldn't bear it anymore. She pushed his head away.

"You're not getting off that easy," he whispered, his hot breath taunting her wet flesh. He hooked his thumbs in her panties and drew them down, then tossed them aside and stood up. The abandoned flashlight rested under the sheet, so she couldn't see what lay beneath those jeans. She began to reach for the light, then stopped herself. He was always the object of desire, the one pursued and ministered to. Let him service her instead.

She slipped her hand back under the covers and flicked off the switch, plunging the caravan into darkness. The novelty of continuing this erotic game left her as boneless as his caresses, but the darkness also meant she needed to make certain he remembered he was dealing with Blue Bailey, not some faceless woman. "Good luck," she managed to say. "I'm hard to satisfy with less than a two-man team."

"In your dirty dreams." His jeans hit the floor with a soft whoosh. "Now where's that flashlight?" His hand grazed her side as he felt for it. Flicking the switch back on, he pulled it from under the sheet, then let the beam trickle over her naked body, from her breasts, to her belly, and below. He stopped. "Open up, sweetheart," he said softly. "Let me see."

It was too much, and she nearly shattered right there. He parted her unresisting thighs, and the flashlight's cold plastic chilled the inner slope of her skin. "Perfect," he whispered, looking his fill.

After that, she knew only sensation. Fingers parting and probing. Lips seeking. Her own hands exploring everything she'd been wanting to touch and stroke and weigh for so long.

Her small body received his with perfect resistance. Tender musk and rugged velvet. They moved together. The flashlight fell to the floor. He pressed deep within her, withdrew, and pressed again. She arched, demanded, dueled with him . . . and, finally, accepted.

♥

Making love without indoor plumbing wasn't nearly as romantic as it seemed. "How did the pioneers handle this?" she complained. "I need a bathroom."

"We'll use your T-shirt. You can burn it tomorrow. Please, God."

"If you say another word about my T-shirt . . ."

"Give it here."

"Hey, watch where you're . . ." She sucked in her breath as he put her T-shirt to a most inventive use.

She didn't make it on top the second time, either. By the third time, however, she managed to invert the power structure. Or, since she had possession of the flashlight, she at least *thought* she'd inverted it. But the truth was, she'd gotten a little foggy about who was servicing whom and exactly what the political ramifications were. One thing was for certain. She could never again taunt him with "Speed Racer."

They dozed off. Her little berth in the back of the caravan wasn't long enough for his tall frame, but he stayed there anyway, one arm around her shoulders.

♥

She awakened very early and crawled over him as carefully as she could. A rush of tenderness claimed her as she lingered for a moment to gaze down at him. The early morning light washed his back, sculpting the curve of muscle and ridge of tendon. All her life she'd had to settle for second best. But not last night.

She picked up her clothes and headed for the house, where she took the world's fastest shower, pulled on jeans and a T-shirt, and transferred a few necessities into her pockets. On her way back outside, she glanced toward the gypsy caravan under the trees. He'd been the unselfish, audacious lover she'd always dreamed of. She didn't regret a moment of last night, but now dreamtime was over.

She wheeled the smaller bike out of the barn and pedaled to the highway. Each hill felt like a mountain, and her lungs started burning long before she reached town. By the time she crossed the final summit and began the descent into Garrison, her legs had turned into overcooked spaghetti.

Nita Garrison, as it happened, was also an early riser. Blue stood in her cluttered kitchen and watched her poke at a toaster waffle. "I charge four hundred dollars for a three-by-three-foot canvas," Blue said, "with a two-hundred-dollar deposit due today. Take it or leave it."

"Chump change," Nita said. "I was prepared to pay a lot more."

"You also have to provide room and board while I'm working." She pushed away memories of the gypsy caravan. "I need to know Tango better so I can capture his true personality."

Tango opened one droopy lid and stared at her through a rheumy eye.

Nita whipped her head around so fast Blue was afraid she'd leave her wig behind. "You want to stay here? In my house?"

It was the last thing Blue wanted, but inevitable after what had happened. "It's the best way for me to produce a quality painting."

A diamond and ruby ring glittered on Nita's gnarled finger as she pointed toward the stove. "Don't think you can leave your mess all over the kitchen."

"You can safely assume your kitchen will be better off with me here."

Nita give her a calculated look that didn't bode well. "Go get my pink sweater. It's on my bed upstairs. And stay out of my jewelry. If you touch anything, I'll know it."

Blue drove a mental knife into Nita's black heart and stomped through the old woman's overly decorated living room to get to the second floor. She could polish off the portrait and be on the road in a week. She'd survived a lot worse than spending a few days with Nita Garrison. This was her fastest ticket out of town.

All but one of the doors had been closed off upstairs, leaving the hallway marginally neater than the rooms below, although the pink plush carpeting needed vacuuming and a collection of dead bugs clouded the bottom of the cut glass ceiling fixtures. Nita's room, with its rose and gold wallpaper, white furniture, and long windows elaborately swagged in rose drapes, reminded Blue of a Las Vegas funeral home. She picked up the pink sweater from a gold velvet chair and carried it downstairs through the white and gold living room, which had a velour chaise, lamps dangling crystal prisms, and wall-to-wall rose carpeting.

Nita shuffled into the doorway, her swollen ankles spilling over her orthopedic oxfords, and held out a set of keys to Blue. "Before you start work, you need to drive me to the—"

"Please don't say the Piggly Wiggly."

Apparently Nita had never seen *Driving Miss Daisy* because she missed the allusion. "We don't have a Piggly Wiggly in Garrison. I don't let any of the chains move in here. If you want your money, you have to drive me to the bank."

"Before I drive you anywhere," Blue said, "call off your dogs. Tell them to get back to work on Dean's house."

"Later."

"Now. I'll help you look up the phone numbers."

Nita surprised Blue by barely putting up a fight, although it took another hour for her to make the calls, during which she ordered Blue to empty all the wastebaskets in the house, find her Maalox, and take a pile of boxes down into the creepy basement. Finally, however, Blue was behind the wheel of a sporty, three-year-old red Corvette Roadster. "You were expecting a Town Car, weren't you?" Nita sniffed from the passenger seat. "Or a Crown Victoria. An old lady's car."

"I was expecting a broomstick," Blue muttered, taking in the dusty dashboard. "How long since this thing's been out of the garage?"

"I can't drive anymore with my hip, but I let it run once a week so the battery doesn't die."

"It's best to keep the garage door down while you're doing that. A good thirty minutes should take care of it."

Nita sucked on her teeth, as if she were drawing venom.

"So how do you get around?" Blue asked.

"That fool Chauncey Crole. He drives what passes for the town's taxi. But he's always spitting out the window, and that turns my stomach. His wife used to run the Garrison Women's Club. They all hated me, right from the beginning."

"Big surprise there." Blue turned out onto the town's main street.

"I got even."

"Tell me you didn't eat their children."

"You have a wisecrack for everything, don't you? Pull in at the pharmacy."

Blue wished she'd kept a leash on her tongue. Hearing more about Nita's relationship with the good women of Garrison would have been a nice distraction. "I thought you were going to the bank."

"First, I need you to pick up my prescription."

"I'm an artist, not your errand girl."

"I need my medication. Or is fetching an old lady's medication too much trouble for you?"

Blue's mood sank from dejection to misery.

After stopping at the drugstore, which had a WE DELIVER sign prominently displayed in the front window, Nita made her run into the grocery for dog food and All-Bran, then stop at the bakery for *one* banana nut muffin. Finally, Blue had to wait while Nita got a manicure at Barb's Tresses and Day Spa. Blue used the time to buy a banana nut muffin of her own and a cup of coffee, which used up three of her last twelve dollars.

She peeled back the tab on the cup lid and waited for a silver Dodge Ram truck to pass so she could cross the street to the car. But the truck didn't pass. Instead, it braked, then angled in front of a fire hydrant. The door swung open and a familiar pair of gay boots emerged, followed by an equally familiar set of lean, denim-clad legs.

She succumbed to a ridiculous moment of giddiness before she frowned at the gleaming truck. "Don't tell me."

Chapter Seventeen

"*Where the hell have you been?*" Dean wore a biscuit-colored cowboy hat and a pair of high-tech brushed metal sunglasses with yellow lenses. A few hours earlier, he'd been her lover, and that made him a walking, talking road hazard blocking the highway that made up her life. From the beginning, she'd given him little pieces of herself, but last night she'd handed over a major chunk, and now she intended to get it back.

He slammed the door. "If you wanted to take a bike ride this morning, you should have woken me up. I was planning to ride anyway."

"That truck is yours, isn't it?"

"You can't have a farm without a truck." Heads were starting to poke up in store windows. He grabbed her arm and drew her against the side panel. "What are you doing here, Blue? You didn't even leave a note. I was worried."

She rose to her toes and planted a quick kiss on the side of that belligerent jaw. "I needed to get to town to start my new job, and my forms of transportation were limited, so I borrowed the bike. You'll get it back."

He yanked off his sunglasses. "What new job?" His eyes narrowed. "Don't tell me."

She pointed her coffee cup toward the Corvette roadster across the street. "It's not all bad news. She owns a great car."

"You are *not* painting that old lady's dog."

"My current net worth isn't enough to cover one of your tips at McDonald's."

"I've never met anybody so obsessed with money." He shoved his glasses back on. "Get over it, Blue. You're giving money way too much power in your life."

"Yeah, well, as soon as I'm a multimillionaire jock, I'll stop doing that."

He yanked out his wallet, peeled off a roll of bills, and stuffed them in the side pockets of her jeans. "Your net worth just took a turn for the better. Now where's the bike? We have things to do."

She withdrew the money. A stack of fifties. Her jaundiced face stared back at her from his yellow lenses. "What exactly is this for?"

"What do you mean, what's it for? It's for you."

"I gathered that, but what did I do to earn it?"

He knew exactly where she was headed, but he was an expert at throwing touchdown passes off the wrong foot, and he let one fly. "You spent all weekend in Knoxville picking out my furniture."

"I helped April pick out your furniture. And I was more than adequately compensated with great meals, a first-class hotel, and a massage. Thanks for that, by the way. It felt terrific."

"You're my cook."

"So far, you've eaten three pancakes and some miscellaneous leftovers."

"*And* you painted my kitchen!"

"I painted part of your kitchen and your dining room ceiling."

"There you go."

"You've fed, housed, and transported me for more than a week," she said. "That makes us almost even."

"Are you keeping a ledger? What about that mural you're painting in my dining room? The *murals*. I want four of them, one for each wall. And I'm having Heath draw up a damned contract today."

She pushed the bills into his front pocket. "Stop trying to manipulate me. You don't care anything about murals. That was April's idea."

"I do care. I liked the idea from the beginning, and I like it even more now. It's also a perfect solution to this problem you've created. But for some reason, you're afraid to go ahead with it. Explain that to me. Explain why you're upset by the idea of painting some murals for a man you're *indebted to*."

"Because I don't want to."

"I'm offering you a legitimate job. It's got to beat working for that crazy old bat."

"Save your breath, okay? So far, the only real service I've provided happened last night, and even a dumb-ass like you has to see I can't take your money after that."

He had the nerve to sneer. "Were we in the same bed? Because, the way I remember, I was the one providing the damn service. You want to reduce everything to commerce? Fine. Then you should pay me. As a matter of fact, I'm sending you a bill. For a thousand dollars! That's right. You owe me a grand. For services provided."

"A thousand dollars? As if. I had to fantasize about my old boyfriends just to get excited."

It wasn't quite the discussion-ending blow she'd hoped to deliver because he laughed. Not a mean laugh, which would have lifted her spirits, but a highly amused laugh.

"Girl!"

Blue winced as Nita chose that moment to emerge from Barb's Tresses and Day Spa, her freshly painted crimson talons curling around her cane. "Girl! Come help me across the street."

Dean gave Nita an obnoxiously cheerful smile. "Good morning, Mrs. Garrison."

"Good morning, Deke."

"It's Dean, ma'am."

"I don't think so." She thrust her purse toward Blue. "Carry this, girl. It's heavy. And watch my nails. You'd better not have been wasting my gas while I was inside."

Dean hooked his thumb in his jeans pocket. "I feel a whole lot better now that I see how well the two of you are getting along."

Blue grabbed Nita by the elbow and steered her into the street. "Your car's parked over here."

"I have eyes."

"I'll swing by the house and pick up the bike on my way back to the farm," Dean called out. "You all have a nice day now."

Blue pretended not to hear.

"Take me home," Nita said as she resettled in the passenger seat.

"What about the bank?"

"I'm tired. I'll write you a check."

Only three days, Blue told herself as she sneaked a look back toward the truck.

Dean stood with a foot propped on the fire hydrant and one of the local beauties hanging off his arm.

When they got back to the house, Nita insisted Blue take Tango for a walk so they could get acquainted. Since Tango was lame and a thousand years old, Blue let him snooze under a hydrangea while she sat on the curb out of sight of the house and tried not to think about the future.

Nita maneuvered her into making lunch, but first Blue had to clean up the kitchen. As she dried off the last of the pans, a silver Ram truck pulled up in the alley behind the house. She watched Dean get out and retrieve the bike she'd left by the back door. He threw it in the rear of the truck, then turned to the window where she was standing and tipped his cowboy hat.

♥

First Jack heard the music, and then he saw April. It was dark, just past ten o'clock, and she sat on the cottage's sagging front porch underneath a crooked metal light fixture, painting her toenails. The years evaporated. In her clingy black top and pink shorts, she looked so much like the twenty-year-old he remembered that he forgot to watch where he was going and tripped on a tree root inside the broken-down picket fence.

April looked up. And immediately looked back down again. He'd been rotten to her last night, and she hadn't forgotten.

All day he'd witnessed her relentless efficiency as she'd directed the house painters who'd finally straggled in, argued with a plumber, supervised the unloading of a truckload of furniture, and pointedly avoided him. Only the men's gazes following her were familiar.

He stopped at the foot of the wooden steps and tilted his head toward the raucous music. She'd perched on an old Adirondack chair with her foot propped on the seat. "What are you listening to?" he said.

"Skullhead Julie." She kept her attention firmly fixed on her toes.

"Who's that?"

"An alternative group out of L.A." Her long, jagged hair fell over her face as she reached back to lower the volume. Most women her age had cut their hair, but she'd never followed trends. When everyone else had worn the Farrah flip, April had adopted a brutal geometric cut that had showcased those amazing blue eyes and made her the center of attention.

"You were always the first to spot new talent," he said.

"I don't really keep up anymore."

"I doubt that."

She blew on her toes, another excuse to freeze him out. "If you came to get Riley, you're about an hour too late. She got tired and fell asleep in the second bedroom."

He'd barely seen Riley today. All morning, she'd followed April around, and in the afternoon, she'd gone off with Dean on a purple bike he'd pulled from the bed of his new truck. When they'd gotten back, she'd been red-faced and sweaty, but she'd also been happy.

He should have been the one to buy her a bike, but he hadn't thought of it.

April shoved the brush into the bottle. "I'm surprised it took you so long to get over here. I could have been spiking her milk with uppers or filling her head with stories of your seedy past."

"Now you're being petulant." He propped his foot on the bottom step. "I was a real prick last night. I came over to apologize."

"Go ahead."

"I thought that's what I just did."

"Think again."

He deserved everything she was throwing out and more, but he couldn't hold back a smile as he stepped up to the edge of the porch. "You want me to grovel?"

"For starters."

"I would, but I don't know how. Too many years of having everybody kiss my ass."

"Try."

"How about I begin by admitting you were right," he said. "I have no idea what I'm doing with her. That makes me feel stupid and guilty, and since I don't know how to deal with either one, I took it out on you."

"Promising. Now say the rest."

"Give me a hint."

"You're scared out of your mind, and you need my help this week."

"Yeah, that, too." Despite her pugnacity, he knew he'd hurt her. Lately he seemed to be hurting a lot of people. He gazed out toward the woods where the fireflies were beginning to show off. Peeling paint scraped his elbow as he leaned against one of the porch's candlestick posts. "I'd give anything for a cigarette right now."

She dropped one foot and pulled the other up. "I don't miss cigarettes so much. Or drugs, for that matter. For me, it's alcohol. Scary to think about living the rest of your life without a glass of wine or a margarita."

"Maybe you could handle it now."

"I'm an addict," she said with an honesty that unsettled him. "I can't ever drink again."

From inside the cottage, her cell rang. Quickly capping the bottle, she jumped up to answer it. As the screen door banged behind her, he shoved his hands in his pockets. Today he'd found a set of blueprints, for the screen porch. His dad had been a carpenter, and Jack had grown up with blueprints and tools lying around, but he couldn't remember the last time he'd held a hammer in his hands.

He gazed through the screen into the empty living room and heard the muted sound of April's voice. The hell with it. He went inside. She stood with her back to him and her forehead resting on the arm she'd propped against one of the kitchen cabinets. "You know how much I care," she said so softly that he could barely make out the words. "Call me in the morning, all right?"

Too many decades had passed for him to feel these old stabs of jealousy, so he focused on the brochure lying on the counter. As he picked it up, she closed her phone and gestured with it toward the brochure. "That's a group I volunteer with."

"Heart Gallery? I've never heard of it."

"It's made up of professional photographers who volunteer their time to take these amazing portraits of adoptable kids in the foster care system. We display them in local galleries. They're more personal than the mug shots social services takes, and a lot of kids have found families through the exhibits."

"How long have you been doing this?"

"About five years." She padded back toward the porch. "I started out styling the sittings for a photographer I know—putting the kids in clothes that reflected their personalities, coming up with props, helping them feel comfortable. Now I'm doing some of the portraits myself. Or at least I was until I came out here. You'd be shocked how much I love it."

He pocketed the brochure and followed her out to the porch. He wanted to ask about the guy on the phone but didn't. "I'm surprised you never got married."

She picked up the nail polish bottle and resumed her perch on the Adirondack chair. "By the time I was sane enough for marriage, I'd lost interest."

"I can't imagine you without a man."

"Stop fishing."

"Not exactly fishing. Just trying to figure out who you are now."

"You want to define me with a head count," she said bluntly.

"I guess."

"You want to know if I'm still the bad girl solely responsible for the fall of countless good men too weak to keep their pants zipped."

"Put like that . . ."

She blew on her big toe. "Who's that brunette I spotted last week traveling with your entourage? Your valet?"

"A very efficient assistant I've never seen naked. So are you serious about anybody right now?"

"Very serious. About myself."

"That's good."

She wiped off a polish smudge. "Tell me about you and Marli. You were married for what? Five minutes?"

"A year and a half. Ancient history. I was forty-two and thought it was time to settle down. She was young, beautiful, and sweet—at least I thought so at the time. I loved her voice. I still do. The demons didn't come out until after we were married and discovered we hated everything about each other. I'm here to tell you that woman did not like sarcasm. But it wasn't all bad. I got Riley."

Following Marli, he'd had two long-term relationships that had been well covered by the press. Although he'd cared a lot about both women, something fundamental had been missing, and with one failed marriage behind him, he hadn't been eager to enter another.

April finished her toes, capped the polish bottle, and unfolded those endlessly long legs. "Don't send Riley away, Jack. Not to summer camp, not to Marli's sister, and especially not to boarding school in the fall. Keep her with you."

"I can't do that. I have a tour coming up. What am I supposed to do? Lock her in a hotel room?"

"You'll figure it out."

"You have too much faith in me." He stared out at the sad excuse for a fence. "Did Riley tell you about last night? With Dean."

Her head shot up like a mother lion sniffing the air for danger to her cub. "What?"

He sat on the top step and told her exactly what had happened. "I'm not trying to make excuses," he said as he finished, "but Riley was screaming, and he was chasing her."

She came out of her chair. "He'd never do anything to hurt her. I can't believe you tackled him. You're lucky he didn't break your stupid neck."

She was right. Although he stayed in shape so he could keep delivering the high-octane concerts that were his trademark, he was hardly a match for a thirty-one-year-old pro athlete. "That's not all of it." He rose from the step. "Afterward, Dean and I had a talk, or at least I talked. I hung out all my sins. Complete honesty. Needless to say, he was thrilled."

"Leave him alone, Jack," she said wearily. "He's taken enough shit from both of us."

"Yeah." He glanced toward the door. "I'd rather not wake Riley. Is it okay if she sleeps here tonight?"

"Sure." She turned away to go back inside, and he almost made it down the steps. Almost, but not quite. "Aren't you the least bit curious?" he said, gazing back at her. "Don't you want to know what it would be like for us now?"

Her hand stilled on the screen door handle. For a moment she didn't say anything, but when she finally spoke, her voice was a ribbon of steel. "Not even a little bit."

♥

Riley couldn't hear what April and her dad had been saying, but their voices had woken her up. She felt cozy lying in bed inside the cottage, knowing they were talking to each other. They'd made Dean together, so they must have loved each other sometime.

She scratched an itch on her calf with her big toe. She'd had so much fun today she'd forgotten to be sad. April had given her cool jobs to do, like looking for flowers to make a bouquet and getting drinks for the painters. This afternoon she'd gone on a bike ride with Dean. Pedaling on the gravel had been hard, but he hadn't called her pokey or anything, and he'd said she had to throw the ball around with him tomorrow so he could get in some practice. Just thinking about it made her nervous, but excited, too. She missed Blue, but when she'd asked Dean about her, he'd started talking about something else. Riley hoped him and Blue weren't breaking up. Her mom had always been breaking up.

She heard April moving around, so she pulled the sheet up to her chin and lay very still just in case April decided to check on her. Riley had already noticed that she did that kind of stuff.

♥

As the next few days passed, Blue told herself it was a good thing Dean was staying away because she needed all her wits to deal with Nita. Still, she missed him badly. She wanted to believe he missed her just as much, but why should he? He'd gotten what he wanted.

A good old-fashioned case of loneliness settled over her. Nita decided she wanted to be in the portrait with Tango, but she also wanted Blue to paint her as she'd been, not as she was. This involved digging through a stack of scrapbooks and photo albums, with Nita's crimson-tipped fingernail stabbing at one page after another, pointing out the flaws of everyone she'd been photographed with—a fellow dance instructor, a slutty roommate, a long series of men who'd done her wrong.

"Do you like anybody?" Blue said in frustration on Saturday morning as they sat on the white velour living room couch surrounded by discarded photo albums.

Nita flicked the page with her gnarled finger. "I liked them all at the time. I was naive about human nature."

Despite Blue's frustration at not being able to get started on the painting, she found a certain fascination in seeing Nita's life unfold from her teenage years growing up in Brooklyn during the war, to the oft-mentioned fifties and early sixties when she'd taught ballroom dancing. She'd had a short-lived marriage to an actor she labeled "a drinker," sold cosmetics, worked as a model at trade shows, and been a hatcheck girl at various high-end New York restaurants.

In the early seventies, she'd met and married Marshall Garrison. Her wedding photograph showed a voluptuous platinum blonde with a beehive, heavy eye makeup, and pale frosted lips gazing adoringly at a distinguished-looking older man in a white suit. Her hips were slim, her legs long, her skin firm and unwrinkled, exactly the kind of woman who turned male heads.

"He thought I was thirty-two," Nita said. "He was fifty himself, and I worked myself into a fit worrying what he'd do when he found out that I was really forty. But he was crazy about me, and he didn't care."

"You look so happy here. What happened?"

"I came to Garrison."

Turning the album pages, Blue watched as Nita's anxious-to-please smiles gradually turned to bitterness. "When was this taken?"

"Our Christmas party the second year we were married. When I'd lost the illusion that I could make everybody like me."

The resentful expressions of the female guests showed exactly how they felt about the brash Brooklyn interloper in her big earrings and too short skirt who'd stolen the town's most important citizen. On another page, Blue studied a photo of Nita standing off by herself at someone's backyard party, a tense smile plastered on her face. Blue flipped to a picture of Marshall. "Your husband was very handsome."

"He knew it, too."

"You didn't even like *him*?"

"I thought he had a backbone when I married him."

"You probably sucked it out of him while you were drinking his blood."

Nita's bottom lip curled, and she took a pull on her teeth, her favorite way of expressing disapproval. Blue had heard that unpleasant sucking sound more times than she could count.

"Get me my magnifier," Nita demanded. "I want to see if Bertie Johnson's mole shows up in this picture. The homeliest woman I've ever met, but she had the gall to criticize my clothes. She told everybody I was ostentatious. I fixed her."

"Knife or gun?"

Suck. Suck. "When her husband lost his job, I hired her to clean my house. Mrs. High and Mighty didn't like that at all, especially since I always made her do the toilets twice."

Blue had no trouble imagining Nita lording it over the unfortunate Bertie Johnson. Nita had been doing exactly that to Blue for the past four days. She demanded homemade cookies, ordered Blue to clean up after Tango, and had even put her in charge of hiring a new cleaning lady—a daunting task, since nobody wanted to work for her. Blue snapped the album closed. "I've seen more than enough to start working. My sketches are finished, and if you'll just leave me alone for a while this afternoon, I can get something done."

Not only had Nita declared she wanted to be in the painting, but she'd also decided she wanted it done on a much grander scale, so she could hang it in the foyer. Blue had special-ordered the canvas and increased the price accordingly. She'd have more than enough money to get started in a new city . . . if she could only get out of Garrison, something Nita was doing her best to prevent.

"How are you going to paint anything decent when you're mooning over that football player all the time?"

"I am not." Blue hadn't caught so much as a glimpse of him since she'd met him Tuesday on the street, and when she'd driven back to the farm to get her things, he'd been gone.

Nita reached for her cane. "Face it, Miss Big Talk. Your so-called engagement is over. A man like that wants a lot more in a woman than you've got."

"As you keep reminding me."

Nita regarded her smugly. "All you have to do is look in the mirror."

"Are you ever going to die?"

Nita's bottom lip curled, and she took a noisy tug on her front teeth. "He's broken your heart, and you won't admit it."

"He hasn't broken my heart. For your information, I use men. I don't let them use me."

"Oh, yeah, you're a real Mata Harry, all right."

Blue grabbed two of the albums. "I'm going up to my room so I can get to work. Don't interrupt me."

"You're not going anywhere until you make my lunch. I want a grilled cheese sandwich. Use Velveeta, not that crap you bought."

"It's called cheddar."

"I don't like it."

Blue sighed and headed for the kitchen. Just as she opened the refrigerator, she heard a knock at the back door. Her heart tripped. She hurried over and saw it was April and Riley. As glad as she was to see them, she couldn't help but be just a little disappointed. "Come in. I've missed you."

"We've missed you, too." April patted her cheek. "Especially your cooking. We would have stopped by yesterday, but I got held up at the house."

Blue hugged Riley. "You look beautiful." Since Blue had seen her five days ago, Riley's long, shapeless tangle had been replaced by a short, curly cut that showcased the oval of her face. Instead of her tight, too fussy clothes, she wore a pair of khaki shorts that fit her comfortably, along with a simple green top that showcased her eyes and complemented her olive skin, which had already lost its pasty look.

"Who's there?" The old woman materialized in the kitchen doorway and took in April with a disparaging glare. "Who are you?"

Blue made a face. "Am I the only one who hears a cauldron boiling?"

April pulled in her smile. "I'm Dean Robillard's housekeeper."

"Blue is still mooning over your boss," Nita said self-righteously. "He hasn't come to see her once, but she won't admit it's finished."

"I'm not mooning. I'm—"

"She lives in fairy-tale land that one, thinking Prince Charming is going to rescue her from her pathetic life." Nita tugged on one of her three necklaces and zeroed in on the eleven-year-old. "What's your name? Something odd."

"Riley."

"It sounds like a boy's name."

Before Blue could put Nita in her place, Riley said, "Maybe. But it's a lot better than Trinity."

"In your opinion. If I'd ever had a child, I would have named her Jennifer." She pointed her cane toward the doorway. "Come into the living room with me. I need a fresh set of eyes to read my horoscope. Somebody else couldn't be bothered." She glared at Blue.

"Riley came to visit me," Blue said, "and she's staying right here."

"You're coddling her again." She regarded Riley with disapproval. "She treats you like a baby."

Riley looked down at her sandals. "Not exactly."

"Well?" Nita said imperiously. "Are you coming with me or not?"

Riley nibbled on her lip. "I guess so."

"Hold it." Blue curled her arm around Riley's shoulders. "You're staying right here with me."

To her shock, Riley edged away after only a moment's hesitation. "I'm not afraid of her."

Nita's nostrils flared. "Why should you be afraid of me? I like children."

"For *dinner,*" Blue retorted.

Nita sucked her teeth, then said to Riley, "Don't just stand there."

"Stop where you are," Blue said as Riley began following Nita toward the living room. "You're my guest, Riley, not hers."

"I know, but I guess I have to go with her," Riley said with a note of resignation.

Blue exchanged a look with April, who gave a nearly indiscernible nod. Blue planted a hand on her hip and pointed toward Nita. "I swear, if you say one mean thing to her, I'll set your bed on fire after you fall asleep tonight. I mean it. Riley, you tell me what she says."

Riley rubbed her arm nervously. "Uh . . . Okay."

Nita pursed her lips at April. "Do you hear the way she talks to me? You're a witness. If anything happens to me, call the police." She gazed at Riley. "I hope you don't spit when you read. I can't stand that."

"No, ma'am."

"Speak up. And straighten those shoulders. You need to learn how to walk."

Blue waited for the defeated look to come over Riley, but the eleven-year-old took a deep breath, pushed her shoulders back, and marched into the living room. "Don't pay attention to anything she says," Blue called after her. "She's mean to the bone."

The sucking finally faded.

Blue stared at April. "Why is she going with her?"

"She's testing herself. Last night she took Puffy outside after dark for an unnecessary walk, and this morning, when she saw a snake by the pond, she made herself walk around the edge so she could get a closer look at it, even though she was pale as a sheet." She took the chair Blue indicated. "It's frustrating. She had the guts to run away from Nashville—the story behind that will curl your hair—and she stood up to her father, but she sees herself as being afraid of every-thing."

"She's a great kid." Blue peered into the living room to reassure herself that Riley was still alive, then pulled the cookie tin out of the cupboard and carried it over to the kitchen table.

"How can you stand living with that woman?" April took one of the homemade sugar cookies Blue offered.

"I'm pretty adaptable." Blue grabbed a cookie herself and sat down in the gilded chair across the table from April. "Riley's an amazing kid."

"I suspect Dean's the reason behind all this testing she's doing. I overheard him talking to her about mental toughness."

A golden-haired elephant had wandered into the kitchen. "He's finally acknowledged her?"

April nodded and filled Blue in on what had happened last Tues-day night, the same night Dean had shown up in the caravan and they'd made love. Blue knew he'd been in pain, and now she under-stood what had caused it. She broke off the edge of her cookie and changed the subject. "How are things going at the house?"

April stretched her catlike body. "The painters finished up, and the furniture is beginning to arrive. But the guys who are supposed to be building the screen porch picked up another job during Nita's boy-cott and can't come back for two weeks. Believe it or not, Jack's taken over. He started framing the porch on Wednesday."

"Jack?"

"Whenever he needs an extra set of hands, he barks at Dean to come help him. Today they worked all afternoon and barely said a word to each other." She reached for a second cookie and moaned.

"God, these are good. I don't know what you and Dean are fighting about, but I wish you'd make up so you could come back and cook. Riley and I are getting tired of cereal and sandwiches."

If only it were that simple. "Once I finish this portrait, I'm leaving Garrison."

April looked disappointed, which was nice. "So your engagement is officially off?"

"We were never engaged. Dean picked me up two weeks ago on the highway outside Denver." Blue told her about Monty and the beaver costume.

April didn't seem all that surprised. "You do live an interesting life."

♥

In the living room, Riley finished reading Mrs. Garrison's horoscope. It said romance was in the picture, which made Riley so embarrassed she wanted to make something else up, but she couldn't think of anything. Riley wished she was in the kitchen with April and Blue, but Dean said she had to stop letting people know how much they scared her. Dean said she should watch how Blue took care of herself and do the same thing, except without hitting anybody, unless she absolutely had to.

Mrs. Garrison grabbed the newspaper like she thought Riley might steal it. "That woman in the kitchen. I thought her name was Susan. That's what I heard in town."

Nobody except Blue knew that April was Dean's mother. "I think April might be her middle name."

"Are you related to her? What are you doing at the farm?"

Riley poked at the couch arm. She wished she could tell Mrs. Garrison that Dean Robillard was her brother. "April's a friend of the family. She's sort of like . . . my stepmom."

"Humph." Mrs. Garrison stared at her. "You look better today than you did last week."

She meant Riley's hair. April had taken her to get it cut, and they'd also gotten some new clothes. Even though it had only been a week, Riley's belly didn't seem to stick out so far, maybe because she didn't have so much time to be bored and eat. Whenever she wanted to go to April's cottage she had to walk, and she had to take care of Puffy. The bike riding was hard with the hills, and then Dean made her throw the football around. Sometimes she wished the two of them could just sit still and talk, but he liked to be doing stuff all the time. She'd started to think maybe he was ADHD like Benny Phaler, or maybe it was just because he was a boy and a football player.

"I got my hair cut," she said. "Plus, there isn't too much junk food lying around, and I've been riding my bike a lot."

Mrs. Garrison's lips got all puckered, and Riley saw that some of her pink lipstick had run into the creases. "Blue turned nasty that day at Josie's just because I said you were fat."

She twisted her hands in her lap and remembered that Dean said she had to keep standing up for herself. "I know I am. But what you said kind of hurt my feelings."

"Then you have to stop being so sensitive when it's obvious someone's having a bad day. Besides, you don't look so fat now. It's good you're doing something about it."

"Not on purpose."

"It doesn't matter. You should study dance so you can move better. I used to teach ballroom dancing."

"I went to ballet for a while, but I wasn't any good, so I dropped out."

"You should have stuck with it. Ballet builds confidence."

"The teacher told my au pair that I was hopeless."

"And you let her get away with it? Where was your pride?"

"I don't think I have too much."

"It's time you get some. Grab that book over there, put it on your head, and walk."

Riley didn't want to, but she crossed the room toward this gold swan table and put the book she found there on top of her head. It slid off right away. She picked it up and tried again with more success.

"Turn your thumbs so they're pointing straight ahead," Mrs. Garrison ordered. "It'll open up your chest and pull your shoulders back."

Riley tried it and decided she felt taller, more grown-up.

"There. You finally look like somebody who has a good opinion of herself. I want you to walk like this from now on, got it?"

"Yes, ma'am."

April poked her head in. "Time to go, Riley."

The book slipped off Riley's head, and she leaned down to pick it up. Mrs. Garrison's eyes squeezed into little slits, like she was getting ready to say something really mean about Riley being fat and clumsy, but she didn't. "Do you want a job, girl?"

"A job?"

"Get the wax out of your ears. Come back next week and you can walk Tango for me. Blue's worthless. She says she's walking him, but all she does is take him around the corner and let him sleep."

"Because he's too old to walk," Blue called out from the kitchen.

Wrinkles folded up between Mrs. Garrison's eyebrows like she might be thinking she was getting too old to walk, too. Somehow it made Riley less afraid of her. She sort of liked what Mrs. Garrison had said about how Riley finally looked like somebody with a good opinion of herself. April, Dean, and her dad were always saying nice things to her, but they were just trying to build her self-esteem, and Riley didn't believe them. Mrs. Garrison didn't care about stuff like self-esteem, so if she said something good, it was probably true. Riley decided to practice more with the book when she got back to the farm.

"Blue, bring me my purse!"

"Is there a gun in it?" Blue shot back.

Riley couldn't believe the way Blue talked to Mrs. Garrison. Mrs.

Garrison must really, really need her or she'd make Blue leave. She wondered if Blue had figured that out yet.

When Mrs. Garrison got her purse, she pulled out a five-dollar bill and held it toward Riley. "Don't buy candy with this or anything fattening."

Riley's dad always gave her twenties, and she didn't need more money, but it would be rude to refuse. "Thank you, Mrs. Garrison."

"Just remember what I told you about your posture." She snapped her purse closed. "Blue will drive out to the farm to get you next week."

"I'm not sure if I'll still be here," Riley said. Her dad hadn't told her what day they were leaving, and she was afraid to ask him because, more than anything, she wanted to stay at the farm for the rest of her life.

♥

On the way home, April reached over and patted Riley's leg. She didn't say anything. She just patted. She also hugged a lot and touched Riley's hair and made Riley dance with her. Sometimes April acted just like a mom, except she wasn't always talking about calories and boyfriends. Also, Riley's mom had never said the curses April did. Mainly Riley liked the way April smelled, like wood and flowers and spiral notebook paper. She would never say it out loud, but sometimes being with April was even better than being with Dean, because Riley didn't have to run around after a football all the time.

She started to smile, even though she had a ton of things to worry about. She couldn't wait to tell Dean that she'd been alone with Mrs. Garrison, and she'd hardly been scared at all.

Chapter Eighteen

Blue's bedroom might be the smallest on the second floor, but it was also the farthest from her employer's, and it had a tiny balcony overlooking the backyard. She sat cross-legged on the pink plush carpet, her back against the puffy floral bedspread as she studied the drawing she'd just finished. Nita's eyes looked like a ferret's. She'd have to fix that. Or maybe not.

The gilt bedside clock pointed to midnight. She set her sketchbook aside, yawned, and closed her eyes. In her mind, she saw the caravan nestled under the trees. She imagined a light flickering in the window, calling her home. But the caravan wasn't home, and she'd get over missing it the same way she'd gotten over missing all the other places she'd left behind. All the other people she'd left behind.

Something hit the balcony door, and she jumped. As she twisted around, she saw a looming figure. Her heart lurched. A melee of emotions—anticipation, dread, anger—struck her all at once. She pushed herself up from the carpet, stomped over to the door, and yanked it open. "What do you think you're doing? I almost had a coronary."

"I do that to women." Dean stepped inside. He smelled spicy and exotic, while she smelled like hash browns. He took in her wrinkled Goodyear T-shirt with old paint stains on the logo. She hadn't even washed her hair this morning because Nita kept banging her cane on the bathroom door demanding breakfast. Still, he seemed a lot more critical of the pink-on-pink bedroom than of her. "Where do you keep your Barbies?"

"You could have called," she retorted. "Or, better yet, continued to ignore me." She sounded like a sulky ex-girlfriend, but it hurt that he'd stayed away, even though that's what she'd wanted him to do.

"Now where's the fun in calling?" He wore faded button-fly jeans and a fitted black shirt with a tuxedo-pleated front. Who would even think of putting together something like that? And pulling it off so perfectly.

"How did you know this was my room?"

He slipped his finger under the bunched sleeve of her T-shirt and straightened it. "The only one with the light still on."

If it weren't so late, if Nita hadn't tested the last ounce of her patience, if Blue hadn't missed him so much, she'd have done a better job of hiding her feelings of ill use. As it was, she snatched her arm away. "You've ignored me all week, and now you decide to show up in the middle of the night."

"I knew you'd miss me if I gave you half a chance."

"Go away."

He gazed down at her with those dreamy blue-gray eyes and brushed her cheekbone with his thumb. "You're worn out. Have you finally had enough?"

She pulled her eyes away from the suntanned V of skin at his open shirt collar. "More than enough."

"Good. I'll let you come back."

She couldn't help it. She sucked her teeth.

His lip curled. "You're going to be your normal pigheaded self, aren't you?"

"I don't know how to be anyone else." She grabbed a stack of clean laundry and stuffed it in the dresser. "Go away. I didn't invite you up here, and I don't feel like sparring with you."

"That's a first." He folded himself into the overstuffed pink ruffled boudoir chair. He should have looked silly, but the chair only made him look more masculine. "Here's the thing, Blue. I'm not saying you're selfish, but I do think you could consider somebody other than yourself once in a while." He extended his legs and crossed his ankles. "Like Riley, for example. She hasn't had a decent meal since you left."

"Hire a cook." Blue knelt down to pick up her sketches from the carpet.

"You know I can't do that while Mad Jack is around. He decided he wants to build that damned porch himself. So far, the workmen haven't recognized him, but that's only because he keeps to himself, and nobody expects to see a rock star standing on a ladder with a hammer in his hand." Long, denim-clad legs stretched in front of her. "But hiring household help is asking for trouble."

She snatched a drawing pencil from under his heel. "Jack's leaving soon, and so is Riley. Your problem's disappearing."

"I'm not so sure about that." He drew his leg in. "I don't ask for favors easily, but we could use a little help."

She picked up the last of her drawings and stood. "I already have a job."

"And it's making you miserable." He rose from the powder puff chair.

As she gazed up at him, the small bedroom seemed to grow even smaller. There was one sure way to get him out of here. "How much will you pay me?"

She waited for him to start pulling hundred-dollar bills from his pockets, so she could kick him out. Instead, he rubbed his thumb over a bandage on his wrist. "Nothing. I'm asking you to do this as a favor. A home-cooked dinner on Sunday."

Just like that, he'd yanked away her moral high ground.

"I know it's a lot to ask," he said, "but all of us would really appreciate it. If you give me a list, I can pick up whatever you need."

She'd been certain he'd offer her money, which would have given her a perfect excuse to throw his Sunday dinner back in his face, but he'd outmaneuvered her, and now she'd feel churlish if she refused. She dropped her sketches on the bed and thought about how much she missed the farm. She wanted to talk to Riley. She wanted to see how the new furniture looked and check up on Puffy and embarrass herself in front of Jack. She wanted to be part of it all again. Her old weakness—trying to belong where she didn't. "Is everybody going to be there?"

His mouth tightened. "You want another chance to act like an idiot in front of Mad Jack, don't you?"

"I'm more mature now."

"Sure you are." He picked up her sketches from the bed. "Yeah, they'll all be there. Tell me what you need."

As long as she stayed with the group, she could go. Just this once. She mentally reviewed the contents of the pantry and gave him a short list, which he didn't bother to write down. He held up her final sketch. "This is great, but I thought you were painting her dog."

"Nita decided she has to be in the portrait, too." Nita cared more about keeping Blue around as her indentured servant than she cared about the painting. "Are you ready to go home yet?"

His gaze wandered to the bed. "Definitely not."

She set her hand on her hip. "I'm supposed to take off my clothes just because you got bored and decided to hop over my balcony railing tonight? I don't think so."

His eyebrows drew together. "It really bothers you, doesn't it, that I stayed away." He jabbed his finger in the general direction of her face. "You're not the only one who's allowed to be pissed off."

"I didn't do anything to you! I needed a job, and don't tell me I had one with you because I didn't."

"I was counting on you, and you turned your back on me. Obviously, you didn't care how I felt."

He looked honestly angry, but she didn't believe him. "You're overprivileged, overindulged, and perfectly capable of holding your own with all of them. What really bothers you is not getting your way." She marched to the balcony door so she could throw him out, but as she pushed the handle, she imagined his body sprawled on the ground with his legs twisted underneath him, and she backed away.

"What really bothers me," he said from behind her, "is believing you were someone I could count on."

She set her jaw against a twinge of guilt and headed across the room. "You're going out the front door. Don't make any noise, or I'll never hear the end of it."

He shot her a hard look, stepped in front of her, and opened the door himself. She followed him out into the pink-carpeted hallway, past an excruciatingly ugly painting of a Venetian canal, and down the steps, so she could lock the door behind him. Just past the landing, he stopped cold and turned. She was on a higher step, and their eyes met. In the light from the dusty crystal chandelier, his face was both familiar and mysterious. She pretended she understood him, but how could she? He lived in the stars, and she was good, solid earth.

She stood without moving as he lifted his arms and channeled his fingers into her hair. The loose rubber band that had been barely holding up her ponytail gave way as he tunneled under it.

His kiss was harsh and thrilling. She forgot everything she knew about herself and slipped her arms around his neck. Tilting her head, she opened her mouth. He cupped her bottom and squeezed. She pressed closer, and her hips rubbed against him.

He broke away so suddenly she got a head rush and had to grab the railing. Of course, he noticed. She flipped her hair, sending the dangling rubber band flying. "You are so bored with yourself."

"I don't feel bored." His low, rough voice scraped her skin like sandpaper. "What I feel . . ." He curled his hand around her bare thigh, just below the hem of her shorts. "What I *feel* . . . is a hot fuckable little body . . ."

Sparks erupted inside her. She licked her lips and tasted him. "Sorry. Now that I've had you, my curiosity is satisfied, and I'm not interested. No offense."

His gaze held steady. He deliberately brushed his fingers across her breast. "None taken."

As her skin pebbled, he gave her a less than friendly smile, turned away, and let himself out of the house.

♥

Blue felt hungover the next morning as she walked out to the curb to get the Sunday paper for Nita. Last night, Dean had tried to change the rules on her. He had no right to be angry just because she wouldn't worship and adore like all the rest. When she went to the farm today, she needed to give him as much trouble as possible.

As she leaned down to pick up the paper, she heard a hissing coming from the other side of the hedge. She looked up and saw Syl, the owner of the local resale shop, peeking at her around the shrubbery through a pair of red cat's-eye glasses. Syl had short salt and pepper hair and thin lips she'd enlarged with dark red lip liner. Blue had enjoyed her sense of humor when they'd met at the Barn Grill after the big fight, but Syl was all business now, hissing like a garden hose and gesturing for Blue to approach. "Come here. We need to talk to you."

Blue tucked the paper under her arm and followed Syl around the corner. A gold Impala sat parked on the opposite side of the street, and two women climbed out: Dean's real estate agent, Monica Doyle; and a slender, middle-aged African American woman Syl quickly introduced as Penny Winters, the owner of Aunt Myrtle's Attic, the town's antique store.

"We've been trying to get you alone all week," Syl said as the women gathered around. "But whenever you show up in town, *she's* always around, so we decided to stake out the house before we went to church."

"Everybody knows Nita has a fit if she doesn't get her Sunday paper first thing." Monica pulled a tissue from the navy and yellow Vera Bradley bag that matched her dressy blue suit. "You're our last hope, Blue. You have to use your influence with her."

"I don't have any influence," Blue said. "She can't stand me."

Penny fingered the gold cross at the neck of her red dress. "If that was true, she'd have gotten rid of you by now like she has everybody else."

"It's only been four days," Blue replied.

"A record." Monica gave her nose a delicate toot. "You have no idea how she runs over everybody."

That was so not true.

"You have to convince Nita to support Garrison Grows." Syl shoved her cat's-eye glasses up on her nose. "It's the only way we can save this town."

Garrison Grows, Blue quickly learned, was the plan the city's leaders had put together to revitalize the town.

"Tourists drive through here all the time on their way to the Smokies," Monica said, "but there's no decent restaurant, no lodging, hardly any shopping, and they never stop. If Nita will let us go ahead with Garrison Grows, we can change all that."

Penny tugged on the small black button between her breasts. "With no national franchises here, we can take advantage of the nostalgia factor and make this place look like everybody's memory of what small American towns were before KFC moved in."

Monica slipped her purse to her shoulder. "Naturally, Nita refuses to cooperate."

"It would be so easy to draw tourists if she'd only let us make a few improvements," Syl said. "Nita wouldn't have to pay for a dime of it."

"Syl's been trying to open a real gift shop next door to her resale shop for five years," Penny said, "but Nita hated her mother and won't rent her the space."

As the church bells rang, the women began outlining other parts of the Garrison Grows plan, which included a bed-and-breakfast, converting Josie's into a decent restaurant, and letting someone named Andy Berillo add a coffeehouse to the bakery.

"Nita says coffeehouses are only for Communists," Syl said indignantly. "Now what would a Communist be doing in East Tennessee?"

Monica folded her arms across her chest. "And who worries about Communists anyway these days?"

"She just wants to make sure everybody in town knows how she feels about us," Penny said. "I don't like to talk bad about anybody, but she's letting this town die out of spite."

Blue remembered Nita's anxious-to-please expression in those early Garrison photographs and wondered how different things might have been if the local women had welcomed her when she'd arrived instead of shunning her. No matter what Nita said, Blue didn't believe she had any intention of selling the town. She might hate Garrison, but she had nowhere else to go.

Syl squeezed Blue's arm. "You're the only person who has her ear right now. Convince her these improvements will mean money in her pocket. She likes money."

"I'd help if I could," Blue said, "but the only reason she's keeping me around is to torture me. She doesn't listen to anything I say."

"Just try," Penny said. "That's all we ask."

"Try hard," Monica said more firmly.

♥

Nita pitched a fit that afternoon when Blue announced she was taking off, but Blue didn't give in and, around four o'clock, amid threats of calling the police, she left for the farm in the Roadster. Since her last visit, the pastures had been mowed and the surrounding fence had been repaired. She parked by the barn, next to Jack's SUV. The warm wind plucked at her ponytail as she crossed the yard.

Riley dashed out. The Silly Putty smile stretched across her face made her look like a different child from the sad little girl Blue had found sleeping on the porch just over a week ago. "Guess what, Blue?" she squealed. "We're not going home tomorrow! Dad says we get to stay a couple more days because of working on the porch."

"Oh, Riley! That's great. I'm so glad."

Riley pulled her toward the front door. "April wants you to go in this way so she can show everything off. And guess what else? April gave Puffy some cheese, and Puffy got stinky farts, but Dean kept blaming it on me, and I didn't do it."

"Yeah, right." Blue grinned. "Blame it on the dog."

"No, really. I don't even like cheese."

Blue laughed and hugged her.

April and Puffy met them at the front door. Inside, the foyer glowed in the late afternoon sun with fresh eggshell paint. A carpet runner patterned with earth-toned swirls ran down the hallway. April gestured toward the splashy abstract Blue had spotted in a Knoxville gallery. "See how great the painting looks? You were right about mixing contemporary art with the antiques."

The chest beneath had a wood and brass tray that already held Dean's wallet and a set of keys, along with a framed early childhood photo of him wearing shorts and a football helmet so big it rested on his collarbones. Next to the chest, a curly iron coatrack waited for one of his jackets, and a rustic twig basket held a pair of sneakers and a football. A sturdy mahogany chair with a carved back offered a convenient place to change into running shoes or glance through the mail. "You've designed everything around him. Has he noticed how personalized this is?"

"I doubt it."

Blue took in an oval wall mirror with a carved wooden frame. "All you need is a shelf for his moisturizer and eyelash curler."

"Behave. Have you noticed that he hardly ever looks at himself?"

"I've noticed. I just haven't chosen to let him know I've noticed."

Blue loved the rest of the house, especially the living room, which had been transformed with pale, buttery paint and a big Oriental rug. The vintage landscapes Blue had discovered in the back of an antique shop looked great with the bold, contemporary canvas April had hung over the fireplace. The worn leather club chairs April had found were in place, along with a carved walnut armoire to hold stereo equipment, and an oversize coffee table with drawers for remote controls and game film. More photos sat on top, some taken of him with childhood friends, others from his teen and college years. Somehow Blue didn't think the pictures were his idea.

♥

Dean unconsciously adjusted his hammering to the music of the Black Eyed Peas coming from the kitchen. He and Jack had been working on the porch most of the day. The exterior walls were up, and tomorrow they'd start on the roof. He glanced toward the kitchen window. Blue had nodded at him when she'd arrived, but she hadn't come out to say hello, and he hadn't gone in. He was pissed with himself for losing it with her last night on the stairs, but at least he had her on his turf now, and nothing beat a home field advantage. Blue loved the farm, and if she was too stubborn to move back, he could at least remind her of what she was missing. One way or another, he was determined to get what he wanted—the affair they both deserved.

Inside, someone turned up the music. April and Riley were supposed to be helping with dinner, but April didn't like to cook, and he could see her dragging Riley away from peeling potatoes to dance. He watched Blue set aside a mixing bowl and join them. She hopped around like a tree fairy, arms waving, her ponytail bobbing. If she'd been alone, he might have gone in to dance with her, but not with April and Jack hanging around.

"I thought you and Blue broke up." Jack's voice momentarily startled him. Other than a request to pass over a tool or hold a board in place, they hadn't spoken all afternoon.

"Not exactly." Dean drove another nail home. He'd been exercising his shoulder, and it was finally loosening up. "We're at a transition point, that's all."

"Transition to what?"

"We're figuring that out."

"Bullshit." Jack swiped his face with his sleeve. "You're not serious about her. She's just a diversion to you."

Blue had been saying the same thing practically since the day they'd met, and Dean had to admit there was some truth in it. If he'd seen her on the street or in a club, he'd never have noticed her, but only because she wouldn't have come on to him. With so many beautiful women trying to catch his attention, how was he supposed to notice the ones who didn't?

"Be careful with her," Jack went on. "She acts tough, but those eyes give her away."

Dean swiped his forehead with his T-shirt sleeve. "Don't confuse reality with your song lyrics, Jack. Blue knows exactly what the score is."

Jack shrugged. "I guess you know her better than I do."

That was the last thing they said to each other until Dean went inside to take a shower.

♥

As Jack watched Dean disappear, he wiped a bead of sweat from his forehead. Although he'd only intended to stay at the farm for a week, he wasn't going anywhere for a while. April had her method of atonement, and he had his—building this porch with Dean. Growing up, Jack had spent summers working with his dad, and now he and Dean were doing the same. Not that Dean gave a damn about any kind of father-son ritual, but Jack did.

He liked the way the porch was shaping up. Everything was solid. His old man would have been proud.

Blue cranked open the kitchen window. Through the glass, he watched April's lithesome, sensual movements and those blades of long hair flying around her head like knives.

"Nobody over the age of thirty should be able to dance like you," he heard Blue say when the song ended.

Riley piped up, breathless from trying to follow April. "Dad is fifty-four, and he dances great. Onstage anyway. I don't think he dances anywhere else."

"He used to." April ran her hands through her hair to sweep it back from her face. "After his concerts, we'd find some out-of-the-way club, and we'd dance until the place shut down. Lots of times they'd stay open just for him. Of all the people I've ever danced with, he was—" She stopped, then shrugged and leaned down to pet the dog. A moment later, her cell rang and she slipped out of the kitchen to answer it.

Yesterday, he'd overheard her address one of her callers as Mark. Before that, it had been Brad. Same old April. Same old hard-on whenever he got near her. Even so, he wanted to make love with her again. He wanted to excavate her layers and discover where her strength came from.

He had meetings in New York and intended to ask her to watch Riley for a few days while he was gone. He trusted her with his kid. The person he didn't trust her with was himself.

♥

Someone started pounding on the door as Dean headed back downstairs from his shower. He pulled it open and saw Nita Garrison standing there. Behind her, a dusty black sedan pulled away. He turned toward the kitchen. "Blue, you've got company."

Nita smacked him in the knee with her cane, and he automatically stepped back, which opened up a hole big enough for her to slip through. Blue emerged from the kitchen, followed by a trail of great cooking smells. "Oh, God, no," she moaned as she spotted Nita.

"You left your shoes on the stairs," Nita said accusingly. "I tripped over them and fell all the way to the bottom. I'm lucky I didn't break my neck."

"I didn't leave my shoes on the stairs, and you didn't fall. How did you get here?"

"That fool Chauncey Crole. He spit out the window the whole way." She sniffed the air. "I smell fried chicken. You never fix fried chicken for me."

"That's because I can't find a place to hide the ground glass."

Nita sucked on her teeth, then whacked him in the shin again for laughing. "I need to sit down. I have bruises everywhere from that fall."

Riley popped in from the kitchen, Puffy trotting behind her. "Hi, Mrs. Garrison. I practiced with the book today."

"Go get it and let me see. But first, find me a comfortable chair. I took a terrible fall today."

"There's one in the living room. I'll show you." Riley led her away.

Blue rubbed the back of her hand over a dab of flour on her cheek. She didn't quite look at him. "I'd better ask April to set another place at the table."

"That woman is not eating dinner with us," he said.

"Then you figure out how to get rid of her. Believe me, it's harder than you think."

Dean followed her into the kitchen, protesting all the way, but Blue waved him off. He looked in the dining room and saw his antique Duncan Phyfe table had been set with fringed yellow place mats, old-fashioned blue and white dishes, a bowl of shiny stones Riley had collected, and a vase of yellow flowers. All the room needed to be complete were the murals Blue refused to paint. April ignored him as she began filling glasses with iced tea. He tried to help Blue out but ended up getting in her way. Jack appeared fresh from his shower. Blue dropped her wooden spoon.

"Good to see you, Blue." He reached into the refrigerator for a beer.

"Uh . . . hi." She knocked over the flour sack as she fumbled to pick up the spoon.

Dean grabbed some paper towels. "We have unexpected company in the living room, Jack, so you'll have to make yourself scarce." He tilted his head toward Blue. "I'm sure your number one fan over there will save you some dinner."

Jack's eyes followed April, but she didn't seem to notice. "I can only hide out for so long," he said. "Your farm's private property. Even if people figure out I'm here, they won't be able to get to me."

But Dean had spent twenty years avoiding anything that could connect him to Jack Patriot, and he didn't want Nita Garrison blabbing to everybody that Jack was staying here.

"Dad went into the beer store today," Riley said from the doorway. "He was in his work clothes, and he wasn't wearing any earrings, so nobody recognized him."

"Recognized who?" Nita appeared behind her. "That football player? Everybody knows he's here." She caught sight of Jack. "Who are you?"

"That's my dad," Riley said quickly. "His name is . . . Mr. Weasley. Mr. Ron Weasley."

"What's he doing here?"

"He's . . . He's April's boyfriend."

April's eyes snapped as she gestured toward the dining room. "I hope you're joining us for dinner."

Blue snorted. "Like you could keep her away."

"I don't mind if I do. Give me your arm, Riley, so I don't fall again."

"Mrs. Garrison thinks Riley is stupid," Riley announced to no one in particular.

"I don't think *you're* stupid," Nita said "Only your name, and that's hardly your fault, now is it." She aimed an accusatory look at Jack.

"It was her mother's idea," he said. "I wanted to name her Rachel."

"Jennifer is better." Nita pushed Riley ahead of her into the dining room.

Jack turned to Blue. "Who the hell is that?"

"Some call her Satan. Others Beelzebub. She goes by many names."

Dean smiled. "She's Blue's employer."

"She's my employer." Blue slapped a drumstick on the platter.

"Lucky you," Jack said.

Blue pulled a pan of roasted asparagus from the oven. They all began carrying in the serving dishes. Blue's eyes narrowed when she saw that Nita had positioned herself at the head of the table. Riley sat to her immediate left. Dean quickly set down the biscuit basket and grabbed a side chair at the opposite end, as far away from the old lady as he could get. Jack got rid of the bowl of warm potato salad nearly as quickly and hurried to sit next to Riley in the place across from Dean. April and Blue realized at the same time that only two empty chairs remained, one at the foot of the table and one directly to Nita's right. They both made a dash for the foot of the table. April had a head start, but Blue played dirty and hip-bumped her. As April lost her rhythm, Blue threw herself into the chair. "Touchdown . . ."

"You cheated," April hissed under her breath.

"Children . . . ," Jack said.

April tossed her hair and marched to take her seat next to Nita, who was complaining to Riley about Blue's bossiness and missed the whole thing. April now sat to Dean's immediate left. They began to pass the food. After April filled her plate, Dean was surprised to see her bow her head over her meal for a few moments. When had that happened?

"Only one biscuit," Nita said to Riley, taking two herself. "Any more will make you fat again."

Blue opened her mouth to jump to Riley's defense, but Riley handled it herself. "I know. I don't get as hungry as I used to."

As Dean gazed around the table, he saw a travesty of the American family. It was like Norman Rockwell on crack. A grandma who wasn't a grandma. Parents who weren't parents. Blue, who didn't fit into any definable role, except as Mad Jack's suck-up. She made sure Jack got the biggest piece of chicken and ran to fetch him a clean fork when he accidentally dropped his. Dean remembered sitting around his friends' dinner tables while he was growing up and longing for a family of his own. He should have been more careful what he wished for.

Everyone complimented Blue on her cooking except Nita, who complained that the asparagus needed butter. The chicken was crispy and moist. A salty crunch of crumbled bacon topped the warm potato salad, which had a tangy dressing. Blue wasn't happy with the biscuits, but the rest of them had several.

"Mrs. Garrison used to teach ballroom dancing," Riley announced.

"We know," Dean and Blue said in unison.

Nita eyed Jack. "You look familiar."

"Do I?" Jack wiped his mouth with his napkin.

"What's your name again?"

"Ron Weasley," Riley said into her milk glass.

She was developing some good street smarts, and Dean gave her a surreptitious wink. He just hoped Nita wasn't too familiar with Harry Potter.

He waited for Nita to resume her interrogation, but she didn't. "Shoulders," she said, and Riley immediately sat straighter in her chair. Nita shifted her eyes between April and Dean. "You two look alike."

"You think so?" April helped herself to another spear of roasted asparagus.

"You're related, aren't you?"

Dean felt himself tense, but his little sister had appointed herself the guardian of family secrets. "Mrs. Garrison's been giving me posture lessons," she said. "I'm getting real good at walking with a book."

Nita pointed her third biscuit at Blue. "Someone else could use posture lessons."

Blue glowered and plunked her elbows on the table.

Nita gave a triumphant smirk. "See how childish she is."

Dean smiled. Blue was definitely being childish, but she looked so cute doing it—a smudge of flour on one cheek, a strand of inky hair trailing down her neck, a mulish expression. How could a woman who was such a mess be so appealing?

Nita turned her attention to Dean. "Football players make a lot of money for doing nothing."

"Pretty much," Dean said.

Blue bristled. "Dean works very hard at what he does. Being a quarterback isn't just physically demanding. It's very challenging mentally."

Riley jumped in as Blue's backup. "Dean's played in the Pro Bowl three years straight."

"I'll bet I'm richer than you are," Nita said.

"Could be." Dean eyed her over a chicken wing. "How much you got?"

Nita let out an indignant huff. "I'm not telling you that."

Dean smiled. "Then we'll never know, will we?"

Jack, who could buy and sell both of them, gave a snort of amusement. Mrs. Garrison sucked a food sliver from her front teeth and zeroed in on him. "And what do you do?"

"Right now, I'm building Dean's porch."

"Come look at my windowsills next week. The wood's rotting."

"Sorry," Jack deadpanned. "I don't do windows."

April smiled at him, and Jack smiled back at her. An intimacy passed between them that shut everybody else out. It only lasted a moment, but no one at the table missed it.

Chapter Nineteen

After dinner, Nita announced that she'd wait in the living room until Blue had finished cleaning up and could drive her home. April immediately rose. "I'll clean up. You go ahead, Blue."

But Dean wasn't ready for Blue to leave. So far, all this little dinner party had accomplished was to remind him how much he missed having her to pal around with during the day and sink into at night. He needed to fix that. "I should burn the trash," he said. "How about helping me carry it out first?"

Riley did her best to upset his plan. "I'll help."

"Not so fast." April began gathering up the plates. "When I said I was cleaning up the kitchen, I meant everybody was helping except Blue."

"Wait a minute," Jack said. "We've been working on the porch all day. We deserve a little relaxation."

Suddenly he and Jack were a team? Not in a million years. Dean grabbed the empty chicken platter. "Sure."

Riley jumped up. "I can load the dishwasher."

"You're picking the music," April said. "And it had better rock."

Blue piped in. "I'm not missing out if there's going to be music. I get to help, too."

Riley escorted Nita into the living room while the rest of them cleared the table. She came back with her iPod and plugged it into April's docking station. "I'd better not hear bubblegum coming out of there," Jack said. "Radiohead would be okay, or maybe Wilco."

April looked up from the sink. "Or Bon Jovi." Jack stared at her. She shrugged. "One of my guilty pleasures, and I'm not apologizing."

"My guilty pleasure is Ricky Martin," Blue said.

They looked at Dean, but he refused to participate in this cozy family confessional, so Blue decided to pipe up for him. "Clay Aiken, right?"

Nita didn't like being left out, and she shuffled in from the living room. "I always liked Bobby Vinton. And Fabian. He was hot." She settled at the kitchen table.

Riley moved toward the open dishwasher. "I sort of like Patsy Cline—Mom had all her stuff—but the kids make fun of me because they don't know who she is."

"Good taste on your part," Jack said.

"So what about you?" April asked Jack. "Who's your guilty pleasure?"

"That's easy," Dean heard himself say. "You're his guilty pleasure, April. Right, Jack?"

The uneasy silence that fell over the kitchen made Dean feel churlish. He was used to being the life of the party, not the end of it.

"Excuse us," Blue said. "Dean and I have some trash to burn."

"Before you go anywhere, Mr. Football Player," Nita said, "I want to know exactly what your intentions are toward my Blue."

Blue groaned. "Somebody please shoot me."

"My relationship with Blue is private, Mrs. Garrison." He pulled the trash from under the sink.

"I'm sure you'd like to think so," she retorted.

April and Jack stopped to watch, more than happy to let Nita do their dirty work. Dean nudged Blue toward the side door. "Excuse us."

But Nita wouldn't let it go that easily. "I know you're not still engaged. I don't think you ever had any intention of marrying her. You just want to take what you can get. That's the way men are, Riley. Every one of them."

"Yes, ma'am."

"It's not the way all men are," Jack said to his daughter. "But Mrs. Garrison has a point."

Dean curled his free hand around Blue's arm. "Blue can take care of herself."

"The girl is a walking disaster," Nita retorted. "Someone has to look out for her."

That was too much for Blue. "You don't care one thing about looking out for me. You just want to make trouble."

"Listen to that fresh mouth."

"Our engagement is still on, Mrs. Garrison," he said. "Let's go, Blue."

Riley jumped forward. "Could I like maybe be a bridesmaid or something?"

"We're not really engaged," Blue felt duty bound to inform her. "Dean is amusing himself."

Their fake engagement was too convenient to let her spoil it. "We're engaged," he said. "Blue is just sulking."

Nita rapped her cane on the floor. "Come into the living room with me, Riley. Away from *certain people*. I'll show you some exercises to strengthen your leg muscles so you can take ballet again."

"I don't want to take ballet," Riley muttered. "I want to take guitar lessons."

Jack set down the pan he was drying. "You do?"

"Mom always said she'd teach me, but she never did."

"But she showed you some basic chords, right?"

"No. She didn't like me touching her guitars."

Jack's expression grew grim. "My acoustic's at the cottage. Let's go get it."

"Really? You'll let me play your guitar?"

"I'll give you the damned thing."

Riley looked as though he'd dropped a diamond tiara on her head. Jack tossed aside the dish towel. Dean pulled Blue outside, not feeling at all guilty about leaving April to Nita's mercies.

"I don't sulk," Blue said as they stepped off the side porch. "You shouldn't have said that. And it's not fair to raise Riley's hopes about being a bridesmaid."

"She'll survive just fine." He stalked toward the oil drum where they burned trash. It was full. He struck a match from the box April kept in a Ziploc bag and tossed it in. "Why won't they all go away? Jack's still around. April's not going until Riley does. That old witch is the last straw. I want all of them out of here! Everybody but you."

"Except it's not that easy, is it?"

No, it wasn't that easy. As the fire caught, he moved back to sit in the grass and watch the flames. This past week, he'd seen Riley's confidence grow. Her indoor pallor had faded, and the new clothes April had bought her were already getting loose. He liked working on the porch, too, even if he had to do it with Jack. Every time he drove a nail he felt as though he was putting his own mark on this old farm. Then there was Blue.

She moved behind him. He picked up a cellophane wrapper that had fallen into the grass and tossed it toward the fire.

♥

Blue watched as the wadded cellophane landed at the base of the drum, but Dean didn't seem to care that he'd missed the shot. His brooding profile stood in perfect silhouette against the twilight. She walked over to sit in the grass next to him. Another bandage had appeared on his hand, this one across his knuckles. She touched it. "Construction accident?"

He propped his elbow on his knee. "I've got a fair-size lump on my head, too."

"How are you getting along with your coworker?"

"He doesn't talk to me, and I don't talk to him."

She crossed her legs and gazed at the fire. "He should at least acknowledge what he did to you."

"He has." He turned his head toward her. "So have you had that particular conversation with your own mother?"

She plucked a blade of grass. "It's different with her." The fire popped. "She's sort of like Jesus. Would Jesus's daughter have the right to complain that he'd ruined her childhood because he was always running off saving people's souls?"

"Your mother isn't Jesus, and if people have kids, they should either stick around to raise them or put them up for adoption."

She wondered if he intended to be around to raise his kids, but the idea of him at home with his family while she was off globetrotting depressed her.

He slipped his arm around her shoulders, and she didn't say a thing about it. The flames leaped higher. Her blood hummed. She was sick of settling for second best. Just once in her life, she wanted to indulge in a dangerous extravagance. The night wind caught her hair. She rose up to her knees and kissed him. Later, she'd put him in his place. For now, she wanted to live in the moment.

He didn't need any encouragement to kiss her back, and before long, they were stumbling behind the barn into the tall grass out of sight of the house.

♥

Dean didn't know why Blue had changed her mind, but since she had her fingers inside his waistband, he wasn't going to ask.

"I do not want to do this," she said as she pulled open the fastener of his jeans.

"Sometimes you have to take one for the team." He whipped her shorts and panties to her ankles, went to his knees, and nuzzled her. She was sweet, spicy, a heady potion to his senses. Long before he'd had enough of her, she fell apart. He caught her and drew her down, keeping her on top to protect her from the weeds that were jabbing him in the butt. It was a small sacrifice for the reward of finally sinking into that warm, writhing body.

She grabbed his head between her hands, clenched her teeth, and said fiercely, "Don't you dare rush me!"

He understood her point of view, but she was so tight, so wet, and he'd been pushed too far . . . He sank his fingers into her hips, pulled her down hard, and let himself go.

Afterward, he was afraid she'd take a swing at him, so he drew her flat on top of him and hooked one of her legs over his hip. Kissing her deeply, he reached between their bodies. She arched and trembled. A surge of protectiveness came over him. He moved his hand and set her free.

When they were done, he stroked her hair, which had come out of its ratty ponytail. "Just to refresh your memory . . ." He traced the small of her back under her T-shirt. "You said I didn't turn you on."

She sank her teeth into his collarbone. "You don't turn me on— not the rational part of me anyway. Unfortunately, I also have slutty parts. Those you definitely turn on."

He wasn't nearly done with her, and he started to touch those slutty parts all over again, but she rolled off him into the weeds. "We can't stay out here fornicating all night."

He grinned. Fornicating, indeed.

She still wore her T-shirt, but the rest of her was naked. She reached around for her panties, which gave him an outstanding view of her bottom as she spoke. "Riley is the only person who won't have figured out what we're doing." She located the panties, stood up to pull them on, and had the gall to sneer at him. "Here's the way it's going to be, Boo. I've decided you and I are going to have an affair— short and nasty. I'll be using you, pure and simple, so don't go all touchy-feely on me. I don't care what you're thinking. I don't care about your feelings. All I care about is your body. Now are you okay with that or not?"

She was the damnedest woman he'd ever met. He grabbed her shorts before she could pick them up. "What am I getting in return for the humiliation of being used?"

The sneer reappeared. "You're getting me. The object of your desire."

He pretended to think it over. "Add a few more dinners like today, and I'm in." He snaked a finger under the leg hole of her panties. "In all the way."

♥

Jack pushed his chair back from the cottage's kitchen table and began tuning his old Martin. He'd recorded "Born in Sin" with it, and now he wished he hadn't been so impulsive about giving it away. Those dings and scratches represented the last twenty-five years of his life. But finding out that Marli wouldn't let Riley near any of her guitars made him crazy. He should have been aware of something that important, but he'd kept himself in deliberate ignorance.

Riley pulled up a chair, sitting so close their knees nearly touched. Her eyes filled with wonder as she gazed at the battered instrument. "It's really mine?"

His regret evaporated. "It's yours."

"This is the best present I ever got."

Her dreamy expression made his throat tighten. "You should have told me you wanted a guitar. I would have sent you one."

She mumbled something he couldn't make out.

"What?"

"I told you," she said. "But you were on the road, and you must not have heard."

He had no recollection of her mentioning a guitar, but then he seldom gave their strained telephone conversations all his attention.

Although he frequently sent Riley gifts—computers, games, books, and CDs—he'd never picked out any of them himself. "I'm sorry, Riley. I guess I missed it."

"That's okay."

Riley had a habit of saying things were okay when they weren't, a practice he hadn't noticed until these past ten days. He hadn't noticed a lot about her he should have. As long as he paid her bills and made sure she attended a good school, he'd figured he was doing his fair share. He hadn't wanted to look beyond that, because getting more involved would have interfered with his life.

"I know most of the open chords," she said. "Except F is hard to play." She watched intently as he tuned, soaking in everything he did. "I looked up stuff on the Internet, and, for a while, Trinity let me practice on her guitar. But then she made me give it back."

"Trinity has a guitar?"

"A Larrivee. She only took five lessons before she quit. She thinks guitar is boring. But I'll bet Aunt Gayle will make her start again. Now that Mom's dead, Aunt Gayle needs a new partner, and she told Trinity they could be like the Judds someday, except more beautiful."

He'd seen Trinity at Marli's funeral. Even as an infant, she'd been irresistible, a rosy-cheeked cherub with blond curls and big blue eyes. The way he remembered it, she'd seldom cried, slept when she was supposed to, and kept her baby formula in her stomach instead of turning it into a projectile as Riley had. When Riley was a month old, Jack had left on tour, glad to have an excuse to get away from a moon-faced, screaming baby he didn't know how to comfort and a marriage he'd already discovered was a big mistake. Over the years, he'd some-times thought he would have been a better father if he'd been given a charmer like Trinity, but the past ten days had enlightened him.

"It was nice of her to lend you her guitar," he said, "but I'll bet her cooperation didn't come free."

"We made a deal."

"Let's hear it."

"I don't want to tell you."

"Tell me anyway."

"Do I have to?"

"Depends on whether you want me to show you an easier way to play the F chord."

She stared at the spot under the sound hole where his fingers had worn off the finish. "I told Aunt Gayle that Trinity was with me when she was really with her boyfriend. And I had to buy them cigarettes."

"She's eleven!"

"But her boyfriend is fourteen, and Trinity's very mature for her age."

"Oh, yeah, she's mature all right. Gayle needs to lock that kid up, and I'm going to tell her so."

"You can't. Trinity'll hate me even more."

"Good. Then she'll keep away from you." Since he didn't have the details worked out, he stopped himself from telling Riley she wouldn't be seeing much of Princess Trinity anymore. He knew now that he could never put Riley under Gayle's dubious supervision. Riley wouldn't like going to boarding school, but he'd plan as much of his travel schedule around her vacation dates as he could so she didn't feel abandoned. "How did you get cigarettes?" he asked.

"This guy who worked at the house. He bought them for me."

Riley, he'd learned, had turned bribery into a survival technique. It made him ashamed. "Did anybody ever watch out for you?"

"I know how to watch out for myself."

"You shouldn't have to do that." He couldn't believe he and Marli had denied her something as basic as her own guitar. "Did you tell your mother how much you wanted to play?"

"I tried to."

In the same fumbling fashion she'd tried to tell him. How could he blame Marli for not paying more attention when he'd been even worse?

"Could you show me that F chord now?" she said.

He demonstrated how to bar only the top two strings, which was easier for small hands. Finally, he offered her the guitar. She wiped her hands on her shorts. "It's really mine, right?"

"It really is, and I couldn't have found a better person to give it to." Suddenly, he meant every word.

She cradled the guitar against her body. He held out a pick. "Go ahead. Give it a try."

He smiled as she slipped the pick between her lips, just as he did, while she repositioned the instrument. When she was satisfied, she pulled the pick from her mouth and, gazing intently at her left hand, struck an F the way he'd shown her. She picked it up right away, then played the other open chords. "You're doing that pretty well," he said.

She beamed. "I've been practicing."

"How? I thought you had to give Trinity her guitar back."

"I did. But I made one out of cardboard so I could work on my finger positions."

His lungs constricted. He pushed himself out of the chair. "Be back in a minute."

When he got to the bathroom, he sat on the edge of the tub and put his head in his hands. He had money, cars, houses, rooms filled with platinum records. He had all that, and his daughter had been forced to practice on a cardboard guitar.

He wanted to talk to April about it. The woman who'd once driven him crazy now seemed to be the only person he could turn to for advice.

Chapter Twenty

June, with all its heat and humidity, began unwinding over East Tennessee. Every night, Blue let Dean in through her balcony for their secret trysts, sometimes appearing only minutes after he'd politely escorted her to the front door from dinner at the Barn Grill. Resisting him had proved to be hopeless, even though she knew she was playing with fire. But now that she wasn't dependent on him for a job, money, and a roof over her head, she'd decided she could take the risk. After all, she'd be gone in a few weeks. She gazed at him sitting naked against the bunched pillows. "You look like you're getting ready to talk again."

"I was just about to say—"

"No talking, remember? All I want from you is sex." She rolled to her side, taking the sheet with her. "I'm every man's dream woman."

"You're a nightmare of mythic proportions." With one clean motion, he whipped the sheet off them both, pulled her facedown across his lap, and gave her bottom a firm smack. "You keep forgetting that I'm bigger and stronger than you." Another smack, followed by a lingering caress. "And that I eat little girls like you for breakfast."

She looked up at him over her shoulder. "Breakfast isn't for at least eight hours."

He flipped her to her back. "Then how about a late-night snack?"

♥

"You might think twice about crossing me, Miss Blue Bailey," Nita said a few days later when Blue announced she intended to work on finishing the portrait instead of baking the chocolate Bundt cake her employer demanded. "That so-called carpenter? Do you think I'm stupid? I knew who he was the minute I set eyes on him. Jack Patriot, that's who. As for Dean's housekeeper . . . Any fool can see she's his mother. If you don't want me calling my friends in the press, I suggest you get into that kitchen and start making my Bundt cake."

"You have no friends in the press," Blue said, "or anywhere else, except for Riley, and only God knows what that's about. Blackmail works two ways. If you don't keep your mouth shut, I'll tell every-body about those papers I stumbled over when you made me clean out your desk."

"What papers are you talking about?"

"Records of the anonymous money you sent to the Olson family after they lost everything in that fire, the new car that mysteriously appeared in some woman's driveway when her husband died and she had to support all those kids, the drug bills that are mysteriously be-ing paid for at least a dozen needy families. I could go on, but I won't. Do you really want everybody to know that the wicked witch of Gar-rison, Tennessee, has the heart of a charred marshmallow?"

"I have no idea what you mean." Nita stalked out of the room, her cane punishing the floor with every step.

Blue had won another battle with the old bat, but she baked the cake anyway. Of all the women Blue had stayed with over the years, Nita was the first one who wanted to keep her around.

♥

That night, Dean sat crossed-legged at the bottom of Blue's bed, her calf draped over his bare thigh. As they recuperated from a particularly kinky round of lovemaking, he massaged her foot, which was sticking out from under the sheet she'd pulled up. She moaned as he rubbed her instep.

He stopped. "You're not going to throw up again, are you?"

"That was three days ago." She wiggled her foot, encouraging him to get back to work. "I knew there was something wrong with Josie's take-out shrimp, but Nita kept insisting it was fine."

He pushed his thumb into her instep a little too hard. "And you ended up spending the night alternating between hanging your head over the toilet and crawling down the hall to take care of that old biddy. Just once, I'd like to see you pick up the phone and ask me for help."

She didn't acknowledge the bite she heard behind his words. "I had everything under control. No need to bother you."

"Are you afraid you'll have to give up your jockstrap if you ask for help?" He dug into the ball of her foot. "Life doesn't need to be an individual sport, Blue. Sometimes you have to rely on the team."

Not in her life. That was a solo game from beginning to end. She fought an uneasy mixture of foreboding, despair, and panic. It had been nearly a month since she and Dean had met, and it was time to move on. Nita's painting was almost finished, and it wasn't as though Blue would be leaving her helpless. A few days ago, she'd hired a terrific housekeeper, a woman who'd raised six kids and was impervious to even the most blatant insults. Blue had no reason to stay in Garrison much longer, except that she wasn't ready to leave Dean. He was the lover of her dreams: imaginative, generous, lusty. She couldn't get enough of him, and for tonight, she shut out everything else.

She eyed his jet-black End Zone briefs. "Why did you put those things on? I like you naked."

"I've noticed." His touch grew lighter as he discovered a magical spot in the sensitive nook behind her knee. "You're a wild woman. This is the only way I can get a little recuperation time."

She dropped her eyes to the real end zone. "Obviously, Thor God of Thunder is fully recuperated."

"Halftime is definitely over." He pulled the sheet away. "And I'm calling the next play."

♥

Jack pulled his overnight case from the trunk of his car, which he'd parked near the barn. It had been a long time since he'd had to carry his own luggage, but he'd been doing it for the past couple of weeks whenever he left the farm for a quick trip to New York or a longer one to the West Coast. The tour was shaping up. Yesterday he'd approved marketing plans, and today he'd done some prerelease publicity for his new album. Fortunately, the county airport was large enough to accommodate a private jet, so he could get in and out fairly easily. With his pilot running interference, he'd even managed to get to and from his car without being recognized.

Dean had agreed to let Riley stay at the farm until he left for Stars training camp a month from now. That meant April was putting off her return to L.A., something he knew Dean wasn't happy about. All of them, it seemed, were making sacrifices for his daughter.

It was nearly seven o'clock, and the workers had left for the day. He set his overnight case by the side door and walked around to the back to see whether the electrician had completed the wiring for the porch's overhead fans. The walls were up, the roof on, and the smell of new wood welcomed him. Out of nowhere, he heard a faint female voice, so innocent, so sweet, so perfectly pitched, that for a moment, he thought he was imagining it.

> *"Do you remember when we were young,*
> *And we'd awake just to see the sun?*
> *Baby, why not smile?"*

He forgot to breathe.

> *"I know that life is cruel.*
> *You know that better than I do."*

She had the voice of a tarnished angel, dewy innocence tinged with disillusionment. He imagined pristine white wing feathers battered at the tips, a halo tilted ever-so-slightly off center. She improvised with the final chorus, moving up an octave, hitting the heart of every note, her range exceeding his rough rocker's baritone. He followed the music around the back of the porch.

She sat propped against the foundation, her legs crossed, his old Martin cradled in her lap, the dog curled at her side. Her baby fat was melting away, and a shiny brown curl brushed her cheek. Like him, she tanned easily, and despite the sunblock April made her wear, her skin had turned nearly as brown as his. She'd fixed all of her concentration on hitting the right chords so that her sublime singing seemed almost like an afterthought.

The final chords of "Why Not Smile?" trailed away. Still not seeing him, she spoke to the dog. "Okay, what do you want me to play now?"

Puffy yawned.

"I love that!" She shifted into the opening chords of "Down and Dirty," one of the Moffatts' biggest hits. But in Riley's hands, the silly country tune had an edgy groove. He heard traces of Marli's bluesy purr and of his drawl, but Riley's voice belonged only to her. She'd taken the best qualities from each of them and made them her own. Puffy finally got around to greeting him with an obligatory trio of yips. Riley's hands dropped from the guitar in midchorus, and he saw her dismay. His instincts warned him to be careful.

"Sounds like all your practice is paying off." He stepped around a pile of wood scraps nobody had gotten around to cleaning up.

She tucked the guitar tighter against her chest, as if she were still afraid he'd take it away from her. "I didn't think you'd be back until tonight."

"I missed you, so I came back early."

She didn't believe him, but it was true. He'd missed April, too, more than he wanted to. In some perverse way, he'd even missed the stab of pain he felt watching Dean playing with Riley, laughing with Blue, or even sparring with the old lady. He sat on the ground next to the one child he did have, the little girl he'd been falling so ineptly in love with. "How are you doing with the F chord?"

"Okay."

He picked up a nail that had fallen into the grass. "You have quite a voice. You know that, right?" She shrugged.

Out of nowhere, Marli's words came back to him from one of their brief phone conversations last year. *"Her teacher says she has a wonderful voice, but I've never heard it. And you know how everybody sucks up to you when you're a celebrity. They'll even use your kid to get close."*

One more mistake on his part. He'd blindly assumed Riley would be better off with his ex-wife than with him, even though he knew exactly how self-involved Marli was. He rolled the nail between his fingers. "Riley, talk to me."

"About what?"

"The singing."

"I don't have anything to say."

"Don't give me that. You have an incredible voice, but when I asked you to sing with me, you told me you couldn't. Didn't you think I'd be interested?"

"I'm still me," she muttered.

"What do you mean?"

"Just because I can sing doesn't make me anybody different."

"I don't understand what you mean." He tossed the nail toward the scrap pile. "Riley, I don't get it. Tell me what you're thinking."

"Nothing."

"I'm your father. I love you. You can talk to me."

Unvarnished skepticism clouded those eyes that looked so much like his own. Words weren't going to convince her of how he felt. Holding the guitar close, she jumped up. The shorts April had bought her dropped down on her hips. "I've got to go feed Puffy."

As she scampered off, he leaned against the porch foundation. She didn't believe he loved her. And why should she?

A few minutes later, April came jogging out of the woods in a crimson sports bra top and body-shaping black workout shorts. She was only comfortable with him if other people were around, and the rhythm of her steps faltered. He thought she might keep going, but she slowed and came toward him. The strength of her body, the way her bare midriff gleamed, made his blood rush.

"I didn't expect you until later," she said, trying to get her breath back.

One of his knees cracked as he came to his feet. "You used to say exercise was for losers who didn't have more creative ways to waste time."

"I used to say a lot of crap."

He dragged his eyes from the trickle of perspiration sliding into the valley between her breasts. "Don't let me interrupt your run."

"I was getting ready to cool down."

"I'll walk with you."

He set off at her side. She inquired about the tour. In the old days, she'd have wanted to know which women would be traveling with the band and where they'd be staying. Now she asked a business-woman's questions about overhead and advance ticket sales. They wandered toward the newly painted white wooden fence surrounding the mowed pasture. "I heard Dean talk to Riley about buying some horses next spring."

"He's always loved them," she said.

He braced his foot on the bottom rail. "Did you know Riley could sing?"

"You're just finding out, aren't you?"

He was getting sick of everyone pointing out all his failures when he was more than aware of them himself. "What do you think?"

April took a pass on going for his jugular. "I heard her last week for the first time." She propped her arms on the fence. "Riley was hiding behind the grape arbor. I got chills."

"Did you talk to her about it?"

"She didn't give me a chance. The second she spotted me, she stopped singing and begged me not to tell you. It's hard to fathom a voice like that coming from someone so young."

Jack didn't get it. "Why is she trying to hide it from me?"

"I don't know. Maybe she explained her reasons to Dean."

"Ask him for me, will you?"

"Do your own dirty work."

"You know he won't talk to me," he said. "Hell, we built that damn porch without exchanging more than twenty sentences."

"My BlackBerry's in the kitchen. E-mail him when you go in."

He dropped his foot from the fence. "This just gets more and more pathetic, doesn't it?"

"You're trying, Jack. That's what matters."

He wanted more than that. He wanted more from Dean. More from Riley. More from April. He wanted what she used to give him so freely, and he brushed the backs of his knuckles over her soft cheek. "April . . ."

She shook her head and walked away.

♥

Dean didn't see the e-mail about Riley's singing until later that day, and it took him a moment to realize it came from Jack instead of April. He read it quickly, then punched in his reply.

Figure it out for yourself.

As he headed outside, he thought about Blue, something he'd been doing with increasing frequency. So many women believed they had to perform like porn stars to turn him on, and it all got so phony. But Blue didn't seem to watch a lot of porn. She was clumsy, earthy, impulsive, exhilarating, and always herself—as unpredictable in bed as she was out of it. But he didn't trust her, and he sure as hell couldn't depend on her.

The ladder rested against the side of the porch. His shoulder didn't protest as he moved it to check the roof. With training camp only a month away, he'd never had anything more than a short-term affair in mind. A good thing, because Blue was fundamentally a loner. He was supposed to take her horseback riding next week, but who could predict if she'd still be around? One night he'd go over that balcony and find her gone.

As he clipped on his tool belt and climbed the ladder, he knew one thing. She might be giving him her body, but she was withholding everything else, and he didn't like it.

♥

Two nights later, Jack came upon April dancing barefoot at the edge of the pond, and the hair on the back of his neck stood up. Only the rustle of reeds and rasp of crickets accompanied her. Her arms rippled in the air, her hair flew in golden filaments around her head, and her hips, those seductive hips, beat out a sexual telegram . . . *Give it to me, babee . . . Give it to me, babee . . .*

Blood shot straight to his groin. The absence of music made her seem bewitched, both eerily beautiful and more than a little mad. April, with her goddess eyes and kitten's pout . . . The girl who'd spent the seventies servicing the gods of rock and roll . . . He knew this disruptive virago dancing at the edge of the pond to the very marrow of his bones. Her excesses, her wild demands, her sexual recklessness had been toxic to a kid of twenty-three. A kid he'd left behind long ago. Now he couldn't imagine her bending to anyone's will but her own.

As she rocked to the imaginary beat, the light spilling from the cottage's back door fixture caught on the cord of a headset. The music wasn't imaginary after all. She was dancing to a song coming from her iPod. She was nothing more than a middle-aged woman kicking up her heels. But knowing that didn't break her spell.

Her hips beat out a final tattoo. Her hair shimmered one last time, and then her arms fell to her sides. She pulled out the earphones. He slipped back into the woods.

Chapter Twenty-one

Blue gazed at the finished portrait before she left the house. Nita wore an ice blue ball gown from a dancing exhibition in the fifties and a sixties beehive that showcased the diamond earrings Marshall had given her as a wedding present in the seventies. She was slim and glamorous. Her skin was flawless, her makeup dramatic. Blue had posed her on an imaginary grand staircase with Tango at her feet. Nita had made her paint out Tango.

"It's not as bad as I expected," Nita said the first time she saw the portrait hung against the gold-flocked wallpaper in the foyer.

Blue correctly translated that to mean she loved it, and, despite its excessive glitz, Blue was happy with how perfectly she'd captured Nita's view of herself: the sex kitten's sparkle in her eyes, the alluring smile on her frosted pink lips, and the perfect shade of platinum in her beehive. More than once, she found Nita in the foyer studying it, an expression of yearning in her aging eyes.

Blue had money in her wallet now. She could leave Garrison anytime.

Nita appeared behind her, and they took off for Sunday dinner at the farm. Dean and Riley grilled burgers and Blue made barbecued beans accompanied by a watermelon salad flavored with fresh mint and lime juice. When Dean started eating his hamburger, he began baiting her about not doing the murals, accusing her of ingratitude, artistic cowardice, and high treason, all of it easy to ignore. Until April spoke up.

"I know how much you love this house, Blue. I'm surprised you don't want to leave your mark on it."

Gooseflesh broke out on Blue's arms, and by the time the rest of them were reaching for second helpings, she knew she had to paint the murals—not to leave her mark on the house as April had said, but to leave her mark on Dean. The murals would last for years. Whenever he walked into this room, he'd be forced to remember her. He might forget what color her eyes were, maybe he'd forget her name, but as long as the murals were on the walls, he'd never be able to forget her. She pushed the food around on her plate, her appetite gone. "All right. I'll do them."

A sliver of watermelon dropped off April's fork. "Really? You won't change your mind?"

"No, but remember that I warned you. My landscapes are—"

"Mushy pieces of crap." Dean grinned. "We know. Good for you, Bluebell."

Nita looked up from her barbecued beans. To Blue's shock, she didn't protest. "As long as you make my breakfast in the morning and you're back in time to make my dinner, I don't care what you do."

"Blue is going to be staying in the caravan now," Dean said smoothly. "It'll be more convenient for her."

"More convenient for you, doncha mean?" Nita retorted. "Blue's dumb, but she's not stupid."

Blue could have argued the point. She was dumb and stupid. The longer she stayed, the tougher it would be to leave. She knew that from hard experience. Still, she had her eyes wide open. She'd miss

Dean desperately when she left, but she had a lifetime's practice saying good-bye to people she cared about, and it wouldn't take her long to get over him.

♥

"There's not a single reason for you to keep living in that mausoleum," Dean said the next night during dinner at the Barn Grill, "not when you're going to be working every day at the farm. I know how much you love staying in the caravan. I'll even put a Porta Potti out there for you."

She wanted to. She wanted to listen to the tap of summer rain on the caravan roof as she drifted off to sleep, to sink her bare feet into the wet grass when she stepped outside in the morning, to spend an entire night curled up with Dean. She wanted everything that would come back to torture her when she left.

She set down her beer mug without taking a sip. "No way am I giving up the sight of Romeo climbing over my balcony railing at night to get to the goodies."

"I'm going to break my neck getting to the goodies."

Not likely. Unbeknownst to Romeo, she'd had Chauncey Crole, who doubled as the town handyman, reinforce the railing.

Syl popped up at the table to check on Blue's total lack of progress getting Nita to agree to the town improvement project. Once again, Blue tried to make her understand how hopeless it was. "If I say it's morning, she says it's night. Every time I try to talk to her about it, I make things worse."

Syl snitched one of Blue's French fries and wiggled her booty as Trace Adkins launched into "Honkytonk Badonkadonk." "You need a positive attitude. Tell her, Dean. Tell her nobody accomplishes anything without a positive attitude."

Dean gave Blue a long, steady look. "That's true, Syl. A positive attitude's the key to success."

Blue thought about the murals. Painting them would be like shedding a layer of skin—not in a good way, like after a peeling sunburn, but in a bad way, while the skin was still alive.

"You can't give up," Syl said. "Not when the whole town's depending on you. You're our last hope."

As Syl walked away, Dean transferred an uneaten piece of broiled perch from his plate to Blue's. "The good news is that people are so busy bugging you they've stopped paying much attention to me," he said. "I finally get to eat my meals in peace."

Not long after, Karen Ann cornered Blue in the restroom. The Barn Grill was no longer serving her alcohol, but that had only marginally improved her personality. "Mr. Hot Shit is screwin' everybody in town behind your back, Blue. I hope you know that."

"Sure I do. Just like I hope you know I'm screwing Ronnie behind yours."

"Asshole."

"Will you try to focus, Karen Ann." Blue yanked a paper towel from the dispenser. "Your *sister* stole your Trans Am, not me. I'm the one who kicked your ass, remember?"

"Only because I was drunk." She propped a hand on her scrawny hip. "Now are you going to get that old bitch to open up this town or not? Me and Ronnie want to put in a bait shop."

"I can't do anything. She hates me!"

"So what? I hate you, too. But that don't mean you shouldn't rise above it to help out other people."

Blue shoved her wet paper towel in Karen Ann's hands and returned to the table.

♥

On the last day of June, Blue loaded up her painting supplies in the back of Dean's Vanquish, backed it out of Nita's garage, and headed to the farm. Instead of leaving Garrison, she was starting work on the dining room murals. She'd been so nervous she couldn't eat breakfast and, with a queasy stomach, she carried everything inside. Just looking at the blank walls made her hands clammy.

Everyone except Dean poked their heads in while she set up. Even Jack appeared. She'd seen him half a dozen times in the past few weeks, but she still tripped over the stepladder.

"Sorry," he said. "I thought you heard me coming."

She sighed. "It wouldn't have done any good. I'm destined to mortify myself where you're concerned."

He grinned and hugged her.

"Great," she grumbled. "Now I can never wash this T-shirt again, and it's my favorite."

When he left, she taped up her drawings so she could refer to them as she worked. With her gray watercolor pencil, she began sketching the broad outlines onto the walls: hills and woodland, the pond, a sweep of mowed pasture. As she marked in a stretch of fence, she heard a car pull up and looked outside. "Dear God in heaven."

She hurried to the porch and watched Nita haul herself from the driver's seat of her red Corvette. April must have heard the car, too, because she popped up behind Blue's shoulder and softly uttered the F-bomb.

"What are you doing?" Blue called out. "I thought you couldn't drive."

"Of course I can drive," Nita snapped. "Why would I have a car if I couldn't drive?" She jabbed her cane toward the brick sidewalk. "What's wrong with good concrete? Somebody's going to break their neck. Where's Riley? She should be helping me."

"Here I am, Mrs. Garrison." Riley raced outside, without her guitar in tow for once. "Blue didn't tell me you were coming."

"Blue doesn't know everything. She just thinks she does."

"I'm cursed," Blue muttered. "What did I do to deserve this?"

Riley helped Nita inside and led her to the kitchen table as directed. "I brought my own lunch." Nita pulled the sandwich Blue had made her earlier from her purse. "I didn't want to be a bother."

"You're not a bother," Riley said. "After you eat, I'll read your horoscope and play my guitar for you."

"You need to practice your ballet."

"I will. After I play my guitar for you."

Harrumph.

Blue gritted her teeth. "What are you doing here?"

"Riley, would you know if there's any Miracle Whip? Just because Blue doesn't like Miracle Whip, she thinks nobody else does. But that's Blue for you." Riley fetched a jar from the refrigerator. Nita slathered it on and asked April for iced tea. "None of that instant stuff. And lots of sugar." She held out half her sandwich toward Riley.

"No, thank you. I don't like Miracle Whip either."

"You're turning into a picky eater."

"April says she doesn't believe in eating things she doesn't like."

"That's fine for her, but look at you. Just because you used to be fat doesn't mean you should turn into some kind of anorestic."

"Leave her alone, Mrs. Garrison," April said firmly. "She's not turning into an anorexic. She's just paying attention to what she eats."

Nita harrumphed, but when it came to April, she picked her arguments.

Blue returned to the dining room with the distinct feeling that today wouldn't be the only day Nita elected to camp out here.

♥

Later that afternoon, Dean came inside, grimy and sweaty from working on the porch. Blue decided there was a big difference between a sweaty male who didn't bathe regularly and a sweaty one who'd had a shower just that morning. The former was repulsive, the second . . . wasn't. While she didn't exactly want to curl up to his damp chest, she didn't exactly not want to either.

"Your shadow's taking a nap in the living room," he said, unaware of the effect he and his damp T-shirt were having on her. "That woman has more balls than you do."

"It's why she and I get along so gosh-darned well."

He examined the sketches she'd taped to the door and window frames, then turned his attention to the long wall, where she'd begun working in the sky. "This is a big project. How do you know where to start?"

"Top to bottom, light to dark, background to foreground, soft edges to hard." She came down off the stepladder. "The fact that I understand technique doesn't mean you're not going to regret pushing me into this. My landscapes are—"

"Cutesy crap. I know. I wish you'd stop worrying so much." He handed her the roll of masking tape she'd dropped and studied the cans arranged on her metal cart. "Some of this is regular latex paint."

"I also work with enamel and oil paints—alkyds because they dry faster, right out of the tube if I want more intense color."

"That bag of kitty litter I carried in from the car . . ."

"It's the best way to get rid of the turpentine I clean my brushes in. It clumps, and then I can—"

Riley shot into the room with her guitar. "Mrs. Garrison told me her birthday is in two weeks! And she's never in her whole life had a birthday party. Marshall only gave her jewelry. Can we like have a surprise party for her here, Dean? Please, Blue. You could bake a cake and make some hot dogs and stuff."

"No!"

"No!"

Her forehead wrinkled in censure. "Don't you think you're both being kind of mean?"

"Yes," Dean said, "and I don't care. I'm not having a party for her."

"Then you do it, Blue," Riley said. "At her house."

"She wouldn't appreciate it. Appreciation isn't part of her vocabulary." Blue picked up the paint she'd poured into a plastic cup and mounted the stepladder.

"Maybe if everybody wasn't so mean to her all the time, she wouldn't be so mean herself." Riley stormed out.

Blue gazed after her. "Our little girl is starting to act like a normal bratty kid."

"I know. Isn't it great?"

It was pretty great.

Dean finally left to look at some horses. Blue pulled white paint onto her brush, and Riley wandered back in, still carrying her guitar. "I bet nobody even sends her a birthday card."

"I'll get her a card. I'll even make her a cake. We'll give her a party ourselves."

"It'd be better if more people would come."

As Riley returned to Nita, an interesting idea struck Blue, a welcome diversion from worrying about what was and wasn't taking shape on the walls. She thought it over for a while and finally called Syl at the resale shop.

"You want the town to throw Nita a surprise birthday party?" Syl said after Blue had explained. "And we're supposed to pull it together in two weeks?"

"Pulling it together is the least of our problems. Getting anyone to show up is the challenge."

"You really think throwing her a party will soften her up enough that she'll go along with the town plan?"

"Probably not," Blue said. "But nobody has a better idea, and miracles do happen, so I think we should give it a shot."

"I don't know. Let me talk to Penny and Monica."

Half an hour later, Syl called back. "We'll do it," she said with a marked lack of enthusiasm. "You just make sure she's there. It would be exactly like her to get wind of this and refuse to show up."

"She'll be there if I have to shoot her first and drag the body."

After half a dozen more interruptions, several of them from Nita,

Blue hung over the dining room's two doorways some of the heavy blue plastic the builders had left. When it was secure, she added a NO ADMITTANCE ON PAIN OF DEATH sign. She was nervous enough without having them looking over her shoulder the whole time she worked.

At the end of the day, she made everyone in the house swear on their iPods, guitars, Tango, Puffy, and a certain pair of Dolce & Gabbana boots to stay out of the dining room until the murals were done.

That evening, she wandered into Nita's bedroom just as the old lady was taking off her wig, revealing a flat cap of thin gray hair. "I had an interesting phone call today," Blue said as she settled on the side of her bed. "I wasn't going to say anything, but you'll somehow get wind of it and then you'll start bitching at me for keeping things from you."

Nita took a brush to her scalp. She hadn't fastened her kimono, and Blue saw she was wearing her favorite red satin nightgown. "What kind of phone call?"

Blue threw up her hands. "A bunch of idiots were planning to throw you a surprise birthday party. But don't worry. I put a stop to it." She picked up the latest issue of *Star* from the foot of the bed and pretended to thumb through it. "I guess some of the younger people in town heard the old stories and decided you got a raw deal when you first came here. They wanted to make up for it—like that could ever happen—with a party in the park, a big cake, balloons, and some asinine speeches made by people you hate. I made it more than clear. No party."

For once, Nita seemed to have been struck speechless. Blue perused the pages innocently. Nita set down her brush and tugged on the sash of her kimono. "It might be . . . interesting."

Blue hid a smile. "It'd be creepy, and you're not doing it." She tossed down the magazine. "Just because they've finally figured out they treated you like dirt doesn't mean you can't keep ignoring them."

"I thought you were on their side," Nita retorted. "You're always telling me how many people I'm hurting. I'm supposed to let them add stores where nobody's going to shop. Open up a bed-and-breakfast where nobody will ever stay."

"That's just good business, but you're obviously too old to understand modern economics."

Nita took one long suck on her teeth, then charged toward Blue. "You call them back right now and tell them to throw their big party. The bigger the better! I deserve it, and it's about time they realized it."

"I can't do that now. It's supposed to be a *surprise* party."

"You think I can't act surprised?"

Blue stomped around for a while arguing, and the more she argued, the more Nita dug in. All in all, a job well done.

Her work on the murals, however, was another matter. As one day gave way to the next, she deviated more and more from her drawings until she finally tore them off the walls.

♥

Dean suggested the two of them celebrate the Fourth of July by hiking in the Smokies. With his long legs and endless stamina, he had to keep doubling back on the strenuous trail to wait, but he never tried to rush her. Instead, he said he liked the slower pace because it kept him from sweating through his hair gel. She couldn't see even a dab of gel in that crisp hair, but he was being too nice for her to call him on it. She hated it when he was nice, so while they ate their trail lunch, she tried to pick a fight. He dragged her into a shady area near a waterfall and kissed her until she was too breathless to think straight. Then he took cruel advantage.

"You," he said gruffly. "Against the tree."

The silvered lenses of his latest pair of zillion-dollar sunglasses kept her from seeing his eyes, but the deliciously menacing set of his mouth made her shiver. "What are you talking about?"

"You've pushed me far enough, lady. It's time to play a kinky game of Prison Break."

She licked her lips. "It, uh, sounds scary."

"Oh, it is. For you, anyway. And you won't like what happens if you try to run. Now turn around and face the tree."

She was tempted to run just to test him, but the tree idea was too enticing. They'd been playing various forms of domination and submission games from the beginning. It kept things light, just the way she wanted it. "Which tree?"

"Prisoner's choice. Your *last* choice before I take over."

She lingered too long admiring the swell of muscles under his T-shirt. He crossed his arms over his chest. "Don't make me repeat myself."

"I want to call my lawyer."

"Out here I'm the law."

He could still manage to surprise her. She was alone with 180-odd pounds of alpha male, and she'd never felt safer or more aroused. "Don't hurt me."

He pulled off his sunglasses and slowly folded in the stems. "That depends on how good you are at following orders."

Wobbly kneed from sexual overload, she moved toward a sturdy red maple surrounded by a mossy carpet. Even the splash from the nearby waterfall couldn't cool her off. When this was over, she'd have to repay him in kind, but for now, she'd simply enjoy.

He tossed aside his sunglasses and gave her a nudge so she was facing the tree. "Put your hands on the trunk and don't drop them unless I tell you to."

She slowly extended her arms over her head. The rough scrape of bark against her skin heightened the sense of erotic danger. "Uh . . . what's this all about, sir?"

"The recent prison break at the maximum security women's prison on the other side of the ridge."

"Oh, that." How could a superstar jock have so much imagination? "But I'm nothing more than an innocent hiker."

"Then you won't mind if I search you."

"Well . . . only to prove how innocent I am."

"Sensible. Now spread 'em."

She inched her bare legs open. He knelt behind her and shoved them farther apart. His stubbly jaw abraded her inner thigh as he pushed down her socks and bracketed her ankles with his fingers. He rubbed his thumb in the hollow just beneath the anklebone, igniting an erogenous zone she hadn't even known existed. He took his time running his hands up her bare legs and along the backs of her thighs. Her skin broke out in goose bumps. She waited for him to reach the hem of her shorts, only to be disappointed when he bypassed those convenient leg openings and pushed up the back of her T-shirt instead.

"A prison tattoo," he growled. "Just as I thought."

"I got drunk at a Sunday school picnic, and when I woke up . . ."

His fingers settled in the smooth curve of her spine, just above the waistband of her shorts. "Save your breath. You know what this means, don't you?"

"No more Sunday school picnics?"

"A strip search."

"Oh, please, not that."

"Don't fight me or I'll have to get rough." He slipped his hands under her T-shirt, pushed up the front of her bra, and dragged his thumbs over her nipples. She moaned and her arms fell.

He pinched her nipples. "Did I say you could move?"

"S-sorry." She was going to die from sexual ecstasy. Somehow she managed to get her rubbery arms back to their former position. He drew down her zipper and pushed her shorts and panties to her ankles. The cool air brushed her bare skin. She pressed the side of her face against the rough tree bark as he played with her bottom, kneading it, skimming the crack with his thumbs, testing to see how far she'd let him go with this wicked game.

Very far, as it turned out.

Finally, when she was so crazy with need, she could barely stand, she heard the slide of his zipper. "One last place to look," he said huskily.

And then he turned her to face him, kicking away her panties and shorts. His eyes were half-lidded, opaque with desire. As though she weighed nothing, he picked her up and set her spine against the tree trunk. Splaying her legs, he stepped between them. She wrapped her calves around his hips and entwined her arms around the strong column of his neck. He opened her with his fingers, tested her arousal, and finally claimed what was, at that moment, indisputably his.

He was so strong that, even as he drove deep inside her, he made sure the rough bark didn't abrade her skin. She buried her face in the crook of his neck, breathed him in, and climaxed long before she wanted to. He expected more from her. After letting her rest for a moment, he began to move inside her again, filling her, luring her, commanding her to join him.

The waterfall streamed beside them. Its crystalline gush mingled with her rough breathing, with his hoarse commands and husky endearments. Their mouths fused, swallowing the words. He dug his fingers into her bottom. A surge . . . a rush . . . and they, too, joined the flood.

Afterward they said nothing. As they headed back down the trail, he moved ahead of her, and she shocked herself by starting to cry. Those old feelings of wanting to belong had once again taken root inside her.

Dean walked faster, increasing the distance between them. She understood him too well. He slid in and out of relationships like other people changed clothes. Friends, lovers . . . It was all so easy. When one relationship ended, he had a long line of people waiting to step into the void.

He turned and called back to her—something about having worked up another appetite. She faked a laugh, but her pleasure in their encounter was gone. What had started out as nothing more than a silly sex game had left her feeling as fragile and defenseless as the child she'd once been.

♥

A letter that had been forwarded from Seattle arrived from Virginia the next day. When Blue opened it, a photo slipped out. Six schoolgirls wearing filthy clothes and teary smiles posed in front of a simple wooden building in the jungle. Her mother stood in the middle, looking exhausted and triumphant. Across the bottom, Virginia had written a simple message. *They're safe. Thank you.* Blue gazed at the picture for a long time. As she took in the face of each girl her money had saved, she let go of her resentment.

On Thursday afternoon, four days after the hike in the Smokies and two days before Nita's party, Blue put the finishing touches to the walls. The murals no longer bore more than a surface resemblance to the original drawings, nor did they resemble the gooey landscapes of her college years. They were something else entirely—all wrong—but she couldn't make herself fix them.

Everyone had honored her demand to stay out of the dining room, and she'd scheduled the grand unveiling for tomorrow morning. She wiped a bead of sweat from her forehead. The air-conditioning in the farmhouse had broken down that morning, and even with a portable fan and the dining room windows open, she felt hot, nauseated, and more than a little panicked. What if— But she wouldn't think about that until after Nita's party. She pulled her damp T-shirt away from her body and stood back to observe her disastrous, misguided work. She'd never done anything she loved more.

She'd finished her last bit of scumbling—using a piece of cheesecloth to blend some shadows for a softer edge—and begun cleaning up when she heard cars approaching. Peering through the open window, she saw two white stretch limos pull up. The doors opened and an assortment of gorgeous people spilled out. The men were all huge, with big necks, bulging biceps, and massive trunks. Despite the differences in the women's skin color and hairstyles, they could have come from a cloning factory for the young and luscious. Pricey sunglasses perched on their heads, designer purses dangled from their wrists, and revealing clothes draped their lithe bodies. Dean Robillard's real life had just come calling.

Dean had gone off to the neighboring horse farm again, April and Riley were running errands, Jack was holed up at the cottage working on a song, and Nita had stayed home for once. Blue pulled out what was left of her ponytail, combed through her sweaty hair with her fingers, and refastened it into a somewhat neater arrangement. As she pushed aside the plastic and stepped out into the foyer, she heard the women's voices drifting through the screen.

"I didn't think it would be so . . . rural."

"There's a barn and everything."

"Be careful where you walk, girlfriend. I don't see any cows, but that doesn't mean they aren't hangin' around someplace."

"The Boo knows how to live," one of the men said. "I should get myself a place like this."

As Blue stepped out on the porch, the women took in her bedraggled appearance: dirty T-shirt, threadbare shorts, and paint-splattered work boots. A man with a tree trunk neck and mile-wide shoulders approached. "Dean around?"

"He's out riding, but he should be back in an hour or so." She wiped her dirty palms on her shorts. "I'm afraid the air-conditioning is temporarily on the fritz, but you can sit on the porch in back and wait for him."

They followed her through the house. The porch, with its new gray slate floor, freshly painted white walls, and high ceiling, felt cool and spacious after the hot dining room. Three graceful Palladian windows set in the walls above the screening sent shade-dappled light

over the wicker chaises and the black wrought-iron table that had arrived a few days earlier. Colorful cushions in soft greens punched
with black lent elegance to the homey space.

There were four men but five women. None of them bothered with
introductions, but she picked up a name here and there: Larry, Tyrell,
Tamika . . . and Courtney, a tall, very striking brunette who didn't
appear to be with any of the men. Blue quickly figured out why.

"As soon as T-camp is over, I'm going to make Dean take me to San
Fran for the weekend," Courtney said with a swish of her gleaming
hair. "We had such a great time there last Valentine's Day, and I deserve a little fun before I have to face another class of fourth graders."

Great. Courtney wasn't even a bimbo.

The women began complaining about the heat, despite the breeze
stirred up by the newly installed overhead fans. They all assumed
Blue was the hired help and started asking for beer, iced tea, diet
soda, and cold water bottles. Before long, Blue was making hot dogs,
slicing cheese, setting out cold cuts along with every snack food in the
house. One of the men wanted the television schedule; another
wanted Tylenol. She broke the news to a gorgeous redhead that Thai
food hadn't yet come to Garrison.

April called while Blue was poking around in the pantry, trying
to find some potato chips. "I saw Dean had company, so I detoured to
the cottage. Riley's with me. We'll stay here until the coast is clear."

"It's not right for you to go into hiding," Blue replied.

"It's reality. Besides, Jack wants me to listen to his new song."

Blue wished she could be at the cottage listening to a new Jack
Patriot song instead of waiting on Dean's friends.

When Dean finally appeared, everyone on the porch jumped up
to greet him. Even though he smelled of horse and sweat, Courtney,
who'd been complaining about the faint scent of manure, threw herself at him. "Dean, baby! Surprise! We thought you'd never get here."

"Hey, Boo. Nice place you got."

Dean didn't even glance in Blue's direction. She retreated to the kitchen, where she began stowing the perishables in the refrigerator. A few minutes later he popped in. "Hey, thanks for helping out. I'll grab a quick shower and be right back down."

As he disappeared, she wondered if he meant that she was supposed to keep waiting on his friends, or that he expected her to join the party. She shoved the refrigerator closed. Screw this. She was going back to work.

But before she could get away, Roshaun popped up at the door asking for ice cream. She fetched more dishes and cleared others away. As she loaded the dishwasher, a freshly showered Dean walked past her. "Thanks again, Blue. You're the best." Moments later, she heard him on the porch, laughing with his friends.

She stood there, taking in the kitchen that she loved so much. This was it, then. Or was it? She had to know for sure. Hands shaking, she set a couple of cans of warm diet soda on a tray, added the last bottle of cold beer, and carried it all out to the porch.

Courtney stood next to Dean, her arm curled around his waist, a strand of her shiny hair caught on the sleeve of his gray polo shirt. In her wedged heels, she was nearly his height. "But, Boo, you have to be back in time for Andy and Sherilyn's party. I promised we'd be there."

He's mine! Blue wanted to say. But he wasn't. Nobody belonged to her, and nobody ever had. She carried the tray over to him. Their eyes met—those familiar blue eyes that had laughed into her own so often. She started to say she'd saved the last cold beer for him, but before she could open her mouth, he looked away, as if she were invisible.

A giant lump grew in her throat. She set the tray gently on the table, went inside, and blindly made her way back to the dining room. More laughter drifted her way. She grabbed her brushes and began cleaning them out. She worked mechanically, tightening paint lids, storing her tools, folding drop cloths, determined to clean everything up so she wouldn't have to come back here. The plastic over the doorway rustled and Courtney poked her head into the dining room. For all her claims of being a teacher, she apparently couldn't read a NO ADMITTANCE sign.

"I have a tiny emergency," she said without even glancing at the murals. "Our drivers went to get lunch, and I'm getting a giant zit. I don't have my cover-up stick with me. Would you mind driving into town and getting some Erace or something? And maybe pick up some mineral water while you're there?" Courtney turned away. "Let me see if the others want anything."

Blue shoved the paint cart out of her way and told herself to give him a chance. But it was Courtney who returned, a hundred-dollar bill pressed between her fingers. "Cover-up stick, mineral water, and three bags of Cheetos. Keep the change." She pushed the money into Blue's hand. "Thanks, hon."

A dozen scenarios flashed through Blue's mind. She chose the one that let her keep her dignity.

An hour later, she returned to an empty house and dropped the cosmetic stick, mineral water, Cheetos, and change on the kitchen counter. Her chest felt as if someone had piled stones on top of it. She finished sweeping the dining room, put the chairs back in place, loaded up Nita's car, and ripped the plastic off the doorways. There was no time like the present to put an end to something that should never have begun.

When she was done, she took one last look at the murals and saw them for what they were. Sentimental bullshit.

Chapter Twenty-two

Dean stood at the edge of the path. They were dancing. All three of them. Behind the cottage, under the stars, with music blaring from a boom box sitting on the back steps. As he watched his father, he saw the genetic source of his own athleticism. He'd seen Jack dance in videos as well as at a live concert he'd been forced to attend with his college teammates. But observing him like this was different. He remembered some lamebrained rock critic comparing Jack's dancing with Mick Jagger's, but Jack had none of that androgynous slink and strut. He was all power.

Riley, who should have been in bed, circled Jack, her movements clumsy, but filled with a puppy dog energy that would have made Dean smile if he hadn't been so unhappy.

April danced barefoot. A long, gauzy skirt twisted around her hips. She arched her spine and lifted her hair. As her lips formed a sensuous pout, he saw the reckless, self-destructive mother of his childhood, enslaved by the gods of rock and roll.

Riley ran out of breath and collapsed in the grass next to the dog. Jack and April locked eyes. He answered her shimmy with some industrial grind. The porch light bounced off her bangles. They kicked it up, moving as if they'd been dancing together for years. April strutted, her lips forming small, moist pillows. Jack gave her a rocker's sneer.

Dean wouldn't have come here at all tonight if April hadn't stopped answering his e-mails a few days ago. Now he was watching the people who'd conceived him get it on right before his eyes. What a perfect ending to a shit hole day. Courtney had been a clingy pain in the ass, and he'd been glad when the women had dragged her back to Nashville to shop. The guys had hung around for a while. For too long. Dean had needed to get to Blue, but by the time he reached Nita Garrison's house, the windows were dark. He'd climbed the balcony anyway, but the doors were locked, and Blue's bed lay empty on the other side of the glass panes. He felt a searing flash of pain before sanity returned. She wouldn't leave until after Nita's party on Saturday. Tomorrow he'd set things right, or as right as they could be.

Nothing had been the same since their Fourth of July hiking trip. Something had gone wrong in that goofy little sex game they'd played. At first, it had all been sexy fun, watching Blue's comic attempts at pretending to be a terrorized female. But at the end, when they'd clung together, a well of tenderness had grown inside him, and something had shifted. Something he wasn't ready to look at too closely.

Riley caught her second wind and joined the dancing again. Dean stood outside the pool of light. Separate from them. Just the way he wanted it.

Jack moved toward Riley, and she started showing off for him, rolling out her entire repertoire of eager, awkward moves. April grinned and danced away. Her skirt swirled. She cocked her head. Spun. And that was when she saw Dean.

With losing a beat, she held out her hand.

He stood immobile. She danced closer, moving her arm, luring him into their circle.

He felt frozen, dizzy, a prisoner of his DNA. The music, the dance drew him to a place he didn't want to be. Those double helix strands of genetic matter imbedded inside him were a hereditary package he'd channeled into sports, but now those ladderlike structures wanted to draw him back to the source. To the dance.

His father jived.

His mother beckoned.

He turned away from them both and strode off to the farm-house.

♥

Jack laughed when April suddenly stopped dancing. "Look, Riley. We're too much for her."

Jack hadn't seen Dean. April made herself smile. Jack and Riley were learning to have fun together, and she wouldn't spoil it with her own sadness. "I'm thirsty," she said. "I'll get us something to drink." When she reached the kitchen, she closed her eyes. It was pain she'd seen on Dean's face, not contempt. He'd wanted to join them—she could feel it—but he hadn't been able to take that first step.

She got busy pouring orange juice for herself and Riley. She couldn't control Dean's feelings, only her own. *Let go and let God.* She poured an iced tea for Jack. He'd want a beer, but he was out of luck. She hadn't expected him to show up at the cottage tonight. She and Riley had been sitting in the backyard talking about boys and listening to an old Prince album when he'd appeared. Before she knew it, they were all dancing.

She and Jack had always been a perfect match that way. They had the same style and energy. Under the spell of the music, she didn't have to think about the folly of being fifty-two years old and still fascinated with Jack Patriot. The music shifted to a ballad. She carried the drinks outside and paused on the steps as Jack tried to pull Riley into a slow dance.

"But I don't know how," she protested.

"Stand on my feet."

"I can't do that! I'm too big. I'll squish your toes."

"A scrawny chicken like you? My toes will be just fine. Come on. Hop up." He pulled her into his arms, and she gingerly placed her bare feet on top of his sneakers. She looked so small next to him. So pretty with her curly hair, bright eyes, and golden skin. April had fallen in love with her.

She sat down on the steps and watched. When she was a kid, she'd seen a girl her age dance like that with her father. April's own father had treated her as an inconvenience, and she remembered locking herself in a bathroom stall so no one would see her cry. But she'd gotten even with him when she was older. She'd found all kinds of boys to give her the love he'd denied. One of them had been Jack Patriot.

Riley had a good sense of rhythm and finally felt confident enough to get off his feet and try the steps on her own. Jack kept it simple. At the end, he twirled her and told her she was a champ, leaving Riley looking giddy and proud. April served their drinks. When they finished, Jack announced it was past Riley's bedtime and took her back to the farmhouse. April was too restless to go inside, so she brought out a blanket and lay down to watch the stars. Blue was planning to leave in four days, Dean in a week and a half, and she'd be going back to L.A. right after. Once she got there, she'd bury herself in work and draw strength from knowing she'd finally learned to keep her soul intact.

"Dean's at the house with Riley," that familiar whiskey-gravel voice said. "I didn't abandon her."

She looked up and saw Jack coming toward her across the grass. "I thought you'd turned in for the night."

"I'm not that old." He went to the boom box and sorted through the CDs lying on the step next to it. Lucinda Williams began singing "Like a Rose." He returned to the blanket and reached down for her. "Dance with me."

"Bad idea, Jack."

"We've had some of our best times with bad ideas. Stop being such an old lady."

She hated that—he'd known she would—and she came to her feet. "If you try to feel me up . . ."

His teeth flashed in a pirate's grin, and he pulled her into his arms. "Mad Jack only feels 'em up if they're under thirty. Although, since it's dark . . ."

"Shut up and dance."

He used to smell like sex and cigarettes. Now he smelled of oak, bergamot, and night. His body, too, felt different from the skinny boy's build she remembered. He was still thin, but he'd picked up muscle. He'd also lost the gaunt look that had hollowed out his cheeks when he'd first arrived. Lucinda's lyrics enfolded them. They drew closer until only a ribbon of air separated their bodies. Soon even that was gone. She looped her arms around his neck. He placed his around her waist. She let herself rest against him. He had a hard-on, but it was simply there. Imposing, but not demanding anything from her.

She let herself drift with the music. She was deeply aroused, floating in a slippery sea. He brushed the hair from her neck and buried his lips in the hollow under her ear. She turned her head and let him kiss her. It was a deep, sweet kiss, far more arousing than their long-ago drunken ones. When they finally separated, the question in his eyes cut through her dreamy state. She shook her head.

"Why?" he whispered, stroking her hair.

"I don't do one-night stands anymore."

"I promise it'll be more than one night." He caressed her temple with his thumb. "You have to wonder what it would be like."

More than he could imagine. "I wonder about a lot of things that aren't good for me."

"Are you sure? We're not kids."

She pushed away. "I don't put out for good-looking rockers anymore."

"April . . ."

Her cell rang from the back step. *Thank you, God.* She moved to answer it.

"You're not really going to pick that up, are you?" he said.

"I have to." As she crossed to the step, she pressed the back of her hand to her lips, but she didn't know if she was wiping away their kiss or sealing it in. "Hello?"

"April, it's Ed."

"Ed. I've been waiting for you to call." She moved quickly inside.

Half an hour elapsed before she got off the phone. She went back out to bring in her things and was surprised to see Jack still there, lying on the blanket, looking at the stars. He lay with one knee bent and an arm crooked behind his head. She was much too glad to see he'd stayed.

He spoke without looking at her. "Tell me about him."

She heard the stiffness in his voice and remembered his old, jealous eruptions. If she hadn't given up playing games, she'd have told him to go to hell, but she sat on the blanket and let her skirt fall in soft folds around her knees. "Them."

"How many?"

"Right now? Three."

She steeled herself as he rolled to face her. But he didn't attack. "They're not lovers then."

It was a statement, not a question. "How do you know that?"

"Because I do."

"I have men calling me at all hours."

"Why is that?"

She saw only curiosity. Either he didn't care whom she kept company with, or he'd begun to understand the woman she'd become. She lay back on the blanket. "I'm a recovering drug addict and alcoholic. I've been in AA for years. I'm sponsoring three men and one woman right now, all in L.A. It's not easy to be there for them long-distance, but they didn't want to change sponsors."

"I can understand why. I'm sure you're very good at what you do."

He propped himself on his elbow so he was gazing down at her. "I've never completely gotten over you. You know that, don't you?"

She had to call it the way she saw it, not the way she wanted it to be. "It's not me you can't get over. It's your guilt about Dean."

"I know the difference, and you're the only woman I've never been able to forget."

As she gazed into his eyes, he dropped his head and kissed her again. Her mouth grew soft and giving under his. But when she felt his hand slip between her legs, she remembered Jack's feelings for her always began and ended in his pants. She rolled out from under him and stood up. "I meant what I said. I don't do this anymore."

"You expect me to believe you've given up sex?"

"Only with rockers." She walked over to the step to turn off the music and gather up her things. "I've had three long-term relationships since I've been sober. A cop, a television producer, and the photographer who got me involved with Heart Gallery. All great guys, and none of them sang a note. Not even karaoke."

Through the darkness, she saw his softly mocking smile as he rose to his feet. "Poor April. Depriving yourself of all that hot rocker love."

"Respecting myself. Probably more than you've been doing."

"I know this'll disappoint you, April, but I stopped being a player years ago. I've gotten used to having real relationships." He picked up the blanket and carried it over to her. "That's the one thing you and I have never tried. Maybe it's time we gave it a shot."

She was so stunned she simply stared at him. He pressed the blanket into her hands, brushed her cheek with a kiss, and left her alone.

♥

At seven the next morning, Dean pulled up behind Nita's house. He hated knowing he'd hurt Blue yesterday. The only reason he'd shut her out was so he didn't have to deal with everyone's questions. How could he explain her to his friends when he couldn't explain her to himself? He knew how to relate to women as friends or as lovers, but not as both.

A dove flew up from Nita's birdbath as he made his way to her back door. He let himself in without knocking. Nita sat at the kitchen table in her big blond wig and a garish floral robe. "I'm calling the police," she said, with more annoyance than anger. "I'm having you arrested for breaking and entering."

He leaned down to scratch a comatose Tango behind the ears. "Can I have some coffee first?"

"It's barely seven o'clock. You should have knocked."

"Didn't feel like it. Just like you don't feel like knocking when you come to my house."

"Liar. I always knock. And Blue is still asleep, so go away and don't bother her."

He filled two mugs with Nita's inky coffee. "What's she doing in bed this late?"

"I'm sure that's not any of your business." Her indignation finally bubbled to the surface, and she stabbed her index finger toward him, a magenta-painted bullet to his head. "You're breaking her heart. And you don't even care."

"Blue's mad, not heartbroken." He sidestepped Tango. "Leave us alone for a while."

Her chair squeaked as she pushed back from the table. "A word of advice, Mr. Hotshot. If I was you, I'd take a look at what she's keeping under her bathroom sink."

Ignoring her, he headed upstairs.

♥

Blue wasn't entirely surprised to hear Dean talking to Nita downstairs. The sun streamed through the balcony doors as she finished zipping up her jeans. She hadn't been able to deal with him coming over the railing, so she'd slept in the bedroom next to Nita's. Now he intended to charm his way back into her good graces. Lots of luck.

As she sat on the side of the bed to pull on her sandals, he appeared in the doorway. Blond, hunky, irresistible. She yanked on a sandal strap. "I have a million errands to run before Nita's party tomorrow, and I don't want to do this now."

He set a mug on her bedside table. "I know you're pissed."

Pissed was only one part of it, the part that wasn't hiding secrets. "Later, Deanna. Real men avoid these kinds of discussions."

"Cut the crap." His field commander's voice always took her aback. "Yesterday wasn't personal. Not in the way you think."

"It sure felt personal."

"You think I was embarrassed to introduce you to my friends because of your crappy clothes and generally shitty disposition, but that couldn't be further from the truth."

She shot up from the side of the bed. "Don't waste your breath. I'm not the kind of woman your friends expect Malibu Dean to hang with, and you didn't want to field all the questions."

"Do you really think I'm that small-minded?"

"No. I think you're basically a gentleman, so you didn't want to spell out that I'm only a buddy with sleeping privileges."

"You're more than a buddy, Blue. You're one of the best friends I have."

"Which makes me what? How about . . . a *buddy*!"

He shoved a hand through his hair. "I didn't mean to hurt you. I just want what's between us to stay private."

"Like all the other things in your life you want to stay private. Aren't you starting to lose track?"

"You don't have a clue what it's like being a public person," he shot back. "I have to be careful."

She grabbed the coffee mug and snatched up her purse from the foot of her bed. "Translated, that means I've become another one of your dirty little secrets."

"That's a rotten thing to say."

She couldn't handle this now, not with a secret of her own. "I'm going to make this easy. Today's Friday. Nita's party is tomorrow. I have some loose ends to tie up around here on Sunday, but first thing Monday morning I'm taking off permanently for parts unknown."

His expression grew thunderous. "This had better be more of your bullshit."

"Why? Because I'm ending it instead of you?" All the emotions she didn't want him to see—sadness, fear, pain—tried to break through her tough girl swagger, but she beat them back. "Life is good, Boo. I got a great deal on a rental car, and I bought a brand-new road atlas. You've been an amusing diversion, but it's time for me to move on."

She'd called a play he wasn't expecting and his hands curled at his sides. "Apparently you need some time to grow up." His words were so cold she half-expected a vapor cloud to form around his mouth. "We'll settle this at Nita's party tomorrow. Maybe by then you'll be able to think like a rational human being." He strode out of the room.

She sat back on the bed, foolishly wishing he'd taken her in his arms and begged forgiveness. Wished at the very least that he'd said something about the murals before he stormed off. He'd seen them by now. Yesterday, she'd found a hand-delivered envelope in Nita's mailbox with a check that April had made out. That was it. No personal note. April and Dean had flawless taste. They hated them. She'd known they would. But somehow she'd hoped they wouldn't.

♥

Dean marched down the pink-carpeted hallway. As long as he concentrated on wringing Blue's neck, he wouldn't have to think about what a jerk he was being. He hated knowing he'd hurt her. She truly believed he'd been embarrassed to introduce her to his friends, but it wasn't embarrassment. If the guys had taken the time to talk to her yesterday instead of treating her like a maid, they'd have fallen in love with her. But Dean didn't want anyone—especially not his teammates—picking over something as personal as his affair with Blue when it was still so new. Hell, he hadn't even known her for two months.

And now she was planning to leave him. He'd realized all along that he couldn't count on her. But after the way he'd treated her yesterday, it wasn't so simple to shift the blame.

He'd reached the landing when he remembered what Nita had said. The old woman loved to make trouble, but she also cared about Blue in her own twisted way. He turned around and went back upstairs.

Blue's bathroom had pink walls, pink tile, and a shower curtain printed with dancing champagne bottles. A towel, still damp from her shower, hung crookedly on the towel bar. He knelt in front of the sink, opened the cupboard door, and stared at the cellophane-wrapped box sitting right in front.

He heard quick footsteps behind him. "What are you doing?" she said in a rush.

As his brain registered what he saw, the blood rushed from his head. He picked up the box and somehow made it to his feet.

"Leave that alone!" she cried.

"You said you were on the pill."

"I am."

They'd been using condoms, too. Except a couple of times . . . He looked at her. She stared back, all big eyes and pale white skin. He held up the pregnancy test kit. "I'm guessing this doesn't belong to Nita."

She tried to give him her mulish look but couldn't carry it off. Her eyelashes swept her cheeks as she looked down. "A few weeks ago when I had food poisoning from Josie's shrimp . . . I threw up my pill. I didn't think anything about it."

A freight train roared straight toward him. "Are you saying throwing up one pill could get you pregnant?"

"It's possible, I guess. My period was due last week, and I couldn't figure out why I wasn't getting it. Then I remembered what had happened with the pill."

He twisted the box in his hands. The train screamed through the bones of his skull. "You haven't opened it."

"Tomorrow. I need to get through Nita's party first."

"No. No you don't." He pulled her the rest of the way into the bathroom and shut the door with the flat of his hand. His fingers felt numb. "Today. Right now." He tore open the box.

Blue knew him well, and it didn't take her long to see this was one fight she couldn't win. "Wait in the hall," she said.

"Not on your life." He ripped open the box.

"I just went."

"Go again." His hands, usually so nimble, fumbled with the directions as he tried to unfold them.

"Turn around," she said.

"Stop it, Blue. We're getting this over with right now."

Wordlessly, she took the box. He stood there watching her. Waiting. Finally, she got the job done.

The directions said to wait three minutes. He marked the time off with his Rolex. It had three dials, one of them a tachometer, but all he cared about was the slow sweep of the second hand. As it inched its way around, a dozen thoughts he couldn't sort out—didn't want to sort out—tumbled through his head.

"Isn't the time up yet?" she finally said.

He was sweating. He blinked and nodded.

"You look," she whispered.

He picked up the stick with clammy hands and studied it. Finally he raised his eyes and met hers. "You're not pregnant."

She nodded, expressionless. "Good. Now go away."

♥

Dean drove around for a couple of hours and ended up on a back road. He pulled the truck off to the side of the crumbling asphalt and got out. It wasn't even ten o'clock. Today would be a scorcher. He heard the sound of moving water and followed it into the woods where he came to a creek. A rusted oil drum lay on its side in the water along with some old tires, bed springs, a smashed highway pylon, and some other junk. It didn't seem right, people dumping their shit like this.

He waded in and began dragging it out. Before long, his sneakers were waterlogged, and he was covered in mud and grease. He slipped on some mossy rocks and got his shorts wet, but the cold water felt good. He wished mountains of litter clogged the creek so he could spend all day here, but before long, the water ran free again.

His world had caved in. As he climbed back in his truck, he couldn't get a deep breath. He'd take a long walk when he reached the farm and straighten out his head. But he didn't make it that far. Instead, he found himself turning into the narrow lane that led to the cottage.

The sound of the guitar drifted toward him as he got out of the truck. Jack sat in a kitchen chair on the porch, his bare ankles crossed on the railing, and the guitar cradled to his chest. He wore three-day stubble, a Virgin Records T-shirt, and black athletic shorts. Dean's muddy socks had collapsed around his ankles, and his feet squished in their sneakers as he approached the porch. The familiar wariness shaded Jack's eyes, but he kept playing. "You look like you lost a pig-wrestling contest."

"Anybody else here?"

Jack strummed a couple of minor chords. "Riley's riding her bike, and April's gone for a run. They should be back soon."

Dean hadn't come to see them. He stopped at the bottom of the steps. "Blue and I aren't engaged. I picked her up outside Denver two months ago."

"April told me. Too bad. I like her a lot. She makes me laugh."

Dean rubbed some caked mud from between his knuckles. "I saw Blue this morning. A couple of hours ago." Now his stomach was giving him trouble, and he tried to suck in some more air. "She thought she might be pregnant."

Jack stopped playing. "Is she?"

A bird called out from the tin roof. Dean shook his head. "No."

"Congratulations."

He stuck his hands in his clammy pockets then pulled them out again. "These pregnancy tests people buy . . . You have to— Maybe you already know this. You have to wait three minutes to get the re-sults."

"Okay."

"The thing is . . . That three minutes while I was waiting . . . I had—I had all these thoughts running through my head."

"I guess that's understandable."

The steps creaked as Dean came up onto the edge of the porch. "Things like how I'd go about setting up medical care for Blue. Whether I trusted my attorney to handle child support or if I should have my agent do it. How to keep it out of the papers. You know the drill."

Jack rose and leaned the guitar against the chair. "A panic reac-tion. I remember the symptoms."

"Yeah, well, when you had your panic reaction, you were— what?—twenty-four? I'm thirty-one."

"I was twenty-three, but the bottom line's the same. If you weren't planning to marry Blue, you had to come up with a plan."

"It's not the same thing. April was crazy. Blue's not. She's one of the sanest people I know." He meant to stop there but couldn't. "She said I've turned her into another one of my dirty little secrets."

"People who haven't lived in the spotlight don't understand."

"That's what I told her." He rubbed his stomach where it was burning. "But those three minutes . . . Everything I was thinking. The plan I was coming up with . . . The lawyer, the child sup-port—"

"All kinds of shit runs through your head at a time like that. Forget about it."

"How am I supposed to do that? Like father, like son, right?"

Dean felt as though he'd ripped himself open, but Jack sneered. "Don't bring yourself down to my level. I've seen you with Riley. If Blue had been pregnant, there's no way you'd have turned your back on your kid. You'd have been right there for him while he was growing up."

Dean should have let it go, but his knees bent, and he found himself sitting on the step. "Why did you do it, Jack?"

"Why the hell do you think?" Jack bristled with derision. "I could candy coat it for you, but the bottom line is that I didn't know how to deal with April, and I didn't want to be bothered with you. I was a rock star, baby. An American icon. Too busy giving interviews and letting everybody kiss my ass. I'd have had to grow up to be a father, and where was the fun in that?"

Dean dropped his hands between his knees and picked at the paint flaking on the step. "But it changed, didn't it?"

"Never."

He came to his feet. "Don't bullshit me. I remember those father-and-son get-togethers when I was fourteen, fifteen. You trying to figure out how to make up for all those lost years and me spitting in your eye."

Jack grabbed the guitar. "Look, I'm working on a song here. Just because you finally decided you want to dig up old garbage doesn't mean I have to grab a shovel, too."

"Just tell me this. If you had to do it all over again . . ."

"I can't do it over, so let it go."

"But if you could . . ."

"If I had to do it again, I'd have taken you away from her!" he said fiercely. "How's that? And once I had you, I'd have figured out how to be a father. Fortunately for you, that didn't happen because, from where I stand, you turned out just fine on your own. Any man would be proud to have you for a son. Now, are you satisfied or do we have to fucking hug?"

The knots in Dean's stomach finally eased. He could breathe again.

Jack dropped the guitar to his side. "You can't make peace with me until you make peace with your mother. She deserves it."

Dean stubbed the muddy toe of his sneaker against the stair tread. "It's not that easy."

"It's easier than holding on to so much pain."

Dean turned away and headed back to his truck.

♥

He left his muddy sneakers and socks on the porch. As usual, no one had remembered to lock the front door. Inside, the house was cool and quiet. A basket in the foyer held his shoes. His caps hung on the coatrack. Next to the brass tray where he tossed his keys and spare change was a photograph of him when he'd been eight or nine. A bony, bare chest; knobby knees sticking out below his shorts; a football helmet engulfing his small head. April had taken it one summer when they'd lived in Venice Beach. His childhood photographs had popped up all over the house, pictures he didn't even remember.

Last night, Riley had tried to drag him in to see Blue's murals, but he'd wanted to see them for the first time with Blue, and he'd refused. Now, he turned away from the dining room without looking in and wandered into the living room. The deep-seated couches were a perfect fit for his long frame, and the television had been positioned so he could watch game film without light reflecting on the screen. The sheets of precisely cut glass protecting the wooden coffee table made drink coasters unnecessary. Drawers held whatever he might need: books, remote controls, nail clippers. Upstairs, none of the beds had footboards, and the bathroom counters were higher than normal.

The showers were spacious, and extra-long towel racks held the over-size bath sheets he preferred. April had done it all.

The echoes of her drunken sobs whispered in his ears. *"Don't be mad at me, baby. It'll get better. I promise. Tell me you love me, baby. If you tell me you love me, I promise I won't drink anymore."*

The woman who'd tried to suffocate him with her twisted, erratic love could never have created this oasis that had become his home.

Today had been too much. He needed time to come to terms with all these muddled feelings, except he'd had years, and what good had it done him? Through the French doors, he saw April entering the screen porch from outside. He and Jack had built that porch, but she'd conceived of it: the high ceiling, the arched windows, the slate floor that was cool on even the hottest day.

She braced the heels of her hands in the small of her back to cool down from her run. Her body glistened with sweat. She wore black shorts, a bright blue racerback top, and she'd pulled her hair into a twisted ponytail far more stylish than Blue's haphazard arrangement.

He needed to get into the shower. He needed to be by himself. He needed to talk to Blue, who understood everything. Instead, he pushed the handle on the French doors and quietly stepped out onto the porch.

The temperature had already hit the mid-eighties, but the tiles were cool against his bare feet. April had her back to him. He'd moved the chairs last night when he'd hosed down the porch, and she was pushing them under the table again. He walked over to the CD player that sat on a black wrought-iron baker's rack. He didn't bother to check which of April's albums was in the changer. If it belonged to his mother, it would be right. He hit the button.

April whirled around as music blared from the small speakers. Her lips parted in surprise. She took in his muddy appearance and started to say something, but he spoke first. "Do you want to dance?"

She stared at him. Agonizing seconds ticked by. He couldn't think of anything else to say, so he began to move to the beat. His feet, his hips, his shoulders. She stood frozen. He held out his hand, but his mother—this woman who lived to dance when ordinary mortals could only walk—his mother had forgotten how to move.

"You can do it," he whispered.

She drew an unsteady breath, the sound somewhere between a sob and a laugh. Then she arched her spine, lifted her arms, and gave herself up to the music.

They danced until sweat dripped from their bodies. From rock to hip-hop, they showed off their moves, each trying to outdo the other. Strands of hair stuck to April's neck, and muddy streaks trickled down his bare legs onto the tiles. As they danced, he remembered this wasn't the first time. They'd danced when he was a kid. She'd pull him away from video games or TV, sometimes even from his breakfast if she'd gotten in late. He'd forgotten there were good times, too.

Right in the middle of a song, the music abruptly snapped off. A crow squawked in the silence. They turned to see a cranky Riley standing by the silent CD player, her hands on her hips. "It's too loud!"

"Hey, turn that back on," April said.

"What are you guys doing? It's lunchtime, not dance time."

"Any time is dance time," Dean said. "What do you think, April? Should we let baby sister dance with us?"

April stuck her nose in the air. "I doubt she could keep up."

"I can keep up," Riley said. "But I want to eat lunch. And you guys smell."

Dean gave April a shrug. "She can't keep up."

Riley's forehead wrinkled in outrage. "Who says?"

Dean and April stared at her. Riley glowered back. Then she snapped the music back on, and they all danced together.

Chapter Twenty-three

Blue swiped a highlighting blush across her cheekbones. The soft pink complemented her glossy new lipstick and darker mascara. She'd also used a little kohl liner along her lash line and some smoky eye shadow. She looked great.

Big deal. This was about pride, not beauty. She had something to prove to Dean before she drove away from Garrison.

As she left the bathroom, she spotted the empty pregnancy test kit she'd stuffed in the wastebasket yesterday morning after Dean had left. She wasn't pregnant. Excellent. Very, very excellent. She couldn't be responsible for a child, not with her vagabond's lifestyle. She'd probably never have a baby, and that was fine. At least she'd never make a child go through what she'd experienced. Still, she felt a new emptiness inside her. One more thing she'd have to get over.

She headed for Nita's room. The hem of the sundress she'd bought for the party brushed her knees. It was sunshine yellow with a ruffled hem and a corset top that made the most of her bustline. Her new purple sandals had satin ankle ribbons tied in delicate bows. The bright purple accents from the sandals and the amethyst-colored earrings Dean had given her provided a funky urban edge to the dress's ultrafemininity.

Nita was doing a last-minute primp in front of her mirror. With her big blond wig, diamond chandelier earrings, and billowy pastel caftan, she looked like a parade float sponsored by a senior citizens' bordello, but somehow she managed to carry it off. "Let's go, Sunshine," Blue said from the doorway. "And remember to act surprised."

"All I have to do is look at you," Nita said as she took Blue in from head to toe.

"It was time, that's all."

"Past time." As Blue came nearer, Nita reached out and fluffed a wisp of Blue's hair. "If you'd listened to me, you'd have let Gary cut it like this long ago."

"If I'd listened to you, I'd be a blonde."

Nita sniffed. "Just a thought."

Gary had been itching to get his hands on Blue's hair since the night they'd met at the Barn Grill. Once he had her in his chair, he'd drastically shortened the length to just past her earlobes, snipped a set of peek-a-boo bangs that highlighted her eyes, and cut a hullabaloo of short layers this way and that around her face. The cut was way too cute for Blue's comfort, but necessary all the same.

"You should have fixed yourself up for that football player from the start," Nita said. "Then he might have taken the two of you seriously."

"He takes me seriously."

"You know exactly what I'm talking about. He might have fallen in love with you, too. The same way you have with him."

"I'm crazy about him, but I'm not in love. There's a big difference. I don't fall in love." Nita didn't understand. This was about Blue leaving with her head high. She had to make sure Dean never looked back at her with even the faintest tinge of pity.

Blue hustled the old woman outside. Nita checked her lipstick in the visor as Blue backed out of the garage. "You should be ashamed of yourself for letting that football player drive you out of town. You belong right here in Garrison, not running all over the place."

"I can't make a living in Garrison."

"I already told you what I'd pay you to stay. A lot more than you can make painting your stupid little pictures."

"I like painting my stupid little pictures. What I don't like is living in servitude."

"I'm the one living in servitude," Nita countered, "the way you boss me around. You're so stubborn you don't see that you're turning your back on a golden opportunity. I won't live forever, and you know I don't have anybody else to leave my money to."

"You're one of the undead. You'll outlive us all."

"Make all the jokes you want, but I'm worth millions, and every one of them could be yours someday."

"I don't want your millions. If you had a shred of decency, you'd leave everything to the town. What I want is to get away from Garrison." She braked at the stop sign before she turned out on Church Street. She was right on time. "Remember," she said. "Be gracious."

"I worked at Arthur Murray. I know how to be gracious."

"On second thought, just move your lips and let me do the talking. It's safer that way."

Nita's snort sounded almost like a laugh, and Blue realized how much she'd miss the old bat. With Nita, Blue could be her own cranky self.

Just like she was with Dean.

♥

The balloon-festooned banner arching across Church Street read HAPPY 73RD BIRTHDAY MRS. G. Dean knew for a fact that Nita was seventy-six, and he had no doubt Blue was behind the deception.

About a hundred people had dutifully gathered in the park. More balloons waved in the breeze, along with red, white, and blue bunting left over from last week's Fourth of July celebration. A ragtag group of teenagers in black T-shirts and matching eyeliner finished playing a punk rock version of "Happy Birthday." Riley had told Dean they were Syl's nephew's garage band, the only musicians who would agree to play today.

Toward the front of the park, near a small rose garden, Nita had already begun cutting into a birthday cake the size of a putting green. Dean had missed the celebratory speeches, but judging from everyone's expression, they hadn't been memorable. More bunting draped long tables holding pitchers of punch and iced tea. He spotted April and Riley standing near the cake table, talking to a woman in a yellow dress. Some of the locals called out to him and he waved, but all the while he was looking for Blue.

Yesterday had been one of the worst and best days of his life. First his ugly encounter with Blue; then his painful, liberating conversation with Jack; and, finally, the dance marathon with April. He and April hadn't talked much afterward, and there'd been no "fucking hug," as Jack had put it, but they both understood things had changed. He didn't know exactly what their new relationship would be, only that it was time for him to grow up and get acquainted with the woman his mother had become.

Once again, he scanned the park, but he still didn't see Blue, and he wanted to. Somehow he had to make things right. Nita carried her plate to a chair reserved just for her while Syl and Penny Winters took over divvying up the cake for the crowd. Nita began shooting darts at the lead singer of the garage band, who was doing a demented Paul McCartney: *"You say it's your birthday."* Both Riley and the woman in the yellow dress had their backs to him. April gestured toward the band, and Riley broke away with her to get closer.

Syl spotted him as she dropped a square of cake on a paper plate. "Come on over, Dean. The frosting roses'll go fast. Blue, drag him over here. I've got a piece with his name on it."

He looked around, but he didn't see Blue anywhere. Then the

small woman in the yellow dress turned, and he got his first sack of the season. "Blue?"

For a moment, she looked as vulnerable as the child he'd accused her of being. Then her chin came up. "I know. I'm cute as hell. Do me a favor and let's not talk about it."

She was more than cute. April had turned Miss Muffet into a fashion plate. The dress fit her perfectly. It was exactly the right length and had the ideal drape for Blue's petite frame. The bodice clung to her curves, and the trendy purple wedge sandals emphasized her trim ankles. He'd imagined her like this. That crazy rumpus of a haircut made the most of her delicate bone structure. Her makeup was flattering and ultrafeminine. He'd known it wouldn't take much to make her look incredible. And she did. Beautiful, stylish, sexy. Pretty much indistinguishable from all the other beautiful, stylish, sexy women he knew. He hated her like this. He wanted his Blue back. When he finally got around to speaking, the wrong thing came out. "Why?"

"I got tired of everybody saying you're the pretty one."

He couldn't even fake a smile. He wanted to stuff her back into her rat-hole clothes, fling those fragile little sandals into the trash. Blue was Blue, one of a kind. She didn't need all this. But she'd think he'd gone crazy if he blurted that out, so he ran his thumb along her narrow shoulder strap. "April sure knows her stuff."

"Funny. That's what she said about you when she saw me. She thought you put me together."

"You did this yourself?"

"I'm an artist, Boo. This is another canvas for me, and not a very interesting one. Now go suck up to Nita. So far, she's avoided stabbing anyone, but the afternoon is young."

"First, you and I need to talk. About yesterday."

She stiffened. "I can't leave her alone. You know how she is."

"One hour, and then I'm coming to get you."

But Blue was already moving away.

April waved at him over Riley's head. The familiar trunk of his old resentments creaked open, but when he peered inside, he only saw dust. If he wanted to, he could walk over to his mother just to shoot the bull. Which was exactly what he did.

April had chosen to wear jeans to the celebration, along with a straw cowboy hat and a figure-hugging top that looked like vintage Pucci. She nodded toward the band. "With a lot of practice, the bass player might be mediocre."

Riley piped up next to her. "Did you see Blue? At first I didn't know it was her. She looks like a real grown-up and everything."

"An illusion," Dean replied tightly.

"Not from where I'm standing." April peered at him from under the rim of her cowboy hat. "And I doubt those men who've been trying to get her attention would agree. She seems oblivious, but nothing much gets past our Blue."

"My Blue," he heard himself say.

April found that interesting. "Your Blue? The same woman who's getting ready to leave town in two days?"

"She's not going anywhere."

April looked worried. "Then you have your work cut out for you."

A man approached with a ball cap pulled low on his head and big silver aviators shading his eyes. Riley gave a little jump. "Dad! I didn't think you'd come."

"I told you I would."

"I know, but . . ."

"But I've let you down so many times that you didn't believe me." He'd left his earrings and bracelets behind and dressed inconspicuously in an olive drab T-shirt and denim shorts, but nothing could disguise that famous profile, and a woman with a baby in her arms looked at him curiously.

April developed a sudden interest in the band. Dean's head wasn't screwed on straight enough right now to figure out what was going on between them.

"Do I see Blue coming toward us?" Jack asked.

"Doesn't she look awesome?" Riley said earnestly. "She's the best artist. Did you know Dean still won't look at her paintings in the dining room? Tell him, Dad. Tell him how beautiful they are."

"They're . . . different."

Blue popped up before Dean could ask what he meant. "Wow," Jack said. "You're a woman."

Blue flushed the way she always did when Jack addressed her directly. "It's temporary. Too much bother." Jack grinned, and Blue turned to Riley. "I'm sorry to be the bearer of bad news, but Nita wants you." Through a hole in the crowd, Dean saw Nita furiously beckoning from her chair. Blue frowned. "She's going to have a heart attack if she doesn't calm down. I vote we don't rush with the CPR."

"Blue always says stuff like that," Riley confided to the rest of them, "but she loves Mrs. Garrison."

"Have you been drinking again, young lady? I thought we talked about that." Blue grabbed Riley's arm and walked off with her.

"Looks like you're getting company," Jack said. "I'd better make myself scarce."

As he left, Judge Haskins and Tim Taylor, the high school principal, came up to Dean. "Hey, Boo." The judge couldn't quite pull his eyes away from April. "Nice to see you here performing your civic responsibility."

"However unpleasant it might be," Tim said. "I had to give up my Saturday morning foursome." Both men gazed at April. When no one said anything, Tim held out his hand. "Tim Taylor."

Dean should have seen this coming. Since April stayed out of places like the Barn Grill, she hadn't met either of them. She held out her hand. "Hi. I'm Susan—"

"This is my mother," Dean said. "April Robillard."

April's fingers twitched. She shook hands with both men, but beneath the brim of her cowboy hat, her eyes began filling with tears. "Sorry." She waved her fingers in front of her face. "Seasonal allergies."

Dean's hand settled on her shoulder. He hadn't planned to do this—hadn't thought this far ahead—but he felt like he'd just won the biggest game of the season. "My mother's been doing undercover work for me, using the name Susan O'Hara."

That required a few explanations, all of which Dean made up on the spot while April blinked her eyes and faked an allergy cough. When the men finally left, April rounded on him. "Don't say a single sappy thing to me or I'll completely lose it."

"Fine," he shot back. "Let's get some cake."

Getting cake, he decided, beat the heck out of having to fake his own allergy cough.

♥

April finally managed to separate herself from the crowd. She found a sheltered spot behind a row of shrubbery in the far corner of the park, sat in the grass against the fence, and let herself have a good cry. She had her son back. They'd need to test the waters for a while, but they were both stubborn, and she had faith they'd work it out.

In the distance, the garage band's lead singer began a painful, white boy's rap. Jack came around the corner of the shrubbery into her shady sanctuary. "Stop that kid before he harms innocent children." He pretended not to notice her red eyes as he sat next to her.

"Promise me you won't ever rap," she said.

"Only in the shower. Although . . ."

"Promise me!"

"All right." He picked up her hand, and she didn't try to draw it away. "I saw you with Dean."

Her eyes started tearing all over again. "He introduced me as his mother. It was . . . pretty wonderful."

Jack smiled. "Did he now? I'm glad."

"I hope someday maybe the two of you . . ."

"We're working on it." He stroked the center of her palm with his thumb. "I've been thinking about your aversion to one-night stands. Bottom line, we're going to have to date like normal adults."

"You want to date?"

"I told you last night that I've gotten used to real relationships. I need a permanent home base now that I have Riley, and it might as well be L.A." He played with her fingers, filling her with a sweet, aching tension. "By the way, I'm counting this as our first date. That gives me a better chance to score the next time we go out."

"Subtle." She shouldn't have smiled.

"I couldn't be subtle with you if I tried." The amusement faded from his eyes. "I want you, April. Every inch of you. I want to see you and touch you. I want to taste you. I want to be inside you. I want it all."

She finally pulled her hand away. "And then what?"

"We do it all over again."

"That's why God made groupies, Jack. Personally, I like a little more structure."

"April . . ."

She rose to her feet and headed off to find Riley.

♥

Dean finally managed to cut Blue from the crowd and pull her around the corner into an old cemetery next to the Baptist Church. He drew her toward the shade of the cemetery's most impressive monument, a sleek black granite plinth belonging to Marshall Garrison. He could see she was nervous but trying to hide it. "How did everybody find out April's your mother?" she said. "The whole town's buzzing."

"We're not talking about April. We're talking about what happened yesterday."

She looked away. "Yeah, what a relief, right? Can you imagine me with a baby?"

Oddly enough, he could. Blue would be a great mother, as fierce a protector as she would be a champion playmate. He pushed the image aside. "I'm talking about your asinine plan to leave town on Monday."

"Why is it asinine? Nobody thinks it's asinine for you to leave for training camp next Friday. Why is it okay for you to go but not for me?"

She looked too much like a grown-up. He wanted Miss Muffet back. "Because we're not done, that's why," he said, "and there's no reason to rush the end of something we're both enjoying."

"We're totally done. I'm a travelin' girl, and it's time for me to move on."

"Fine. You can keep me company when I drive back to Chicago. You'll like it there."

She ran her hand over the corner of Marshall's monument. "Too cold in the fall."

"No problem. Both my places have fireplaces and furnaces that work just fine. You can move in."

He didn't know which of them was more surprised by his words. She went completely still, and then her purple glass earrings jerked in her dark curls. "You want me to move in with you?"

"Why not?"

"You want us to *live together*?"

He'd never let a woman live with him, but the thought of sharing his space with Blue felt just fine. "Sure. What's the big deal?"

"Two days ago, you wouldn't introduce me to your friends. Now you want us to live together?" She didn't look as tough as usual. Maybe it was the dress or those soft curls framing her sharp little face. Or it could have been the distress he glimpsed in her Bo Peep eyes. He tucked a wisp of hair behind her ear. "Two days ago, I was confused. Now I'm not."

She pulled back. "I understand. I finally look respectable enough for you to show me off in public."

He bristled. "How you look doesn't have anything to do with it."

"Just a coincidence?" She looked him squarely in the eyes. "That's a little hard to believe."

"What kind of jerk do you think I am?" He hurried on before she chose to answer. "I want to show you Chicago, that's all. And I want a chance to think about where we are without a clock ticking."

"Hold on. I'm the thinker, remember? You're the one who stands in department store aisles and hands out perfume samples."

"Stop it! Stop trying to deflect everything important with a wise-crack."

"Look who's talking."

His current tactics weren't working, and he could feel himself losing his cool, so he called an audible. "We also have some business to take care of. I paid you for those murals, but I haven't approved them yet."

She rubbed her temple. "I knew you'd hate them. I warned you."

"How could I hate them? I haven't seen them."

She blinked. "I took the plastic off the doors two days ago."

"I haven't looked. You were supposed to show me, remember? That was part of our deal. For what I have invested in those walls, I deserve to see them for the first time with the artist who painted them."

"You're trying to manipulate me."

"Business is business, Blue. Learn to distinguish."

"Fine," she snapped. "I'll drop by tomorrow."

"Tonight. I've waited long enough."

"You need to see them in daylight."

"Why?" he said. "I'll mainly be eating in there at night."

She turned away from the monument, from him, and headed for the gate. "I have to get Nita home. I don't have time for this."

"I'll pick you up at eight."

"I'll drive myself." Her ruffled hem whipped her knees as she left the cemetery.

He poked around the gravestones for a while, trying to get his head together. He'd offered her something he'd never offered another woman, and she'd tossed it back as if it meant nothing. She kept trying to play quarterback, but she was a lousy leader. Not only didn't she know how to look out for the team, she couldn't even look out for herself. Somehow he had to change that, and he didn't have much time.

♥

Riley dumped a load of paper plates into the trash and returned to sit next to Mrs. Garrison. A lot of people were leaving, but it had been a good party, and Mrs. Garrison had been pretty polite to everybody. Riley knew she was happy that so many people had showed up and talked to her. "Did you notice how nice everybody's been to you today?" she said, just to make sure.

"They know what side their bread's buttered on."

Mrs. Garrison had lipstick on her teeth, but Riley had something on her mind, and she didn't tell her about it. "Blue explained to me about what's happening in the town. This is America, and I think you should let people do what they want with their stores and everything." She paused. "I also think you should start giving free ballet lessons to kids who can't afford them."

"Ballet lessons? Who would come? All kids care about nowadays is hip-hop."

"Some of them would like ballet, too." She'd met two middle school girls today who were nice, and that had given her the idea.

"You have a lot of opinions about what I should do, but what about what I want you to do? It's my birthday, and I only asked for one thing."

Riley wished she'd never brought up the subject. "I can't sing in public," she said. "My guitar playing isn't good enough."

"Piffle. I gave you all those ballet lessons, and you won't do one little thing for me."

"It's not little!"

"You sing better than any of those hoods in that band. I never heard so much racket in all my life."

"I'll sing for you back at your house. Just the two of us."

"You think I wasn't scared the first time I danced in public? I was so scared I almost fainted. But I didn't let that stop me."

"I don't have my guitar."

"They have guitars." She jabbed her cane toward the band.

"They're electric."

"One of them isn't."

Riley didn't think Nita had noticed the lead guitar player trading his electric for an acoustic when they tried to sing Green Day's "Time of Your Life." "I can't borrow somebody else's guitar. They wouldn't let me."

"We'll see about that."

To Riley's horror, Nita pushed herself off the bench and shuffled toward the band. Less than half the crowd was left, mainly families letting their kids play and some teenagers hanging out. Dean came in through the park's side entrance, and she rushed across the grass to get to him. "Mrs. Garrison's trying to make me sing. She says it's her birthday present."

Dean didn't like Mrs. Garrison, and she waited for him to get mad, but he seemed to be thinking about something else. "Are you going to do it?"

"No! You know I can't. A lot of people are still around."

He looked over her head, like he was trying to find somebody. "Not so many."

"I can't sing in front of people."

"You sing for me and for Mrs. Garrison."

"That's different. That was private. I can't sing in front of strangers."

Finally, he seemed to be paying attention to her. "You can't sing in front of strangers, or you won't sing in front of Jack?"

When she'd explained how she felt, she'd made him promise never to say anything about it. Now he was using it against her. "You don't understand."

"I understand." He wrapped his arm around her shoulders. "Sorry, Rile. You'll have to figure this out for yourself."

"You wouldn't have got up and sung when you were my age."

"I can't sing like you."

"You sing pretty good."

"Jack's trying," he said. "If you sing, it won't change the way he feels about you."

"You don't know that."

"Neither do you. Maybe it's time to find out for sure."

"I already know for sure."

His smile looked a little fake, and she thought he might be sort of disappointed in her. "All right," he said. "Let me see if I can get the old bat to leave you alone."

As he headed over to talk to Mrs. Garrison, Riley started to feel dizzy. In the old days before she'd come to the farm, she'd always had to stick up for herself, but now Dean was sticking up for her, just like he had when her dad wanted to take her back to Nashville. And he wasn't the only one. April and Blue stood up for her around Mrs. Garrison, even though she didn't need them to. And her dad had stuck up for her the night he'd thought Dean was chasing her for real.

Mrs. Garrison was talking to the lead guitar player when Dean reached her side. Riley bit her fingernail. Her dad was standing by himself next to the fence, but she'd seen a couple of people look at him funny. April was helping clean up, and Blue had just wrapped some leftover birthday cake for Mrs. Garrison to take home. Mrs. Garrison said that if people kept their light under a bushel, the candle went out, and that Riley would shrivel up into a nobody if she didn't start being true to herself.

Her armpits were wet, and she felt like throwing up. What if she started to sing and she totally sucked? She stared at her dad. Even worse, what if she didn't suck at all?

♥

Jack straightened as he saw his daughter walk toward the band's microphone, a guitar in her arms. Even from the other side of the park, he could see how frightened she was. Was she really going to play?

"My name is Riley," she whispered into the mike.

She looked small and defenseless. He didn't know why she was doing this, only that he wouldn't let her be hurt. He began to move, but she'd already started to play. No one had bothered to plug the acoustic into an amp, and, at first, the crowd ignored her. But Jack could hear, and even though the intro was barely audible, he recognized "Why Not Smile?" The pit of his stomach contracted as Riley began to sing.

> *"Do you remember when we were young,*
> *And every dream we had felt like the first one?"*

He didn't care if he blew his cover. He had to get up there. This was no song for an eleven-year-old, and he wouldn't let her be embarrassed.

> *"I don't expect you to understand*
> *With everything you've seen. I'm not asking for that."*

Her soft, lilting voice was such a marked contrast to the band's off-key yowling that the crowd began to fall silent. She'd be crushed if they laughed. He quickened his steps only to have April appear at his side and reach out to stop him. "Listen, Jack. Listen to her."

He did.

"I know that life is cruel.
You know that better than I do."

Riley missed a chord change, but her voice never wavered.

"Baby, why not smile?
Baby, why not smile?
Baby, why not smile?"

The crowd had grown silent, and the band members' adolescent sneers faded. Listening to a little girl sing those adult words should have been funny, but no one laughed. When Jack performed "Why Not Smile?" he turned it into an angry, confrontational assault. Riley was pure vocal heartbreak.

She brought the song to an end, hitting an F instead of a C. She'd been concentrating so hard on the chord changes that she hadn't made eye contact with the crowd, and she seemed startled when they began to applaud. He waited for her to flee. Instead, she moved closer to the microphone and said softly, "That song was for my friend, Mrs. Garrison."

People in the audience began calling out for more. Dean smiled, and so did Blue. Riley stuck the guitar pick between her lips and re-tuned. With no regard for copyrights or the secrecy that always accompanied the release of a new Patriot song, Riley slipped into "Cry Like I Do," one of the songs he'd been working on at the cottage. He couldn't have been prouder. At the end, the crowd clapped, and she went into the Moffatts' "Down and Dirty." He realized her song choices were based more on whether she thought she could manage the chord changes than the song itself. This time when she finished, she said a simple thank-you and handed the guitar back, ignoring the crowd's demand for an encore. Like any great performer, she was smart enough to get out while they wanted more.

Dean reached her first and stuck to her side as people gathered to compliment her. Riley had a hard time meeting anyone's eyes. Mrs. Garrison looked as smug as if she'd been the one doing the singing. Blue couldn't stop beaming, and April kept laughing.

Riley wouldn't look at him. He remembered the e-mail he'd sent Dean when he'd been trying to understand why she was so secretive about her singing.

Figure it out for yourself, Dean had said.

At the time, he'd thought Riley was afraid he wouldn't love her if she didn't sing well enough, but he understood his daughter better now. She knew exactly how well she sang, and she wanted something entirely different.

As the crowd began to drift away, more people openly stared at him. Someone snapped his picture. A middle-aged woman edged over to him. "E-excuse me, but . . . Aren't you Jack Patriot?"

Dean had seen it unfolding, and he immediately appeared at her side. "How about giving him a break?"

The woman flushed. "I cain't believe it's him. Here in Garrison. What are you doin' here, Mr. Patriot?"

"It's a nice town." He glanced past her to see Nita and Blue guarding Riley.

"Jack's a friend of mine. He's staying at my farm," Dean said. "I know the thing he likes most about Garrison is having some privacy."

"Sure, I understand."

Somehow Dean managed to keep the rest of the curious onlookers away. Blue and April herded Nita toward her car. Dean nudged Riley toward her father and then disappeared, leaving her no choice but to approach. She looked so anxious that Jack's heart ached. What if he was wrong about this? But he had no time for second-guessing. He gave her a quick peck on top of her head. She smelled like birthday cake. "You were great up there," he said. "But I want a daughter, not some teenybopper rock star."

Her head shot up. He held his breath. Her eyes turned into puddles of disbelief. "Really?" she said on a single long exhalation.

He'd come so far with her this summer, and the slightest misstep could wipe all that out. "I'm not saying I don't want you to sing— that's entirely up to you—but you need to keep a clear head about it. You have an amazing voice, but your real friends are the people who'd love you even if you couldn't sing a note." He paused. "Like me."

Her dark brown eyes, so much like his, widened.

"Dean and April, too," he said. "Blue. Even Mrs. Garrison." He was laying it on thick, but he needed to make sure she was clear. "You don't have to sing to earn anybody's friendship. Or their love."

"You know," she whispered.

He pretended to misunderstand. "I've been in the business a lot of years. I've pretty much seen it all."

Now she was getting worried. "But I can still sing for people, can't I? After I don't suck so much at the guitar."

"Only if you want to. And only if you don't let anybody judge who you are just by that voice of yours."

"I promise."

He wrapped his arm around her and drew her close. "I love you, Riley."

Her cheek fell against his chest. "I love you, too, Dad."

It was the first time she'd said the words.

They walked toward the car with their arms around each other. Just before they got there, she said, "Could we talk about my future? Not the singing, but school and where I'm going to live and all that."

Right then, he knew exactly how he was going to handle this. "Too late," he said. "I've already made up my mind."

The old guarded look sprang back into her eyes. "That's not fair."

"I'm the dad, and I make the decisions. I hate to be the one to break the bad news, star baby, but you're not getting anywhere near Aunt Gayle and Trinity no matter how much you beg."

"Really?" The word came out as a soft gasp.

"I don't have the details worked out, but we're going to L.A. together. We'll find a good school for you out there. Not a boarding school, either. I want you around where I can keep my eye on you. We'll hire a housekeeper both of us like so you'll have somebody to keep you company when I have to travel. You'll get to see April sometimes—I'm still working on that part. What do you think?"

"I think—I think it's the *best thing ever*!"

"So do I."

As he climbed in his car, he smiled to himself. Rock and roll might keep you young, but there was something to be said for finally growing up.

Chapter Twenty-four

Blue arrived at the farm an hour late. She'd traded in this afternoon's yellow sundress for a plain white tank and a new pair of khaki shorts, both of which actually fit her. Dean hoped Jack and Riley would stay away like they were supposed to. "I don't want to do this," Blue said as she came into the foyer.

Dean resisted kissing her and closed the front door instead. "My advice is to get it over with fast. Go into the dining room ahead of me and turn on all the lights so I get the full miserable effect as soon as I walk in."

He couldn't coax even the shadow of a smile from her. It was strange to see Blue so undone.

"You're right." She and her new purple sandals strode past him into the dining room. He wanted to pitch those shoes into the trash and make her wear those ugly black biker boots. The dining room lights went on. "You're going to hate them," she said from inside.

"I think you've mentioned that before." He smiled. "Maybe I should get drunk first." He walked around the corner and into the dining room. His smile faded.

He'd been prepared for a lot of things, but not for what he saw.

Blue had created a woodland glade of mist and fantasy. Straws of pale custard light peeked through the leaves of gossamer trees. A swing made of flowering vines swayed from a curving branch. Blooms never seen in nature grew in a bright carpet around a gypsy caravan perched by the side of a fantasy pond. He couldn't think of one thing to say. Except the wrong thing. "Is that a fairy?"

"J—just a small one." She gazed up at the tiny creature peering down at them from above the front window. Then she buried her face in her hands. "I know! It's awful! I should never have done it, but my brush got away from me. I should have painted her out. And . . . the others, too."

"There are more?"

"It takes awhile to see them all." She sagged into a chair between the windows and spoke in a small, stricken voice. "I'm so sorry. I didn't mean to do it. This is a dining room. These murals belong in a—a kid's bedroom or a—a preschool. But the walls were so perfect, and the light was exquisite, and I didn't know how much I wanted to paint like this."

He couldn't seem to take it in. Wherever he looked, he saw something new. A bird with a beribboned basket in its beak flew across the sky. A rainbow arched near the doorframe, and a cloud with the face of an apple-cheeked old woman gazed down on the gypsy caravan. On the longest wall, a unicorn dipped its nose into the water at the edge of the pond. No wonder Riley loved these murals so much. And no wonder April had looked worried when he'd asked her about them. How could his tough, razor-tongued Blue have created something so soft, so magical?

Because she wasn't tough at all. Blue's toughness was merely the armor she'd drawn around herself to make it through life. Inside, she was as fragile as the dewdrops she'd painted on a spray of floral bells.

Her fingers poked through her curls as she dropped her forehead in her hands. "They're terrible. I knew how wrong they were while I was painting them, but I couldn't stop myself. It was like something broke loose inside me, and all this poured out. I'll return your check, and if you give me a few months, I'll reimburse you for whatever it costs to have the room repainted."

He knelt in front of her and pulled her hands from her face. "Nobody's repainting anything," he said, gazing into her eyes. "I love them."

And I love you.

The knowledge passed through him as easily as a breath of air. He'd met his destiny when he'd stopped on that highway outside Denver. Blue challenged him, fascinated him, turned him on—God, did she ever turn him on. She also understood him, and he understood her. These murals let him see the dreamer inside, the woman who was determined to run away from him on Monday morning.

"You don't have to pretend," she said. "I've told you how much I hate it when you're nice. If your friends saw this—"

"*When* my friends see this, I won't have to worry about any lags in the dinner conversation, that's for sure."

"They'll think you've lost your mind."

Not after they meet you.

Looking as serious as he'd ever seen her, she slipped her hand into his hair. "You have a flawless sense of style, Dean. This house is masculine. Everything in it. You know how wrong these murals are."

"They're completely wrong. And incredibly beautiful." *Just like you.* "Have I told you how amazing you are?"

She searched his face. She'd always been able to see through him, and her expression gradually turned to wonder. "You really do like them, don't you? You're not just saying it to be kind."

"I'd never lie to you about anything important. They're wonderful. You're wonderful." He began kissing her—the corners of her eyes, the curve of her cheek, the bow at the top of her lip. The room cast a spell over them, and soon she was in his arms. He picked her up and carried her outside, moving from one magical world into another— the haven of the gypsy caravan. Under the painted vines and fanciful flowers, they made love. Silently. Tenderly. Perfectly. Blue was finally his.

♥

The vacant pillow beside him the next morning was his own fault for not getting around to ordering that Porta Potti. He pulled on his shorts and T-shirt. She'd better have the coffee going. He intended to sit on the porch with her, drinking the whole pot and talking about the rest of their lives. But when he walked across the yard, he saw that the red Corvette was missing. He rushed inside and was greeted with a ringing telephone.

"Get over here right now!" Nita exclaimed when he answered. "Blue's leaving."

"What are you talking about?"

"She set us up, telling us she was going on Monday. All the time, she planned to slip away today. Chauncey Crole went with her to pick up her rental car, and she's heading out toward the garage now to load it up. I knew something wasn't right. She's been—"

Dean didn't wait to hear the rest.

Fifteen minutes later, he turned in to the alley behind Nita's house and skidded to a stop next to the garbage cans. Blue stood by the open trunk of a late-model Corolla. Despite the heat, she wore a black muscle shirt, jeans, and her biker's boots. He wouldn't have been surprised to see a spiked leather collar around her neck. The only thing soft about her was that fluffy little haircut. He sprang out of the truck. "Thanks for nothing."

She dropped a box of painting supplies into the trunk. The backseat was already loaded up. "I had my fill of good-byes when I was a kid," she said stonily. "I don't put myself through that anymore. By the way, you'll be happy to know I got my period."

He'd never hurt a woman in his life, but he wanted to shake her until her teeth rattled. "You're insane, you know that?" He stalked over to her. "I love you!"

"Yeah, yeah, I love you, too." She tossed in her duffel.

"I mean it, Blue. We belong together. I should have told you how I felt last night, but you're so damned skittish, I wanted to work up to it so I didn't scare you off."

She planted a hand on her hip, playing the badass but not quite pulling it off. "Get real. You don't love me."

"Is it so hard to believe?"

"Yes. You're Dean Robillard, and I'm Blue Bailey. You wear designer labels, and I'm happy with a Wal-Mart bargain. I'm a drifter, and you have a career that lights up the sky. Do you need to hear more?" She slammed the trunk lid closed.

"That's superficial crap."

"Hardly." She pulled a pair of cheap black sunglasses from the purse she'd left on the roof of the car and slipped them on. Her bluster faded, and her lower lip trembled. "You had your life turned inside out this summer, Boo, and I was the go-to girl helping you get through it. I've loved every minute of these last seven weeks, but it hasn't been real life. I've been Alice living in your Wonderland."

He hated feeling helpless and he went on the attack. "Believe me, I know the difference between reality and fantasy better than you do, judging from my dining room. You haven't even figured out how frickin' talented you are!"

"Thanks."

"You love me, Blue."

Her jaw jutted forward. "I'm crazy about you, but I don't fall in love."

"Yes, you do. But you haven't got the guts to see it through. Smack-talking Blue Bailey lost her courage years ago."

He waited for her counterattack, but she dipped her head and rubbed the toe of her boot in the gravel. "I'm a realist. Someday you're going to thank me."

All her sass and strut had disappeared. Her strength had been an act. She was a fake—soft inside, full of hurt and fear. He struggled to get his cool back but couldn't manage it. "I can't do this for you, Blue. You either have the guts to take a risk or you don't."

"I'm sorry."

"If you leave, I'm not coming after you."

"I understand."

He couldn't believe she was doing this. Even as he watched her climb into the car, he waited for her to find her courage. But the engine turned over. A dog barked in the distance. She backed out into the alley. A bee buzzed past him toward a stand of hollyhocks, and she pulled away. He waited for her to stop. To turn around. She didn't.

The back door banged and Nita came down the steps, her robe flapping open over a crimson nightgown. He jumped into his truck before she could get to him. Something unthinkable pulled at the edges of his brain. He tried to push it away, but as he sped down the alley, it only gathered strength. What if Blue had told him the truth? What if he was the only one who'd fallen in love?

♥

Was it true? Blue asked herself as she drove down Church Street for the last time. Was she a coward? She pulled off her sunglasses and swiped at her eyes with the back of her hand. Dean believed he loved her, or he'd never have said the words. But people had said they loved her before, and every one of them had let her go. Dean wouldn't be any different. Men like him weren't meant for women like her.

She'd known from the beginning this affair put her in jeopardy, but even though she'd struggled to keep her emotions in check, she'd given her heart away. Maybe someday his words of love would be a sweet memory, but now they were a rusty knife twisting in her heart.

The tears rolled unchecked down her cheeks. She couldn't shake off his hurtful words. *Smack-talking Blue Bailey lost her courage years ago.*

He didn't understand. Regardless of how hard she tried, no one ever loved her enough to keep her around. No one ever—

She sucked in her breath. The town limit sign flashed by. She fumbled in her purse for a tissue. As she blew her nose, she took a hard look inside herself and saw a woman who was letting fear dictate the course of her life.

She eased back on the accelerator. She couldn't leave town like this. Dean wasn't a fool. He didn't give his heart away to anyone. Was she really too damaged to recognize love, or was she simply being a realist?

She looked down the road for a place to turn around, but before she could find one, she heard the siren.

♥

An hour later, she gazed across the gray steel desk at the chief of police, Byron Wesley. "I didn't steal her diamond necklace," she said for what seemed like the hundredth time. "Nita planted it in my purse."

The chief looked over her head to the television, which was tuned to *Meet the Press*. "Now why would she do that?"

"To keep me in Garrison. I told you." She slapped her fist on the desk. "I want a lawyer."

The chief pulled the toothpick from his mouth. "Hal Cates plays golf on Sunday morning, but you can leave a message."

"Hal Cates is Nita's lawyer."

"He's the only one in town."

Which meant Blue would have to call April.

But April didn't answer her phone, and Blue didn't have Jack's number. Nita was the one who'd had her arrested, and she was hardly likely to bail her out. That left Dean.

"Lock me up," she said to the deputy. "I need to think."

♥

"Are you going to get Blue today?" Jack asked Monday afternoon, the day after Blue's arrest, as he and Dean stood on side-by-side ladders giving the barn a fresh coat of white paint.

Dean wiped the sweat from his eyes. "Nope."

April gazed up at him from the ground, where she was painting window trim. The red bandanna she'd twisted around her hair was already speckled with white. "Are you sure you know what you're doing?"

"I'm sure. And I don't want to talk about it." He wasn't sure at all. He only knew that Blue wasn't tough enough to stay in the game. If Nita hadn't stopped her, she would have been halfway across the country by now. When Dean got up this morning, he'd decided he could either get drunk and stay that way, or slap paint on this damned barn until he was too tired to feel the pain.

"I miss her," Jack said.

Dean annihilated a cobweb with his paint rag. Despite everything he'd told her, she'd walked away from him.

Riley piped up from the ground below. "I don't think Blue and Dean are the only ones who had a fight. I think you and April did, too, Dad."

Jack kept his eyes on the area he was painting. "April and I didn't fight."

"I think you fought," Riley said. "You hardly talked to each other all yesterday, and nobody's dancing."

"We're painting," April said. "You can't dance all the time."

Riley cut to the chase. "I think you two should get married."

"Riley!" April, who never let anything embarrass her, turned red. Jack was harder to read.

Riley persisted. "If you got married, Dean wouldn't be a . . . You know." She whispered, "A bastard."

"Your father's the bastard," April snapped. "Not Dean."

"That isn't very nice." Riley picked up Puffy.

"April's mad at me," Jack said, dipping his roller in the pan attached to his ladder. "Even though all I did was tell her I think we should start dating."

Dean forced himself to put his own misery aside. He looked down at Riley. "Beat it."

"I don't want to."

"I need to talk to them," he said. "Grown-up stuff. I'll tell you everything later. I promise."

Riley thought for a moment, and then she and Puffy made their way to the house.

"I don't want to date him," April hissed as Riley disappeared. "This is nothing more than his thinly disguised attempt to get me into bed. Not that I consider myself so irresistible these days, but try convincing him."

Dean winced. "Please. Not in front of the child."

April pointed her brush at Jack, and a trickle of paint ran down her arm. "You like a challenge, and I won't put out for you. That makes me a novelty."

As repulsive as it was to hear about his parents' sex life—or apparent lack of one—he had a stake in this conversation, and he forced himself to stay put.

"What makes you a novelty," Jack said, "is the way you can't shake off the past."

They started tossing around insults, both of them so intent on self-protection they didn't see the hurt they were inflicting, but Dean saw it. He climbed down the ladder. Just because his own life was a mess didn't mean he wasn't clear about what other people needed to do. "It would mean a lot to me if the two of you really liked each other," he said, "but I guess that's my problem. I know you don't want to make me feel like a mistake, and putting up a front whenever I'm around has to be getting old."

Sucker's bait, and Blue would have seen right through it, but she was currently locked up in the city jail for stealing a necklace Nita had planted in her purse, and these two were awash in guilt. "A mistake?" April exclaimed, getting rid of her brush. "Don't ever feel like you were a mistake."

Jack came down the ladder and moved to her side, the two of them suddenly a single unit. "You were a miracle, not a mistake."

Dean rubbed at some paint on his hand. "I don't know, Jack. When your parents basically hate each other . . ."

"We don't hate each other," he said sharply. "Even when we were at our worst, we never hated each other."

"That was then, and this is now." Dean rubbed off more paint. "From where I stand . . . Never mind. I shouldn't let it bother me. I'll be satisfied with what I can get. When you come to my games, I'll shuffle the tickets around so your seats are as far apart as I can get them."

Blue would have been rolling her eyes, but April pressed her hand to her chest, leaving a paint smear behind. "Oh, Dean . . . You don't have to separate us. It's not like that."

He pretended to look perplexed. "How is it then? Maybe you'd better tell me because I'm confused. Do I have a family or not?"

She whipped off her bandanna. "I love your father, as stupid as that might be. I did then, and I do again. But that doesn't mean he can pop in and out of my life whenever he pleases." She was sounding more confrontational than loving, and he wasn't entirely surprised when Jack took offense.

"If you love me, why the hell are you giving me such a hard time?"

The old man wasn't handling this as well as he should, so Dean slipped his arm around his mother's shoulders. "Because she's done with fly-by-night relationships, and that's pretty much all you're offering. Isn't that right, April?" He turned back to his father. "You'll take her to dinner a couple of times and then forget she exists."

"That's bull," Jack shot back. "And whose side are you on anyway?"

Dean thought it over. "Hers."

"Thanks a lot." Jack's earring bobbled as he jerked his head toward the house. "Make yourself scarce, too. Your mother and I have a few things to settle."

"Yes, sir." Dean snatched a water bottle and disappeared. He wanted to be by himself anyway.

♥

Jack grabbed April by the arm and hauled her inside the barn where they could have a little privacy. He was burning up, and not just from the midday heat. He was burning up from guilt, from fear, from lust, and from hope. The dusty barn still held the faint scent of hay and manure. He backed April against a stall.

"Don't you ever again say that all I want from you is sex. Do you hear me?" He gave her a little shake. "I love you. How could I not love you? We're almost the same person. I want a future with you. And I think you should have let me figure that out on my own without trying to convince our son I'm a sleaze."

April couldn't be intimidated. "Exactly when did you realize you loved me?"

"Right away." He saw the skepticism in her eyes. "Maybe not the first night. Maybe not exactly right away."

"How about yesterday?"

He wanted to lie, but he couldn't. "My heart knew it, but my head hadn't completely sorted it out." He brushed her cheek with his knuckles. "You were braver than me. The moment you said those words out there, it was like this big egg cracked open and I could finally see what was inside."

"Which was . . . ?"

"A heart filled with love for you. My sweet April."

His voice choked with emotion, but she was tough, and she looked him straight in the eye. "Tell me more."

"I'll write you a song."

"You've already done that. Who could forget your memorable lyric about 'blond beauty in a body bag'?"

He smiled and let a lock of her hair slip through his fingers. "This time I'll write you a nice song. I love you, April. You've given me back my daughter and my son. Until these past few months, I've been living in a world where all the colors had run together until they were muddy, but when I saw you, everything started to glow. You're a magical, unexpected gift, and I don't think I could survive if that gift disappeared."

He waited for her to give him more trouble. Instead, a smile gradually tugged at the corners of her soft mouth, and her hands dropped to the waistband of her shorts. "Okay. I'll put out. Take off your clothes."

He gave a hoot of laughter and pulled her deeper into the barn. They found a mangy old blanket and stripped off their sweaty, paint-spattered clothes. Their bodies had lost the tautness of youth, but her softer contours pleased him, and she drank him in as if he were still twenty-three.

He couldn't disappoint her. He lay her back on the blanket where they kissed for an eternity. He explored her curves and recesses while the blades of light filtering through the barn's slats fell in thin golden ropes over their bodies like bondage cords.

When they could no longer tolerate the torment, he lowered himself gently upon her. She opened her legs. Let him in. She was wet, tight. The hard floor tested their bodies—tomorrow they'd pay—but, for now, neither of them cared. He began to move. This was missionary love. Straightforward, love inspired, pure. Without the randiness of youth, they had time to gaze into each other's unshielded eyes. Time to speak wordless messages and make unspoken pledges. They moved together. Rocked together. Surged. And, when it was over, they rejoiced in the miracle that had happened to them.

"You made me feel like a virgin," she said.

"You made me feel like a superhero," he said.

Enfolded by earthy smells of sex and dust, of sweat and long-forgotten farm animals, they held each other. Their joints ached from the hard floor. Their hearts sang. Her beautiful long hair skimmed his body as she eased herself onto her elbow and kissed his chest. He stroked the beads of her spine. "What are we going to do now, my love?"

She smiled up at him through the golden web of her hair. "One day at a time, my love. We're going to take it one day at a time."

♥

Being incarcerated wasn't quite the nightmare Blue had imagined. "I like the sunflowers," Deputy Carl Dawks said, rubbing his short afro. "And the dragonflies are real pretty."

Blue wiped off her brush and went to the end of the hallway to check the proportions on the wings. "I like painting bugs. I'm going to add a spider, too."

"I don't know. People are funny about spiders."

"They'll like this one. The cobweb will look as if it's made out of sequins."

"You sure do have some ideas, Blue." Carl studied the mural from a new angle. "Chief Wesley thinks you should paint a skull and crossbones in the lobby as a warning to obey the law, but I told him you didn't paint that kind of stuff."

"You told him right." Her stay in jail had been oddly peaceful, as long as she didn't let herself think about Dean. Now that she'd started painting what she wanted, ideas were flooding her brain so fast she couldn't keep up with them.

Carl wandered out into the office. It was Thursday morning. She'd been arrested on Sunday, and she'd worked on the mural in the jail's hallway since Monday afternoon. She'd also made lasagna for the staff in the community kitchen and answered the phone for a couple of hours yesterday when Lorraine, the clerk, had picked up a bladder infection. So far April and Syl had visited, along with Penny Winters, Gary the hairdresser, Monica the real estate agent, and Jason, the bartender at the Barn Grill. All of them were sympathetic, but except for April, no one was anxious for her to get out of jail until

Nita had signed the final papers agreeing to the town improvement project. That was the bargaining chip Nita had played to trigger Blue's arrest. Blue was furious with her . . . and touched beyond words.

The person who hadn't visited was Dean. He'd warned her that he wouldn't come after her, and he wasn't a man for idle threats.

Chief Wesley stuck his head into the hallway. "Blue, I just got word Lamont Daily is stoppin' by for a cup of coffee."

"Who's he?"

"The county sheriff."

"Gotcha." She put down her brush, wiped her hands, and went back to her unlocked cell. She was currently the jail's only prisoner, although Ronnie Archer had been here for a couple of hours after Carl had picked him up for driving with a suspended license. Karen Ann had bailed out her lover, unlike Dean. But then Carl's bail was only two hundred dollars.

Her jail cell had proven to be a good place to think about her life and sort through the rubbish that was shackling her. Syl had sent over an easy chair and a brass floor lamp. Monica had brought a couple of books and some magazines. The Bishops, the couple who would now be able to turn their Victorian house into a bed-and-breakfast, had provided her with decent bed linens and fluffy towels. But Blue couldn't enjoy any of it. Tomorrow, Dean left for training camp. It was time for a jail break.

♥

A perfect fingernail moon shone down from the midnight sky onto the dark farmhouse. Blue parked by the barn, which had a fresh coat of white paint, and headed for the side door, only to discover it was locked. So was the front. A creeping sense of dread trickled through her. What if Dean had already left? But when she reached the back-yard, she heard a porch glider squeak, and she could make out a broad-shouldered shape sitting there. The screen door was unlatched.

She stepped inside. The clink of ice cubes drifted her way. He saw her but he didn't say a word.

She twisted her hands in front of her. "I didn't steal Nita's necklace."

The glider squeaked again. "I never thought you did."

"Neither does anyone else, including Nita."

He kept his arm draped over the back of the cushions. "I've lost track of how many of your constitutional rights they've violated. You should sue."

"Nita knows I won't." She moved toward the small iron table at the end of the glider.

"I sure would."

"That's because you don't feel as close to the community as me."

The edges of his cool chipped away. "If you feel so close, why were you running?"

"Because—"

"Point made." He set his glass on the table with a heavy thud. "You run away from everything you care about."

She couldn't work up the energy to defend herself. "I really am a coward." She hated feeling so exposed, but this was Dean, and she'd hurt him. "The thing is, a lot of really good people have cared about me over the years."

"And they all gave you up. Yeah, I know." His expression said he didn't care. She snatched up his glass, took a big gulp, and choked. Dean never drank anything stronger than beer, but this was whiskey.

He rose and flipped on the porch's new floor lamp, as though he didn't want to be alone with her in the dark. His stubble had grown a good quarter of an inch past the fashionable point, his hair was flat on one side, and he had a paint smear on his arm, but he could still have posed for an End Zone ad. "I'm surprised they let you out," he said. "I heard that wasn't supposed to happen until Nita signed off on the town plan next week."

"They didn't exactly let me go. I sort of broke out."

That caught his attention. "What does that mean?"

"As long as I get Chief Wesley's car back before he goes off duty, I doubt he'll notice. Just between us, he runs a fairly loose operation."

He snatched the tumbler from her. "You broke out of jail, *and* you stole a squad car?"

"I'm not that stupid. It's the chief's personal car. A Buick Lucerne. And I only borrowed it."

"Without telling him." He took a swig.

"I'm sure he won't mind." Her sense of being ill-used rose to the surface. She plunked into the wicker chair across from the glider. "Thanks for rushing over to bail me out."

"Your bail is set at fifty thousand dollars," he said flatly.

"You pay nearly that much for hair products."

"Yeah, well, you're pretty much the exact definition of a flight risk." He resumed his former seat.

"You were going to take off for Chicago tomorrow without seeing me, weren't you? Leave me here to rot."

"You're hardly rotting." He settled back into the cushions. "The word is that Chief Wesley loaned you to the Golden Agers yesterday morning for an oil painting demonstration."

"It's his work-release program." She clasped her hands in her lap. "You're glad I was arrested, aren't you?"

He took another slow sip, as if he were thinking it over. "Ultimately, it doesn't mean much, does it? If Nita hadn't done her worst, you'd have disappeared by now."

"I wish you'd at least . . . come to see me."

"You made your feelings more than clear the last time we talked."

"And you let a little thing like that stop you?" Her voice caught.

"Why are you here, Blue?" He sounded tired. "You want to drive the knife in a little deeper?"

"Is that what you think of me?"

"I guess you did what you had to. Now I'm doing the same."

She pulled her legs tight against the rocker. "It's hardly surprising that I have a few minor trust issues."

"You have trust issues. Artistic issues. Fake-toughness issues. Then there are the fashion issues." His lip curled. "No, wait, that's part of the fake-toughness thing."

"I was getting ready to turn around when Chief Wesley pulled me over!" she exclaimed.

"Sure you were."

"It's true." It hadn't occurred to her that he might not believe her. "You're right. What you said in the alley." She drew a deep breath. "I do love you."

"Uh-huh." Ice cubes clinked as he drained his glass.

"I do. Really."

"Then why do you sound like you're getting ready to puke?"

"I'm still sort of getting used to the idea." She loved Dean Robillard, and she knew she had to take this one terrifying leap. "I've—I've had a lot of time to think lately, and . . ." Her mouth was so dry she had to push out the words. "I'll go to Chicago with you. We'll live together for a while. See how things work out."

Stony silence followed. She started to get nervous.

"That deal is no longer on the table," he said quietly.

"It's only been four days!"

"You're not the only one who's had time to think."

"I knew this would happen! It's exactly what I said all along." She came to her feet. "I haven't been anything more to you than a novelty."

"You've just proven my point. Exactly why I don't trust you."

She wanted to take a swing at him. "How could you not trust me? I'm the most trustworthy person in the world! Just ask my friends."

"The friends you only talk to on the phone because you never stay in the same city with them for more than a few months?"

"I just said I'd go to Chicago with you, didn't I?"

"You're not the only one who needs security. I waited a long time to fall in love. Why it had to be with you, I don't know. God's big joke, I guess. But I'll tell you this. I'm not waking up every morning wondering if you're still around."

She felt sick. "Then what?"

He regarded her stubbornly. "You tell me."

"I already did. We start with Chicago."

"You'd like that, wouldn't you?" He practically sneered at her. "You thrive in new places. It's growing roots that gives you trouble."

He'd nailed her.

He rose. "Let's say we went to Chicago. I introduce you to my friends. We have a great time. We laugh. We argue. We make love. One month goes by. Another. And then . . ." He shrugged.

"And then you wake up one morning, and I'm gone."

"I'm away a lot during the season. Imagine how that'll wear on you. And the women. They throw themselves at anyone with a uniform. What are you going to do when you find lipstick on my shirt collar?"

"As long as it's not on your End Zone briefs, I think I can handle it."

He didn't break a smile. "You don't get it, Blue. Women are after me all the time, and it's not in my nature to walk away without at least giving them a smile and telling them I like their hair or their eyes or some other fucking nice thing about them because it makes them feel good, and that makes me feel good, and that's the way I'm made."

A natural born charmer. She loved this man.

"I'd never screw around on you." He gazed down at her. "That's also the way I'm made. But how can you believe that, when you'll be waiting for proof that I don't love you—that I'm like all the others who rejected you? I can't watch everything I do, censor every word I say because I'm afraid you'll walk away. You aren't the only one carrying a few scars around."

His irrefutable logic scared her. "I'm supposed to *earn* a spot on Team Robillard? Is that it?"

She expected him to back off, but he didn't. "Yeah, I guess that's it."

She'd spent her childhood trying to prove herself worthy of other people's love, and she'd always failed. Now he was asking her to do the same thing. Resentment choked her. She wanted to tell him to go to hell, but something in his expression stopped her. A bone-deep vulnerability from the man who had everything. In that moment she understood what she needed to do. Maybe it would work, or maybe it wouldn't. Maybe she was about to take heartbreak to a whole new level. "I'm staying here."

He tilted his head, as if he hadn't heard her right.

"Team Bailey is staying right here," she said. "At the farm. Alone." Her thoughts raced. "You don't even get to visit. We won't see each other until"—she searched for some significant point in time—"until Thanksgiving." *If I'm still around. If you still want me.* She swallowed hard. "I'll watch the trees change color, I'll paint, I'll definitely torture Nita for what she's done to me. I might help Syl set up her new gift shop, or—" Her voice broke. "Let's be honest . . . I may get panicky and drive away."

"You're going to stay at the farm?"

Was she? She managed a jerky nod. She had to do this for them, but mainly she had to do it for herself. She was tired of her aimlessness, scared of the person she might become if she kept on like this—a woman with a life so small it could fit into the trunk of a car. "I'll try."

"Try?" His voice sliced through her.

"What do you want from me?" she cried.

The man of steel thrust out his jaw. "I want you to be just as tough as you pretend."

"You think this won't be tough?"

His mouth tightened. An ominous foreboding crept through her.

"Not tough enough," he said. "Let's raise the stakes." He loomed above her. "Team Robillard won't visit the farm, but Team Robillard also won't call you, won't even send a fricking e-mail. Team Bailey will have to live every day on faith." He dug them in deeper, daring her to fold. "You won't know where I am or who I'm with. You won't know whether I'm missing you, or screwing around on you, or trying to figure out how to break it off." For a moment, he was silent. When he spoke again, his aggression had faded, and his words brushed across her skin. "It'll feel like I'm walking away from you, just like everyone else."

She heard his tenderness, but she was too fragile to accept it. "I have to get back to jail." She turned away.

"Blue . . ." He touched her shoulder.

She hurried to the door and out into the night. Then she began to run, stumbling through the grass until she got to the chief's car. Dean wanted everything from her, and he was giving her nothing in return. Nothing except his heart, which was just as fragile as hers.

Chapter Twenty-five

First Blue painted a series of gypsy cara-
vans, some tucked into secret coves, others traveling down country
roads toward distant arrays of minarets and gilded onion domes.
Then she moved on to bird's-eye views of magical villages with
crooked streets, prancing white horses, and an occasional fairy
perched on a chimney pot. She painted like a madwoman, barely finishing one canvas before she began another. She stopped sleeping,
barely ate. As she completed each piece, she tucked it away.

"You're hiding your light under a bushel just like Riley was doing," Nita declared to Blue over the noise in the Barn Grill on a Sunday morning in mid-September two months after Dean had gone
back to Chicago. "Until you've got the courage to let people see your
work, you've lost my respect."

"That'll keep me up at night," Blue retorted. "And don't act like
no one's seen them. I know you sent Dean copies of those digital photos you made me take."

"I still can't believe him and those parents of his sold their private
story to that filthy tabloid. I nearly had a heart attack when I saw that

headline. 'Football Star Is Jack Patriot's Love Child.' They should have had more dignity."

"That filthy tabloid was the highest bidder," Blue pointed out. "And you've subscribed to it for years."

"Doesn't matter." Nita sniffed.

The print story had broken the second week of August with Dean, Jack, and April's sole television interview not long after. April told Blue that Dean had decided to give up his secrets the day of Nita's birthday party. Jack had gotten so choked up he'd barely been able to talk. They'd decided to sell the story to the highest bidder, using the money they received to set up a family foundation supporting organizations that helped hard-to-place children find permanent families. Riley alone had protested. She'd wanted to give the money to puppies.

Blue talked to all of them on the phone—everyone except Dean. April didn't volunteer much information about him, and Blue couldn't ask.

Nita tugged on a ruby earring. "The whole world's gone crazy, you ask me. There were *four* RVs hogging up the parking spaces in front of that new bookstore yesterday. Next thing you know, we'll have a McDonald's on every corner. And why you told the Garrison Women's Club they could meet at my house from now on, I'll never know."

"And I'll never know why you and that awful Gladys Prader—a woman you used to hate—have struck up a friendship. Although some might call it a coven."

Nita sucked on her teeth so hard Blue was afraid she'd swallow an incisor.

Tim Taylor popped up next to them. "The game's starting. Let's see if the Stars can finally pull one out." He pointed toward the big-screen TV that the Barn Grill had added so everyone could follow the Stars on Sunday afternoons. "This time try to stop closing your eyes every time Dean takes the snap, Blue. You look like a sissy."

"You mind your own business," Nita shot back.

Blue sighed and dropped her head to Nita's shoulder. She stayed like that for a while. Finally, she said, so only Nita could hear, "I can't do this much longer."

Nita patted her hand, brushed her cheek with a gnarled knuckle, then poked her in the ribs. "Sit up straight or you'll get a hump."

♥

By October, Dean's game had improved, but not his mood. The snippets of information he wormed out of Nita weren't reassuring. Blue was still in Garrison, but no one knew for how long, and those brilliant, magical paintings of gypsy caravans and faraway places he'd seen in the photos Nita forwarded weren't encouraging. The initial firestorm of publicity over Jack and Dean's relationship had begun to die down. At least one member of his family attended every game, depending on their work and school schedules. Still, as much as he loved them all, the hole inside him kept growing larger. Every day Blue seemed to be slipping further away from him. A dozen times he picked up the phone to call her, but he always set it back down. Blue had his number, and she was the one with something to prove, not him. She had to do this on her own.

And then, on a rainy Monday morning at the end of October, he opened the *Chicago Sun-Times*, and all the blood drained from his head. A big color photograph showed him at Waterworks, his favorite dance club, with a model he'd dated last year. He had a beer bottle in one hand and the other wrapped tightly around her waist as they engaged in an intimate kiss.

Dean Robillard and his former girlfriend, model Ally Tree-bow, got cozy last week at Waterworks. Now that they're back together, is the Stars' quarterback finally ready to give up his title as Chicago's most eligible bachelor?

Dean heard a roaring in his ears. This was exactly what Blue had been waiting for. He knocked over his morning coffee grabbing for the phone, all his resolutions to give her space forgotten. But Blue didn't answer. He started leaving messages. Still no response. He called Nita. She subscribed to every Chicago paper, so he knew Blue would see the photo, but Nita didn't answer, either. He was due at Stars headquarters in an hour for the required Monday-morning meeting. He jumped in his car and drove to O'Hare instead. On the way, he finally faced the truth about himself.

Blue wasn't the only screwed-up person in this partnership. While she used her pugnacity to keep people at a distance, he used his amiability just as effectively. He'd said he didn't trust her, but now that felt like a cop-out. He might be fearless on the football field, but he was a coward in real life. He always held back, so afraid of coming out a loser that he voluntarily put himself on the bench instead of playing the game to the end. He should have brought her to Chicago. Better to risk having it all fall apart than to cop out the way he had. It was long past time he grew up.

An ice storm in Tennessee canceled his original flight, and by the time he reached Nashville, it was late afternoon, cold and drizzly. He rented a car and took off for Garrison. On the way, he saw fallen tree limbs and utility trucks repairing downed power lines. Finally, he turned in to the muddy lane that led to the farm. Despite the bare trees, wet brown pastures, and his churning stomach, he felt as if he'd come home. When he saw the light shining through the living room windows, he drew his first clean breath since he'd opened the morning paper.

He left the car near the barn and made a dash through the rain for the side door. It was locked, and he had to let himself in with his key. "Blue?" He kicked off his wet shoes but kept his coat on as he moved into the chilly house.

No dirty dishes sat next to the sink, no cracker boxes lay open on the countertops. Everything was spotless. A chill trickled through him. The house felt hollow.

"Blue!" He headed toward the living room, but the light he'd seen through the windows came from a lamp plugged into a timer. "Blue!" He took the stairs two at a time, but even before he reached his bedroom, he knew what he'd see.

She was gone. Her clothes were missing from his closet. The dresser drawers where she'd stored her underwear and T-shirts were empty. A cake of soap, still in its wrapper, sat on the shelf in his unused shower, and the only toiletries in the medicine chest belonged to him. His legs felt heavy as he entered Jack's old bedroom. Nita had mentioned that Blue worked in here to take advantage of the light coming through the corner windows, but not even a tube of paint remained.

He made his way back downstairs. In her haste to leave, she'd forgotten her sweatshirt, and she'd left a book in the living room, but even the cherry yogurt she always kept in the refrigerator had vanished. He ended up in the living room, staring at the flickering light of the television but seeing nothing. He'd thrown the dice and lost.

His cell rang. He hadn't gotten around to taking off his coat, and he pulled the phone from his pocket. It was April, calling to check up on him, and as he heard the concern in her voice, he dropped his forehead into his hand.

"She's not here, Mom," he said unsteadily. "She ran."

♥

Eventually, he fell asleep on the couch with QVC droning in the background. He awakened late the next morning with a stiff neck and an acid stomach. The house was still cold, and rain pummeled the roof. He stumbled into the kitchen and made a pot of coffee. It burned all the way down.

The rest of his life stretched in front of him. He dreaded the drive back to the airport. All those miles with nothing to do but count the missteps he'd made. The Stars were playing the Steelers on Sunday. He had film to study, a strategy to plan, and he didn't care about any of it.

He forced himself into the shower, but he couldn't summon the will to shave. His empty eyes stared back at him from the mirror. This summer he'd found his family, but now he'd lost his soul mate. He wrapped the towel around his waist and drifted blindly into the bedroom.

Blue sat cross-legged in the middle of his bed.

He faltered.

"Hey, you," she said softly.

His knees went weak. It had been so long since he'd seen her that he'd forgotten how beautiful she was. A few curls from that short, inky fracas brushed the corners of her grapesicle eyes. She wore a petite green wrap sweater and neatly fitted jeans that hugged her small hips. A pair of darker green ballet flats lay on the rug next to the bed. Instead of looking devastated, she seemed to be drinking him in, and her smile was almost shy. It hit him like a thunderbolt. After all the agony he'd put himself through, *she hadn't seen the photo!* Maybe the ice storm had screwed up paper delivery. But then, why had she moved out?

"Did you let me know you were coming?" she said.

"I—uh—left a couple of messages." About a dozen.

"I forgot my cell." She regarded him searchingly.

He wanted to kiss her until neither of them could breathe, but he couldn't do that. Not yet. Maybe never. "Where's—where's your stuff?"

She cocked her head. "What do you mean?"

"Where are your clothes? Your paints?" He raised his voice without meaning to. "Where's that lotion you use? Your damn yogurt? *Where is it?*"

She looked at him like he was crazy. "All over the place."

"No, it's not!"

She unfolded her legs, the motion awkward. "I've been painting at the cottage. I'm working with oils now instead of acrylics. If I paint over there, I don't have to sleep with the fumes."

"Why didn't you tell me?" Oh, God, he was screaming. He tried to calm himself down. "There's *no food here!*"

"I eat at the cottage so I don't have to run back every time I get hungry."

He pulled in some air to get his adrenaline rush under control. "What about your clothes? They're missing."

"No, they're not," she replied, still looking confused. "I moved my stuff into Riley's room. I hated sleeping in here without you. Go ahead and laugh."

He eased his hands off his hips. "Trust me. I don't have a laugh anywhere in me right now." He needed to be sure. "Have you given up bathing, too? You're not using my shower."

She dropped her legs over the edge of the bed, her brow knitting. "The other bathroom's closer. Are you feeling all right? You're starting to scare me."

It hadn't occurred to him to check the other bathrooms or walk over to the cottage. He'd let himself see only what he'd expected to find, a woman he couldn't depend on. But he'd been the undependable one, not willing to put his heart on the line. He tried to regroup. "Where have you been?"

"I drove to Atlanta. Nita kept nagging me about my paintings, and there's this incredible dealer there who—" She stopped herself. "I'll tell you later. Did they bench you? Is that what this is about?" Her indignation flared. "How could they? So what if you weren't on your game in September? You've played brilliantly ever since."

"They didn't bench me." He pushed his hand through his damp hair. The bedroom was cold as hell, and he had goose bumps everywhere, and nothing was settled. "I need to tell you about something, and you have to promise to hear me out before you get crazy."

She gasped. "Oh, God, you have a brain tumor! All this time, while I've been holed up here—"

"I don't have a brain tumor!" He plunged in. "There was a picture of me in yesterday's paper. Taken at a benefit for cancer research I went to last week."

She nodded. "Nita showed it to me when I stopped to check on her."

"You've already seen it?"

"Yes." Blue continued looking at him as if he were demented.

He moved closer. "You saw the picture in yesterday's *Sun-Times*? The one where I'm kissing another woman?"

Her expression finally clouded. "Who was that anyway? I should kick her ass."

Maybe he'd suffered one too many concussions because he got light-headed and had to sit down on the edge of the bed.

"Nita was in a snit, believe me." Blue waved her hand and began to pace. "Despite the fact that she's started to like you, she still believes all men are scum."

"And you don't?"

"Not all men, but don't get me started on Monty the Loser. Do you know he had the nerve to call me and—"

"I don't care about Monty!" He jumped back up. "I want to tell you about that picture!"

She looked vaguely annoyed. "Go ahead then."

He did not understand this. Wasn't Blue the woman who woke up every morning afraid of being abandoned? He tightened the knot on his towel, which was in danger of falling off. "I was standing at the bar when she came up to me. We'd dated a couple of times last year, but it never amounted to anything. She was drunk and she threw herself at me. Literally. I grabbed her so she didn't fall."

"You should have let her. People don't have enough respect for your personal boundaries."

Now her attitude was starting to piss him off. "I *let* her kiss me. I didn't push her away."

"I understand. You didn't want to embarrass her. There were people standing all around, and—"

"Exactly. Her friends, my friends, a bunch of strangers, and that damned photographer. But as soon as I got my lips unlocked, I pulled her aside, and we had a private chat about our lack of a relationship. I didn't think any more about it until I saw the paper yesterday. I tried to call you, but . . ."

She regarded him searchingly, and then her expression went stony. "You didn't finally fly down here because you thought I'd run away over something like that, did you?"

"I was *kissing another woman!*"

"You thought I'd run! You did! Over that stupid picture. After all I've gone through to prove myself!" Her eyes flashed grape-flavored thunderbolts. "You're an idiot!" She stormed out of the bedroom.

He couldn't believe this. If he'd seen a photo of Blue kissing another man, he'd have torn the world apart. He hurried into the hall after her, the clammy towel getting colder by the minute. "Are you telling me you weren't worried—not for a minute—that I might be screwing around on you?"

"No!" She started down the steps, and then spun around. "Do you really expect me to fall apart every time another woman throws herself at you? Because, if that's so, I'll be a nervous wreck before the honeymoon's over. Although, if they do it in front of me . . ."

He went still. "Did you just propose to me?"

She bristled. "Do you have a problem with that?"

The scoreboard lit up, and he gave the world a high five. "God, I love you."

"I'm not impressed." She stomped the rest of the way down the steps. "Why is it that I have faith in you, but—after everything I've gone through—changing my whole life for you!—you still don't have any faith in me?"

Prudence suggested this wasn't the best time to bring up her past history. Besides, she had a point. A really good point, and he'd have to tell her what he'd learned about himself, although not right now. He went after her. "Because . . . I'm an insecure jerk too good-looking for my own good?"

"Bingo." She stopped next to the coatrack. "I've given you way too much power in this relationship. Obviously, it's time for me to take over."

"Could you start off by getting naked?" Her eyebrows shot together. She wasn't letting him off that easily, and he quickly retrenched. "Where did those clothes come from?"

"April orders everything for me. She knows I can't be bothered." Her curls bobbed. "And I'm too mad—too *furious*!—to get naked."

"I understand. You have to put up with a lot from me." A sense of absolute peace stole through him, disturbed only by the powerful erection that even his chilly towel hadn't been able to discourage. "Tell me about Atlanta, sweetheart."

A wise move on his part because she temporarily forgot he was an insecure, love-struck idiot. "Oh, Dean, it was wonderful. He's the most prestigious dealer in the South. Nita wouldn't shut up about the paintings, and she made me so mad that I finally sent him photographs. He called me the next day and demanded to see everything."

"And you couldn't pick up a phone and clue me in about something that important?"

"You have enough to think about right now. Honestly, Dean, if your offensive line doesn't give you better protection, I—"

"Blue . . ." He reached the end of his patience.

"Anyway, he loved everything!" she said. "He's giving me my own show. And you wouldn't believe the prices he's going to charge."

Enough was enough. "We'll work the wedding around it." He closed the distance between them in two strides, pulled her into his arms, and kissed her exactly as he'd been dreaming about doing for months. She kissed him back, too. Damn right she did. "There is definitely going to be a wedding, Blue. The minute the season is over."

"Okay."

"That's it?"

She smiled and cupped his jaw. "You're a steadfast man, Dean Robillard. The more I painted, the more that became clear to me. And you know what became just as clear?" She ran her finger over his bottom lip. "I'm a steadfast woman. Loyal to a fault, and as tough as they come." He pulled her against him. She rested her cheek against his chest. "You told me I needed to grow roots, and you were right. It was so easy to be happy when we were together. I needed to make it difficult. Knowing I have a permanent family helped a lot. It's . . . made me stop being so afraid."

"I'm glad. April is—"

"Oh, not April." She tilted her face up to him. "April is one of my dearest friends, but, let's face it, you'll always come first with her." Blue looked faintly apologetic. "The truth is, Nita loves me for better or for worse. And, trust me, she's not going anywhere until somebody drives a stake through her heart." Her smile grew a question mark. "Would it be okay if we asked April to plan the wedding? I'll just muck it up, and frankly, I'd rather paint."

"You don't want to plan your own wedding?"

"Not too much. Weddings don't interest me." She gazed up at him with the most tender, dreamy eyes he'd ever imagined. "On the other hand, being married to the man I love . . . That interests me very much."

He kissed her more fiercely until she gasped and pushed him away. "I can't stand it any longer. Wait right here."

She ran upstairs, and despite the fact that he was approaching hypothermia, he was more than willing to wait her out. He moved around to get warm and saw that more magical creatures had appeared on his dining room walls, including a benevolent-looking dragon. He also noticed that the caravan door was painted wide open and two tiny figures stood silhouetted in the window.

Her footsteps tapped behind him. He turned. If he discounted her black biker boots, she wore only a lacy pink bra and tiny matching panties. His Blue in pink. He could hardly take it in. She'd found the courage to wear soft clothes and paint soft pictures.

"Race you!" With a teasing smile, she shot ahead of him into the kitchen and out the side door, her small buttocks peeping from beneath her panties like halved peaches. He lost a few seconds enjoying the view but still managed to catch up with her halfway across the yard. The rain had turned to sleet again, and he'd lost his towel, which left him buck naked, barefoot, and freezing to death. She moved ahead again so she reached the caravan first. She laughed, as mischievous as any of the imps she painted. Icy drops sparkled in her hair, and the shadows of her nipples showed through the wet, silky cups of her bra. He followed her inside.

The caravan was frigid. She kicked off her biker boots. He peeled off her damp pink panties. Pulling her beneath him, they fell into the cold bunk. He drew up the comforter so that it covered their wet, shivering bodies, then tugged it over their heads. In their dark cave, they warmed each other with their hands, their kisses, their bodies, and the pledges they needed to make.

The sleet pounded on the curved roof, tapped at the small windows, rapped at the blue door. They lay together, perfectly sheltered.

Epilogue

♥ ♥ ♥ 🏎️ *Tuxedos must have been invented just to be* worn by Dean Robillard, Blue thought as she stood next to him at the altar. He was so dazzling she had to mentally undress him to keep from feeling intimidated, although she looked pretty amazing herself, thanks to the Vera Wang bridal gown April had found for her. Putting this wedding in April's hands had been Blue's second smartest decision, right after marrying this man, who'd turned out to have as many insecurities as she did.

Hundreds of white orchids flown in from halfway around the world filled the sanctuary. Hand-sewn crystals sparkled on the pale blue bows decking the pews and floral pedestals. More crystals spelled out the bride's and groom's initials on the blue aisle runner. The church was jammed with Dean's friends and teammates, who'd flown in for the February ceremony, plus the new friends they'd made in Garrison. Thanks to Dean, the Stars had only fallen one game short of the AFC Championship, an incredible feat, considering their slow start.

Jack stood next to Dean as his best man. His tuxedo was immaculately fitted like his son's, but Jack had accessorized it with silver and jet earrings. As Blue's matron of honor, April's long, ice blue gown was more formal than the sundress she'd already chosen for her upcoming Hawaii nuptials. That wedding would be a family-only affair, although April and Jack were letting Riley bring her best friend from school so she had somebody her own age to hang out with. Dean had already given his parents the land around the pond for their wedding present, and they'd be tearing down the cottage soon to build their own vacation house.

"Who gives this woman to be married to this man?"

Nita rose from the front pew. She was majestic in a flowing blue caftan. "I do," she said in a voice that left no room for debate. Nita had walked Blue down the aisle, which seemed perfect to both of them. Virginia was still in Colombia, standing up for those with no voices. Dean had shipped her a disposable cell phone, and she and Blue had been talking more frequently, but Blue knew the phone would soon end up at an orphanage or helping out a medical care worker.

Riley rose from the front pew. She looked beautiful and happy in her pastel blue gown with white rosebuds in her dark hair. Jack picked up his guitar to accompany her on the ballad they'd written together for the ceremony. Riley's amazing voice filled the church, and when Jack joined her on the chorus, tissues rustled everywhere.

It was time to speak their vows. Dean gazed down at her, his eyes shining with tenderness just as she suspected her own were. Everything beautiful surrounded them: the candlelight, the orchids, their family and friends. Blue eased to her tiptoes. "Thanks to April," she whispered, "you have the wedding you've dreamed about ever since you were a little girl."

Dean's boom of laughter was one more reason she loved this man with all her heart.

♥

They spent their wedding night alone at the farmhouse. Tomorrow, they'd leave on Jack's plane for their honeymoon at his house in the south of France, but for tonight they were content to lie naked and sated on the bed of comforters they'd made in front of the living room fire.

She slipped her knee between Dean's thighs. "For two guys who make fun of men hugging each other, you and Jack sure did your share of it today."

Dean pressed his lips to her hair. "At least we didn't almost start a brawl, which is more than you can say."

"Not my fault. How did I know Karen Ann would decide to crash our reception?"

"I'll bet she'll never threaten another wedding cake. You dove over two linebackers to get to her."

Blue grinned. "My favorite part was when April started yelling, 'No, Blue! You're wearing Vera Wang!' "

He chuckled. "My favorite part was when Annabelle jumped in to help you out."

They started nuzzling each other. One thing led to another, and some time passed before they resumed their conversation. "I'm still trying to adjust to having a rich wife," he said.

"Hardly." Still, her paintings were selling like crazy. Ordinary people who knew nothing about great art, but knew what they liked, were buying them as quickly as she could finish them. Her work had also given Dean the future direction he'd been looking for. He and April were going into business together, marketing a whimsical line of clothes based on Blue's designs. April would kick things off next year with a few basic items. By the time Dean retired, they hoped to be ready to expand into furniture and home decor. Considering their impeccable eye for style and Dean's business acumen, Blue had no doubt they'd be successful.

Dean gazed at the huge canvas that dominated the longest wall of the living room, the reason they were celebrating their honeymoon here instead of upstairs in their bedroom. He stroked her shoulder. "I don't think any bridegroom ever got a better wedding present."

"I saw it in a dream." Blue tucked her head into the crook of his neck. "Exactly how it was going to be for us. I hardly slept while I worked on it."

She'd painted the farm, but like all the rest of her creations, this was a magical world of summer and winter, spring and fall. She'd opened the walls of the farmhouse to show everything going on inside. In one room, all of them sat around a Christmas tree. In another, they surrounded an old woman blowing out birthday candles. Puppies romped in the kitchen. A Super Bowl victory party took place in the backyard, and the town's Fourth of July celebration filled the side yard. On the front porch, a tiny figure in a beaver suit, minus its head, sat on a Halloween pumpkin. A well-worn path led from the farm to the pond, where a father and daughter played their guitars next to the water and a woman with long blond hair raised her arms to the sky. Horses grazed in the pasture. Fanciful birds perched on the roof of the barn. And right above the farmhouse, a hot air balloon descended with a pair of smiling babies peering over the basket, natural born charmers each one.

Dean's wedding ring glimmered in the flames as he pointed toward the left side of the canvas. "After the hot air balloon, that's the part I like best."

Blue didn't have any trouble figuring out what he meant. "Somehow I knew you'd feel that way."

The gypsy caravan sat beneath a canopy of trees. Thick vines held the wheels firmly in place. She and Dean stood nearby, and the people they loved danced all around them.

Author's Note

I know writing is supposed to be a solitary profession, but so many people support and encourage me, it doesn't feel that way. I'm grateful to the readers who send me such lovely e-mail and also keep me company on the SEP Bulletin Board at susanelizabethphillips.com. That's where I got to know Beverly Taylor, who was kind enough to share her vast knowledge of East Tennessee with me. ("No, Susan. You can't call it Eastern Tennessee.") Thanks also to Adele San Miguel for her Tennessee insights and to Dr. Bob Miller for once again advising me on football player injuries. Several teachers helped me understand eleven-year-olds, including Kelly LeSage and my dear friend Susan Doenges. Also, some charming fourth and fifth graders did their best to set me straight. Thank you, all.

My emotional support begins with my husband, Bill; my sister Lydia; my wonderful sons; and the best daughters-in-law in the world, Dana Phillips and Gloria Taylor. In addition, I give thanks every day for my gifted, funny, insightful writer friends, especially Jill Barnett, Jennifer Crusie, Jennifer Greene, Kristin Hannah, Jayne Ann Krentz, Jill Marie Landis, Cathie Linz, Lindsay Longford, Suzette Van, Julie

Wachowski, and Margaret Watson. Then there are all the booksellers and librarians who continually find new readers for me. I truly appreciate it.

Professionally, I have the most fabulous team in the world supporting me at William Morrow and Avon Books, beginning with my editor, Carrie Feron. It is a joy to work with so many extraordinary people in the art, editorial, marketing, production, publicity, and sales departments. Yes, I know how lucky I am. Steven Axelrod has been my agent since he was in elementary school. It's been a great partnership. Sharon Mitchell, my able assistant, knows how to do *everything* and I'd be lost without her.

Finally, a huge thanks to my son Zach Phillips for letting me use two of his songs, "Why Not Smile?" (copyright 2006) and "Cry Like I Do" (copyright 2003). Zach, you truly rock.